# Briguella

# Briguella

*Vicki FitzGerald*

# Acknowledgements

Heartfelt thanks to all those who helped make my dreams finally come true.

I am enormously indebted to my exceptional publisher Miika Hanilla at Next Chapter for believing in me from the outset and bringing Briguella to life. Thank you for having faith.

Greatest thanks to Steve Green, former Home Office Forensic Scientist & Head of the Investigative Crime Team at Chepstow Forensic Science Laboratory, for invaluable insight into forensics and exceptional guidance. You truly helped shape this book.

Sincere thanks to Richard Sleeman, Scientific Director at Mass Spec Analytical Ltd and Forensic Advisor's Vicki Rowsell & Steve Robinson, for your evidence ideas and helping to bring authenticity to the book.

Enormous thanks to John Pitchers for the interesting mortuary tour and your valuable assistance with autopsy procedures.

To the wonderful registered paramedics, Sarah and Natalie, who ensured the accuracy of my medical text, huge thanks.

I owe a great thanks to Chris Weigold, former head of Local Policing Directorate, Avon & Somerset Police, Police Sergeant Jenkinson and former Crime Scene Investigator Bindy Cardy, for your expertise.

To Andrew Toogood, who allowed me to sit and imagine inside the 15th century tithe barn, thank you for providing the setting that gave such inspiration.

The life of a writer is a solitary one, therefore I am hugely grateful to all my friends for their encouragement - Deena Shelton, Victoria Kirtley, eagle-eyed copy-editors, Darren Bane, Linda Tanner, and Andrew Ramsey. Thank you, first readers, - Ben & Sally Harris, and John Thompson for his contacts.

To mum, dad, nan & gramps, and my in-laws, who have always supported my ambitions, I hope I've made you extremely proud.

My deepest appreciation goes to my husband, Kevin, for being there for me, keeping me going and being my rock. I wouldn't be here without you. You made it possible for me to chase my dreams. I love you, always.

To my wonderful, funny, children, who never complained while I 'finished another chapter'. I love you to the moon and back.

Thank you, lovely reader, for buying my book and recommending it to others. Your support means the world to me.

*For Kevin, for believing in me and helping me to follow my dreams.
For Matthew & Emily, who light up my life.*

*In loving memory of my gramps, Colin Francis
who would have been proud*

# Chapter One – DCI Beckley

*Monday 14 December 2015*

Death lingers like fog weaving through frosted branches across the ashen sky.

The mangled doll-like corpse forms a stark silhouette against the estate; limbs sprawled gracelessly and bathing in blood stolen from her veins. The stench of rotting flesh blankets the air with a suffocating abattoir aroma. Crimson streaks solidify, congealing on her mottled skin, seeping beneath her and down between cracks in the pavement.

No one can save her; the deathlike pallor of her face indicates she's long been devoid of life. Her previous beauty marred by violence; nose shattered and plugged by crisp obsidian blood. It has been ten days since the last victim. This is not the end of his killing spree - it's only just begun.

Her blanched hand reaches out; four fingertips severed and taken as trophies to add to his growing collection. The calloused finger remains pointing, as if offering a clue to her murderer.

She stares at me with haunted eyes; panic and defiance locked in her pupils. This girl didn't die without a struggle. Her beaten body is partially frozen by the minus four-degree temperature. Ice shards cling to her bruised lips like sugar granules, her breath forever gone. She has been dead for several hours; left rotting proudly on display like contemporary art to be admired.

The scene projects into my mind, one I'll never be able to erase. It adds to the ghouls already lurking in my head. I don't remember the last time that I felt angst; it is clawing through my body torturing my guts in tense cramps.

I thought the first victim was an isolated incident, a one off; I was wrong. My eyes slam shut, and I see her bluish lips hung wide open, begging for mercy. Her cries echo in my ears. I want to vomit; bile is already seeping into my dry mouth thinking about the fear they encountered in their final moments.

The stunned faces rubbernecking and capturing the gore with their iPhones are as unwelcome as the blade that pierced her heart and severed her fingers. It's his signature move; mutilation for his own gratification. We are clueless as to his identity and can only surmise that a serial killer has darkened our door. A warped monster is lurking on the streets, blade clutched in his bloody hand ready to butcher his next victim. The thought instils anger and dread. I'm dealing with a ticking time bomb and the countdown to his next kill has already begun.

Press helicopter rotor blades slash the layered candyfloss clouds breaking the eerie stillness to film the morbid scene from above. Erratic camera flashes encroach the boundary as satellite trucks arrive in droves. Reporters are drawn to the police tape like maggots to flesh.

My heart contorts, panicked and afraid by the intrusion in to her privacy. I turn my back on the media glare, eyeing her snapped stilettos resting on the silvery glass blades. I imagine how the attack ensued, the killer smashing her skull from behind and catching her off guard. She crashes to her knees awaiting her execution.

Evidence triangles secure the girl's decomposing corpse and surrounding blood pool. Her clothing is disheveled; top lifted above her breasts to expose her heart and allow the knife to impale it. I picture the killer astride her, viciously choking her and coldly watching the light go out in her eyes.

A black bird swoops low, cackling raucously, distracting the vision. Crime Scene Investigators rush to secure polythene bags over the victim's head, hands and feet after copiously photographing her decomposing corpse in situ. Her statue-like body is transferred, and lays co-cooned in a dark navy body bag, strapped snugly to a stretcher, as it's lifted into the black private ambulance for transportation to the mortuary.

Two forensic pathologists, Deena Shelton and Daniel Delaney, continue to document the scene. Dr Shelton is meticulous. Her acumen is razor sharp and I admire her assiduous attitude. Dr Delaney is crouched on the ground examining the blood-suffused tarmac where the victim lay dying. He's experienced but new to the unit. Paired together, they work in a harmonious fashion.

Shelton's glare is riveted, taking detailed notes with her surgical-gloved fingers. She bags the victim's coat into a large brown paper biohazard evidence bag, seals and labels it for lab analysis.

The killer is escalating fast, but his eagerness may hinder him and leave behind one vital piece of DNA, or evidence that we need to nail the son of a bitch.

CSI Investigator Amy Foster is beside the pooling bloodstain that Delaney is analysing, blood coating his sterile gloves. She packs away tools into her ribbed aluminium transit case; it's enormous against her petite frame.

Patiently, I observe Shelton, who's moved alongside the Ford CSI van. She removes blue disposable overshoes from her brown boots and secures them to avoid losing trace evidence. She's mid-thirties with brunette curls. Shelton looks at me with knowing eyes whilst unzipping the overalls over her jeans and adding them to the package.

"I'd put time of death at more than eight hours ago," she dictates, peeling away her gloves.

"Is it the same perpetrator?"

"It's very likely. The injuries sustained are consistent with the first victim; this girl, however, is missing four fingertips rather than three. She shares a similar profile; blonde, late twenties and attractive. I'll provide more detailed findings once her body has thawed and undergone an autopsy," Shelton answers confidently. Her tone is calm, her demeanour not perturbed by the gore.

DI Wakeman is behind her at the tape boundary deterring the press from scavenging.

Have you recovered any evidence?" I probe.

"SOCOS haven't recovered any notable hair or prints from the scene. We may find DNA or fibres when we process the body."

She's dedicated and has a real passion for her job, you can see it in her eyes. We are similar in that sense. I need a lead in this investigation and closure, not only for the victims' families but for myself. I can't have another death on my conscience.

# Chapter Two – Kate

*Monday 14 December 2015*

Someone once told me that I didn't have to be afraid. Fear isn't real. Like the ghosts of my childhood nightmares, it's an illusion. My father lied to comfort and protect me from the real world, so I would fall back to sleep.

I want to be little again; innocent and naïve. Today's world is cruel. Anxiety and fear are an intrinsic part of life. We fear the unknown, losing who we love, and we fear death. The only thing we ought to fear is fear itself, the feeling of unrelenting terror that paralyses your soul.

She felt it when he killed her.

I share her fear, a violent wave of adrenalin flushing through me. Two bodies have been unearthed on the Millbrook Estate in Weston-super-Mare, both stabbed in the heart within days of each other. They were young, with full lives ahead of them. Now they are just statistics among the 600-700 annual UK murder count.

Only these women are not just data to me, they were killed on my patch and now I must face the bloodshed and report the horrific details.

A child, aged six or seven, sits alone in the graffiti-covered playing area alongside a discarded syringe. I want to scoop her into my arms and take her away to safety. I stare into her gentle, watery eyes. She softens me, but I feel icy cold.

My eye line shifts to a hooded figure draped in gold chains outside Londis, dealing cocaine to a scrawny teenager. Beside him rests a homeless man clutching a frayed blanket up to his matted, bearded chin. His bloodshot eyes dart at me momentarily from beneath his worn woollen hat. Panic fills me. I don't like it here. I don't feel safe.

A swarm of police uniforms inhabit Lasmerton Drive. A tall, athletic detective stands authoritatively in the distance, tucked safely behind the police tape to elude the press. I suspect he's in charge and cannot catch his attention.

The sharp wind and its icy pellets penetrate my silk blouse and grip my pale flesh. I think of the victim lying alone in the dark, gradually freezing like an ice pop. No one deserves to suffer a brutal death, let alone be abandoned, like a chicken carcass for foxes to devour.

The forensic figures photograph the crimson and slowly darkening bloodstains. Sparse ash leaves rustle in the trees above, inhabited by a lone ill-omened magpie. It directs a malevolent gaze over its beak and our eyes interlock. In the morbid surroundings, its presence unnerves me and sets my heart racing, my mind reciting the nursery rhyme "One for Sorrow." The incessant tune replays in my ears. I flinch and shudder it away.

"This is a crime scene, you cannot go beyond this point," a voice orders.

I break our stare, encountering a plump police officer with vapour billowing from his mouth. His stern, russet eyes probe my presence. I offer my hand instinctively, which he ignores. His formidable stare burns holes in my face from behind his beard, which has white wisps. His sky-grey suit trousers are too short, hugging his chubby ankles and exposing off-white socks. He's pushing 50 and, despite his dumpy appearance, he has a threatening demeanour which throws me off guard.

My eyes are drawn away to the sea of white suits rummaging through the alleyway gathering forensics. Tiny yellow numbered triangles dot the pathway as evidence markers. Attentively, I peer through my new purple Michael Kors glasses, focusing on the blood-tinged ice and an article of clothing. It's dark in colour, either navy or black. The tape pulls across my waist as I hover, scrutinising the scene wondering what else has been unearthed.

Low stratus clouds loom above, sending me into a trance. A storm is impending.

I think about the killer and what motivates him to inflict pain and suffering on women. The chilling faces of Jeffrey Dahmer, Arthur Shawcross and Dennis Nilsen flash across my mind. Dahmer raped, tortured and strangled his 17 victims during his reign of terror before dismembering their bodies and reducing their remains in drums of acid.

Shawcross, AKA the Genesee River killer, murdered countless women and ate their genitalia, while Nilsen mutilated students and homeless men and flushed their body parts.

Each of them is superseded by chilling images of Fred and Rosemary West, Britain's biggest serial killers. The "ordinary" couple tortured, raped and murdered at least ten women, including their own children, in a spree that lasted over a quarter of a century. They concealed their dismembered treasures inside their "House of Horrors".

Such acts of sadism are incomprehensible. My nerves tingle at the vivid recollections and I shake my head instinctively, forcing the imprint of their disturbing faces to the back of my mind.

Fear tremors crawl through me and ricochet up my spine. I wonder if he's lurking, watching the CSIs conduct their investigations. It's common for killers to obsess with the police investigation, revisit the scene and relive their gratification.

You envisage the appearance of a psychotic killer; how they would behave. They're more likely to be one of the anonymous faces you pass on the street or sit across from you on the train. You'll never remember them because they are the average Joe or Jane, with an ordinary appearance camouflaging their tormented minds.

I wonder whether the killer has been building up to this new deviant personality, if he's a tourist or an ex-con; theories roam my mind. Someone must know who he is or have noticed him lurking out of place.

I wonder if he's a thrill killer, sneaking up on random lone women. According to my source, that seems improbable. It appears that he has a type; blonde, young and pretty. He's meticulous and hunts his prey.

My numb fingertips twist my hair tips as I revisit the deadly stare of the magpie. I turn my back on the bloodshed and quicken my footsteps to safety. I contemplate the women and guilt detonates and discharges through my body like a lightning bolt because deep in the pit of my belly, I'm relieved I don't fit the profile.

# Chapter Three – DCI Beckley

*Tuesday 15 December 2015*

Shrouded in dense woodland, The Riverside Centre lies within the remote village of Flax Bourton. It's the most advanced forensics mortuary centre in the South West and is tucked behind HM Coroner's Court, an impressive late Gothic-style stately home with a sweeping drive and lawns centred with feather reed grass.

Inside, it swanks technological excellence. Shelton is carrying out the autopsy. I find the process repugnant. An initial examination was performed after the body was discovered; however, the procedure was delayed due to the body being partially frozen.

Hilary Evans, the centre's receptionist, greets me with a warm smile. Her chubby cheeks plump out her facial creases, offering a more youthful appearance than that of her actual age; around sixty. She ushers me through double doors toward the CSI Suite, where the glass window and TV camera screen offer an optical viewpoint of the Forensic Autopsy Room.

Shelton and Delaney are ready to proceed, in their burgundy medical scrubs and disposable plastic visors with transparent facial guards. Anatomical pathology technologist, John Richardson, is also present.

The body, suffused with a meshwork of purple contusions, rests upon a stainless-steel autopsy table.

Shelton flashes me an acknowledging smile and begins to dictate into a hand-held recorder. She looks weary.

"The deceased is a 27-year-old female identified as Cheryl Gray. There are no distinguishing features present on the body. This victim endured a violent death. There are 32 injuries to her face, neck and torso."

Amy Foster photographs the bruising. Her dark hair is fixed into a bun, highlighting her accentuated cheekbones. She's the youngest of the trio; late twenties. The deceased's eyes bulge and protrude on to grazed cheeks. Her strawberry-blonde wayward hair is matted with coagulated blood.

"There are defence wounds. Her nails are broken and conceal stone chippings, suggesting that she tried to crawl away from her attacker," Shelton states, her expression pensive.

She removes the grit with a swab, places it into a clear plastic tube and seals it. Cheryl Gray is petite, the same build as the previous victim, Nicole Hall, and around 5ft 4ins in height. Shelton moves to inspect the deceased's right palm.

"The distal phalange has been severed on the index, middle, ring and little finger. Each was cut cleanly with a sharp blade. These injuries are consistent with those found on Nicole Hall's body, except that Nicole's index finger remained."

"What's the significance?" I ask.

"A trophy. He's numbering them."

"Based on the number of fingers that have been severed, and the chronological order in which they were discovered, these women could potentially be his third and fourth victims," Shelton conjectures.

Every muscle in my face clenches with anxiety.

"There may be two more bodies unaccounted for?"

"This is just an assumption," Shelton replies, resting Cheryl's palm back down. "There's bruising to the left eye, a lacerated wound on the right bottom lip, and abrasions on both cheeks. She was subjected to significant force. There are haemorrhages on her eyelids and face."

Foster rests the digital SLR camera upon her chest while Delaney offers a theory.

"The assailant subjects his victims to a vicious attack and then pins them by their throats, long enough to cause minor strangulation."

"Correct."

"These petechial haemorrhages indicate a venous obstruction. There are also hairline fractures to her right and left clavicle, and a skull fracture."

"So, he beat and strangled the victim before stabbing her and severing her fingers?" I query.

Shelton nods and crosses behind the table. She's tall, about the same height as Delaney, around 5ft 8ins.

Clutching an L-shaped forensic scale, she examines the chest wound while Foster captures images.

"There's a vertical, single-edge, linear stab wound to the chest caused by a thin, non-serrated blade."

"Delaney passes a beige rubber body block to Shelton, who palces it under the deceased's spine, causing the head to fall backwards and the trunk to lift. She grips a scalpel and makes a Y-shaped incision from each shoulder to the lower point of the sternum.

Shelton continues opening the chest cavity with rib shears, cutting through the costal cartilages laterally. I look away; the cracking sound grates on my ears. The sternum is removed as one complete chest plate and set aside on a silver tray.

Shelton's hands are back inside the chest, the scalpel blade gnawing to remove soft tissue and expose the heart. The room remains silent, awaiting her findings. She's studying the cavity meticulously and inserts a stainless-steel probe.

"The blade penetrated the aorta and severed the left anterior descending artery. It measured 3-5 inches in length," she continues.

"The blood spatter on her clothing started right and ended left, suggesting the assailant was right handed," Delaney interrupts.

A flash of recognition washes over Shelton. Her green apron is tarnished with ruby red fluid. Her elbows are tucked close to her hips, directing her bloody hands upwards like an abattoir worker.

"It's the same modus operandi. Both victims' tops were lifted above their breasts to expose their underwear. Both were stabbed in the heart and both had their distal phalanges removed."

"Was she sexually assaulted?" I ask.

"No. There are no signs of inflammation or forcible penetration."

"So, we are looking at a violent assailant who is becoming increasingly vehement with each attack?"

"Yes," Shelton concurs.

"Why stab them in the heart?"

"He wants revenge against women," Delaney interjects, face impassive.

Anatomical, pathology technologist, John Richardson, assumes his role. He creates an upside-down U-shaped incision in the scalp, stretching from left to right, and opens it in two flaps. The front fold rests over the deceased's face, the lower flap falls to the nape of her neck. Delaney hands him the cutting hand-piece of a Medezine oscillating saw, and he begins sawing the skull. Its grinding vibrations produce a high-pitched mechanical resonance which mauls at my eardrum as the pitch fluctuates.

Minuscule blood specks splatter on Richardson's visor as he persists with the incision. The saw is disregarded, and the skull cap removed to expose Cheryl's brain.

Shelton and Delaney closely observe the rubbery tissue in situ before Richardson severs its connection to the cranial nerves and spinal cord. His gloved hands retrieve the organ.

He carries it to a chrome forensic scale on the dissection table and records a weight of 1120g. Shelton proceeds with the removal of the heart, weighing 260g, and other body structures.

"All are within normal limits, suggesting the deceased was a perfectly healthy female," she recites.

Delaney and Shelton step aside, allowing Richardson to suture the victim neatly with twine.

"What about any DNA trace?" I ask.

Foster lifts her head, her eyes express profound disappointment.

"There are no surface traces of the assailant on the victim. No hair or prints. The blood traces all belong to the victim. He's forensically aware and able to avoid detection," Foster answers.

Her words slice through me like cheese wire. We have two bodies, no motive and no suspect. There is also a possibility that two other women lay undiscovered. This, I fear, is just the beginning of my nightmare.

# Chapter Four – DCI Beckley

There is not a single crime scene that I don't recall. Each photographed tableau is divided and stored in sections of my brain overriding my own soul, acting as a constant vivid reminder.

No matter how hard I try to erase them from my memory they remain etched there. Nicole and Cheryl's faces are the latest to join my corpse library, and sadly they won't be the last.

Nicole's tormented eyes reach out to me from the plasma screen with pure, unadulterated terror. Her face stripped of smiles and laughter, pupils locked with fear. The image makes me feel dead inside. My fists clench angrily, every nerve ending tinging with unease. Panic bubbles inside my chest and I break into a cold sweat, visualising other victims. A deathly silence lingers in the air, interrupted only by my uneasy breaths.

Criminal psychologist Victoria Archer shatters the stillness of the conference room.

"Is it the same MO?" She's dressed in a black suit with leather stilettos.

"The injuries are consistent. Blunt force trauma to the head, neck bruising consistent with strangulation, and a stab wound to the heart. She bled out after enduring a vicious beating," Shelton answers.

Her blood-tarnished scrubs have been replaced with skinny jeans and a baby pink jumper.

"Four fingertips were severed. Nicole Hall was missing three. This could suggest the killer is numbering his victims and taking their fingers as trophies. The stab wound is consistent with the weapon used in Miss Hall's attack. Severs to the distal phalange also appear similar in nature," Shelton states firmly.

"The victims were not sexually assaulted and there was no evidence of ejaculate," Delaney interjects.

"The killer must gain sexual excitement from the experience of attacking and killing women. Rather than fantasising over a consenting partner, he wants to dominate and act out extreme aggression against strangers."

Archer describes an offender profile; her demeanour exudes confidence.

"Your theory is highly possible. The offender is likely to suffer a sexually deviant-based personality disturbance. Creating terror and inducing pain would give the killer immense pleasure; it's a substitute for sex. He may feel sexually inadequate and lonely. Loneliness can lead offenders to develop a sadistic fantasy life, involving a violence context. By stabbing them in the heart, he experiences vengeance," Archer states.

"The wounds indicate the assailant is physically strong. He's becoming more vicious, brutalising his victims. He's daring, too. Both victims were attacked out in the open. There was a huge risk of being caught. This suggests he was highly aroused and willing to take the chance," Shelton conjectures.

Delaney's teeth gnaw and grate on the tip of his biro, his mind digesting the facts.

"Pre-crime factors that precipitate murderous actions include everyday pressures; job loss, relationships, money worries or bereavement. Most people cope with such stressors. The killer creates a fantasy world where his anxiety is relieved. But the pressure mounts, he dreams about committing a violent act until something triggers him to cross the line. The fantasised attack becomes real. He went on a homicidal test run, re-enacting his dreams. Once this threshold is crossed the offender reaches the point of no return. He was frightened and thrilled, experiencing a state of heightened arousal. But his relief was short lived during the cooling-off period. The urge to kill caressed his mind and he struck again. It's become a compulsion," Archer elaborates.

Fear slithers through me like snake venom, weaving its way through the blood in my veins.

"So, this is just the beginning?" I ask. My jaw locks with anticipation.

"Once a killing cycle is triggered it's rarely broken. He will continue to act out his sexual dominance and sadistic tendencies through aggression. By numbering his victims, he's telling you there will be more bodies to come. It also suggests another two victims lie undiscovered."

Nicole's stare plagues me. I hear her heart beat against the icy pavement she lay upon.

"Who is he?" I whisper.

"He's a sociopathic male. Not a loner though, that character would have stood out on the estate. He's mature, aged 30-50. I'm suggesting the likes of Ted Bundy; popular, attractive and deceptive. He could be in a relationship or is single, and he has intercourse. It just isn't enough to satisfy him. Each kill was planned, he's meticulous and is therefore a person with above average intelligence," Archer states.

"The offender has developed hatred toward women and has a predilection for young, blonde, attractive girls. This detestation could stem back to his childhood. It's likely he endured a harsh upbringing or suffered emotional abuse. Revenge can manifest itself in many ways and simmer for lengthy periods until something triggers the offender to act out. He wants to dominate women as a form of punishment," she continues.

Perpetrators are all the same in my experience; screwed up because of a warped childhood involving abuse. That doesn't warrant the excuse to torture and kill. A vivid image of my wife Jen supersedes the victim; her blonde hair framing her concave cheek bones and her mouth, which seeps blood. I blink, obliterating the morbid hallucination and return my attention to the victim before me.

"Is there any workable evidence?" I ask. Foster stares wide-eyed.

"No, we have nothing of significance. He's astute and forensically aware. It's going to be tough to apprehend him," Foster warns.

* * *

The killer is inside my head; he's all I think about. I suspect he's been fantasising for some time, but something triggered him to graduate from an observer to a perpetrator. Nicole Hall endured the least violent attack. He rushed, got it over with quickly to relieve his impulses. But the urge remained, he craved the feeling again, which prompted him to kill Cheryl Gray.

Overhanging branches either side of the carriageway create the illusion of a tunnel. I mull over the case, wondering where the other bodies are. If the women are not connected, what made him choose them? Nicole Hall, 28, was a receptionist. Cheryl Gray, 27, a trainee nurse. Their places of employment were in different locations, miles apart, and each lived separate lives. The only connection is their similar profile and their place of death.

Their social media profiles indicate both took pride in their appearance, though their clothing could be conceived as a little provocative. Both wore short skirts and low plunged tops when they were stabbed. Perhaps he chose them because of his own preconception of the type of women they were. He's turned on or infuriated, by their revealing dress sense. Maybe he judged them to be cheap and therefore, in his twisted mind, they asked for it.

The sun is obscured by dense cloud. It's 1pm. I'm hungry and agitated. The congested traffic moves slowly nearing Hampton. I bypass the Greek restaurant where I took Jen for her birthday. A dull ache swells inside me as I recall her disappointment; I was called out to a fatal shooting. It was my job that ruined us and our four-year marriage. I regret that deeply. My life is full of regrets; losing the best thing that ever happened to me. And the lives of the Harroways.

# Chapter Five – Kate

The newsroom feels custodial. Quite often I feel imprisoned, only allowed to leave when my editor, Cecilia, dictates. Today isn't one of those instances, though; I'm elated that my story is front page.

This case has become a national media frenzy. The daily reporters are hijacking as usual, thinking they're the hotshots. It fills me with rage. They traipse in, take over and leave us to pick up the pieces. It's no wonder we are all tarnished with the same brush and generally despised as a profession.

I remember observing the horror on the faces of an elderly couple, appalled having witnessed a TV crew crawl through bushes to get a clear shot of two children's dead bodies being recovered from a house fire. I felt equally repulsed. It is actions like this that make me question whether I'm cut out for this job.

There will be no praise for my efforts today; it's the norm.

I grab my coat and slip into darkness. The shadows of the trees sway forcefully in the wind, producing eerie shapes across the carpark. It's Arctic and, as I draw cold air into my lungs and exhale, a ghostly breath hovers.

I quicken my heels towards the car, clutching my jangling keys in my warm palm. Clevedon promenade is deserted, aside from two empty cars. The swaying string promenade lights frame the pier and its jetty. Its twisted metal structure stands proudly in the ocean, which glistens below the moonlight.

Normally I admire its delicate beauty but tonight it looks sinister, angry in the dark shadows. I shudder, and an anxious feeling consumes me. The crime scene replays; blood glistening in frosted shards. I step on the accelerator; the deadly nightfall follows in the rear-view mirror.

I'm overwhelmed with disappointment. The house stands in darkness, with no sign of Taylor. I long for him to fulfil his promise and make more effort. I can't remember the last time I felt his touch or the warmth of his hand in mine. I miss the way that he used to look at me; completely mesmerised as if I was his world. I cherish those memories, the ones inside our bubble before it was burst by tragedy.

Work has helped him to refocus, but the enduring sadness lingers in his eyes, it's locked inside.

I want to find a way in, to help him, but the shutters remain down, guarding his soul. It has been almost a year since Paul died. His death left a huge void and I can't fill it. They were close; all twins are. But ever since the accident, Taylor's not been the same man that I fell in love with and married.

I remember the moment as if it were yesterday. The conversation relaying the news that brings the world as you know it, crashing down. I could barely make out his words through the awful howls; an unrelenting resonance that crushed my heart. That's when it sunk in; Paul was dead, killed by a female motorcyclist who veered on the A370. Paul's car crossed the carriageway and plunged into a ditch. He died on impact from severe head trauma, at 28.

I couldn't intrude on Taylor's grief, so I locked my secret away. It still hurts and haunts me every day.

My tears resurface, my heart hollow, as I gulp Merlot. It warms my throat. I feel as though I'm driving along aimlessly with no sense of direction; my body controlling the car, my mind hovering, suspended above, paying no attention.

That summarises my life; detached and uncertain how to get a grip. I can't lose control and let my life fall apart. I smear my teardrops, bury my sadness and turn on the Sonos speaker. Adele's 'Hello' plays softly, as the glass kisses my lips. Cooking will help me to forget.

It's 8.20pm. I've been constantly checking my phone but every time I stare at the blank screen, the more rejected I feel.

The oven alarm bleeps, alerting me to the garlic bread. I reach for a tea cloth and retrieve the baking tray. Heat quickly penetrates the fabric, the hot metal surface pricking my wrist. I run my hand under the tap; the cold water offers relief and alleviates the blistering pain. If only it could take away all my agony.

My stomach emits a raucous roar, begging for food and I relent. I'm angry at him for making false promises, and I hate eating alone. Sam Smith's 'Lay me Down' plays softly. After a few mouthfuls, I push my plate away. With my chin on my wrist, I relate to the lyrics; miserable and exhausted. My manicured nails twirl the wineglass stem. My gaze drifts, watching the liquid cling to the sides as I listen to the singer divulge his emotions. My heart aches; the pain unbearable.

The uplifting piano tempo offers a distraction and I cup the glass vase and gulp the berry fluid. Tears caress my cheeks. I want my pain to evaporate, to feel happy again, but sadness overwhelms me. I don't see how I can escape my grief; it entraps me.

I drag myself toward the staircase and lean on the banister before encountering the empty chill of our room. I fall onto the bed, staring up at the windowpane watching dark clouds float aimlessly by. They are calming. I feel myself drifting, my weary eyes succumbing to the darkness.

When I wake, Taylor is next to me, asleep. His muscular arm is draped across my waist and his warm breath is tickling my neck. It's 2.15am.

My anger dissipates, and I feel happy and safe that I'm no longer alone. He promised me things would be better and I know they will, in time, I just need to be patient. My eyes surrender, falling back asleep.

We will get through this and everything will be alright. It has to be.

# Chapter Six – Kate

*Tuesday 15 December 2015*

White satellite Mercedes trucks emblazoned with national television and satellite news channel logos overrun the street outside Weston Police Station. Their giant circular dishes span the vehicle roofs and dominate the grey skyline.

The spicy aroma of jerk chicken infiltrates the air, reminding me of a shack on Bavaro beach, as do palm trees outside the Bath Stone Grade II Listed Magistrates Court. The warm, honey tones and white Georgian sash windows radiate a glow, in contrast to the incongruous 1970s, five-storey block of the neighbouring police station.

A desk sergeant is poised behind the glass-protected counter. The fluorescent ceiling lights illuminates his receding hair. He has brown eyes cornered with deep crow's-feet, which draw diagonal lines away from his face and emphasise his bulging nose and thin lips, which offer a sincere smile.

I inform him that I'm attending the press conference and he instructs me to sit. I pace the reception; my heels snag in the nylon carpet. I'm too agitated to sit on the bench, where a drawn woman waits nervously, chewing her fingernails. Her sunken eyes emit dark circles onto her gaunt face.

I smile and turn away. I hate waiting, it irritates me. Taylor says I'm too impatient. He laughed at me over lunch for getting anxious over the wait. I didn't want to gulp it, given he'd taken me out as a surprise by way of an apology.

Ryan had cajoled him into a quick pint last night, which quadrupled. It does when he's involved. I don't resent Taylor spending time with friends; it helps him to move on. Equally, he doesn't mind me going out with Dawn, though our social outings have become far less frequent since the birth of her children. I don't share her world where nappies, night feeds and crying have hijacked her life.

Taylor took me to Cronwells, a trendy bar on Hill Road. It's chic, with driftwood chairs, black chaise longue sofas and opaque glass pendulum lighting. He held my hand for the first time in months and we spent much of the hour laughing. As soon as he looks at me with his vivid blue eyes, and smiles, my anger dissolves.

It resembled our earlier years, saturated in happiness, creating footsteps on powdery beaches. I'd give anything to be that perfect couple again. Before death ruined us.

The inner glass panelled door buzzes. A young female police officer emerges, ushers me inside and along the vacant corridor. Her fingers swipe an identity card through the metal reader and we climb a twisting staircase to the second floor.

Journalists rush to set up equipment. Three cameras are being fixed to heavy-duty tripods, while radio journalists adjust fleeced boom mics on the press stand. I sit on a single seat at the front. The room is impersonal and feels institutional, with intense whitewashed walls and neat oblong tables. A backdrop stands behind a table at the end of the room centered with the constabulary logo; a red dragon coat of arms upon a blue and white shield, framed inside a diamond design beneath Her Majesty's crown.

Flashes of black and white emerge; two uniformed officers take their positions. My blouse is uncomfortably tight, clinging against my perspiring skin. A suited man enters and pours water into a clear plastic cup. He's striking, around 37, with subtly gelled Ivy League hair and faint stubble on his chiselled jawline. I recognise him from the Lasmerton crime scene. He's sophisticated and well-groomed. His strong build and protective demeanour reminds me of Taylor. To his left is a male officer in his late 40s with a black crew cut.

"Good afternoon ladies and gentlemen," says the crew cut copper. "Thank you for your attendance. I would like to introduce Detective Chief Inspector William Beckley. Will is the senior investigating officer in this enquiry. He will read out a short statement."

He turns his attention to DCI Beckley and I follow him with my gaze.

"Good afternoon. We are treating the death of 27-year-old Cheryl Gray as part of a serial murder investigation. The autopsy has taken longer than usual, because of the frozen condition of her body. It has now been completed and the cause of death concluded as a single stab wound to the chest. As a result of the autopsy findings, we are linking Cheryl's death to that of Nicole Hall, 28, who was discovered 10 days ago in the Weston vicinity. Our heartfelt condolences are with their families, friends and all those who knew them, at this incredibly difficult time."

He pauses and takes a drink from the plastic cup. He swallows hard, and then continues his statement.

"The last few days have seen us handling one of the most complex and fast-moving cases the force has dealt with in recent years. We are citing this case as a serial investigation, as it is our understanding that these may not be the only victims. Due to the autopsy findings, we believe there could potentially be two other women lying undiscovered. I would state that this may not be the case at all, but we are keeping an open mind. Our efforts will remain meticulous, as they have been right from the outset of this enquiry."

My heart swells against my breastbone, adrenalin flooding my blood at the thought that the killer could have struck four times. Other journalists in the room gasp at this grim revelation. Anxious furtive glances are exchanged, all thinking the same thing; four girls? And these are just the ones the police think they know about! Who knows how many others there might be!

DCI Beckley fiddles with his suit lapels. I watch his face closely; he licks his fleshy lips and swallows before continuing.

"We have already established more than 900 lines of inquiry from information provided by the public; 167 of these are considered high priority. I can assure you that no stone will be left unturned during this investigation. We will bring Nicole and Cheryl's killer to justice."

DCI Beckley toys with his left wrist and I catch a glimpse of his silver watch. It looks expensive, perhaps a Tag Heuer or a Breitling.

"One of our lines of enquiry concerns the night of Sunday 13th December. We are aware of Cheryl's last movements. Cheryl socialised with colleagues at the Balmoral Pub in Northville Road and left the venue alone, at around 10pm. She stopped at a Londis store in Byron Road, at 10.15pm, where she was captured on CCTV purchasing cigarettes. Cheryl is seen exiting the shop and turning right, in the direction of her home in Selworth Road, a five to ten-minute walk away. She never arrived."

There's another pause. DCI Beckley sips from his cup again, observing the reporters feverishly scribbling notes in their pads. He wants to give us time to take down every detail accurately.

He clears his throat and continues. "The autopsy findings suggest Cheryl's body lay in the lane off Lasmerton Drive overnight before being discovered in the early hours of Monday 14th December. Her handbag was recovered in undergrowth near the railway line. It contained personal effects and the cigarettes. I am keen to hear from anyone who witnessed or heard anything suspicious in the area, particularly between the hours of 10pm and 6am. No matter how small or insignificant you think your information may be, we would urge you to come forward."

DCI Beckley takes three more sips of water and rests the cup near the cluster of mics.

"We understand women on the estate and, equally, across the whole of Weston are extremely concerned and we have been doing all we can to reassure them and make them feel as safe as possible. Officers have distributed 2,000 personal attack alarms and we are urging women not to walk anywhere on their own, particularly in dark, unlit areas."

I stretch my aching fingers during another pause. My eyes sting from the camera flashes; their snapping reverberations invade my ears.

"Someone knows what happened to Nicole and Cheryl and we ask you to search your conscience and come forward. We need to piece together what happened to these young women and why, so we can bring closure for their families. The huge public and media interest in this case is understandable and we thank you all for your assistance. We do, however, ask that you respect the privacy of the grieving families, both of whom have expressed a wish not to be contacted by any media."

DCI Beckley's sapphire eyes lock on mine, and my heart flickers, the feeling akin to a trapped butterfly. I seize the opportunity.

"Why do you believe there are potentially more victims? And do you have a suspect?"

My cheeks flush, the rush of blood warming my skin. All eyes turn on me.

"It would be inappropriate to comment any further as this is an ongoing investigation," he says calmly, as if the question had been anticipated.

"We are keeping an open mind. We believe that these are random attacks; the victims are not connected. They do, however, share a similar profile; blonde and late twenties."

DCI Beckley fiddles with his wrist again; confidence altered. He snaps a wrist band concealed under the white margin of his shirt.

"There are many active lines of enquiry and at this stage I'm not prepared to speculate as to whether any suspects have been identified. Again, I would urge anyone with information regarding the deaths of Nicole or Cheryl, to come forward and help us with our enquiries."

"Ladies and gentlemen that concludes the conference for today," the man with the crew cut steps in. "Any updates regarding this investigation will be issued via the normal media channels. No further questions, thank you."

The duo stands. DCI Beckley is tall with a muscular frame. His tailored navy suit has a slight sheen that snugly grips his toned quadriceps. My cheeks retain warmth, my heart pounding with excitement and a sense of awe. In a split second, he's gone from the panel and the reporters lower their hands in disappointment.

I don't share their dissatisfaction, I'm buzzing with adrenalin; we have a serial killer roaming the estates.

# Chapter Seven – Kate

Cheryl Gray's pretty face stares from below the headline, 'Weston Killer Claims Second Blonde Victim'.

Her family released a statement via the Police Press Office, along with several pictures of Cheryl.

She was a trainee nurse at Weston General, just five years younger than me and lived with her best friend, Selina Martin. Judging by her Facebook profile she was well liked; countless tributes flood her wall. The impression I form is one of a party girl. She reminds me of myself partying with my Southampton university pals in Bedfords Bar.

I swallow cold tea. It leaves a sharp undesirable taste in my mouth.

I kick off my stilettos under the desk to stretch my toes after an exhausting morning.

"There's a dead kid. Get on it," Cecilia yells abruptly in my direction. She's leaning on her office doorframe sneering, fingertips playing with the ends of her long blonde hair.

Tom, Lucy, Sara and Kieran lower their heads, avoiding contact. I thought given we were a similar age, we would become friends, but I am forming the opinion that Cecilia has a strong antagonism toward me.

The constabulary website confirms the death of an 18-month-old, scalded in the bath at her home in Pithful Drive. The toddler was taken to Weston General but died upon arrival. Her death is being treated as suspicious and the Child Protection Unit has been alerted.

The details are harrowing. A sickness crawls inside of me like an insect. Cecilia expects me to visit the scene and "door knock". I fumble for my shoes, stuff my notebook into my Michael Kors tote bag and head out in search of the whole story.

\* \* \*

My nerves are on edge, I'm walking alone on the roughest part of Millbrook in the fast fading daylight, with an apparent serial killer roaming freely.

I quicken my steps and turn right into Pithful Drive where I'm almost ploughed down by an obese pensioner on a mobility scooter. I'm not sure whether I am more startled by the near miss, or the fact that her mouth is drawing on a roll-up below a nasal cannula that's attached to a portable oxygen tank.

It's freezing, and the fine drizzle quickly mutates into a heavy downpour. Droplets cling to my glasses and saturate my hair, leaving my curls limp. I bunch and sweep them together around my neck in one bundle.

A woman approaches through an alleyway on my right, pushing a pram. Her childlike face suggests she's only a teenager herself. She's not had the chance to experience life as an adult, before motherhood.

"Excuse me, I'm from the Southern Chronicle. Could you help me?" I enquire.

The girl halts and steps on the muddy buggy brake with her damp, scuffed Kappa trainers.

"You here about the dead kid, yeah?" She asks, drawing on a crinkled spliff.

"Yes."

"Everyone's talking about it." Her attitude is blasé.

"She killed him, that's the rumour; drowned it in the bath or some sick shit like that."

I watch her closely, inhaling the burning butt; fingers tarnished jaundice yellow with nicotine.

"Who?" I ask.

"Sam Cross."

"Where does she live?"

"Couple doors away from me."

"Can you show me where, please?"

"Sorry, got to see my Probation Officer. Number six," she replies, pointing toward the top-level block of flats across the cul-de-sac.

At the end of the pathway, I wipe wet streaks from my cheeks and cautiously climb the concrete stairwell. It's littered with lager cans and empty crisp packets, and it reeks of stale urine. I hasten my footsteps, holding my breath, continuing my ascent. I step around a discarded used condom, which clings to the floor, and continue to number six.

There's a large crack in the frosted door panel and paint flaking off in shards. I tap my knuckles against the glass and step back, awaiting a reply.

Scouring over the railing I observe overgrown gardens filled with rusted junk. An old Asda shopping trolley is tipped on its side alongside a mobility aid and a broken seesaw, left discarded underneath.

Pacing up and down the walkway, I chew my thumbnail, chipping the white tip varnish. My stomach twists gripped with apprehension. I loathe 'door knocking', it's the worst part of the job, taking advantage of people at their most vulnerable.

It was something I never thought the job would entail. But it's a frequent occurrence and has led to me being threatened and followed on countless occasions. I wouldn't admit those occurrences to Taylor, he'd be furious that I've put myself in danger.

Striking up conversation with the mother will be hard and I suspect she won't take too kindly to me knocking at her door. My own pain resurfaces, as I think about her baby's death. I caress my stomach; my lip buckles and tears begin, reminiscing about my secret.

It has been devouring and rotting my insides for almost a year now. I think about it every day. I discovered I was pregnant just before Paul's death. I'd planned on presenting Taylor with a football Babygro, even pictured his face, deep curiosity morphing to joy.

But then I answered the call informing me Paul was dead. I kept our baby a secret, waiting for the right moment; I couldn't intrude. Nine days later our baby was gone.

I crouch and peek through the letterbox into the hallway. Cuddly toys lie sprawled across threadbare carpet.

A hard pebble fills my throat. I would have been a good mum, if, perhaps a little clueless at the outset. I certainly wouldn't have left my baby alone in the bath. I blink, forcing the thoughts away, and post a business card through the letterbox. I shouldn't be here. I wish I was at home snuggled on the sofa wearing my ridiculously thick pink fluffy slipper socks.

The engorged lump explodes as I stand. Hairs bristle on the nape of my neck as I encounter a disconcerting figure. He's inches from me, face concealed with a football scarf and a baseball cap. His alarming eyes are riveted on mine. He leans closer and tugs at his scarf.

"You should be careful out here," he whispers, menacingly.

I stumble and fall backwards; spine jabbing the door pane. My throat closes over with panic. I stand wordless, staring at him. The lines around his eyes become more apparent. I force a smile to suppress my fear.

I breathe deeply to quash the panic rising from my gut as he saunters away. Seagulls squawk in the damp air; the abrupt sound amplifies my fear. I stand incapacitated watching him, as the sky behind turns a thunderous grey.

His black Lonsdale trainers skulk toward a stairwell. I delve for courage, press my palms against the door and regain my composure. Nausea and panic flush through me as I stagger down the grimy staircase.

I accelerate, my heart raucously stabbing against my chest on the verge of explosion. I look over my shoulder before racing on through the waterlogged path. My heel halts me, restraining my escape. I fall, crashing to my knees; hands slamming against wet slabs. Minuscule stone chippings tear at my skin. I yank my lodged shoe from its snare but it's immobile.

My frenzied eyes dart sideways, searching for his presence. I abandon the shoe, will my injured ankle to push me to my feet and limp out of Pithful Drive on bare nylon tights. The water penetrates the sheath and quickly absorbs, latching around my toes and ankles.

I fumble for my keys, unlock the car and shut myself in. Staring through the rainfall my mind throbs, increasingly tormented with the realisation that my life is centred on both fear and tragedy. I drive home barefoot at high speed. My mind replays the scene and the sound of his footsteps, obsessively. I can barely see through my tears. My frantic hands grip the steering wheel tightly and I step on the accelerator.

\* \* \*

I force my bedraggled body from the car and limp through the front door. Black mascara lines smudge under each eye and draw vertical lines down my face. My side fringe is cemented to my forehead. Tears resurface; I'm unable to suppress my pain.

Taylor appears from the kitchen; expression fixed with disbelief, studying my eyes as the tears burst their banks. I bellow an uncontrollable howl.

"Who did this to you?" Taylor spits. His brow is knotted, eyes angry, defensive.

"No one, I fell," I falter.

"What were you doing?" He asks, interrogating.

"Covering a baby death on Millbrook," I stammer. My head dips.

"You went down there on your own?"

I can't look at him. I can't speak. My words evaporate in my dry mouth.

"Why would you put yourself in danger?"

I examine my raw, clawed palms. My throat closes over again; I don't want to talk about it. My foot throbs, the ankle bone has swelled.

"How did you even drive like that?" he continues.

I take a breath, searching for my voice. I can't tell him about the stranger.

I search my soul for courage. Taylor brushes my hair from my cheeks and wipes away my tears; our eyes interlock. His face has warmed; lines evaporated. His eyes shimmer like inviting rock pools. He rubs my ankle. My foot recoils from the pain of his touch.

"I tripped and fell on my way to the car," I say, softly.

He notices my thumb fondling my wounded left palm and takes my hand into his. His tender lips kiss the surface. It stings but is welcoming. I can't recall the last time I felt his kiss.

"I'm going to take care of you Kate, I promise."

\* \* \*

Warm bubbles with the subtle aroma of white lily swathe my aching body. My tears return as flashbacks haunt me; his breath infiltrating my ear. I sink under the water, washing him away, and close my eyes to erase his face, but the memories cling to my skull.

Floating aimlessly, I inhale the scent of curry spices. I stare up at the intense spotlights; water reflections dance across the ceiling in kaleidoscopic patterns. I feel safe and embarrassed for succumbing to the stranger's intimidation. The water laps around my ears as I lie saturated under the sparkly froth.

A shadow suddenly obscures the lights above; my eyes flicker open. Panic floods me, as I encounter eyes staring down at me and I immediately sit bolt upright.

"You scared me," I screech.

Taylor ejects a loud belly laugh, which mutates to an ape-like shriek, enjoying my misfortune. He has no idea why I'm afraid, and I won't tell him. I can't.

"I'm sorry," he chortles.

He hands me a glass of wine. Soapsuds cling to the glass and drip back into the bath. Its sweet, fruity, cold tang offers a refreshing welcome.

"Thank you."

Taylor kisses my forehead; it warms my heart. He pulls away; chin covered with froth. I bellow my own chuckle.

Taylor gestures me to the table, smirking at the row of tea light candles dotted between foil containers.

"And they say romance is dead," I tease.

"I did promise you dinner," Taylor answers proudly, as he refills my glass.

We talk briefly about work and I agree to be more sensible. He says I get too involved. I do, and I know should keep my distance, but it's hard when dealing with people's emotions. I'm not made of stone or cold hearted. Every one of my stories touches me and leaves a lasting impression. I just need to find room to store everything in before I lose my mind.

# Chapter Eight – DCI Beckley

*Wednesday 16 December 2015*

"There's a man in the house. He's hurting my mummy. I'm scared."

"Where are you?"

"I'm in my bedroom."

"Where do you live?"

"11 Buckland Drive."

"Does the man know you are in the house?"

"I don't know. I saw him downstairs. He had a knife. I saw blood on the floor. I think he's hurt mummy, she's crying."

"OK. What's your name?"

"Toby."

"How old are you Toby?"

"I'm nine. Hurry. Please hurry."

"Is there anyone else in the house? A brother or sister?"

"No. Just me and mummy, and the man."

"OK Toby, listen to me, don't hang up. Do you have a lock on your door?"

"No. Mummy's screaming. Please come fast."

"I want you to stay in your bedroom until I tell you it's safe, OK?"

Silence.

"Can you hear me, Toby?"

"Um."

"It's going to be OK Toby, help is on the way."

"He's yelling at mummy. Please help her."

"Help is coming, Toby. Do you recognise the man?"

"No. Can you come really fast?"

Crying.

"Listen to me, Toby, take a deep breath. You are doing really well."

"He's going to find me. I'm scared."

"Try to stay quiet so he doesn't know you are there, OK?"

"OK. I-I'll try."

"Where are you in your room?"

"Under my desk."

"OK, stay there. Tell me what you can hear."

"The man is yelling at mummy downstairs. She's still crying. Are you nearly here?"

"We're almost with you Toby, try to stay calm. You are being very brave."

"He's coming. He's coming! I can hear him."

Crying.

"Ssh Toby."

Crying.

"Toby, please try to stay quiet. I want you to stay safe, OK?"

Silence.

"I can see his feet. He's coming to get me."

"Be quiet Toby. The police are right outside. They are coming to help you and your mummy."

Silence.

"Toby?"

Screams.

"No. No. Help!"

"Get off him you bastard."

"Shut your fucking mouth."

"Mummmmmmmmmmy!"

Screams.

My body violently jerks into consciousness. I'm blinded by the radiant sun seeping through the blind, as it continues its climb to illuminate the dull sky.

I'm trembling, copious sweat beads swarm my temples; shirt fused to my back. I squint and lift my heavy head, studying the wall clock.

Pain throbs the base of my neck, the muscles entwined. I breathe deeply to steady my raging heart, which rattles against my ribcage and cartilage.

Their deafening screams remain trapped in my ear drum, echoing with every breath. His death plagues me. The guilt hurts more than hailstones. I shouldn't have listened to the emergency call; it didn't help me to better understand how the events unfolded that night.

We had a clean shot. I told the armed officers to hold fire; I believed I could negotiate. I was wrong. He had no intention of letting them go. I am to blame for the death of Toby Harroway and his mother, Marie, and I'll have to live with that for the rest of my life.

My hands tremble as if I'm going cold turkey.

I flick my elastic wristband to quash my anxiety, but it doesn't relieve my pain. The force instructed me to speak to a counsellor after that night. It's been eight months now but talking about the incident with Dr Patterson only worsens matters. It keeps both the ordeal and their faces fresh in my mind. I want to bury it, but I can't, I have their deaths forever buried on my conscience.

I see them in my dreams, I see their faces everywhere I look. Sometimes they pass me in the street. I watch the blood seeping from Toby's slashed neck and fixate on the frozen terror locked in his mum's eyes. I recall flashbacks of her cream carpet saturated by pooling arterial blood from the repetitive stab wounds, and the disappointment in Detective Chief Superintendent Harding's face when I delivered the outcome. The Harroway case is the reason Harding withdrew my promotion to Detective Superintendent. Or, in his words, "put it on hold". I failed everyone.

My head falls; temple rested upon my clammy fist. I eyeball the lifeless faces of Cheryl and Nicole across the desk. Their sombre eyes stare back at me pleading for help, as they lie twisted like broken dolls.

I study the crime scene photographs, their corpses proudly on display. Every inch of their flesh has been photographed in microscopic detail from varying angles. He robbed them of their dignity and their privacy when he took their lives, initiating every orifice to be swabbed, tested, scrutinised and dissected by pathologists.

But their cruel torment doesn't end there. Their bludgeoned bodies are being closely examined by every member of the Major Crime Investigation Team and they are displayed in the Incident Room for all to see.

And when we catch the vile bastard responsible for their brutal deaths, their bodies will be shown to the judge and jury. When he stole their last breath, he not only took their life, he ripped their dignity and pride from their souls.

DI Wakeman knocks gently on the door and saunters in to inform me Delaney and Shelton have arrived. He looks drained; his under eyes resemble bruises.

I can't remember the last time either of us went home and slept. We don't have anything to go home for. Wakeman also prioritised his job before his family to move up the ranks. Now we're paying for our mistakes. He's put on two stone since his wife Catherine left; his weight gain attributed to an abundant diet of takeaways and whisky. His kids barely find time for him and the hurt is beginning to show. We both fucked up.

If I can solve this case, maybe I can salvage my career. It's too late for Jen and me. She's stopped taking my calls and my texts go unanswered. If there was a remote chance she would take me back, it would involve me changing job. I can't; the force has been my life for 17 years. If I left, I'd resent Jen. I want her to be happy, so if that means ending our marriage and letting her move on with someone else, then so be it. I need to find my way back to normality.

Cold air-conditioning awakens my senses. Today is a new day; we must make progress towards catching this son-of-a-bitch. Shelton and Delaney are sipping coffee.

"What have we got?" I ask, tone upbeat. Both look despondent.

"The recovered fibres don't tell us much. There was a single dark hair strand, foreign to her, but there was insufficient DNA present to yield a profile," Shelton answers.

"What about the nail samples?"

"Further analysis revealed solely mud traces and stone chippings, nothing from the killer." "So, we've got nothing?"

"The crime scenes were controlled and planned. He's methodical and emotionless, making no attempt to conceal their bodies. He has no remorse for his actions," Shelton responds.

"He selects secluded, darkened alleyways, allowing him to dominate and degrade his victims over a prolonged attack. The locations fell within his comfort zone; the Millbrook Estate," Delaney adds.

"Killers commit murder close to their residence or kill in an area familiar to them from their past. Could the killer live, or have once lived on Millbrook?" I ask.

Shelton looks perplexed; head rested upon her delicate wrist, adorned with a dainty silver Pandora bangle.

Delaney places his mug on the table. "Perhaps. What we do know is that both victims were discovered in isolated areas confined to the Millbrook estate. He has good local knowledge and has an overwhelming need to protect himself, indicated by his ability to disappear quickly after the offences. Both of their deaths were organised, thoroughly planned. He knew where he could attack each victim with minimal risk of being caught. The area is intimately familiar to him. He could live there, or it may be an association through work."

"What else do we know about the victims, DI Wakeman?"

"Due to their similar appearance, it's possible he chose them because they met strict criteria of his psychological construct. Both victims were blonde, late twenties and pretty," he answers confidently.

"So, he hunted them out for their looks, preyed and stalked them extensively to acquire knowledge of their routines?"

"Yes."

"So, there's premeditation."

"Yes. He humiliated both victims during a long-standing attack and fled the scene without being captured on CCTV," Delaney adds.

"We need to learn more about Nicole and Cheryl, so we can understand why he chose them as targets. What was it about them that he despised? Look at every aspect of their lifestyle; their routines, past and present relationships. Were the victims' extroverts or shy individuals? This will help us gauge how they would have reacted to a stranger. Would they have been friendly or evasive? Were they sexually promiscuous or involved in escort work, porn or prostitution? Their social media profiles imply both were outgoing. Was the killer drawn to them for their personalities?"

"Interview friends, colleagues and family, the better we understand them, the more we can learn about the killer."

Wakeman nods. "I'll brief the team."

Shelton's fingertips twiddle with a pink bead on her bangle in slow circular motions. I notice she doesn't wear any rings on her fingers.

"He will become over confident, his guard will slip, and he'll come unstuck at some point," she says, offering a reassuring smile. "And then, we'll have him."

"But how many more victims is he going to claim first?"

"I don't know," she says, softly, lowering her head.

"There may already be two other bodies unaccounted for," I say. "Wakeman, I want uniforms doubled on the estate and properties canvassed again. Look at missing persons for anyone sharing a similar profile. That way we can ascertain whether he's likely to have claimed another two women locally. Release the Londis store CCTV footage to the media too, with another appeal for information. All details must be made public. It may send him to ground temporarily and buy us a little time to try to find out who he is."

# Chapter Nine – Kate

I'm back on Millbrook, despite promising Taylor that I wouldn't return alone. Cecilia wants an update, and there's a wall of heavy silence shielding the enquiry. As always, if there's no updates coming from the official sources, then we journalists have to find something for ourselves.

A warm glow of auburn sunrays bathes the estate. The sun, however, does little to repel the chill in the air. I pull on my leather gloves. Their black and sapphire fur trim enclose my wrists, shielding them from the vehement wind. They were a birthday gift from my sister Louise.

The level of fear seems to have decreased, as residents go about their day to day business as if nothing happened. It's that old British spirit, stiff upper lip and all that. A balding, unshaven man carries a torn bin bag toward the kerb. His obese hairy stomach protrudes from under his soiled grey patterned tank top and rests on his baggy, faded black joggers, crotch overstretched and sagging toward his knees. He's smirking, stroking sparse greasy hair tendrils while X-raying my body. His perverted eyes follow me down the street.

A swathe of police officers' issue personal attack alarms to female passers-by. Others question tenants and scribble into their black Personal Note Books.

Remnants of torn, weathered police tape flap in the breeze at the crime scene perimeter.

I imagine how the attacks played out, and how the killer caught his victims off guard. Both victims were young; neither had had the chance to find love, marry or start a family. Their lives were cut short in the most horrific circumstances.

If I died now, I would look down on my life and see how unfulfilled it is. I don't want that. I will get our marriage back on track, and the past few days have proved it's possible. Taylor is finally coming to terms with Paul's death and he's starting to act like his old self again. If he can do that, then I can find myself too.

Muffled sounds resonating from a police airwave radio distract my thoughts. A short police officer is poised beside his car, instantly recognisable with its blue and yellow retro-reflective square Battenberg markings. His chubby hand rests on the roof, ear tilted towards his left shoulder, listening to the transmission.

His back is shielded by a black canvas stab resistant vest. A young female officer approaches a youth who is talking on his iPhone, shuffling along in ripped jeans that sag and expose his boxers. She tries to strike up a conversation with him, but he brushes past, colliding shoulders with her. I catch his eye; he offers a leering wink. I'm ashamed to say this, I'm not surprised those women were attacked here, this estate is infested with cretinous letches and it makes my skin crawl.

The inaudible radio whispers fall silent, and I approach cautiously. Sometimes cops screw up and reveal information that they shouldn't. His diminutive frame turns; I retreat sharply on my heels, encountering the testy officer from the crime scene. My intestines cartwheel to my throat, recalling his threatening demeanour. His expression is fierce, staring disdainfully from beneath his crumpled brow.

"Whatever it is that you want, I strongly suggest you follow the proper procedure," he snaps, looking down his 'drinkers nose' and projecting an array of alcohol tarnished saliva spots onto my cheeks.

"You'll find all the information you need via the press office."

His tongue is lubricated by the stench of stale liquor, confirming my suspicions.

"The press office isn't offering any updates on the investigation."

"You won't get anything from me; we have protocol for good reason," he hisses.

"I'm not trying to be awkward or to cause trouble, I'm just trying to keep the investigation prominent in people's minds and help to keep women safe."

"I don't have time for this. You're interfering with a police investigation."

I quickly subdue an almost overwhelming impulse to roll my eyes.

"I'm not interfering. My presence here is not hindering the investigation in any way," I reply, my tone equally petulant.

"Listen, love, I suggest you totter away on your heels back to your toasty office and await an update," he patronises; fingers mimicking walking legs. My teeth clench angrily.

"I'll let you get back to work because so far you haven't done a great job," I scorn, unable to contain my rage.

"Missy, we've been working around the clock collating information with 57 active, high priority leads."

Bingo; there's my update. That's all it needs. One little snippet of new information. The rest of the article can be filled by repeating some of the information that's already been published.

"Those leads would have followed the public appeal announced via the media. The investigation needs us both," I exclaim.

I'm not normally assertive but this DI is a parasite of a man and gets my back up.

I'm tense and irritable from our encounter. A scrawny woman approaches, carrying weighty shopping bags. A toddler follows behind her, lacking a coat. Her cheeks and hands are flushed crimson, her lips tinged blue. The woman shouts at the toddler, telling her to stop skulking, as she draws on a cigarette. Smoke wafts from her thin lips onto the child's face. The mother is painfully thin, her drainpipe legs accentuated by skinny pale blue denim jeans and a crop top that exposes a silver belly bar. She yanks the child's wrist, pulling forcefully.

"Hurry up, daddy gets mad if we take too long."

The girl peeps at me with sad blue eyes. Her dreary face pulls at my heartstrings and tugs at my insides, which coil tightly, recollecting my pain which, no matter how hard I try to hide it, is never far from the surface. I want to take the toddler home, away from this sorry excuse for a life.

"Excuse me, can I talk to you please?"

The mother halts, placing her carriers on the kerb with frostbitten fingers.

"Sure," she replies eagerly.

"I'm from the Chronicle. How are women on the estate feeling? Are the police doing enough?"

I avert my stare towards the DI. His head is twisted awkwardly, eavesdropping, eyes firing daggers.

The mother's red raw wrists are deeply indented by the overstretched plastic bags, and she takes the opportunity, while I've stopped her, and she put her bags down, to rub her wrists for comfort.

"They're only back because they want information. To be honest I'm scared. Most women here don't feel safe being out and about."

I gratefully jot down her comments, like a hungry animal which has just been thrown a few eagerly-awaited tidbits of food.

"You never think something so horrible will happen on your doorstep. I'm too scared to go out at night and even in daylight, I'm always looking over my shoulder," she continues.

"The police claim they have some high priority leads," I state, offering reassurance.

"They need to hurry up and catch the sick bastard." She then confirms the spelling of her name, Hayley Bourton, along with her age, 25.

I press her to tell me where she lives.

"Over there, flat three," she confirms, pointing behind me. "That's my boyfriend, waiting for me."

I turn and spot the putrid balding man smiling, fist fidgeting at his crotch. I smile politely and thank her for her time. I'm grateful that, despite the difficult time Taylor and I have been experiencing, our lifestyle is a far cry from theirs.

# Chapter Ten

*Friday 18 December 2015*

He was more than satisfied with his latest spree. His dry, cracked lips stretched into a wry smile, recalling vivid footage of her desperate eyes pleading with him to stop.

He craved fresh meat. The enjoyment of their torment dispelled the rage he felt. His teeth ground together, as recollections of his tormented past resurfaced. He felt agitated and increasingly angry at the mounting attention his activities were attracting. Yet at the same time, he felt a sense of smug satisfaction, as he knew that the police had nothing on him.

He fumbled inside his pocket, the brushed chrome surface of a Zippo lighter touched his palm. He wrapped his fingers around the cold shell and plucked it from the jacket lining. His thumb flicked the lid, exposing the flint wheel ignition system, which ejected an amber flame when he activated it.

He transfixed upon the warm glow in a state of trance, thinking about his next kill. His arm reached for the Southern Chronicle, and he allowed the fire to engulf it.

* * *

Fear coiled around her frantic heart, her eyes riveted on his deadly stare, violently penetrating her pupils through oblique, sombre eye sockets.

Urine slid down her legs, pooling at her feet, and seeped between her toes, as she observed the malicious spirit of his contorted olive mask. Immobilised by fear, she stared at the fleshy cheeks and hooked nose. A second blow of pain to her skull intensified. Her vision became scarlet.

He smiled, watching her tears fall. She lifted her quivering hand to fight back but a vicious kick forced her to her knees. A third blow knocked her, face down, onto the frosted grass. She lay, barely conscious, his erratic hands flipping her onto her back and ripping open her top, allowing the wintry air to snap at her exposed flesh. He leaned close, admiring his work, watching her chest rise and fall with every frantic heartbeat.

The rattling vibrations of an oncoming train stirred her senses, averting her gaze from the ice shards blanketing the concrete, upwards towards the light of its passing carriages. The beams pierced her pupils and she slammed her eyes shut.

She lay, paralysed by fear, and gagged, feeling his intense grip crushing her windpipe. He remained silent, absorbing her terror, enjoying her fight for breath as he slowly suffocated her. She inhaled the stench of stale liquor as he licked his lips.

As her senses began to fail her, she recognised the distant sound of a barking dog. Its howl grew closer. He wanted more time to watch, to admire, to degrade her and to see the light go out in her eyes. He stared attentively at her lacy bra. It repulsed him, the same way the other women had. They needed to be taught a lesson. He would teach them, show them their worth.

The dog howl neared the alleyway. He stood inert; blade fused to his glove. His mind raced, feeling incensed. A male voice ejected a plea, calling after the animal. He panicked and ran into the shadows.

\* \* \*

Removing his polythene gloves, he noticed a speckle of blood. He disposed of them in a petrol forecourt bin.

His body twitched, enraged. She was still alive. He slid back into his car and sped away, tyres screeching around the Sainsbury's roundabout. His knuckles whitened as he gripped the steering wheel. If only he had gripped her throat more savagely and collapsed her windpipe.

His heartbeat became erratic, increasingly anxious because of his error. He recalled the muffled voice echoing along the pathway; the voice that would find her. His canine teeth chewed the inside of his cheek, sinking deeper with rage until they drew blood. He plucked a cigarette from a crumpled packet on the passenger seat, licked his lips and inserted the filter into his mouth. Normally he savoured the aftermath, felt aroused at the sexual pleasure derived from their deaths.

Tonight, he was numb.

# Chapter Eleven – DCI Beckley

*Saturday 19 December 2015*

Cheryl and Nicole are the first two faces of Operation Paramount. I swipe my proximity card to access the Incident Room and eye the wall-mounted LG TVs, as I bypass the surveillance hub.

It's a hive of activity; officers behind control panels listen closely to live updates via earpieces. At the Intel 24 desks, intelligence officers focus intently on their computer screens. The Gold commander, Martin Greensdale, is with the TAC advisor, Steve Kent, to my right. I eye the room, scrutinising street maps, photographs and detailed case notes; no surface untouched by the investigation.

Both bodies were discarded in public locations, where the killer was certain they would be found by passers-by. He wanted attention. DI Morton, part of the Live Cell team, presents a file on missing persons. I peruse the folder. The majority are brunettes, with just a few blondes.

"Delve into the blonde Mispers. Ascertain whether there are any resemblances between their last known locations and our crime scenes," I instruct.

"Sir, we've got another vic," Wakeman interrupts, a sense of urgency and excitement written on his face.

"What?"

"But she's alive, Sir."

Panic erupts, traveling up my windpipe in a volcanic motion.

"What do you mean?" I ask, my tone incredulous.

"Weston General alerted us. Sounds as though the killer was disturbed and fled the scene. The victim is in ICU."

Wakeman is sweating, his shirt underarms stained with yellow crusty patches. I unconsciously inhale his unpleasant body odour. This is the breakthrough we've been waiting for. This lead could nail the bastard.

"The killer might not know that she survived. We need to keep this fact under the radar," I say.

* * *

The clinical stench of Weston General floods my nasal cavities. I hate the hospitals, they remind me of sad times. Watching someone you love die is heartbreaking and an experience that I do not care to repeat any time soon.

DI Wakeman and I pass the reception; telephones continually ring. A fresh aroma from Costa Coffee offers a temporary relief from the medical odour. We proceed through the glass-panelled atrium, passing a small pond and decorative donkey sculpture, named Phoenix. Her yellow face is accentuated with a fiery flamed red mane and her body depicts a snapshot of the seaside with its pier, crystal ocean and boats.

Wakeman is panting heavily beside me. His heavy footsteps drag over the veined marble flooring. He wipes sweat from his brow onto the back of his hand. We stand patiently, my gaze studying an unusual limestone 16-point compass star floor design. It draws me in and dispels the noise and chaos around me. I no longer see porters wheeling lifeless souls on hospital trolleys. I only see the star's centre, a circular black pupil, staring up at me. That is the last thing they saw, his sinister eyes transfixed on theirs, as he stole their last breath.

The lift opens on the third level. We proceed to the Critical Care Unit. Kimberly, a young slender nurse in her 20s, offers us a warm smile, having examined our warrant cards. She's pretty, with blue eyes and blonde hair fixed in a ponytail. She informs us that the 28-year-old female patient, Hannah Green, remains on ICU, and accompanies us to the senior sister, Mary Porter. She's mid 50s and has a welcoming face. Her greying bobbed hair is tucked behind her ears.

"We understand a young female was admitted to A&E."

"The patient, Hannah Green, was admitted shortly after midnight, having sustained a physical attack. Her condition remains critical. She suffered a subdural haematoma from a severe head injury and underwent surgery."

"Burr holes were drilled into her skull, enabling the haematoma to be drained through a tube. She is currently in a medically induced coma, as she will require close monitoring and specialist device support to maintain her normal body functions."

"What's her prognosis?"

"The operation was a success, there's no reason to think that she won't regain consciousness in due course. She suffered a sustained attack and aside from the subdural haematoma injury, she also has numerous lacerations."

"We need to get SOCOS to document her injuries, is that possible?"

"Yes, of course."

I follow Mary to ICU and instruct Wakeman to deploy teams immediately to the crime scene.

\* \* \*

Hannah's battered face is a fusion of purple and black tones, a stark contrast to the bright white pillow on which her bandaged head rests. Her eyelids protrude, bulging from deep black circular tunnels surrounding each eye.

A nasogastric tube occupies her nose and an endotracheal tube is inserted between her bruised lips, fuelling her lungs from the ventilation machine. Wires protrude from the neckline of her hospital gown, monitoring her heart rate, pulse and oxygen levels.

I study her petite neck, surveying the bruising, consistent with strangulation. It's the same MO and she fits the profile; late twenties and blonde. My eyes dart to her hands, passing over the hypoallergenic Micropore tape, securing an intravenous drip in place. All her fingertips are intact.

Foster enters the room. She logs Hannah's injuries, continually snapping macro shots of each laceration. I feel uneasy, treating Hannah like a piece of evidence, but that's what she is. If there's a remote chance he's left any DNA, then we must seize it. Prompt evidence collection is crucial, though it's highly likely that any trace evidence has already been contaminated.

Foster swabs under her fingernails and gathers samples into plastic tubes. Her face conveys deep concentration. She's looking for any bruising, which details partial prints and can be later used for a visual comparison.

The rational part of my brain tells me however, that this is extremely doubtful; he wears gloves. Our only real hope is that Hannah regains consciousness.

# Chapter Twelve – Kate

The clinical stench pricks my nose and absorbs onto my skin, despite having arrived at Weston General only moments ago.

I shouldn't be at work, but I've been given a tip-off that there was another attack, but that, this time, the victim survived. My source is highly trusted and has assured me that he has not alerted any other news outlet. A living victim willing to share such a graphic survival story is front page material and will impress Cecilia.

My eyes sting triggered by a lack of sleep. I was out with Dawn last night; Taylor with Ryan. We dined at our favourite Bistro, Le Château. Built in the 1900s as an Edwardian Folly, the exterior resembles an authentic castle overlooking the estuary. Inside, it's cosy with a contemporary menu. I opted for Halloumi with sundried tomatoes and strawberries, followed by spicy mango fish curry. We had a great time and promised to make more effort to get together more often in the future.

I rarely get out these days unless it involves running or gym sessions. Had I not received this tip-off, I would still be lounging in my PJs and fluffy socks. Instead, I'm here, with a fuzzy prosecco head feeling out of place passing nursing personnel in medical scrubs.

My uneasiness stems from the fact that I shouldn't be here in a professional capacity, without the full consent of the hospital Trust's communications department.

My clammy hands twitch as my heels clip the corridor. I continue onwards regardless, unperturbed by the gaunt, gowned patients. On the third level, I catch my breath and settle my nerves before continuing onwards.

Confronted by a set of double doors, a tsunami of nausea passes over me. Suppressed memories flood the surface; ones that I've tried so desperately to bury. I gingerly step closer; armpits sweating profusely. I swallow hard forcing away a lump constricting my throat.

The ultrasound department entrance lies on the other side. It is where my grief began when I lost our baby. I'll never forget the feeling, half of my soul ripped from within me. I'd felt different that day; I couldn't place or shake an awful feeling. Then the unbearable cramps came, and I started bleeding. I told Cecilia I'd vomited. She told me to leave the office. I waited over two hours for an ultrasound, hoping we were OK; I was in denial.

The midwife dissected the screen, vacated and re-emerged with a second consultant. It was her sunken eyes that confirmed the gut-wrenching news before her clinical words left her lips.

I'd miscarried at 13 weeks due to a chromosomal abnormality. That's how she informed me that my baby was dead. She finished by saying 'the pregnancy tissue would pass out naturally within a week or two', unless I wanted to have it surgically removed.

I left feeling empty and alone. I lost a part of me that day and I remain consumed with grief.

Taylor and I are both messed up. I hadn't had the chance to tell him he was going to be a dad. Adding to his grief would only have caused him further, unnecessary heartbreak. That's why I made the decision to keep my loss a secret.

I search for courage and bypass the department towards ICU, wiping a tear from the corner of my eye. I need to forget the past if Taylor and I are to get back on track. But losing a baby isn't something you can erase from your memory.

I've wanted to confide in Dawn so many times, but she was pregnant with the twins. She may have felt awkward being around me with her enormous bump and I wouldn't impede our friendship. It is better that I keep it to myself and focus on my career.

At ICU, I peer through a circular glass windowpane. Nerves tighten their grip on my chest.

Tentatively, I step inside and hear dialogue echoing nearby. I pause, panicked and uncomfortable, having recognised the man's voice.

DCI Beckley and DI Wakeman appear. Cemented to the floor, my feet are unable to retreat. The men halt and stare, and I feel the walls close in on me. DI Wakeman's lips contort into a sneer. He nudges DCI Beckley, muttering under his breath. My cheeks redden, the surface pricked with blood. I have no justifiable reason for being here; an encounter is unavoidable.

I direct my eyes over to DCI Beckley, who offers a reassuring smile and motions forward.

My teeth bite my forefinger nail, unable to break eye contact. He's wearing the smart navy suit again. In comparison to DI Wakeman, he looks well-groomed and the suit fits his muscular frame snugly.

His eyes smoulder, glinting something sexy and dangerous. My heart is on the verge of detonation. He's inches away, assessing me. I feel somewhat surprised, encountering unexpected delicate tingles creeping up the nape of my neck.

"Can I help you?" he asks, offering me his right hand instinctively.

My jaw is locked, teeth clenched with anxiety. I stretch my lips into an uncomfortable smile. My blouse clings tightly to my breasts, perspiration beads sucking its silky fabric against my skin.

"I recognise you from the press conference," he says.

My scarlet cheeks radiate an intense heat, my ankle twists inwards awkwardly. I offer him my hand, which he grips. The senior sister standing behind him eyes me with a contemptuous glare.

I search the hollow pit of my stomach, finding courage to break my reticence.

"Kate Rivendale, Southern Chronicle," I whisper.

"I understand there's another victim, who survived."

He leans closer, intruding into my personal boundary. My hand remains entrapped inside his buttery palm. I bite my bottom lip timidly. "Where did you acquire your alleged information?" he enquires; his warm breath tickling my cheeks.

He's about 6ft 4ins tall and, despite my three-inch nude stilettos, he towers above me.

He's older than I had originally assumed, around 37. I recognise his Armani Code aftershave. The scent radiates adrenaline and seduction. A delicious concoction of emotion ignites a sweet fire in my stomach, burning fear and nausea to ashes, their particles morphing to flecks of excitement.

He's stunning, with perfect stubble adorning his chiselled jaw and above the cupid's bow of his kissable lips. His eyes are intricate and enchanting, commanding my full attention. I struggle to breathe.

His irises are translucent, minuscule white rays dance harmoniously among striking aquamarine tones, drawing me into his jet-black pupils, which eject a cognac glow. He's hypnotising, I'm captivated by his charm. My legs are weak; toes scrunched inside my shoes.

"Miss Rivendale?"

I have no idea how long I have been standing before him, mesmerised.

"Sorry, I'm not at liberty to say," I manage to blurt out. "I must protect my source. Are you implying that my claims are founded?"

DCI Beckley rests his hand upon my arm. The touch sends a bolt of electricity through me. His lips stretch into a cheeky smile and drift toward my ear. My teeth sink further into my lip. He breathes his provocative words against my skin.

"Neither am I," he teases, retreating and freeing me from his arousing spell. He fixes my gaze, and clarifies, "at liberty to say."

My cheeks remain flushed, my breathing slow. I'm embarrassed, and guilty, yet excited by the sudden revival of incarcerated passion lurking in the depths of my soul.

* * * DCI Beckley * * *

The attacker's forbidding presence remains at the crime scene. I feel his fist smash into my face; unrelenting punches knocking me to my knees. I sense the violent stamps, as I lie helpless on the floor.

His fingertips crush my throat, restricting my breath. I bend to inspect the ground in greater detail, continuing to imagine how the events unfolded. The bloodstains have dried taking on an obsidian tone.

Hannah would have been our third, or possibly our fifth, victim, if the theory is accurate.

She was very lucky to survive her ordeal. I feel an immense need to protect her identity and I am incensed by the leak of information to Kate Rivendale. She has no firm intelligence on the record and is only trying to do her job, but I'm leading this investigation. I decide what information is released and when.

I recall Kate's cheeks reddening during our encounter. She appeared sweet and naive, aged in her thirties, and reminded me of Shelton. No doubt Rivendale will re-emerge; gossip mongers are at the tape and the press will certainly follow.

Stratus clouds obscure the skyline, hanging low overhead. Snowfall is imminent. My eyes scour the street lampposts searching for CCTV cameras. There are none.

A blue patch of material captures my attention at one of the evidence triangles. CSI Tom Ford approaches it with a clear zip seal bag and tweezers.

"What is it?"

He carefully retrieves the object from a puddle, eyes riveted, closely studying it.

"It's the tip of a glove," he observes.

He hands the bagged item to me; its diameter is smaller than a five pence piece.

"Do you think we could lift a print from it?" I ask, as I examine it.

"It's wet. Retrieving any evidence is improbable, but we'll get it analysed."

"Did you discover anything else?"

"Not really."

I stand pensively, disappointed. I'd hoped we would have more to go on, given he was disturbed mid-attack. Once again, I find myself willing Hannah to regain consciousness. She's our best – and right now, our only - hope in cracking this case.

# Chapter Thirteen – Kate

*Saturday 19 December. Evening*

I stare at my reflection in the Art Deco mirror on my dressing table; I don't like what I see. I shouldn't have gone to the hospital, it is not something I would normally do.

I'm too eager to impress Cecilia instead of being true to myself. Going to ICU made me no better than the national hacks. Not only did I embarrass myself, by getting caught by DCI Beckley and DI Wakeman, but I made myself relive my own harrowing ordeal.

My blood runs cold. I knock back rosé medicinally and enjoy its fruity tang. Mascara stains adorn my cheeks, which I remove with a soft cotton pad in circular motions.

I look drained and pitiful.

Instead of hiding away in the bathtub I should have run off my embarrassment. Running helps clear my head. There's no better feeling than putting in your earphones, shutting out the world and running through the countryside with the wind howling against your face.

Taylor will be home soon. I don't want him to see me like this. We're going out for a pre-Christmas family meal with my parents and sister. It's a long-standing tradition on the last Saturday before Christmas Day. I don't feel festive or remotely feel like celebrating.

Beyond my reflection hangs an electric blue dress; an early present from Taylor. It's beautiful with fine laced sleeves. I take another gulp; the wine level falls beneath the baby pink flowers on the wine glass surface. The glass was a present and one that I cherish. I keep sipping, enjoying the cold liquid on my tongue until it's empty.

Wine has become one of my vices. It's a distraction, an easy way to ebb away my emotions. I drink far more than I used to, probably far too much for my size 8 frame. But then again, none of us know what lurks around the corner. I could be dead tomorrow, so why not indulge in life's simple pleasures?

I certainly didn't expect my baby to die, so I am of the view that life is too short, and we should live every moment to the full. Only right now, I don't feel like living it. I've been living a lie and one day my secret will unravel like a ball of wool. I want to unburden myself and tell the truth, but I can't.

I wish I could go back and erase the past year and start over again.

Sometimes I wonder how Taylor would have reacted if I'd told him. Would he have blamed me or comforted me? I imagine us lying in bed, his arms snaked around my waist, our eyes locked. I tell him, and he kisses me softly, wipes my tears and caresses my cheek.

But then the illusion is shattered, superseded by his scornful face; arms shoving me away with utter contempt. His eyes burn holes in me as though I'm a piece of shit. In that moment, my heart shatters and I know I must keep the secret locked away.

I reach for the foil blister packet hidden in my make-up bag and pop one of the round pills into my palm. They help me some days. It's only a small dose and one that I'd never admit to anyone that I'm taking. According to my doctor 10mg of Citalopram will make all the difference to how I am feeling.

Only I can bring back the old assured, successful Kate, but right now I have neither the strength, nor the determination to do that.

* * *

Taylor arrives home as I reach the bottom stair. With my make-up perfected and hair curled and pinned to one side, I look glamorous. The girl before him is not the woeful creature who stared back at me from the mirror earlier. Taylor is beaming.

"Wow. You look beautiful."

He hasn't smiled at me in this way for a long time. I return the gesture, as he kisses my forehead before rushing upstairs to shower.

My heart twitches, recalling my encounter with DCI Beckley. The chemistry between us was electrifying and unexpected. My cheeks warm a gentle blush as I evoke memories of his captivating eyes locked on mine. I take a deep breath; the feeling evaporates, replaced with overriding guilt. That's the exhilarating spark missing between Taylor and me. We will reignite it. We must.

# Chapter Fourteen – DCI Beckley

*Christmas Eve 2015*

Intricate snowflakes float weightlessly from the sky, dancing in the air, as they weave through the stark tree branches. Freshly lain snowfall blankets the driveway to HM Coroner's Court and the Riverside Centre, beautifying the ornate structure. The feather reed glass resembles snow cones, glistening in the morning light.

I'm refreshed, having slept in my bed for the first time since Cheryl Gray was discovered. I needed a break; tiredness was starting to cloud my judgement. I'd hoped to wake up to more positive news but instead another body has been discovered.

By all accounts, she could be his second victim, indicated by a missing forefinger and middle finger.

She's been dead for a while, decomposing under a bridge near the railway tracks, not a million miles away from where Cheryl was found.

Archer's theory is accurate, implying one more victim remains undiscovered. TAC advisor Steve Kent suggested a full-scale search of the estate to ensure no dense area is left unturned. It will be a difficult operational task, given the weather conditions, but necessary.

None of the girls deserved to die, let alone be left to rot; wild animals gnawing away at their skin and bones. We will find her.

My car tyres indent the wintery scene outside the mortuary entrance. I step out; bitter air stings my face as snow crunches subtly underfoot.

It's Christmas Eve and none of us should be dealing with such an atrocity, especially at this time of year, but we chose our pathways, where death and destruction are an intrinsic part of life. Only today, it feels worse than usual.

Once the body has been identified, I will need to inform her next of kin and not only ruin their Christmas, but the rest of their lives.

The inner surroundings of the Riverside Centre do little to repel the plummeting outside temperatures. I keep my coat on and continue past the fridge room, leaving a trail of ice shards behind.

Despite countless visits, I'm still not accustomed to the 135 bodies that are stored here; four per freezer. It repulses me knowing I'll join the body count one day, sharing a confined space with three strangers.

Foster unloads bagged evidence from the crime scene onto the worktop of the CSI suite. She offers me an acknowledging smile as I open the viewing window into the autopsy room.

APT John Richardson has his back to me, wearing burgundy scrubs and an apron. He retrieves the body from the fridge tray with a mortuary stacking trolley roller. The smell isn't profuse. A sour bubble gum odour produced by a mixture of decaying bodies and the centre's cerise cleaning fluid. I should be used to it by now but it's hard to ignore.

Richardson unzips the body bag. The air quickly degenerates, replaced with an overpowering stench of rotting human flesh, similar in nature to that of slaughtered animals at a butcher's counter. I inadvertently place my palm against my nostrils to shield my airways.

Shelton and Delaney appear in their usual autopsy attire and matching olive Dunlop wellies. The pair assist him with the body transfer onto the steel autopsy table.

The deceased is in a severe state of decomposition, with black lips. Her abdomen, shoulders and head are discoloured green; face bloated around the eyes. Her skin is marbled, an intricate pattern of blood vessels visible on her green and black flesh, with liquid-filled blisters spanning her torso. It's burst in places where the surface has cracked due to the pressure of internal gases and the breakdown of the skin itself. She has been dead for weeks.

As they slide her across, clumps of loose blonde hair fall onto the floor. Her corpse looks a similar build to the other women.

"The deceased has been identified as Shelley Carter, aged 25," Shelton informs me.

She and Delaney X-ray the body first, followed by her skull. The real-time imaging is captured on the camera system, which I witness on the LCD TV screen. They proceed to a full body inspection, having been joined by Foster and her SLR Camera, to document the injuries.

"There are bruises consistent with grip marks around the deceased's neck. Significant force was applied to the windpipe, intended to flatten it, and causing mucus to form. This would effectively seal the throat so that air cannot flow in or out. But he didn't apply enough pressure to achieve a complete collapse, as this is not the way he wanted her to die; rather, this method was to silence her screams," Shelton explains.

"His coup de grace was a single, horizontal stab wound between the fourth and fifth rib. The penetrating trauma, caused by a non-serrated, single edged blade, passed through the chest wall and pierced the heart. Unable to pump blood to the brain at a pressure necessary to maintain cerebral blood flow, and keep her conscious, brain death would have followed within several minutes."

"So, it's the same MO?" I ask.

"Yes, and she was found with her clothing disheveled, in the same manner as the other victims."

Shelton moves to the left side of the table and takes fingertip scrapings from the deceased's hand with a cotton bud. With the corpse in a state of advanced decomposition, some of the nails fall away in the process. Shelton switches to the opposite side of the deceased, lifting her palm upwards for closer inspection.

"The distal phalanges have been severed on the forefinger and middle finger. The cut is clean, as with the other victims, suggesting that the same weapon was used."

Foster continues snapping away, the clicking resonance, combined with the camera flashes, irritates me.

"I submit that we are looking at his second victim, given the fact that two fingertips are missing and also the level of decomposition. Her PMI is approximately three weeks ago."

Shelton looks in my direction, her face deadpan. The autopsy procedure has no impact on her despite the putrid condition of the body. I find it revolting and degrading, no matter how many I bear witness to.

The stench overpowers my lungs. I step backwards, putting distance between myself and the procedure.

Delaney grips a forensic scale and moves to the chest, documenting the incised knife wound measurements. Shelton inserts a scalpel into the deceased's chest, slicing through her flesh, creating a Y-shaped incision across the torso, and then cracks open the chest.

After studying the evidence bags sprawled across the CSI suite for a few moments, I redirect my focus back to the autopsy, just as Shelton removes a steel probe from the heart.

"The weapon used matches the same shape and size as those used on the other victims. The blade penetrated the right ventricle causing death."

She withdraws her hands from the chest cavity, cradling the heart in her bloody palms, which she passes to Richardson. He records the weight at 435 grams. The procedure is repeated for the remaining internal organs.

"All the organs are within normal limits, suggesting the deceased was otherwise healthy prior to death."

Richardson is behind the deceased's head. He's mid 30s and is a highly regarded APT, having been headhunted from a hospital in the city. He's prolific with his procedures and works seamlessly alongside Shelton and Delaney. His face is perplexed as he clutches a scalpel, head tilted and pressed against his left shoulder, inspecting the skull. He pauses; eyes fixed on her ear. The room is silent as he shifts around to the left-hand side of the table and tilts the deceased's head further away from him.

"Look," he urges, directing his eyes at Delaney and Shelton.

"There's dried blood within the ear and an incision."

They swap places to examine the ear canal. Foster captures a few snaps.

"There's a small puncture wound in the ear canal, perhaps the result of a long, sharp instrument being inserted," Delaney confirms.

"For what purpose?" I inquire.

"It's an unusual MO. The killer inserted an object upwards through the ear canal, through the temporal bone at the base and side of the skull to pierce the brain. The incision would have caused a hemorrhage."

"What killed her? The stab wound or the hemorrhage?"

"Given the killer's desire to torture and punish his victims, I would suggest he stabbed her first and then, as her body shut down, he inserted the object into the brain for his own personal gratification," Delaney answers.

"What about the other victims? This injury was not present on any of them, was it?"

"No." Shelton replies, her cheeks flush a subtle crimson tone, flustered.

"It's not something we detected. But I think we should re-examine their corpses."

Richardson walks towards the three white internal doors, sliding out Cheryl Gray's body from one of the forensic case fridges. He unzips the body bag to her chest and shines a small torch into her left ear. He feigns a sombre expression while studying the ear canal closely. The room remains quiet. He averts his gaze over to Delaney and Shelton and nods his head.

Shelton looks panicked, losing her usual composure as she rushes over to inspect for herself. Richardson moves to the adjacent forensic fridge, pulling on the flip handle to retrieve Nicole Hall's corpse. Delaney strides across the wet room flooring, his wellies dragging blonde hair strands over the floor drain. He's beside Richardson, analysing her ear.

"It's subtle but the incision is present," Delaney blurts, breaking the silence.

"We need secondary autopsies on both victims; a full, closer inspection of their craniums."

# Chapter Fifteen – Kate

*Christmas Eve 2015*

The force will still not officially confirm that a third victim has been found. My source works within the constabulary, therefore, I'm assured it's true. But I can't run with it though, not unless I have it on the record.

I've never been let down in the past by this person, who helped me expose several high profile scandals in the past; "Copping Off", the PC caught having sex at the station and "The Dogging Copper", who engaged in a carpark tryst on duty, were two of the biggest stories I broke, through my source.

There are good cops, bad cops and a few naughty ones too, who, despite their allegiance to the law, let their own vices cloud their judgment.

I feel guilty remembering the faces of the uniformed officers splashed across the front page. Their careers were already over; their fate sealed by their own actions. I merely exposed the reason for their suspension.

"Copping Off" was shortlisted for a national award, a momentous achievement for me. Every national daily followed my lead.

I understood that the story went far deeper than I could publicly divulge. Had I shared key details about the women involved, you'd understand why there was no hesitancy on my part in printing it. That however, is a secret I'll take to my grave in order to protect them.

I'm in a state of reverie; eyes fixed on the luminous light flashing on the landline. It's 6.42am. I'm alone and uneasy, fearing it's the Health Trust lodging a formal complaint against me for visiting ICU.

The caller is determined; the light displays incessantly. I answer reluctantly encountering silence. My forefinger traces my bottom lip, goose bumps swarm sending a shiver through me. The silence seems to last a lifetime.

"Hello?"

My tonsils swell with fear. I swallow.

"Can I help you?"

Silence is replaced by ragged breaths. Ominous thoughts tease my mind, terror latching around me wondering if it's the killer, toying with me. The news exposure has angered him and now I must face the consequences. I'm choking on my dry tongue; lungs overactive drawing in short panicked breaths.

"Can I help you?" I ask again.

Faint sobs emerge, breaking the muteness. My fear is overridden with confusion.

"Hello, is anyone there?" Feminine howls intensify, and relief surges my body.

"Please talk to me, are you OK?" I plead.

"It's my baby, my baby is dead," a voice blurts; words barely audible.

The abrupt statement renders me speechless. I hang on the line listening.

"My baby died at the safe house. It's their fault he's gone." I snatch a pen and start scribbling notes.

"Doctors say Tommy died from gastroenteritis caught from the dirty conditions."

"Where did this happen?"

"Gresham House. It's a safe house for women fleeing domestic abuse. Other children are sick and could die too," she warns.

I feel ashamed to admit it, but I want to hang up. The thought of yet another story involving a dead child repulses me. I know I can't, and I would never do that to someone who is clearly so distressed. I guess that's the nature of my job, never knowing what card I'm going to be dealt.

I just seem to be having a bad run of luck right now.

* * *

Fresh lain snow compresses underfoot against the kerb as I navigate the carpark, toward the Crown Inn.

Ice shards penetrate my soles, seeping cold air around my toes, as snowflakes drift aimlessly from the morning sky, landing on my hair like confetti.

My face is raw; ice kissing my tender cheeks as I continue towards the entrance. As I tap my heels against the doorstep shards fall and glisten like pearl sequins.

I open the pub door and sudden warmth strokes my face like intense humidity greeting me from an aircraft door. Unwanted regulars' eyes dissect my body as I tread over the sticky archaic Renaissance woven Axminster carpet.

An obese barman engulfs the bar. His huge stomach protrudes from underneath his shirt, projecting the illusion of a full-term pregnancy. I look past him, continuing my search for the mother, Charlie. I spot a lone woman sobbing.

She's painfully thin, her arms and legs twig-like, eyes sunken and her face skeletal. Life has been tough. She appears downtrodden, with greasy mousy hair and torn, faded jeans. Tentatively, I walk past a man in his 60s with a glass eye.

The woman lifts her petite head, directing a stare. Her blood vessels are dilated with blood flowing through them, producing red lines across the whites of her eyes.

"I'm sorry for your loss," I say, offering what I hope is a comforting smile.

"I can't believe he's gone. Please help me," she begs, grasping a glass of amber whisky in her shaky hand to her chapped lips.

"You need to tell me everything."

She's 23 but looks childlike. "I know I can't bring Tommy back, but you need to stop this from happening to someone else's kid," she muffles; tears overflowing from her desolate eyes.

I pluck a tissue packet from my bag, hand it over and listen courteously. Her gaze studies the liquor; she's had several judging by the collection of glasses piled on the scratched mahogany table. Still, I'm not one to judge.

Her baby's death is disturbing, and I fear, if what she is telling me is true, that other children could be at risk. A tear falls over my lashes, hearing her describe his lifeless body and the alleged squalor, in which they were both forced to sleep. Her dirty fingernails slide a 6x4 photograph across the table. I presume it is Tommy. His lips are blue, his face moon white and emaciated. It's been taken after death.

"It's the only picture I have of him," she whispers.

I hastily wipe my face to conceal my emotions, feeling heartbroken inside.

Gresham House denies that the virus stemmed from their premises, and the manager argues that the blame lies with the mother. It's a tricky situation, with both parties attributing blame over the boy's death upon the other.

I'll discuss it with Cecilia, but given we will soon have an official comment, and the mum's side of the story, I know she'll run with it. Clutching the harrowing image in my fingertips, I leave Charlie behind. We can't print a photograph of a dead child, but she's insistent that I make an exception and return the picture later.

There is nothing else I can do for her.

Back in the newsroom I draft the article, headed: "Mum Complains of Dirty Conditions after Baby Death".

Cecilia is more than satisfied with the Gresham House response and earmarks the article for front page, minus the distressing image. I should feel elated at another page one scoop, yet the content does nothing to excite me.

I need to direct my focus back to the Millbrook murders and get a new lead, or, at least, official confirmation of the third victim. I know she exists, I feel it in my bones. My source has no reason to lie.

Feeling bold and determined, I call the station and ask for DCI Beckley.

I'm certain that he won't take my call; it's not protocol. But I have to try.

My eyes itch. I'm tired, having been on hold for ages, latching the telephone cord around the length of my forefinger. The office is sweltering, extreme heat pumping from the radiators to repel the outside chill. Tacky gold and berry tinsel hangs above them. Christmas has snuck up fast; I've been so preoccupied. It's 4.17pm.

"Just one moment please," a voice muffles before the classical symphony restarts, irritating my eardrum.

"DCI William Beckley."

I freeze; body pricked with panic. I inhale, searching for my words, while frantically pulling my finger free from its snare.

"Oh, er, hi, it's Kate, Kate Rivendale, Southern Chronicle."

"How can I help?"

"Could I discuss the enquiry I made earlier regarding a third victim?"

"You realise contacting me directly is against procedure?"

"Yes." I say softly, as my heart sinks. I feel like a young schoolgirl, being told off by the headmaster. My mouth is dehydrated. I lick my lips, generating saliva.

"You should be liaising with the press office."

His tone is forceful. My stomach churns; cheeks burn. My underarms moisten, perspiration sweeping across my skin.

"I'm aware of that, I just wanted to apologise for going to the hospital. It's not something I have ever considered in the past."

"We all make mistakes."

There's an awkward silence. I'm uncertain whether I should probe further.

"I can see that you are just doing your job, Ms Rivendale. I just wouldn't advise going to ICU again without prior consent."

I feel sick. I guess he feels he has now put me in my place. I am about to apologise again, and end the call, when he continues.

"Listen, there are facts that we can release, and there is information which could hinder our investigation if it were made public at this present time. Do you understand what I am trying to say?"

I inhale slowly, my chest gripped with nerves.

"I think so."

"At a point in time when I'm able to disclose such facts, I could ensure that you are the first to be made aware." His tone has altered and is more sympathetic.

"I would appreciate that very much, thank you."

"I understand the need to see the wider picture of this investigation. I need your help to release relevant case data as much as you need my input. Once I have key information, I will happily provide you with it, if you are willing to work together?"

"Yes, yes of course."

"We can meet, or I can call you with updates as they arise," he offers, his voice sultry.

"Umm."

My words become incarcerated behind my tonsils. I'm fully aware that my face is radiating a scarlet glow. Tom looks intrigued, staring from across the reporters' station. I sip stale coke; its oversweet tang sends a shudder down my back.

"You can reach me on this landline, or my mobile, which is 07752464747," I say, trying hard not to sound flustered or breathless.

"I'll be in touch Ms Rivendale."

"Great, thank you."

There's a momentary pause and then silence on the line.

Flustered, I hang up and swivel my chair back to the computer screen. Tom is smirking while continuing to type. I pretend I'm un-fazed by my embarrassed expression, and place Tommy's picture in my handbag.

The last thing I want to do is see his mother again, but I never break a promise.

# Chapter Sixteen – Kate

*Christmas Eve 2015*

The dark sky illuminates the powdery crystals sweeping the length of the pebbled beach. Snowflakes continue to fall, sliding against the windscreen.

Clevedon Pier is barely visible through the dense conditions.

*"Driving home for Christmas"* plays on the radio. The cheery melody evokes a smile. I've finished early to return the photo to Charlie. The M5 motorway is quiet, having avoided rush hour. I slow my speed on the dual carriageway into Weston, passing a gritting lorry, which spits tiny shards against my car.

Weston is a seaside town stuck somewhere between the 1970s and the present day. At the height of summer, it's full of pensioners on day trips from Birmingham and Wales, enjoying fish and chips and drinking from flasks along the promenade. Families enjoy ice creams and donkey rides, spend endless 2p coins in the gaudy amusement arcades and ride The Grand Pier attractions.

The town experienced a boost in visitors thanks to Banksy bringing his Dismaland attraction to The Tropicana, an old abandoned lido. But it's long gone, along with the crowds.

In the off-peak winter season, Weston bears its own its own resemblance to Dismaland. The concessions are shut, the land train non-operational and the seafront deserted, aside from solitary dog walkers who've forgotten how to smile. In the winter, it's a ghost town that has lost its beating heart.

I'd be far better suited to somewhere tropical where the sun can dance across my skin. But home is where the heart is, and I couldn't be away from my family.

Charlie is slouched against the wall of the Crown Inn drawing on a cigarette. Her denim jacket is unbuttoned, exposing her midriff. She clocks me and staggers over. Her bloodshot eyes stare through the glass. She opens the door and slumps beside me. I return the photograph, but Tommy's blue lips and waxy complexion remain imprinted in my mind. I share her grief, though her loss is more vivid.

"I'm Sorry, we couldn't use the picture, but the story will be front page," I explain.

"It's okay, I guessed as much. Do you think it will help?"

"The council must take the matter seriously and investigate your allegations against Gresham House. Then, if necessary, take action."

She seems lost, her face blank.

"I take it you're not going back there?" I ask.

"No, I can go home to my flat now that my ex-boyfriend has left. It's safe now."

She informs me that she lives on Millbrook, and I step on the accelerator. Technically, I shouldn't offer her a lift, but I can't leave her alcohol-fuelled and grieving, on Christmas Eve.

Lasmerton Drive emerges on the right. Torn police tape remnants remain visible, flapping from the lamppost.

"Hope they catch the dirty fucking bastard," Charlie exclaims, breaking the silence.

"Sorry?"

"The fuckwit who's attacking women."

"It's horrendous." My voice trails off, distracted by siren wails and cobalt lights blinding my rear-view mirror. My heart bolts.

Two police cars and a trio of women await us. Charlie's hands shake, shoving chewing gum between her lips. Tears fall down her cheeks.

"Come on, I'll walk with you."

She gets out, rests her hand on the bonnet, feet treading through slush. I link her arm, accompanying her.

"You need to leave," a tall, officer yells, staring down his pointed nose. I look beyond him, focusing on the women.

"Please don't leave, I'm begging you," Charlie pleads, face grief-stricken and panicky.

My heart is torn, head pounding. My subconscious whispers in my ear, telling me to forget her and leave. I don't want to be arrested for obstruction. My teeth gnaw my lip, deliberating.

"Please." Charlie repeats. Her expression conveys extreme distress. Her cheeks are clammy, her bulging eyes fixed on me. I won't leave her. If that means I'm slung into a police car and banged up for the night, then so be it.

Charlie grips my hand and laces fingers with mine. I feel awkward but follow her towards a stairwell with a police escort in tow. Scant lighting flickers intermittently; most of the lights have been smashed. Glass shards crack underfoot as I continue my ascent, inhaling a profuse urine odour. Poised on the last step, I scrape my soles against its edge, dislodging any fragments before continuing onwards with Charlie.

We enter flat 4. My desiccated mouth falls open as my eyes gawk at the squalid conditions. The putrid smell of mould taints the air. I step over bespattered carpet to reach the kitchen. Filthy dishes are piled upon the worktop and a cat litter tray overflows onto the lino with lumps of faeces and puddles of rancid urine.

I hold my breath, trapping any fresh air inside my lungs to withstand the nauseating stench. Clumps of sick rise and flush against my palate. My hand moves unconsciously resting over my lips.

Two women enter. One stands inches from Charlie's sombre face, her huge shapeless bust and stomach rolls ooze against her floral dress, forcing pressure onto the gaping plastic front fasteners. Her fingers pluck a handful of papers from her tan saddle handbag. She shoves them under Charlie's nose.

"We're taking your children into care, due to suspicious circumstances surrounding your baby's death," she announces coldly, hands touching up her heavily lacquered perm.

"You can't, they're all I have left. Tell them," Charlie pleads, searching my eyes from the depths of her desolate soul.

I'm dumbstruck, studying the social worker's expressionless, wrinkled face. Her eyes are menacing.

"We have a court order," she replies, stretching her plump lips into a smirk. I retrieve the document and skim the printed pages. I can't find the words and simply nod at Charlie, who looks as if the world has fallen from beneath her.

Screams from the hallway shatter the silence. Two toddlers are being snatched from the arms of a skeletal woman, presumably their grandmother. Charlie crashes to the floor, her knees pound into urine. Her hands grip my trousers, pleading.

"Stop them!"

Vomit erupts again, filling my mouth. I force it back down.

"Give them back. I'll kill myself," she threatens.

Her tears saturate my legs. My eyes sting, welled with my own tears, witnessing the children's fingers being cruelly peeled away from their grasp. I wipe my eyes and loosen Charlie's grip, feeling heartbroken.

"I have to leave, I'm sorry."

I avoid eye contact.

"Please, you can't go," she whimpers. "Stop them, I can't lose my babies."

"I'm sorry Charlie, I can't get involved in this."

I retreat swiftly and hurry down the stairwell. I gasp, snatching fresh air. The street is deserted, aside from the unoccupied police cars and my Cherry Peugeot. I fumble for my keys, my breath hovering.

Loitering beyond my car, I glimpse a figure.

I walk hastily, my hands quivering. His silhouette skulks closer. Petrified, the keys slip through my fingertips into the gutter; my heart thrashing.

His footsteps quicken as my hands grapple in the darkness, scratching against tarmac chippings. I'm next. My life is over. Taylor warned me not to come here, I should have listened. Now I won't have the chance to make things right. His breath hovers over my ear; he kneels beside me.

"You shouldn't be out here alone," he whispers.

His face is concealed by the hood of his jacket. His gloved hands dangle my keys; the silver nickel glistens in the moonlight. I snatch them, flee and unlock the car door.

I insert the keys into the ignition, daring myself to glance out. He's gone. Air blasts against my trembling body. I ache with fear and guilt, tasting my tears on my lips.

Leaving Charlie is the right decision, but it hurts. The social workers have their reasons for taking the children into care and maybe this time I was duped, and Charlie is to blame.

I feel vulnerable and disappointed with myself, as I truly believed I could spot evil.

# Chapter Seventeen

*Christmas Eve 2015*

The burning rage inside him spiralled, igniting a fire in the pit of his gut.

Her survival remained unclear, but whether she was dead or alive was no longer of importance. The uncertainty was overridden by an uncontrollable urge to kill and fulfil his desires.

Tonight, he felt like the proverbial kid in a candy shop, the choice on Christmas Eve was boundless. Dirty whores are everywhere, seeping out of their scant clothing. No shame, no pride. Stumbling around the streets intoxicated, alone, asking for it.

The shadows concealed his presence. Her high heels clipped the pavement. He felt aroused, the urge to control and degrade her, irresistible. His breath lingered over his skin, suffused against his mask. He felt excited, watching her slender legs move closer, towards him.

She was now in reach, sauntering along the lane, her inner thighs exposed, passing him inattentively. His fist smashed her skull. Her ankles crumbled, falling off her heels, and she slammed face down onto the snow.

Blood gushed from her nose and seeped into her mouth. She coughed to clear her throat, sending blood spatter across her lips, tarnishing the feathery snow. Her vision blurred while his unrelenting hands thrashed her body onto her back.

She tried to scream but his hand jammed against her throat, smashing her skull against the tarmac. The pain jolted her eyes back open, encountering the flicker of the steel blade slashing the drifting snowflakes.

He rose to his feet, stamping repeatedly on her stomach. She lay immobile, studying the masked figure and the blade. Her heartbeat accelerated as the knife tip slashed her clothing. His breathing quickened, growing excited.

Paralysed by fear, she watched him pause, examine the terror in her eyes, and then smile as the blade plunged into her chest with the exact precision intended. His smile widened, and he exhaled slowly in awe.

* * * DCI Beckley * * *

*Christmas Day 2015*

I should be accustomed to this way of life after all the years in the job. My profession doesn't allow people to enjoy normal holidays.

I can't remember the last time I celebrated Christmas Day with all the trimmings. Still, I may as well be here, I've got no one to spend Christmas with. Both my parents are dead, and Jen will be enjoying the festive season with her own mum and dad.

I peruse the reports on my desk, outlining the traits of the four victims we've identified.

Nicole was naturally pretty, confident and well liked. She was the sort of person who could easily captivate attention.

Cheryl was equally beautiful and popular. She worked as a trainee nurse and was socially outgoing.

Both, according to their friends and family, were single. There is no history of problematic past relationships. Neither was linked to the sex industry or escort work. They were both normal young girls enjoying life.

We know little of Hannah yet, or Shelley Carter. But it appears as if he's targeting women based on their looks and personalities, which make them more naïve and trustworthy.

Archer, Foster, Delaney and Shelton sit patiently in the interview room to outline their findings from the secondary autopsies. From the bemoaned expressions across Delaney and Shelton's faces, it's clear that they had missed a vital part of the killer's MO the first time round.

"Merry Christmas," I mock, trying, but failing, to lighten the mood.

Shelton offers a hint of a smile. She's exhausted, with dark shadows underlying her eyes. Delaney and Foster both look equally unenamoured to be sharing Christmas Day with me.

"What's the latest?"

"The secondary autopsies did, in fact, uncover trauma to their ear canals. We believe that the killer inserted a long, sharp instrument, similar in diameter to a skewer, through the temporal bone and pierced the brain. To penetrate the bone, the assailant would have used significant force and the victims would have endured prolonged pain. We believe this is his signature; a calling card to let us know they were his."

"How did you miss it?"

"I can only apologise."

Shelton's gaze studies her lap, her fingertips fiddle nervously with the surface of a new aquamarine glass bead.

"We have three bodies; Nicole, Cheryl and Shelley. Plus, our survivor, Hannah Green, who remains unconscious. There has been no change in her condition. It's likely she will remain on ICU for several days," I outline.

Wakeman enters, interrupting. "Make that four," he says, solemnly.

I turn to face him, examining his puffed cheeks. Remarkably, he's changed attire, and is now wearing a dark grey suit, and thankfully, his distinct body odour is absent.

"Live Cell has been alerted to a body in Weston, outside the Millbrook estate."

"Is it the same MO?"

"A single stab wound to the chest. Victim is blonde, around the same age as the other women. She was found in a secluded pathway, off Hamlear Grove, near the town centre."

"For fuck's sake!"

Sweat saturates my underarms. This is getting out of control.

"We need to get to the crime scene," Shelton exclaims.

"Why swap location?" I quiz.

"Hannah Green," Delaney answers confidently, placing his pen down on the table.

"His satisfaction was short lived. He doesn't know whether she's dead or alive. He's worried about getting caught, doesn't want to take the risk there. Women across Weston think that's his killing ground, so they feel safer walking around in other parts of town. Swapping his comfort zone to another location is perfectly logical."

"Reverting back to the other victims, what can you tell me forensically? Any new evidence, Amy?"

She's on the edge of her chair clutching a report, keen to disclose information.

"I've some rather remarkable findings," she announces. "The blue rubber has been identified as the tip of a disposable glove, provided at petrol stations. The manufacturer is Healthguard. Unfortunately, it had been submersed in water and therefore no latent fingerprint could be lifted. More interestingly, we recovered a small population of extraneous fibres during the secondary autopsy from inside each of the victims left ears. Normally few fibres are recovered from body orifices, therefore these were deemed to be potentially significant. To be honest we were baffled by them in the lab."

She pauses, allowing the others to absorb her information, before continuing.

"It's not something any of us have encountered before. Thus, samples were sent to undergo industrial enquiry. It appears we unearthed rare red Casein yarn fibre. Casein yarn is chemically similar in appearance to wool, only distinguishable under the microscope. It was blended with rayon, wool, mohair and cotton during the 1930s and 1940s to create woven and knitted fabrics. It was a cheaper substitute for wool but fell out of use at the end of World War II, when newer, cheaper synthetics such as nylon emerged. Today Casein yarn is obsolete."

"Where the hell did it come from then?"

"While Casein yarn is not readily available, it doesn't mean that it couldn't still exist in some shape or form, perhaps as a red blanket or jumper."

"Sorry I'm struggling to comprehend the significance."

"I'm saying the Casein yarn fibres are old, having been stored for years, in perhaps an attic or basement, and now they have resurfaced after all this time."

"So how did the fibres get inside their ears?"

"Through contact with the weapon. The killer must wrap his tools up for concealment, which is why I believe you are more likely to be looking for a red blanket. Once he inserted the skewer into their ears and removed it, the friction left behind these extraneous fibres. Find a match and we find our killer."

\* \* \*

Hamlear Grove lies one mile from the town centre and 1.7 miles from the Millbrook estate. It's not a huge distance in terms of expanding his comfort zone, yet, it's far enough for women walking alone to feel relatively safe.

Despite our advice not to walk unaccompanied, our warnings were ignored. It was Christmas Eve, revellers partying and fuelled with alcohol, without a care in the world, don't want to know that they may be in danger. The alcohol fuels their bravado, a sense of invincibility. Bad things happen to other people, not to them.

The last victim has been identified as Jesse Cooper, 26, a nurse, according to the hospital ID badge found inside her purse.

It's cold, the glacial air has ripped through my suit, wrapping itself around my vertebrae. Her body lay here overnight in this alleyway, off Hamlear Grove. Shielded by dense snow, her body was virtually concealed but visually still apparent to the dog walker who discovered her.

Foster and her colleague, Darren Fairview, gently dust the snow layering Jesse's partially frozen corpse with their latex gloved hands. The surrounding snow on which she rests has absorbed her blood, resembling cherry cola slush puppy.

Foster captures images throughout the removal process.

The body is in a state of full rigor mortis; upper torso purple, hands blue and her eyes sunken into her skull. Her lower limbs are in a state of lividity, the skin stained dark purple-black. Every inch of her is photographed, the wounds and incisions documented in microscopic detail by Shelton.

Jesse rests in the same position as the other victims; upon her back, her clothing slashed, and her underwear exposed.

Shelton wastes no time checking for a puncture wound inside the ear canal. I do not need verbal confirmation; her eyes tell me she's uncovered trauma inside.

It's our killer.

## Chapter Eighteen – Kate

*Christmas Day 2015*

I can't tell Taylor about my horrendous ordeal with Charlie, or the terror I felt.

The stranger unsettled me, leaving me panicked. I thought it was the killer, believed I was next. The Millbrook estate terrifies me.

Having been fortunate to grow up in a respectable, trouble-free area, I'm not used to the dramas that I encounter on that estate. Death, drugs and violence are rife and while it may make for a great story, the atrocities only deepen my fear of venturing down there.

Still, I chose my career. I wanted to be the roving reporter I'd seen on TV, out capturing the story as it happens. You imagine a job, only it isn't the same in real life. Journalism is ruthless, a constant battle to prove yourself. Always fighting for the best stories to get your name out there and be noticed.

I try my best but my conscience battles with my heart. I can't be the hardnosed bitch that I'm stereotyped to be. I have feelings. Every single story touches me, leaving a lasting memory. I never really understood until I got out on my patch how hated we are as a profession. That's what really twists my gut, the feeling of being despised, the look I have seen in the eyes of many strangers because of what I do.

I should be happy today, it's Christmas. I can't wait to sit in front of the fire with Taylor, opening our presents. I sneak out of bed, peer out of the window and feel my lips stretch into a smile at the thick snow.

It's 7.58am. I feel childlike, wanting Taylor to wake up. He looks peaceful with his head snuggled on the pillow. The festive period has been killing him; he's been working around the clock. But today is ours, no work for either of us. Later, we're off to my parents for Christmas dinner. Sometimes I wonder what Taylor's parents would have been like, had they been around. It's not something he likes to talk about.

I climb back onto the bed; my knees sink into the memory foam. I place a kiss on his lips.

"Merry Christmas."

He remains still. My naughty inner temptress throws her toys out of the pram at the lack of reaction. I'm sulking, studying his face closely, watching his eyes finally flicker open. He plants a huge kiss back on my lips.

"Merry Christmas, Mrs Rivendale," he teases.

He quickly flips me onto my back and lies on top of me, tracing warm kisses up my neck until he reaches my lips. His electric eyes are on mine glistening in the morning light.

He's back! I can see the warmth in his gaze, his soul re-emerging from the depths of despair.

Taylor is becoming the man that I knew was trapped inside. I'd hoped that he would find his way back to me, that we would find our way back to each other. It just took far longer than I'd anticipated.

His hand reaches under my pillow; lips smirking, feigning a mischievous smile. Old embers smoulder. He looks happy. I want to capture his expression, store it in my mind and override one of the traumas.

"Merry Christmas," he says again. as he withdraws his hand, which is now holding a dainty gift box.

I lean against my duck-feathered pillow examining the box, covered with shiny red wrapping, tied with an organza gold bow. I pull the ribbon and peel off the paper, only to encounter a second and third layer. The suspense is killing me. Finally, I reach a suede box containing a diamond solitaire ring. It's beautiful. My eyes well, eyeing the gem. I ache with elation, feeling the wall between us cascading down.

"What's the matter? Don't you like it?"

"It's stunning. I adore it, I just didn't expect it. Thank you."

He wipes my tears and kisses me softly.

"Where's mine?" he teases.

"Under the tree, come on," I urge, leading the way.

We race along the landing, pushing and shoving one another like children, before halting at the top stair.

"Go on, I'm just messing with you," Taylor insists, reaching his hand out allowing me to lead the way once more.

As I search under the tree, I hear a cork pop in the kitchen. Nestled amongst wrapped gifts under spruce branches is a black and gold box. I'd planned to tease him first with a few stocking fillers, but after receiving my ring, I can't wait to let him open it. The tree lights twinkle in the early morning dawn.

'*Rocking Around The Christmas Tree*' suddenly blasts across the room. Taylor emerges, carrying flutes of Bucks Fizz, and dances his way across the living room carpet. His lack of attire and puerile behaviour sends me into fits of laughter. I take my glass and sip the cold bubbles, enjoying the citrus tang.

"Are you going to keep me in suspense?"

I realise that I'm cradling his gift on my lap. Taylor wastes no time deconstructing the packaging and gawks at the contents. A smile emerges as he retrieves the brushed gunmetal Bulova Marine Star watch.

"Do you like it?"

"Oh Kate, I love it."

"Turn it over."

Taylor studies the back eyeing the engraving, '*Every second I love you more.*' His smile is radiant, eyes cheerful and full of passion. He pulls me close and places his soft lips on mine for what feels like an eternity.

I recall a saying I once heard; '*Patience is a virtue and the best things in life are worth waiting for*'; it couldn't be more accurate.

## Chapter Nineteen – DCI Beckley

*Boxing Day 2015*

The Riverside Centre is second home to me. The autopsy process was delayed yesterday due to the frozen condition of the body and now Delaney, Shelton, Foster, Richardson and I are dissecting a corpse on Boxing Day.

I should be exhausted and bloated from over-indulging on roast turkey, all the trimmings and copious amounts of wine. Instead, Christmas dinner consisted of a packet of crispy bacon Wheat Crunchies and a bottle of Coke.

Strangely, I have no appetite today, studying the bludgeoned body laid out before us. Oddly, the press isn't aware of this latest kill. But I'm grateful. I'd rather keep it that way, for as long as possible.

"There's positional blanching on her back, indicating her body lay pressed on her spine for around 12 hours," Shelton states, resting the deceased back down upon the autopsy table.

"She was murdered on Christmas Eve."

Her skin is waxy; the lividity process has discoloured her flesh a deep plum, almost black shade.

Debris and grit cling to her swollen lips. Her eyes are sunken, skin puffed underneath.

I study the hospital ID card which is sealed in a clear polythene bag next to her personal effects and evidence collected at the scene. Jesse was attractive, fitting the same profile as the others, although I can barely see the resemblance now.

Why are women not taking heed of our warnings about venturing out alone? I know it was Christmas Eve but for fuck's sake, the pure ignorance beggar's belief. I'm not implying that she deserved this, merely pointing out that common sense should prevail.

At 26, Jesse, had her full life ahead of her. Now, she's just his fifth victim and we are still no closer to identifying him.

"It's the same MO. The stab wound to the heart and the incision through the temporal bone," Shelton reiterates.

I turn back to face the autopsy table, my eyes on Shelton's blood-stained apron. The autopsy has progressed fast; chest cavity open and the heart on the steel dissection table. I've heard all I need to; confirmation that's she's one of his.

I desperately need Hannah Green to regain consciousness and start talking. But she's been on ICU with no condition change for six days, my hopes are fading.

Shelton and Delaney finish up. I head to the viewing room feeling exhausted and in need of caffeine. The Bosch Tassimo dispenses an Americano.

Ceiling spotlights brighten the room as do the magnolia walls against the oak flooring. The room is tranquil, with heavy velour brown curtains framing the glass viewing window. Staring through the pane I observe an empty Bier trolley. Jesse will be laid out there, once Richardson has finished suturing, and has washed her hair. The smell of the raspberry shampoo and coconut conditioner that he uses on the corpses, lingers in the confined air.

Richardson does a remarkable job of cleaning them up; given the prolonged violence they have been subjected to. Jesse's parents will be visiting shortly, to say their final goodbyes, on a day when families normally come together for fun and laughter.

There is a distinct lack of exuberance in my life right now. My world revolves around mortality and while that vile bastard is still out there, I can't see my circumstances changing any time soon.

## Chapter Twenty – Kate

*Monday 28 December 2015*

The past few days have been the happiest moments that Taylor and I have shared in the past year.

Not only did we enjoy time with my family, we also celebrated Christmas with a party. Everyone came; Ryan and Sara, Todd, Helen and Pete, even Dawn and James, who brought the twins over.

They say time is a great healer and it's true when it comes to us. We both took a virtual holiday, escaped from life to deal with our grief. Whilst neither of us will ever forget Paul, and I'll never erase our baby's death from my memory, we can, it seems, finally move on. Christmas has brought us closer and reunited our hearts as one.

It's sad that we both let things get this far. We were beyond happy once, mapping out our future together after getting engaged. Some would have called us crazy, but it felt right. We planned our dream wedding, then set about buying our house and creating our perfect home.

I remember the days when I would get over excited and nip out for paint while Taylor was at work and makeover a bedroom by the time he was home. He'd pretend to be annoyed with me for starting another transformation but was secretly glad that he hadn't had to do it. DIY is not his forte.

I, on the other hand, am creative, more imaginative. That's what they say about Pisces. I have an idea in my head of how I want something to look, and then put every ounce of energy into bringing that image to life.

We've worked hard turning the house into our home, though we kept the third bedroom neutral. Not that either of us had brought it up, we just quietly earmarked it for baby Rivendale. It brings tears to my eyes; I must try to stop thinking about it.

We will be happy again. We've certainly got off to a good start these past few days. The time spent at my parents house over Christmas was entertaining, full of party games, dancing and too much alcohol. Mum bought enough food to feed the entire street, a trait she inherited from Nan, who always stores at least five bags of sugar and six tins of custard in her food cupboard. Her food storage obsession must be linked to the war rationing she experienced as a child.

I look better, much happier; but I'm bloated, ready to burst at the seams. Breakfast, lunch, dinner and late-night supper for two consecutive days has taken its toll. My suit trousers are tight, squashing my stomach.

I'm back at work today. I just hope that being apart from Taylor again doesn't burst our bubble. I'm certain it won't. The progress we have made has been immense, despite us not actually broaching the subject of us having drifted.

We just seem to have slotted back together, like a jigsaw. We're soulmates, only our souls temporarily wandered apart, but have now, thankfully, been reunited once more.

On closer inspection, my eyes look deprived of sleep and I layer on Este Lauder Double Wear camouflage foundation to conceal the dark shadows. My tongue is stained berry from the Cabernet pigments and craves rehydration.

I need to resume normality and whilst I shouldn't admit it, I'm excited about getting up to speed on the Millbrook murders. I'm distracted by a text from an unknown number. I click the envelope icon: *'I have an update on the case, can you meet?'*

The timing is uncanny. Given the context, I presume that it's DCI Beckley.

'*Yes. Where?*' I reply promptly.

'*Costa Coffee. Flower Mead Retail Park.*'

My tiredness has evaporated, replaced with a surge of adrenalin.

I'm not nervous at the prospect of seeing him face to face, I'm excited at the potential working relationship we can establish. If we can build trust between us, it could help me to progress my career and gain exclusive information, which will make me stand out from the journalist pack.

'*What time?*'

'*Asap.*'

It's 7.40am.

'*8am?*'

'*Perfect*'.

That will give me chance to meet him and arrive to work before 9am. I want to keep our meeting confidential and protect him as a valuable source. I suspect his superiors would not approve of him sharing information without following the normal procedures.

I wish I didn't feel so awful. I run to the bathroom and brush my teeth and tongue fiercely to remove the profuse stale alcohol odour from my breath.

\* \* \*

Commuters pack the roads driving through the mist layering the dual carriageway toward the motorway after the holiday season.

It feels like Christmas was just a surreal figment of our imagination, as normal daily routines are resumed. We all know it happened, of course, and enjoyed it but it's over in a flash after weeks of momentum and feverish preparation.

I manoeuvre through the coffee-stained slush, around the roundabout by the old helicopter museum and onwards over the flyover, passing the new Premier Inn. The traffic slows, queuing at the traffic lights.

A surge of nausea vents inside, my teeth chew my cheek, feeling overwhelmed by a concoction of nerves and excitement building and pumping through me.

The lights turn green; I make my approach, mounting the speed bumps outside Frankie & Benny's and park in an empty space outside the mobile phone outlet. I turn off the ignition with my trembling fingers and snatch a glance through the passenger window. My heart reaches an impetus speed, excitement coiling around it as I observe DCI Beckley in a window seat.

I step out; the cold air nibbles my neck, sweeping under my hairline and down my back. I dig my hands deeper into my satin pocket lining as I stride across the melting snow towards the entrance in my new heels.

He's talking on the phone. I sense he's agitated and angry. His brow is furrowed, head rested upon his right palm, exposing the brushed chrome of his wristwatch.

My palm presses against the coffee bean insignia on the handle; it's freezing. Inside, the fresh coffee aroma swirls around me, invades my nostrils and warms my chest. I pause, maintaining a clear distance to avoid encroaching on his personal space.

Two builders in high-vis jackets and tatty, paint-stained jeans shield my view. They wink, brush past and exit. Arctic air blasts through, slicing over my cheek. I inch further forward, chewing my thumbnail awkwardly.

DCI Beckley redirects his eyes to the doorway before shifting his gaze on to me. I'm blushing. He continues speaking for a few seconds before ending the call and offering a smile.

I thought the lust that I had felt before would have diminished but his eyes are intoxicating, drawing me in. I surprise myself, as I recognise that, rightly or wrongly, it is lust that I am feeling. I saunter over, he meets me half way. My body feels every heartbeat echo in my chest, propelling the blood through my veins.

"Miss Rivendale," he greets, holding out his hand, which he grips firmly around mine.

"DCI Beckley."

"Please, call me Will."

His eyes glisten, are full of intrigue, capturing and reflecting the radiant spotlights. They appear a deep sapphire today, punctuated with minuscule flecks of green. He wears a slim fit, dark charcoal suit with notch lapels, two welt pockets and a crisply-ironed white shirt underneath.

Our handshake lasts far longer than it should. My entrapped hand becomes clammy against his touch. When he finally frees me, he moves his palm to the small of my back, ushering me alongside him towards the counter.

I imagine his fingers tracing slowly down my back, caressing my face and running through my hair. My lips pout into a smile, which I force away. The lingering coffee aroma is infused with taints of his alluring aftershave, which I inhale. It sets my heart racing. My lips remain interlocked, my mind re-picturing the two of us together in a forbidden embrace.

Cups clang and startle me, propelling me back to reality. The male Barista turns to serve us. He's around 27 but the wispy coarse blonde and ginger stubble on his face makes him appear older. He's clad in a neatly pressed brown Costa shirt, adorned with a rectangular gold badge, embossed 'Harry'. He completes our order, sprinkling the top of my hot chocolate with a fine cocoa dust and adds the coffee bean design to Beckley's regular single black shot, via a stainless-steel stencil. I inhale the rich roasted scent wafting from the china cup.

We collect our order and sit at the window table. I cup my hot chocolate in both palms; it feels deliciously warm.

DCI Beckley's eyes are on me. Heat returns; pricking the surface of my cheeks. He's electrifying, stirring my inner desires. There's something dangerously attractive about him. I find him intense. I'm unable to strike up conversation. He empties two brown sugar sachets into his cup and mixes with a wooden stirrer.

"I had a vital update with regards to the investigation, which has changed considerably within the last few minutes."

My eyes remain fixed on his, listening to every word.

"I was going to confirm your suspicions regarding the third victim and her survival. This knowledge was on a strict need to know basis to protect her from the offender and allow her time to regain consciousness and tell us whatever she could about the assailant. Sadly, I have just been informed that the victim died in the past hour."

I absorb his sentences, which roll off his soft lips. I need to get a grip of myself.

"The past few days has seen the investigation advance quickly, with the discovery of two further bodies."

Two more? I lean closer, my mind confused and intrigued by the quickly unravelling information.

"There are now five victims?" I probe.

"Yes. We believe that Nicole Hall and Cheryl Gray, the first two victims that we identified, were actually his third and fourth kills. Subsequently, he attacked Hannah Green, who escaped, but who has tragically just died. Another victim, identified as Shelley Carter, was found on Christmas Eve. She had been dead for three weeks, and we suspect she's the second victim. Furthermore, on Christmas Day the body of Jesse Cooper was found outside of Millbrook, having been killed in the same manner."

"How can you tell the order of the victims?"

"The autopsies have pinpointed the approximate time of death for each victim, and the killer is severing their fingers to number them. He pauses, giving me enough time to properly absorb this macabre revelation, and then reveals more. "Nicole was missing three fingertips, Cheryl was missing four, Shelley, two. Jesse, the latest victim had five fingers missing."

"Where's the first victim?" I ask, not wanting to dwell on the thought of the killer apparently mutilating the bodies of his victims, just to help keep count.

"We don't know. Search teams have conducted sweeps across Millbrook, but they haven't unearthed another body. The investigation is becoming very complex and is escalating at immense speed. He's now struck outside of his comfort zone, attacking elsewhere in Weston where women thought they were safe, which is deeply disturbing."

"Can I go on the record with this?"

"Yes. On the proviso that I can read your copy first, with the right to make amendments if I feel it compromises me in any way."

"I can agree to that." My body is buzzing; every nerve ending tingling in an intense rush. I know that this could be a career-defining story, and I now appear to have a hotline to exclusive central!

"I'll be holding an official press conference this afternoon, details of which will be released via the press office at 9am. But you have the story first."

"I'm really grateful for your assistance." I smile, and he returns the gesture. He has tiny dimples, which accentuate his cheekbones and perfect stubble. I sip my hot chocolate; froth clings to my top lip. I lick it off, feeling mortified as the realisation of everything he has told me sinks in.

"Just to clarify, this investigation has jumped from two to five victims, one of whom survived but who has since passed away, and the attacks are no longer confined to Millbrook?"

"Correct."

"And what exactly is he doing to women?"

"The killer beats and stabs them in their heart. Even more peculiarly, during the prolonged attack he punctures their eardrums with a skewered instrument causing a brain haemorrhage. We believe this is his signature."

"Shit." I squirm, my eyes screw trying to shield myself from the gore.

"Can I quote you, on the record?"

"No. Attribute the information to a police source. Anything I say this afternoon during the press conference can, of course, be attributed to me, which you can use as a follow up story."

"I'm very grateful, thank you."

Perhaps he doesn't hate me after all and understands the competitive nature of my profession.

"Like I said earlier, I'm happy for you to divulge the facts that I have discussed with you, on the condition of copy approval."

"Sure, only please don't let my editor know of our arrangement, she wouldn't approve."

"Agreed," he says, before adding, with a wry smile, "I don't think my Chief Constable would, either."

His fingers are laced. I notice he doesn't wear a wedding band, and this pleases me. My eyes move upwards back to meet his gaze. He looks forlorn. I sense that he is lonely or disturbed by something. It's a look I have seen in Taylor's eyes; grief eroding his heart.

I barely know him but feel an overriding interest to get him to share his pain and help free his soul. He breaks our contact, sips his coffee, drawing away the roasted bean design into his mouth before placing the cup back to rest on the saucer.

"Can I ask you one more detail about the attacks please?"

"Sure."

"Does he sexually assault the women?"

"No, he doesn't touch his victims sexually. However, we believe the attacks are sexually motivated, in that he gains sexual gratification from their deaths and vicious mutilation."

"Do you have a suspect?"

"I can't disclose that at this time. All I can say is that the investigation is ongoing and that we have a vital piece of evidence which links each of the attacks to the killer."

"A significant rare fibre has been found on each victim, but I don't want to further divulge what it is, as it may cause the killer to destroy the source to which fibre belongs."

"I'm intrigued."

"I'll tell you, but it's strictly off the record, for now"

I lean closer, hovering my ribs against the table edge. He's testing my loyalty, examining my character to see if I am trustworthy. He is purposely dangling key information to see if I'll take the bait and publish it regardless of our agreement.

I wouldn't do that to him. I want this relationship to work and create an unbreakable trust.

# Chapter Twenty-One – Kate

My instincts were correct; the killing spree is escalating fast.

Heading on to the motorway I recall Beckley's words regarding the killer deriving sexual gratification from their deaths. Research suggests Killers fall into categories.

Visionaries leave behind chaotic crime scenes and physical evidence, and they tend to select victims at random. All the Weston victims share a similar profile, suggesting they were carefully chosen. Beckley hasn't made any suggestion to confirm that they have a great deal of evidence to go on.

Missionaries feel compelled to kill a certain type of person, usually the homeless, prostitutes, or gay men. Their aim is purely to kill; they have minimum contact with the victims. Given the killer's MO - the beating and the skewer to the brain he doesn't fit the missionary type.

Hedonists, on the other hand, kill for profit; the victims are known to them and their deaths are carefully planned, and their bodies neatly disposed of. The Millbrook killer leaves his victims on show; they are are unknown to him, as far as we can tell, and therefore there's no profit to be gained from their deaths.

That leaves the Control Killer, who, whilst enjoying causing pain and suffering, gains immense pleasure from dominating and being in charge.

I feel queasy recalling memories of the bloodstained concrete and imagining their brutalised bodies sprawled alongside. Yet, at the same time, I am excited to be at the centre of a media frenzy, and honoured that Beckley has chosen me as his preferred media contact.

My journey has taken no time at all, probably because my thoughts have been roaming. The snowfall is heavier here than at home, spread across the pavement like a cancerous growth.

I hurry from the carpark, skating over powdery patches, and input the entry code on the keypad, fixed to the crumbling Victorian façade. Jenny, the blonde bubby receptionist, offers a wave while talking on the phone. She's lovely, always working with a smile on her face, and is the type of person that makes you feel better about yourself; always complimentary and interested in your life.

The warmth of the foyer embraces my cheeks, as I dash past the advertising department into the newsroom. Tom's face exudes surprise. He's never arrived at work before me in the last three years and always jokes that I must sleep under my desk.

I offer no explanation and slot in to my seat. My fingers are frantic, banging the keys raucously writing my exclusive story. I don't require my notes; Beckley's words still echo in my ears, the graphic accounts quickly unfolding on screen.

My stomach contracts; nausea, excitement and fear compressing every organ, thinking about the killer's unique signature. The pain those women must have endured, having been skewered in the ear and brain, is unthinkable.

He's now claimed five young women. They were beaten, degraded, tortured and killed, their fingers taken as trophies. I'm angry and fully aware that my typing is vicious as I continue to outline the case developments. Tom is monitoring me closely, he is intrigued but does not interrupt.

Cecilia's presence brushes by me, as she ambles to her office. She's wearing her army green parka coat again. The same coat she's worn every winter since I started here, after my journalism degree three years ago. The suedette lapels and scruffy cuffs are now heavily faded, as is the belt around her waistband, which gathers too tightly under her colossal fake bust.

I want to present the article to her, observe the surprise on her face before she calls everyone for morning conference. I'm not at all conceited, but this story is huge. Every national and TV outlet will be following my lead wondering how I got the inside scoop.

I ensure the story contains my by-line and upload it to the news basket. Cecilia is aware of my presence at the doorway, but her face remains fixed on her computer screen; mouth chewing on a Twix bar. I cannot comprehend how she stays a size 10. She leaves me hovering, just long enough to ensure I'm mindful of the hierarchy.

She's poised in her usual austere manner, arms folded across her chest glaring at me coldly. My heels snag in the carpet as I gingerly approach the desk. She eyes me.

My face is burning, her unwelcome gaze scrutinising me.

"Where did you get this information?" she asks, eyes scanning the article on screen.

"A trusted police source."

"You're certain that it's true. It's not going to come back and bite me on the ass?"

"The story is 100 per cent factual. The information will be officially released this afternoon. I have been given this exclusively, so we can take the lead."

"Tell the subs to work on it now."

Her eyes stare blankly, fixed upon mine. She finds me repugnant, I'm certain of it. No matter how hard I try to please her, her attitude toward me exudes a profound distaste. I turn on my heels annoyed at her lack of appreciation. I really don't know what it will take to please her. Perhaps nothing will.

## Chapter Twenty-Two – DCI Beckley

*Monday 28 December 2015. Morning*

This case is a fucking nightmare. We have no suspects and the body count is mounting. Our only glimmer of hope was Hannah and now she's dead.

The senior sister informed us that she had developed a sudden bleed on her brain and she was pronounced dead at 7.35am.

I'm in the Incident Room staring at each of their faces and their bludgeoned corpses on display.

I'm both puzzled and intrigued by the red Casein yarn fibres. He must encase his kill tools inside it to neatly conceal and store them. They are a part of his fantasy world that he must keep closely guarded. The items will be kept tucked away at his home or in his car, out of sight.

What about his trophies? If he's keeping their fingers, rather than just severing them and dumping them to label the victims, where and how would he store them? And why would he want to keep decaying bone and flesh?

Archer will help to answer my questions. She's waiting in my office; shoulder length blonde hair cascading neatly, resting on her suit jacket. She's studying the documents clasped in her fingertips.

"Miss Archer."

She turns, overlooks her shoulder and greets me with a cheery smile.

"DCI Beckley."

"Can I get you a coffee?"

"No, I'm fine, thank you."

"Now you're up to speed with the latest victims, I wonder if we can discuss the profile in further detail. Unfortunately, our survivor died earlier this morning."

"Yes, I'm aware," she replies, empathetically.

"Do you have anything new to offer?"

"The offender gains sexual arousal, or gratification, from committing murder, and the feeling of utter control over his victims. It is the most extreme form of sexual sadism. Erotophonophiliacs tend to fantasise about beating, stabbing, strangling and mutilating their victims, which is exactly what we have seen demonstrated on each of the women. They're also more likely to engage in cannibalism, torture and trophy keeping."

"Is that why he severs their fingers?"

"For many killers', part of their ritual consists of taking a souvenir to remind them of the crime. It is proof that they have acted out their fantasy in real life, and they use them to perpetuate the pleasure and excitement encountered during the kill. In this instance, we are talking about body parts, which he's taking to number his victims. I expect he's preserved them, perhaps in a solution of formaldehyde and ethanol, as a keepsake. It's not difficult to purchase, it's readily available online and therefore he could have bought the chemicals with ease without raising any eyebrows."

"So, he's toying with us. Labelling his victims numerically and keeping their fingertips as trophies."

"Yes, that's exactly it."

"What kind of fucked up bastard does that?"

"He'll probably use them for repetitive sessions of compulsive masturbation to relive the attacks."

I feel embarrassed at my foul outburst in front of Archer. She's always so polite but this killer has got right under my skin. I detest him and despise having to share the air that we breathe.

"Who is he? What character are we looking for?"

"He's an organised offender, in that he plans his crime, selects and stalks his victims. He'll exude extensive control over the victim through manipulation and gaining a sense of fear. To fulfil this criteria, the killer must be educated and is of above-average intelligence, attractive with a conventional home life, and is employed. Either he has some degree of social grace, and lures his victims, or he patiently waits for an opportune moment to strike. He'll have a vehicle to get to and from the scenes unnoticed. Foster recovered a petrol station glove sample. Perhaps it would help to obtain CCTV footage from local petrol forecourts on the nights of the murders."

"DI Wakeman's already on it, examining stations using Healthguard gloves."

Archer nods and continues with her summary.

"When he feels the urge to kill and acts out his fantasy, it will be accompanied by a facilitator; pornography, a stimulant, such as cocaine, or a depressant to lower inhibitions, such as alcohol. He could have drink-driving, or drug convictions. He also demonstrates the traits of a disorganised killer in that he leaves the body at the scene to be discovered. He wants to be admired and be an honourable opponent to the police. He'll maintain a murder kit. He'll come prepared with his weapons and torture instruments. We know that the Casein fibres were found in their ear canals, and that the only way they could have been there is from direct contact. Therefore, he must carefully conceal the knife and skewer inside a Casein fabric of some description."

She pauses, then takes a deep breath before continuing her detailed report. "He's going to be difficult to apprehend if I am entirely honest with you. He is forensically aware and is going to inordinate lengths to cover his tracks. There was a slip up with Hannah Green, of course, for which he will no doubt have punished himself. But he's been careful and left no trace of himself on any of the bodies. No hair, prints, or semen, just those few rare fibres. He's meticulous."

"So, our only real connection is the Casein fibre?"

"Yes, and I'm no expert with regards to that, you'll need to discuss it in far greater detail with Amy Foster. What I would suggest is that you release a breadcrumb of information to the press. Say you have a rare fibre, perhaps from an old red blanket or jumper. It may encourage someone to come forward, who has seen an unusual item matching the description in their home environment."

"If we tip him off that we are aware of the red garment, surely he'll dispose of it? That's what I would do."

"Perhaps, but you have to weigh up the likelihood of the details of such an unusual item triggering the conscience of a loved one."

My brain aches, I'm tired of this investigation. It's draining my soul, day by day. We are still no further forward with our progress since Nicole's death and I can't see us making a major breakthrough any-time soon.

# Chapter Twenty-Three – Kate

*Monday 28 December 2015. Afternoon*

Members of the press have been summoned to police headquarters for the media conference.

I confess I feel a little smug, having already written my article. DCI Beckley has helped me enormously, for which I am deeply indebted to him. I stuck to our agreement and allowed him full copy approval first, obviously through a discreet process, and without Cecilia's knowledge. She would not have approved.

Police HQ is closer than Weston station, a mere five miles up the coast located among hilltops and secured with gated barriers to prevent unauthorised access. Spread over 47 acres, the site is home to over 1,000 operational personnel and support staff. It's modern in comparison to the unsightly appearance of Weston Station, which has been likened to a council estate tower block.

I have attended HQ on countless occasions, most recently regarding a man missing from his home for one year. Sometimes police renew appeals for information on the anniversary of a person's disappearance. But I am of the view that it's pointless. If someone purposely walked out of their life, it's because they wanted to, and they don't want to be found.

At my lowest I've wondered how it would feel to walk away from everything and start over again. Either just pack up and go without telling a soul where, or, in my more mischievous moments, I've pondered what it would be like to fake your own death so that no one would ever come looking for you.

But those feelings only appeared when I was heavily depressed and after a couple of bottles of wine, no longer compos mentis. I wouldn't do it, I wouldn't inflict that pain and sadness on Taylor or my family. Those who choose to turn their back on their families are selfish. They don't think of the torment and suffering they inflict on those they leave behind.

The traffic is slowing; queuing vehicles turn left up Valley Road, the access slipway to HQ. Sweeping fields dotted with snow residue stretch for miles across to the edge of the M5 motorway in the distance. Storm clouds loom above, darkening the skyline. Oncoming car headlights illuminate the impending dusk as they approach and then pass.

I wonder who the other victims are, and what they were like. I assume they looked similar in appearance to Nicole and Cheryl, who were both were pretty, young blondes.

I'm grateful for the fact that I transformed my appearance from a natural mousy blonde to a brunette a few years ago. Right now, it's my only protection. I've had a couple of scares lately on the Millbrook estate, but that was just my subconscious reading too much into the situations and the surroundings in which I placed myself.

Something must make the killer detest his victims; circumstances rooted from his past, or a situation that has triggered him to act out his frightening fantasies.

Two small cookie-toned brick towers house security personnel granting inner access to the site. I follow protocol; provide my name and media organisation, which the guard crosschecks. He nods and lifts the barrier. I drive aimlessly, locating a car parking space, while listening to Ellie Goulding's *'How Long Will I Love You.'*

When I'm parked, I message Taylor to let him know that I'll be late home. My phone bleeps on route to the semi-circular glass entrance with Taylor's response. *'I'm on a late. Eat without me beautiful. Sorry x.'* I'm annoyed, I'll be asleep by the time he's home. I was looking forward to being reunited again.

Marela, one of my rival reporters is ahead in the distance. She's attractive, slim and tall but oozes arrogance in equal measure. I follow behind, stepping over the nude Cotswold buff patio and approach Nick Fermont, a police press officer. He uses his proximity card to gain inner access the building. We join camera crews armed with boom mics and around 35 reporters with spiral notebooks. It's 4pm. My exclusive report is now already online.

Nick ushers the entire press pack up a sweeping staircase, along a corridor and directs us into a room on our right. It's set up in a similar fashion to Weston; table positioned at the front of the room below the constabulary logo backdrop. Film and radio crews set up their tripods, cameras and microphones on the press stand. Nick vacates the room, I presume to inform Will of our arrival. Marela is cross-legged, tapping her pointed burgundy patent stiletto. She's a couple of years older than me and a clear follower of fashion. Her highlighted blonde hair is fine and exudes a crystal sheen, reflecting the light as it moves.

She looked down her nose at me once, just after I first joined the paper, while we were waiting to go back into the Magistrates Court. It was once too often, particularly when I had done nothing to warrant her distaste. Some people are born with a persona that radiates arrogance. She's certainly no better than me; if anything, I think she's probably jealous of some of the exclusives I've cracked. Treat people the way you wish to be treated, that's my motto in life. If she can't act like a decent human being, then I have no time for her.

The wait is irritating, as is Marela's glare. She has a look of distress and burning rage. Her phone rests in her palm; screen displaying the Chronicle website. I offer a sweet smile and turn away. She's seething and I'm enjoying it. The silence is replaced with chatter and whispers. Mobiles ring an array of melodies. My article is circulating fast. I lean back in the chair and enjoy the huge buzz. Marela answers her phone. I suspect she's getting a bollocking from her editor; her cheeks are scalding and she's now out of her seat and pacing on her expensive heels.

Nick re-joins us, signaling that the conference is about to get under way. The room falls silent as DCI Beckley enters alongside two other senior officers, whom I do not recognise.

Will sits at the centre of the panel. He adjusts his jacket and tie, and refrains from all eye contact. He's not ignoring me due to any contempt; he's trying to maintain his distance as my story source.

"Good afternoon ladies and gentlemen. Thank you for your attendance. I'm DCI Will Beckley, leading this live, dynamic investigation. Further to our earlier appeal for information in relation to the deaths of Nicole Hall and Cheryl Gray, I would like to provide you with an update. I cannot emphasise enough that this is an extremely complex case, which is both wide ranging and fast moving, changing course considerably in the past few days."

He pauses, clears his throat, and surveys the room, ensuring he has everybody's full attention, before continuing.

"Unfortunately, I can now confirm that three further bodies have been discovered and we are currently unravelling the circumstances surrounding their deaths. Formal identification has taken place with regards to each victim and autopsies carried out in the past day. We would like to offer our condolences to all the families at this incredibly distressing time. Family liaison officers have been appointed to the affected families, who are understandably deeply shocked and saddened by these tragic events. Due to the autopsy findings, particularly the nature of their deaths, we are linking each of the murders to the deaths of Nicole and Cheryl."

Will pauses again and takes a mouthful of water. His eyes squint in the glare of the intruding camera flashes. There had been gasps from the attentive audience when he had revealed the discovery of a further three bodies. I listen intently, jotting down his speech in shorthand, as he continues once more.

"I can confirm that on the 20<sup>th</sup> December, Hannah Green, aged 27, was subjected to a vicious assault in an alleyway on the Millbrook estate. She was walking home alone from Lasmerton Drive, at approximately 11.45pm but never arrived. On this occasion, however, the attacker was disturbed."

"Hannah was discovered by a passer-by and taken to hospital, where she underwent surgery. We believe, due to the nature of her the injuries, that she was attacked by the same person who killed Nicole Hall and Cheryl Gray. The details surrounding her ordeal were not made immediately public to protect her identity, and to conceal her survival from her attacker. Hannah suffered serious head injuries, and despite the best efforts of medical staff at Weston General, sadly she died this morning before regaining consciousness. Our thoughts remain with her family and friends at this extremely difficult time."

He pauses again. Several journalists exchange glances with each other. Will's tone of voice makes it clear that he had been hoping very much that Hannah would survive and would be able to talk to them.

"I can also confirm that the body of Shelley Carter, aged 28, was found on Christmas Eve, under a railway bridge near to Lasmerton Drive. The autopsy puts her time of death three weeks earlier, on or around, December 3rd. Shelley had not been reported missing, as her family believed she had returned to her home in Devon. She was last seen on the 2$^{nd}$ December, having visited her parents for the weekend. She endured a similar attack and died at the scene. A further body was discovered on Christmas morning. As in the case of Shelley, due to the condition of the body, the autopsy process has taken longer than normal, hence why we are only able to release these details now. The victim has been formally identified as Jesse Cooper, aged 26. Jesse was murdered on Christmas Eve and had endured a sustained attack, and fatal stab wound to the chest. Jesse was last seen as she made her way home from the town centre following celebrations with work colleagues. She left the Back Bar alone and was captured at 11.58pm on CCTV, walking along the Boulevard towards her home in Springlands, a 10 to 15-minute journey. She never arrived."

Will takes another drink. The air in the room is dry, and heavy with anticipation.

"Jesse's body was discovered on Christmas morning. We are aware that the crime scene is outside of the Millbrook Estate, where the other victims died, but are linking her death to the same assailant. Due to the similar nature of all the attacks, and the fact that the killer is labelling his victims by severing their fingertips, we firmly believe the same offender has claimed all five lives. Once again, I would like to stress that our heartfelt condolences remain with all their families."

His comments about the fingers being severed draw more gasps from the audience. Every detail like this makes the story more sensational, from a national paper's point of view. This will generate more media attention, and also put even more pressure on Will's team to find the killer quickly. The national newspapers have an insatiable hunger; if Will doesn't satisfy that hunger quickly, the spotlight will turn on him and his apparent failure to protect the people of Weston and secure justice for the families of the victims.

"Our investigations are ongoing, and I would like to further emphasise that we are making significant progress," he says. "We currently have 70 officers involved on this case, including those deployed to support the families of the deceased, and those conducting forensic searches. As well as the victims sharing similar injuries, we have unearthed further evidence linking each attack; rare, red Casein yarn fibres. We believe this evidence to be highly valuable, as it will help identify the killer."

There are more gasps from the press pack. It's unusual for a media conference to reveal so much new information.

"Casein yarn fibres are extremely rare and were used to make clothing and household items in the 1930s and 40s. Production of this fibre ceased after the end of World War 2, in 1945. We understand the killer is using an item made of this rare yarn, perhaps a red blanket or jumper, to conceal his weapons. We need the public's help in trying to identify this garment. If you believe you may have such an item in your home or at work, search your conscience. I would ask charity shop employees to pay attention and try to recall perhaps selling such an item in recent weeks or months. This garment is the key to identifying the culprit. I would like to sincerely thank the public for helping the police with our appeals for information to date. Without such assistance, we cannot do our job of assisting those who live in our community. I would also like to reiterate our appeal for any new information into the deaths of Nicole Hall, Cheryl Gray, Hannah Green, Shelley Carter and Jesse Cooper. If you were in the vicinity of any of the attacks, or have any information, no matter how small, or irrelevant you think it may be, please to come forward and contact us on Crimestoppers on 0800 555 111."

Marela is wildly flapping her arms, signalling her wish to ask a question. The other reporters follow suit, pens poised in their fingertips, all bidding for Will's attention. He points at Marela, which irritates me.

"There is a story circulating that the victims are being skewered. Can you confirm the accuracy of such claims?"

Will finishes the remaining water in his beaker.

"I can confirm that numerous injuries were inflicted. Each victim suffered a single stab wound to the heart, and the autopsy process unearthed puncture wound incisions to each of their ears, suggesting the use of a sharp object."

"Do you have any suspects at all?" A male voice interrupts.

"I am sure that you'll understand that I am not able to further elaborate, as this is an active investigation. I would appeal to the individual responsible for these crimes to do the sensible thing, the right thing and give yourself up. If you don't, we will find you. It's only a matter of time. We WILL catch you."

# Chapter Twenty-Four

*Tuesday 29 December 2015. 10.20pm*

The light flickered, offering intermittent illumination inside the bus shelter.

She sat fiddling with her delicate watch strap, shivering in the vehement wind as it seeped through her Angora scarf. The overhead light buzzed unexpectedly. She gazed up, her pupils dilated, shielding them.

A hand gripped her throat and slammed her skull into the metal shelter. His grip tightened, silencing her screams. He smashed her head once more, yanked her wrists and dragged her away. Tree branches tore at her face as he hauled her through brambles into an alley enclosure.

Her vision was hazy; she couldn't see him but could sense his presence, admiring his catch. His hand smashed her face into the wet soil, suffocating her. As she struggled for air, she ingested clumps of mud into her mouth and inhaled particles which lodged in her nostrils.

Her left hand grappled the ground in search of a weapon. His foot slammed down on it, snapping a bone, immobilising her. Tears teemed as his knuckles pummelled her face. The pain paralysed her catatonic body, which he tore at erratically.

A knife slashed her shirt open, exposing her white bra. She flinched, feeling polythene-clad fingertips drag over her breasts toward her navel.

She tried to focus and study his contorted face as he trailed his hands over her thighs. He paused, absorbing her panic. She blinked until she could see clearly; a mask, protecting his identity. She scrutinised its burnished features, with deeply inset frown lines framing cock-eyed eyebrows and an awry upper lip, stretching into a snarl up against his left cheek.

She arched her back attempting to fight back but couldn't. He grew closer, gripped her throat again. Alcohol wafted over her face. "Tell her to fucking back off," he hissed, before retreating back into the shadows. She rolled onto her front, clawing her fingers through the earth as she crawled back towards the light.

* * * DCI Beckley * * *

*Wednesday December 30, 2015*

A wave of guilt flushes through me. I thought exposing the details of his crimes, and the lead we had with the rare fibres, would send him to ground, and give us the time we need to crack the case.

Only, it didn't. He's reacted angrily; this victim purely a messenger, directed at Kate in the most personal circumstances.

I can't bear to break the news. The victim is alive and fully cooperating, but she's suffered horrifically. The guilt that I am experiencing doesn't override the feeling of onus eating away at me over Toby and his mother, it has proliferated it tenfold. I want to be free of my torment but I'm never going to escape it.

Wakeman manoeuvres the car around the Six Ways roundabout and pulls up outside Eton House. A modern, purpose-built reception, clad with blue signage, has been added beneath the towering Victorian building.

The blonde receptionist offers a nervous smile as we mount the disabled ramp and enter. She ends her call and directs us through to the newsroom. Journalists fiercely tap their keyboards, and phones bleep from every corner.

The room falls silent; our presence acknowledged. Kate turns to see what has prompted the sudden, unusual, silence. She's sat inside the door, tucked away on a tatty chair. Her desk is neatly organized, housing a framed picture next to the monitor in which she's smiling, alongside a man, presumably her husband. I continue my observations before my eyes fall onto her face. Her cheeks flush and she bites her lower lip with her pearly teeth. In other circumstances, it would be quite alluring. But not now.

"Mrs Rivendale, can we talk to you in private?"

Her eyes widen in profound alarm.

"We need to talk to you as a matter of urgency, could you please accompany us to the station?"

She's ghostlike; the colour drained from her face. Her hands tremble, which she attempts to conceal through laced fingertips. The silence is overridden by faint whispers, staff speculating as to what we want with Kate.

"Has something happened to Taylor? Tell me," she blurts, unable to hide the fear in her voice.

"No, Mrs Rivendale. If you could just please come with us, we can talk to you in private."

I feel awful withholding the news, but I'm certain she would prefer that the details weren't divulged in front of the entire newsroom.

Kate rises to her feet with her handbag, leaving behind her notebook and pen. She walks nervously on her heels, maintaining a tearful gaze with the receptionist through the window. She sinks into the car, claustrophobic, segregated behind the front seats.

I coyly stare at her in the rear-view mirror. Her eyes well and trickle tears; face gaunt. She quickly wipes her cheeks with her forefinger while staring out of the window as we pass the tree-lined promenade. Her expression remains numb for the entire motorway journey.

Kate's clearly troubled by the flashes of black and white uniforms rushing like Zebras to their fluorescent chequered vehicles. I open her door and offer my hand on her shoulder. She stares back at me, clueless and distressed by her ordeal.

"You haven't done anything wrong Kate," I assure her.

Her eyes remain riveted on mine.

"Then why am I here?"

"Let's just go inside."

Her head nods with a dubious expression and she walks in slow motion as though her soul is detached from her body. I want to comfort her but it's inappropriate. She looks like a fox, frozen in the path of oncoming traffic.

# Chapter Twenty-Five – Kate

This is a dream, or a nightmare, from which I can't awaken. My heavy legs drag and clip the floor as we proceed inside. Voices broadcast over police Airwave radios, but I can't concentrate, or make sense of anything.

I pass Gareth Hawkings and Mark Pearce, whom I worked undercover with on a drug raid; both look perplexed. Embarrassed, I bow my head, studying the scuffed lino. Heavy-duty double doors slam against the wall startling me.

A woman sits hunched over ahead of us; face collapsed in her palms. Her identity is concealed but I recognise her electric blue coat.

My heart is thrashing against my breastbone. We near the custody suite, my stilettos breaking the silence in which she sits. Our eyes meet. She's almost unrecognisable and appears to have aged ten years.

"Kate, thank God." I study mum's face and then look back at Will. My head hurts and feels clamped with confusion. I don't know what the hell is going on. Mum stands, and clutches hold of me tightly.

"What's happened?"

"Haven't they told you?"

"No. I was dragged out of my office and escorted here," I sneer at DI Wakeman, who folds his arms across his stomach.

"Is it Dad?"

"No."

"What's all this about then?" I plead.

Her mascara has smeared under both eyes and her foundation is tarnished with tear stains.

"Mum, for goodness sake just tell me what's going on!" I look down horrified as she collapses to her knees, crying uncontrollably. Will takes hold of her upper arms and lifts her back on to the plastic chair, and then gives DI Wakeman a nod. He places his palm in the shallow of my back and ushers me away into an interview room on the right. Two double hefty doors slam and lock behind us.

It's disconcerting inside and I'm enormously constricted by the confined space. The walls are adorned with noise-deadening white metal panels; their brightness sting my eyes. A table rests against the wall with two charcoal chairs positioned either side. I take minuscule steps toward them, clutching a crumpled, sodden tissue.

"I can't take this anymore," I blurt, tracing my footsteps backwards.

I bump in to him; my back colliding with his chest. He places his hands on both my arms and ushers me forward, then sits opposite, offering a sincere expression.

His eyes are plagued by sadness. I'm not frightened, just lost and overwhelmed.

"Kate, there's no easy way to tell you this. I have some bad news," he says. A tremor runs through my body, my armpits moist.

"Please, just tell me."

Will pauses momentarily, he can't find his words. I dig my nails deeper into my thighs.

"I need to inform you of an incident involving your sister."

"Is - is she dead?"

Panic electrocutes my spine; I bolt to my feet sending my chair flying backwards.

"When? How?"

"She's not dead, Kate."

"If she's not dead, then what is it?" He walks around the table and retrieves the chair.

"Please, sit back down," he instructs.

"There's no easy way to say this. Your sister has been the victim of a serious assault and is receiving medical treatment at Weston General."

His words puncture my heart.

"Why am I here? I should be at the hospital."

"I will take you there shortly, after we discuss the circumstances."

"I don't understand."

"Your sister was attacked waiting at a bus stop last night. We fear that her assailant is the individual responsible for the Millbrook murders."

The vice on my head tightens. I rub my forehead and stare across at him over the microphone positioned upon the table.

"Are you saying the serial killer attacked Louise?"

Will places his hands on the table.

"We believe that is the case. There are similarities with regards to the injuries she sustained."

"Did he?"

"Your sister wasn't stabbed, and her fingers remain intact."

"Then how do you know that it was him?"

"Because he attacked Louise as a warning to you."

"What do you mean, as a warning to me? Why?"

"Your sister was able to give us a very detailed account."

I can't take it all in, it doesn't make sense. Beckley scoops a witness statement perched at the far end of the table. The text is lengthy, but my eyes cannot focus on the typeface. His eyes glance through the document.

"Your sister claims the offender made a clear and concise threat; '*tell her to fucking back off*'. She believes this threat is directed at you, due to your coverage of this case, and your exclusive story yesterday."

Tears drip onto my collarbone, I shiver at their cold touch. I'm horrified, his words snarl my stomach into a fierce knot. I can't breathe, my chest is tightening. My belly feels like a drum of acid; full of dread. Vomit erupts uncontrollably from my mouth on to the floor. I stand, doubled over, clutching my stomach. I'm unable to focus; wall panels merging into distorted shapes.

He's still talking; voice muffled.

My legs are numb, weighty as lead, crumbling beneath me. I'm falling. The light fades and I slip into darkness.

## Chapter Twenty-Six – DCI Beckley

My fist slams the red circular panic button; it's deafening. Kate needs urgent medical help. She could choke on her own vomit. She's cocooned, lying unconscious in a foetal position.

DI Wakeman and PC Matt Holtby emerge. Holtby administers first aid, while Wakeman informs me that a first responder has been dispatched. Holtby studies Kate through his black metal rimmed glasses, closely assessing her condition. He lifts Kate's chin and tilts her head backwards. He uses his forefinger to dislodge any vomit latched to her tongue and ensure that her airway is clear.

Her left hand is placed under her right cheek. He grips her left shoulder and leg, and gently rolls her towards him to rest in the recovery position.

This has never happened to me during an interview, I'm a bag of nerves.

Holtby presses his index and third finger on her neck to the side of the windpipe, feeling for a pulse. Her chest begins to rise and fall; she's still breathing. The fetid vomit stench fills the confinement of the interview suite. I did this to her. If I hadn't told her about her sister, then she wouldn't have collapsed.

Another death on my watch is the last thing that I need.

My eye catches sight of a fluorescent high-vis jacket emerging in the doorway. A first responder rushes in carrying first-aid equipment. He takes over and unbuttons her suit jacket; she remains unresponsive.

My heart contracts watching her sprawled the floor. Remnants of sick cling to her chin and latch on her perfectly tousled curls. After checking her pulse, the technician uses a medical pocket torch light and lifts Kate's eyelids to examine her pupils for signs of a seizure. She reacts; flinching. I linger my eyes over her face. She blinks again, eyes fixed upon the chequered polystyrene ceiling panels.

"Give her some space," the responder urges. "She needs to stay still to allow blood flow to return to her brain."

I step back to the table, refill her glass and place it back down. DI Wakeman has acquired a large roll of three-ply blue Wypall absorbent paper and is clearing up the sick. I check back at Kate; she's dazed and pale.

"What's her name?"

"Kate."

"Listen to me Kate, you fainted a few moments ago, but you're going to be fine. You need to remain on the floor for a few more minutes and then we can get you back on your feet, OK?" the responder dictates. Kate doesn't answer, just nods slowly. I feel awful like I've taken a momentous blow in the boxing ring.

My shirt is stuck to my armpits, seeping up the vapour. I snap my wristband to curtail my anxiety, but it does little to repel my emotions. I step out of the room, into the hallway where I gratefully I gasp fresh air, while restlessly pacing the uninhabited passageway.

The situation is out of my control.

I march back inside and see Kate is now sat upright. She takes the cup of water in her shaky palm, and slowly takes small mouthfuls. Her mouth retches again but no fluids emerge. She wipes her mouth on the back of her hand.

"What happened to me? I don't understand," she whispers.

"You passed out; it was shock."

Kate's face falls to the floor, recalling the memories prior to her collapse.

"Come on, let's get you off the floor." I reach out with my hand, offering her assistance. She places her left hand in mine and I lift her slowly back to her feet, and onto the chair. The first responder appears satisfied with her condition and vacates the room.

"Is there anything I can get you?" I ask.

"No. I'm fine. Thanks."

Her appearance says otherwise; cheeks colourless. I pluck a tissue and wipe the side of her chin; she's unfazed by my contact. I'm not entirely convinced that she's fully aware of what's happened to her.

"Kate, can you remember what we were talking about before you fainted?" I probe.

There's an awkward silence hanging in the air. Her fingers twiddle a diamante tennis bracelet on her wrist. She refrains from making any eye contact.

"Yes, you basically told me my sister was attacked and it was my fault," she blurts.

"No Kate, no. I'm not blaming you at all. I was just stating the facts that were presented in the witness statement. This is not your fault, it's mine. I enlisted your help. Rather than the additional publicity deterring the killer, the media coverage angered him. He's taken particular offence to you and your story; the most detailed account of the investigation."

"I was just doing my job. If I thought for one minute he would come after me or my family, I would never have written the damn piece."

She seems affronted. A small tear glides over her cheekbone.

"I understand how you must be feeling but you may have helped us." I refresh Kate's cup again.

"How could I have possibly helped? Louise will never forgive me." Mascara stains trace their way down her pallid face.

"You can help us. To have known who your sister was, the killer must have been observing you closely; watching your every move."

"Great! He's stalking me. Am I next?" Kate snaps, chewing her thumb.

"He could have attacked you, but he didn't. What I am trying to say is that you could help bring him in."

"What are you suggesting?"

She looks at me, eyes wretched. A pang of guilt floods me.

"We want to put you under surveillance, watch your movements to see if you can lead us to him. It's also for your protection. Though I must stress, I don't believe he wishes to harm you."

Kate sips her water, her tense frame wracked with pain, sadness and guilt. She lacks the astute confidence I admired when I first encountered her during the press conference.

"Kate, I understand this is a big ask, but we truly believe you could help us achieve a major break in this investigation. You could help prevent any more lives being taken. Your sister has given us a vague description of her attacker; that, alone, is a significant step forward. But with your help, too, we could catch the sick son-of-a-bitch."

Her concentration drifts, her eyes close contemplating my request. Kate is my final hope. There cannot be any more lives lost.

## Chapter Twenty-Seven – Kate

I'm cold and afraid, rendered speechless. Life has been sucked out of me. My heart aches feeling every ounce of the damage that I've caused.

I scrutinise Will, who's awaiting an answer, but I can't read him. A clump of vomit is lodged inside my cheek. I force it away with my tongue, swallow hard and gulp water. I must look horrendous.

Will offers a smile and reaches across the table, placing his hand upon mine. It's warm and comforting. He doesn't mean any affection by his mannerism, he's purely trying to coerce me into helping him. My cheeks warm, blood pricking the surface.

He has a kind nature; I wonder why he's single.

"Kate, your involvement in our investigation could be paramount to us solving the case."

His pleading eyes draw me in as I begin to feel vaguely normal. I take deep breaths while resting my head on my fist.

"We really need your help. Think of the victims, your sister especially."

My feelings of warmth and security are instantly dispelled by rage discharging through me. How dare he use my guilt over Louise to force me into a decision, and commit to his operation?

"Basically, you want to use me as bait." I snap.

"No. You will be safe; you'll have armed officers monitoring you. It's for your protection also."

"Earlier you implied that he wouldn't harm me, now you are saying I need protection, which is it?" I yell, pulling my hand away from his.

He's stunned at my outburst. I lean back on the chair, arms folded defensively across my chest. He's never seen me angry.

"Kate, I apologise. I didn't mean to scare you."

"Insinuating that I need protection makes me fear my life is in danger."

"I don't believe that you are Kate, truly. You don't fit his profile."

"Killers have been known to change their MO. The Boston Strangler raped and killed pensioners before transgressing to younger women, both white and black. Anything's possible."

"I get your point, Kate. But had he wanted to hurt you, he already would have."

"Perhaps, or maybe he just hasn't had the opportunity yet."

"I understand that you have grave reservations, but I want to assure you that I won't put you in any unnecessary danger. You can call me at any time, day or night."

He looks crestfallen. I can tell that he's worried that he's upset me and ruined our working relationship. He has a valid point. If I can lure the killer in, that's positive for him. Only, I'm not ready to die; not for the sake of a story or a murder investigation. I just got my life back on track and now everything is ruined again.

"I'm not agreeing to anything until I've seen Louise."

"I understand. You are free to leave at any time, this is not an interview."

I stand, my legs precarious, as I pass DI Wakeman. He unlocks the inner and outer door and allows me to proceed out into the corridor. Mum is no longer present; I presume she's gone to the hospital.

Wakeman buzzes me through an internal door and another officer releases the second set. My tears erupt, as I spot Taylor in the distance, waiting for me. I run and collapse against his chest.

"Kate, your mum called me. You cannot blame yourself."

"Can you take me to Louise?"

"Yes. Why did they bring you to the station?"

"I'll explain everything, just get me the hell out of here."

\* \* \*

Paramedics in artichoke polyester shirts and combat trousers retrieve a patient from the rear doors of an ambulance and rush the casualty into A&E.

Taylor takes my hand in his, trying to diminish my anxiety as we approach the main entrance. I have no idea where Louise is. Rain droplets infiltrate my cheeks and cling to my hair, which has an aroma of sick. I examine my curls, noticing strands hardened with a crispy texture. I feel revolting.

Costa Coffee is crowded with customers. Taylor releases me, and I wait while he approaches a volunteer manning the reception desk. She twiddles a biro in her fingertips before searching the system. I cannot hear their conversation. I feel lost and afraid. None of this feels real. I'm scared, visualising what he could do to me, although I'm more petrified of coming face to face with Louise and encountering her wrath.

Taylor reappears and slips his arm around my waist, directing me down the atrium. We pass an elderly gentleman in a wheelchair. His hospital gown is gathered over his scrawny thighs exposing his white knee-high compression stockings. He has a delicate breathing tube fitted under his nostrils; the pipes connected to an oxygen tank. He looks close to death but offers me a sincere smile. I return the gesture and continue, headed for Steepholm Ward.

"Try not to worry, she'll be fine," Taylor assures, kissing my forehead as I cuddle his chest.

The lingering medical odour repels the smell of my vomit. We pause outside the ward, pumping clear hand sanitiser into our palms before proceeding.

Twelve patients rest in hospital beds.

"She's not here." I look at Taylor, confused.

"Can I help you? Are you looking for a relative?" A busty middle-aged nurse enquires.

"I'm looking for Louise Harvey. I was told she was on this ward, but I think we may be mistaken." She leans close, her face hovering near my ear. "She is in bay two. Her injuries look rather significant," she quietly whispers.

I stare beyond her, and Taylor's grip tightens around my hand as I study a motionless body; barely recognisable. White gauze is taped to the side of her neck, blood encroaching the surface.

I feel as though I've been gutted by a machete. I hesitate before approaching; armpits perspiring against my blouse.

Louise is alive but looks broken. Her right arm is set in plaster cast. Her left arm rests on the bed, heavily bruised and slashed. An off-white blanket conceals her legs and any lower injuries.

"Don't let her see you staring," Taylor whispers.

My lips lock awkwardly. I redirect my eyes back to her face. Her eye sockets are black and bulbous, giving the impression she's squinting. Her lips are cut and swollen.

"Louise, it's me, Kate."

She strains her head, eyes water-logged and desolate.

"I'm so sorry," I whisper.

I collapse beside her bed. Taylor intervenes and lifts me back up on to an orange visitor's chair.

"You two should be alone, I'll give you some space," he says softly, kissing my cheek.

My voice box has lost its ability to function. I place my palm on her arm; she withdraws it, as though I've scolded her with boiling water. Her rejection crushes my heart.

Louise stares out of the window, her gaze fixed upon water droplets pounding the glass.

"I knew your job would get you into shit one day," she blurts, breaking the silence. She's right, this is my fault. "But I didn't think it would get me, too."

"I'm so sorry. I would never have knowingly put you or anyone else in danger."

"It's too late for apologies. My life is ruined thanks to you."

"Louise, please look at me. I'm sorry."

She maintains her gaze on the window refusing to make any eye contact.

"The police have asked me to help catch him. I'll do it for you." "Too bloody right you will, or I'll never forgive you."

Her head shifts, resting back on her pillow. She eyes me with a cruel stare. I'm horrified. Her once perfect white smile has been smashed; three of her front teeth are missing, revealing gaping gums.

"Listen to me, I'll go undercover. This is down to me and I promise you that I won't let him get away with this."

I reach for her hand again but halt upon noticing a plastic tube inserted on the surface.

"Do whatever it takes to get the fucking bastard," she hisses.

## Chapter Twenty-Eight – Kate

*Wednesday 30 December 2015. 5.15pm*

My thoughts aimlessly swirl in my head like a child running to catch a floating fairy. If I could catch one now I'd wish, with all my heart, for everything to revert to normal.

Taylor turns on the radio to break the awkward silence on our journey home.

A news bulletin blasts from the speaker, which he switches over to Heart FM. Typically, he doesn't know what to say, or do. The truth is nothing he can say will change what's happened or make me feel better. I followed the story and it's led me down a treacherous path.

Taylor always warned me about getting too close and for the first time in my career, I realise that he's been right all along.

My phone logs 12 missed calls from DCI Beckley. My head is throbbing, I can't focus. Taylor reaches across and gives my thigh a gentle squeeze.

"I'm sorry you had to see her like that."

"I just can't get my head around it, I've ruined her life."

"Kate, you have done nothing of the kind. It wasn't your fault, stop blaming yourself."

"Everyone else is blaming me."

"Time will heal her. She'll be OK."

"Time might mend her injuries, but her mind is another matter. You should have seen the way she looked at me."

"Whatever happens, I'm by your side. I love you." "I love you too." The car halts on the driveway.

"Come on, let's get you inside."

I drag myself out of the car, walking on strained footsteps toward the house. I'm safe here but it doesn't stop me feeling afraid. I can't shake the feeling that he's watching me. I look out of the window into darkness and shield the glass with the curtains.

I tell myself that he's not here, but it doesn't prevent me from inspecting every room in the house.

"Stop being paranoid," Taylor says, frowning.

I snatch a bottle of Merlot from the wine rack and slam it on the breakfast bar angrily. My hands rummage through the top drawer in search of a bottle opener. Frustrated and incensed, I rip the drawer forcefully; the contents smash against the granite flooring in a cacophony of clattering metal.

I collapse alongside them; cold infiltrates my legs as I sit hunched in a ball, my head rested on my knees. Taylor rushes in and embraces me.

"Calm down, everything will be fine."

He sets about picking up the utensils, pops the wine cork and pours me a large glass.

"What am I going to do?" "You promised your sister you would help, and she is adamant that she wants you to cooperate with the police."

"I don't like the idea of being followed."

"I can't say that I'm enamoured with the idea, but if it keeps you safe then surely that's what matters. Call DCI Beckley in the morning."

I force a smile and gulp the wine. Its plum and mulberry undertones warm my throat. I know that it's the right thing to do but I'm terrified.

After drinking I feel calmer.

I reject an offer of take-away curry and cook us Turkish Testi Kebabs. It was one of our favourite dishes that we discovered while holidaying in Iclemer, last year. Although I don't have a huge clay pot to cook it in and won't be setting it on fire or slicing the top off with a giant sword, it will still taste almost as good.

I need time to think and cooking always relaxes me.

Just when we found happiness again something like this comes and slaps me in the face.

Cooking reminds me of my mum. It's somewhat of family trait. Weekends were for family gatherings growing up as a child, three generations sat around the table indulging in roast dinner.

In the summer months, it was dads turn, sizzling up a monumental feast on the barbecue. After serving up sausages, pork kebabs, burgers, lamb kofte and halloumi, accompanied with salad, dips and pitta bread, he'd proceed to ask everyone if they wanted a pork chop. I'm surprised that I'm only a size eight; I ought to weigh 20 stone. These family moments formed some of my best childhood memories and helped conjure my own love for cooking.

I pray that my actions haven't torn our family apart.

The fact that mum didn't wait for me at the station doesn't bode well. I know that she will blame me for Louise's ordeal.

I'm tearful listening to the soothing lyrics of '*Iris*', by the Goo Goo Dolls, while sipping wine. I don't know how long I have been standing here; my mind lost in thought thinking about what he did to Louise. She was always so proud of her pearly smile. She's a dental nurse, so hopefully her dentist will repair the damage.

I want to help Will I'm just not sure I can.

\* \* \*

Taylor tries his best to help me remain upbeat; telling me that being a part of the investigation could yield stories. I hadn't even had chance to tell him about my exclusive provided by Will.

He was working late at the time, and perhaps a part of me felt guilty for meeting Will, given the spark that I'd felt during our encounter.

We finish a second bottle over dinner and Taylor offers to clear the dishes. I head upstairs and undress in darkness, quickly pulling my cold satin nightie over my body. I slip under the duvet and lie still listening to Taylor clattering around the kitchen.

I feel as though my world is shattering; guilt devouring me.

I roll onto my side, trying to ease the pain while staring up at the window. I can't see the moonlight tonight, it's shrouded by dark clouds and an eerie lingering fog. I close my eyes.

Vivid flashbacks of Louise's battered face haunt me.

I've acted selfishly, only thinking about the next scoop and not the impact that it could have on people I love. Louise was an innocent party in all this, she didn't deserve to be dragged into it. My tears saturate the pillow.

Taylor joins me under the duvet and pulls me close, stroking my hair. It's soothing and makes me feel safe.

"You'll feel better in the morning," he says, tenderly.

I close my eyes and darkness grows, as I slip away into a deep black hole.

# Chapter Twenty-Nine – DCI Beckley

*New Year's Eve 2015. 8am*

I cannot stop staring at her horrific injuries. Her face is barely recognisable from those that I've seen of her prior to the attack.

The guilt that Kate must be feeling is unimaginable, which was his clear intention. He's an absolute bastard for putting that on her.

I share her guilt. It's my fault that she published the story. I provided the exclusive that diverted his attention towards her, and ultimately her family. If he was infuriated with her actions, I don't understand why he didn't tackle the issue head on and claim Kate as a victim. I'm glad he didn't, of course. Perhaps he felt that attacking a relative would hurt more. Logically though, Louise fitted the profile; Kate doesn't.

I sly another glance at Louise, her face covered with bruises and lacerations. The wounds will fade in time, and her teeth can be repaired. It could have been worse; she could be dead. At least Louise won't be permanently disfigured from her ordeal; though the mental scars are another issue.

We're joined by a sketch artist, who tries to capture details of the mask the attacker wore from the description Louise provides. The drawing emerging on the artist's pad resembles to a Venetian mask, the kind worn at masked balls.

My mind aches, trawling the depths of my knowledge for an appropriate substitute.

I search for sculpted masks in Google on my iPhone, which returns results for characters of the Commedia dell'Arte; the improvised Italian theatre. Each colourful character portrays a stereotype, boasting a distinct set of attributes.

I revise my search to images; the masks of Pantelone and Arlechino appear first in the search results.

I move round to the opposite side of the bed. Louise follows me with her eyes, studying me closely. She pushes her timid body further upright against the pillowcase. I sense her fear and discomfort.

"Could I show you some images?" I venture, cautiously.

"What images?"

"A selection of masks. Perhaps one of them looks like the one your attacker wore. That could prove incredibly helpful."

She nods and reaches out her lacerated right hand. I place my phone in her palm, which is protected with gauze and Micropore tape. Faint aging maroon bloodstains tinge the surface. She flicks the screen with her left forefinger.

"Do any of these images look like mask that you saw?"

Her breathing accelerates and sweat beads form on her temples, eyes transfixed on the screen. Her finger swipes the screen upwards, examining image after image offered by my Google search. The anticipation is nauseating. We're going to get a hit; I can feel it.

DI Wakeman sits opposite, slurping from his cardboard Costa cup. He's clearly uninterested in the lengthy process and turns his head, following the nurse who had just tended to Kate's dressing. She's a busty blonde with a friendly face and a kind nature. Wakeman looks far more interested in her bedside manner than he is in anything else.

I turn back to Louise, who recoils from the phone, hurling it away in distress. It falls and rests on the blanket. I retrieve it and study a full-screen image of an olive mask captioned Briguella; a malicious crafty character. It's menacing; eyes disturbing, mouth baleful.

Her trembling hands wipe the cascading tears away from her cheeks.

"Is this it, Louise? Is this what he wore, something like this?"

She is powerless to speak, and sits pitifully, cowering against the pillow.

I don't press her any further, I already know the answer. The horror of her reaction tells me all that I need to know. We have a significant break-through. We're getting closer and I'm going to nail the bastard to the wall.

* * * Kate * * *

*New Year's Eve 2015, 8am*

Vivid flashbacks of Louise's distorted face propel me from my nightmare back to reality. I've awoken covered in sweat, my body trembling all over.

My heart's erratic; I'm struggling to breathe, thinking about him touching her. I blink, trying to force her traumatised face away from my memory but it's etched in my mind's eye, like a terrifying mental tattoo.

Swaddled under the duvet, I hear the wind howling angrily. My throat is parched; alcohol traces cling to my taste buds. I pull the duvet over my head and lie motionless underneath. I want it to be a bad dream.

My stomach flips, pins and needles prick my skin, imagining the reaction I'll get at work. I was last seen being escorted out of the office by DI Wakeman and DCI Beckley. I don't want to tell them about it. If I speak and relay the graphic accounts, it becomes real all over again.

I toss and turn, fighting in the darkness to drift back to sleep. My efforts are in vain; all I can think about is Louise.

I flip back the covers and tip-toe into the ensuite. Cold air sweeps across my flesh as I undress and step into the shower cubicle. Icy droplets spear my back, growing increasingly intense as the pressure mounts. I lean against the cool porcelain tiles shielding my skin from the blast, until the temperature warms. Steam clears my stuffy sinuses. I close my eyes allowing water to blast over my face. The jets merge with my tears. I'm wretched, angry and culpable.

My weak legs judder, sending me crashing to my knees. The pain is unbearable.

Why didn't he attack me? It's a game. Instead he's damaged my family and torn Louise's heart. This will ruin our relationship; she won't ever forgive me. Why would she? If the shoe were on the other foot, I wouldn't be forgiving.

I feel deflated; my tears increase the intensity of my headache to the point where it feels like my brain could explode at any moment. I dig my fingertips on my temples, rubbing to erase the pain. My body rocks back and forth under the water; my howls uncontrollable.

The door crashes open startling me, Taylor emerges.

He pulls frantically at my arms, dragging me upwards from beneath the waterjets. I stumble, smashing my back into the thermostatic shower bar valve. I yelp at the excruciating jab and Taylor pulls me free from the cubicle. My body clings to his chest; hair stuck to his stubble. He retrieves a fluffy white towel and envelops, me trying to provide calmness and comfort.

"It's OK, baby, I'm here."

My weight rests against him, as my tears continue to spill.

"Why did it happen? I didn't do him any harm."

"Kate, listen to me, this wasn't your fault. If I could find the bastard, I'd fucking kill him myself."

Water beads trickle down my legs and pool at my feet on the polished granite tiles.

"I don't have a choice, do I? I must help DCI Beckley. If I don't, Louise won't ever forgive me."

Taylor grips my arms tightly, pushing me away. I can see in his eyes that he agrees with me.

"They won't let any harm come to you," he offers.

"Can you call him and ask him to come to the house?" "DCI Beckley?"

"Of course, get ready and I'll make you a cup of tea."

Taylor passes me a hand towel and vacates the bathroom. I skulk back to the bedroom and perch on the edge of the mattress; knees tucked tightly against my bare chest. The warm towel cocoons my body, offering some relief.

I catch my reflection. I barely recognise my own pitiful self, and better resemble a heroin addict; skinny and gaunt with dark under eyes. My mind flashes back to Weston Station and my embarrassment resurfaces. Not only did I vomit everywhere, but I passed out in front of Will.

He must regard me as a weak imbecile. I realise now that only I can rectify this situation and make things right, but given the damage caused, I already know that our lives will never be the same again.

# Chapter Thirty – Kate

*New Year's Eve 2015. 8.55am*

I stare at the round pills in my palm and gulp them down. I wish they contained a bigger dose to help take the edge off. I close my eyes, sip water and feel the tablets float aimlessly on my tongue.

I tuck the blister packet back inside my make-up bag before Taylor re-emerges. It is better he doesn't know; he'll only end up asking me too many questions that I don't want to answer. If the truth came out now, he would be heartbroken that I had kept it from him, perhaps angry even. At the time, I believed I'd made the right decision, though it would have helped having someone to talk to. Keeping a secret of this magnitude is the hardest thing I have ever had to do.

It's changed me and not for the better.

Sometimes I don't recognise myself. Perhaps I'm still in mourning. Though technically, I'm not sure if you're allowed to mourn for someone that you've never met. But that's how I feel, the same devastated emotional wreck that I was after my gramps died.

I finish curling my hair and stare aimlessly into the mirror. My appearance conceals the way I feel inside. Women are lucky in that sense; can paint a different picture on the outside with make-up to hide the ugly truth. I don't know how to find myself again. I wish I had the answers, but I don't. Perhaps I ought to get some help, but I don't like the thought of that. I'm too private to divulge my inner secrets to a stranger.

Voices echo in the hallway, and it's all becoming real again. The conversation grows louder. I recognise Will's voice and heat flushes my cheeks. This was a bad idea. How can I maintain my composure around Taylor? He's going to notice that I'm attracted to Will; he's not stupid. I feel sick at the prospect of being in the room with the pair of them at the same time. It's not a situation I could have ever envisaged.

"Kate," Taylor calls. I'm catatonic, chewing nervously on my nails.

They look disgusting; varnish chipped and flaking. I take another mouthful of water, wishing it was wine.

"Kate," he calls again, voice growing louder.

His footsteps creak along the landing.

"Didn't you hear me calling you? DCI Beckley and DI Wakeman are waiting downstairs."

"Yes, sorry. I'm coming."

"It'll be fine. Don't worry."

He offers his hand and helps me to my feet.

Tentatively, I follow him down the stairs and spot Will out of the corner of my eye. He's on the large sofa nearest to the fireplace. His fingers are laced, arms resting on his lap. I can't believe he's in our house. It's surreal and my heart is frantic.

Wakeman has his back pressed against the sofa. His fat stomach overhangs his belt. I hate the fact that he's in my house. I can't bear to be around him. He had no right to treat me the way he did, I've never acted inappropriately at a crime scene.

His stern, icy eyes bore into me. There's stillness behind them; he dislikes me.

I'm nervous at the prospect of being under surveillance. In the past, I've accompanied officers on various operations, but I've never been the subject of one. Taylor continues into the kitchen, presumably to make tea and coffee.

Will and I make eye contact. He smiles, my stomach contracts and my heart twitches. I'm still mortified about what happened at the station.

"I'm sorry about yesterday," I stammer, gaze slipping to the floor, head hung with shame.

"Kate, there's no need to apologise, your reaction was perfectly understandable. You were in a state of severe shock. I'm just glad to see you're OK."

I sit on the two-seater sofa opposite them feeling uncomfortable in my own home and unnerved by their presence. I hope they drove an unmarked vehicle, otherwise I'll be the centre of idle street gossip, everyone alluding as to why officers are inside my house. I'll be tarnished a criminal.

"Have you thought any more about the surveillance?" Will probes. His eyes lock on mine; I wish he wouldn't do that.

"Yes. It's not something that I feel entirely comfortable with, to be honest, nor something that I ever thought I'd have to do."

"Of course," he nods. "And I can understand your concern, but I cannot emphasise enough how valuable your help could be to us."

"I know, and I've thought long and hard when reaching my decision." I pause, allowing myself one last chance to change my mind. I close my eyes, and see Louise staring at me, demanding that I do the right thing.

"I'll agree to it, but I'm only doing it for my sister. There are also some conditions to my involvement that I want agreed."

"Sure, please elaborate."

"I want to be kept fully informed. If you think he's within 100 metres of me, I want to know. I am not letting that sick bastard ever get close enough to touch me."

I leap overdramatically from the sofa and pace barefoot on the carpet.

"Kate, don't worry, we'll keep you safe. It is our job to protect you."

I halt in front of Will; he raises a reassuring smile.

"What exactly will it entail?" I ask, biting my thumb nail with agitation.

"We want you to continue with your normal routine and go to work. An unmarked police car will follow you at all times, and we'll have undercover officers in position monitoring your movements."

"So, I won't be accompanied in the newsroom by an officer? I don't want everyone knowing."

"No. Trust me, Kate, we know what we're doing. With regards to your home environment, we will also have undercover officers observing the house throughout the night. Is it alarmed?"

"Yes, it's a new system," Taylor interrupts, as he re-enters the room and hands Will and Wakeman a coffee.

"Excellent."

"Can you assure me that my wife is not being put in any danger?"

"Obviously, every operation comes with associated risks, but we don't believe Kate is in any significant danger. We'll be monitoring her closely and constantly," Will assures, tone confident.

"I'm placing my trust in you and I'm telling you now that if he touches a single hair on Kate's head, you'll be held personally accountable."

My cheeks redden at Taylor's outburst. I'm both embarrassed and impressed.

"He won't, not on my watch."

\* \* \*

Bronzing pearls inject colour and life onto my cheeks. I'm already late for work. Warily, I descend the stairs and notice Will and DI Wakeman standing by the door. Will stares directly at me.

"Are you certain about this Kate?"

"Yes."

I grab my handbag from the dining room table and ignore the rigid toast. Taylor stands by the kitchen sink, back pressed against the countertop, arms folded across his chest. His agitated eyes meet mine.

"Taylor?"

"Please be careful," he begs.

"I'll be fine, don't worry," I assure, tone unconvincing. I fight back my swelling tears and re-join Will and Wakeman.

Fear grips my torso as I step out of my sanctuary. A breeze whips past and I button my coat, quickening my pace towards the car. I slide into the driving seat and lock the doors. It eases my discomfort and offers a safety net. My pulse is racing, breathing increasingly intense, imagining a bullet penetrating the windscreen and blasting a gaping cavity in my chest. Blood splatters the opaque glass.

I snatch a deep breath, peer in the rear-view mirror and watch Will and Wakeman retreat to their vehicle. I drive away, leaving them at the end of the road. I'm uncertain where the undercover officers are positioned, but I know they are in pursuit, maintaining a safe distance.

The radio offers a distraction.

I can't lie. I'm petrified at the situation in which I have been thrown but I brought it on myself.

The snow has melted there's not a single trace left on the roads. I join the M5, closely monitoring my speed. It puzzles me how the killer found out about Louise. I can only think that he stalked me on social media. I need to review my security settings and will make that a priority.

An Audi Q7 follows closely behind. There's also a black BMW 5 series ahead, maintaining a close distance. I suspect they're both surveillance vehicles.

The newsroom falls silent; blood pricks my face, reddening. I feel both angry and betrayed, as faint whispers emerge. Tom stares at me momentarily before redirecting his glare behind me. I already feel Cecilia's aura, triggering a dull ache inside of me. I'm 30 minutes late for work and know I'm about to be reprimanded.

"Kate, could you step inside my office?" She asks, tone harsh.

I refrain from making eye contact, walk past the reporters station and enter, closing the door behind me.

"Please explain why you were escorted from the office by the police yesterday."

She twiddles the tips of her long blonde hair. I feel as though a spear has torn my stomach open, slitting me in two. My legs are quivering; I steady myself by placing a hand upon her desk. She eyes me curiously before continuing with her interrogation.

"Well, what do you have to say for yourself?"

"I don't know where to start," I stammer.

"What trouble have you brought to my door?"

I pause, taking measured breaths to refrain from crying.

"It's my sister. She's the latest victim," I blurt.

Cecilia's chin drops in dismay, perhaps mixed with a little guilt over how abrupt she had been with me, and for not giving me the benefit of any doubt.

"She was attacked as a warning to me," I mumble.

"I don't understand."

"He threatened her, instructing me to back off with regards to news coverage."

Cecilia leans back in her padded office chair, dumbfounded.

"That's why the police took me to the station. I'm really sorry, I wasn't given an option."

She remains silent, arms crumpled across her buxom chest.

"I'm under police surveillance for my own protection; they think he's watching me. The detective leading the investigation wants to observe me; he hopes I can lead them to the killer."

She remains mute and stomps towards the door, smashing it against its frame. I follow her with my eyes. She steps into the newsroom clapping her hands vigorously, vying for attention. The keyboard tapping halts, everyone fully aware of her raging presence.

"I'm holding an urgent conference in the boardroom."

All the reporters and subs obey her order and quickly vacate their desks. I feel queasy. She's going to tell everyone. Why would she do this to me? How could she humiliate me like this? It's nobody's business but mine. This is my life and she has no right divulging it so publicly. I want to yell at her, tell her to mind her own fucking business but I don't have it in me to confront her; she scares me.

I follow on hollow legs up the staircase and enter the cornflower blue conference room. Cecilia positions herself at the head of the oblong oak table, her huge bust squashed against the surface edge. Her face is stern, scouring silent faces. I lower my head to avoid all eye contact.

"I need to inform everyone of an extremely serious matter. I'm sure there was speculation yesterday with regards to the police visit, therefore I am clarifying the situation."

Eyes penetrate me as I sit twiddling my gold wedding band anxiously. It's hot and sticky in this confined space; I need air.

"I'll be blunt. The latest victim of the Weston serial attacker is Kate's sister," she blurts. Her words sicken me to the core. I swallow and subtly slide my palms under my hair to shield my ears. I can't bear to listen.

"Kate's sister survived but had been targeted due to their relationship. The attacker struck as a warning regarding further news coverage. Kate is under police surveillance as part of the ongoing investigation into the Millbrook murders. This information is to go no further than these walls. Everyone will continue their normal duties while Kate is monitored, understand? My sympathies are with you and your family, Kate."

I'm shocked, she's never offered me an ounce of kindness before.

I force myself to straighten my aching neck, meeting an array of sympathetic and stunned expressions. I slip away to the toilets, locking myself behind a cubicle, unable to control my emotions. I sit on top of the toilet seat lid, resting my head on my palms. Tears draw lines in my foundation, as the door creaks open.

"Kate?" Cecilia calls abruptly.

"Yes."

I wipe the water droplets with the cheap toilet paper. Its rough surface hurts my raw cheeks and reminds me of the toilets at school.

"There's been a shooting on your patch. Can you cover it?"

"Sure."

I wait for the door to close, unbolt the cubicle and creep out. My complexion has reverted to its pallid façade; eyes crimson with raging blood vessels. I splash cold water on my face and pat away the mascara stains.

Back at my desk I locate the police bulletin, '*Witnesses Sought to Pellet Gun Shooting.*' The press release details an incident regarding a 12-year-old boy. I ignore the hushed gossiping around me, grab my pad and vacate the newsroom feeling relieved to be alone, where I can let my tears run free.

* * *

The Grantham estate is similar in nature to Millbrook, only less violent. Its 70s concrete precincts are filled with teenage kids skiving off school. They stand in groups smoking fags and spliffs outside of McColl's and Coral.

It's horrific to hear the vulgar obscenities they inflict on elderly passers-by. I want to tell them to have some respect, but I know better than that. They will almost certainly each be carrying a blade tucked inside their tracksuits. I know their type; not to be messed with. I can imagine the future that lies ahead for them, and it isn't pretty.

I catch the eye of a frail pensioner as she saunters slowly past them, pulling her shopping trolley behind. I'm impressed with the way she manoeuvres through them, undeterred. I guess that's how you should act around here; show you're confident and not afraid.

Sometimes I wonder whether I should carry a weapon for self-defence. It's sad that I think in that way. The trouble is, a: I think I'd be rendered immobile with fear and b: I'd probably be unable to fight back. I just wouldn't know how.

A Ford Transit van waits in the distance with two plain clothed officers observing from behind the dash. They've changed the covert car to blend with the estate. There's also an old-style Metro on the opposite side of the cul-de-sac. I count four figures inside all monitoring my movements.

I scuttle through the drizzle to the address, treading over the rickety pavement outside the unsightly end-terrace house. Overgrown grass blades brush against my legs as I wade through, passing a rusting Yamaha motorbike. The nicotine-stained net curtains hang loosely on overstretched wires in the windows, their frames warped. I sly a glance over my shoulder and feel my heart accelerating.

The front door is slightly ajar and centred with a glass window concealed with an obscene hand gesture sticker. I cringe, wondering what lies ahead. I remove my jacket, down dressing to adjust to my surroundings.

An emaciated woman emerges, wearing an off-white vest with no bra underneath; the fabric tucked into her faded 90s jeans.

"Hi, I'm from the Southern Chronicle regarding the shooting incident involving your son."

"A reporter is here about Jason," she yells over her shoulder.

My eyes are transfixed upon her blackened, gappy teeth. I wait patiently, as rain seeps through my blouse. The Ford Transit moves closer, keeping me in sight.

"OK, come in."

I step inside, manoeuvring through the small gap into the living room, watching as she scoops up scattered dirty dishes. My eyes squint, focusing through a smoke haze, which breaches my lungs. The smog clogs the back of my throat; I struggle to breathe and cough to clear my airways.

Beyond the fog, an obese unshaven man sits in a shabby armchair watching TV, with cornflake traces apparent in his bearded chin. I study the brown nicotine-stained walls, once terracotta in colour. I can make out a fine flower print under the copious layers of grime.

My pupils widen, encountering a mammoth tiger staring down at me from within a tarnished golden frame. It hangs above the fireplace taking prize position. I cringe at the distasteful fixtures and dirty conditions wondering how people live like this.

"Sit down," the woman urges.

The chair, which was also once terracotta, is now sullied and covered with rigid cigarette welts. I'm uncomfortable, feeling my clothes absorbing dirt. The woman sits opposite picking her blackened fingernails. I form the view that she's a heavy drug user.

"I was sorry to hear about your son. Tell me what happened, is he OK?"

"Yeah, he was shot by an air rifle. Bloody force pushed him right over," she replies, tone almost tinged with excitement as she plucks her half-smoked roll-up from the overflowing ashtray.

"Is he badly injured?"

"His back is bruised but the pellet didn't go into his skin."

She maintains her eyes on the TV, watching Jeremy Kyle.

"Did he recognise the person responsible?"

"Nah, he didn't see them, just heard a bunch of lads running off, laughing."

I realise that I'm not going to get much detail, she's clearly uninterested.

The lingering stale smoke repulses me. I study the man, who remains unfazed by me. He emits a vulgar burp.

"Is your son here?"

"No, he's at a mate's house.

He's fine now."

"Can I talk to him later? Perhaps send a photographer when he's home to take his picture? I can run an appeal for information."

"Do we get paid?"

Her eyes suddenly light up, and she takes her eyes off the TV screen for a moment, looking at me with an expression of greedy anticipation on her face.

"Sorry, no."

"OK, fair enough." Her momentary interest fades as quickly as it had arrived, and she returns her gaze to Jeremy Kyle.

I jot down her phone number and rise to my feet to leave. My heels strike floorboards as I stride over the threadbare carpet toward the door.

"Thank you for your time." They barely acknowledge me.

Outside, I gratefully gasp fresh air to refuel my lungs, but the stench lingers on me. I feel vile and want to wash it off my skin. I march back to the car to escape the unpleasantness of Grantham. As experiences go on the estate that episode ranks up there as one of the worst.

Inside the car, I feel alone and afraid once more. Panic surges through me, the realisation that I'm exposed again, and that he could strike at any time.

My world is chaotic, and I'm terrified about what lies ahead.

# Chapter Thirty-One – Kate

*New Year's Eve 2015. 5.15PM*

The rain slaps my face as I dash through the office car park. Louise's words, *"Do what it takes to get the fucking bastard"* resound in my ears, I'm unable to silence them.

Fast-approaching footsteps quicken behind me. I panic, eyeing the faint outline of the Victorian care home and the reflecting moonlight. I increase my pace as the brisk sea air howls from the promenade.

Sudden intense beams pierce my eyes, illuminating my path. I blink, adjusting to the light and detect two covert silhouettes beyond the rubber wiper blades.

"Night, Kate," Tom mutters, overtaking.

I lock myself in my vehicle and routinely examine the rear seat. Everything unnerves me. I'm desperate for it all to be over and life to be normal.

\* \* \*

My drenched trousers cling like a leech sucking flesh. Fresh grapes rest on the hospital tray along with an array of women's magazines. A bouquet of pink roses is displayed in a vase on the bedside locker.

Louise's face has worsened overnight. I skulk toward her and mum, my head hung low like an outsider intruding. My eyes well, knowing my actions have damaged our relationship.

Mum's protective hand rests upon to Louise's arm. The gauze on her neck has been removed exposing black snaked stitching in a 10cm diagonal slash. Her face is swollen, patches tarnished jaundice yellow.

"Did you hear me?" Louise repeats, angrily.

I shake my head.

"I asked if they've caught him."

"No."

"Then why are you here?"

"I've come to see you, to see how you are," I stammer nervously.

I look to mum for support, but she glances away, turning her back on me. I feel hollow and completely alone for the first time in my life.

"How do you think I am? Look at me," Louise's crumbled mouth screeches.

"And you coming here telling me they haven't caught him makes it worse."

"I'm sorry."

I bow my head with shame.

"Sorry doesn't cut it Kate. It doesn't even begin to come close."

I hover agitated with my hands tucked awkwardly in my pockets, longing for booze. Nurses gather at the reception, whispering and pointing.

"I'll leave. I can see this is not a good time," I mutter, retreating.

"No, wait. I want to know what you're doing to sort this mess out."

They both stare, hatred raging in their eyes. Remorse grates my insides.

"I'm trying to help. I'm under surveillance."

"Then why haven't they caught him?"

My cheeks redden, angry that my efforts are being dismissed.

"I don't know."

"Surely, they have some leads? she yells. Then she drops her voice, and adds, "go, Kate. Just go."

"I think it is best that you leave." Mum's words crush my heart. I flee on tremulous legs feeling wounded and desolate.

* * *

Rain slaps the windscreen as I stare into darkness. I've never felt so sad or alone; rejected by my own flesh and blood.

I reach into the Tesco carrier bag in the passenger footwell, crack the wine seal and take a slug with my back turned to the surveillance car. I couldn't care what they think, but I certainly don't need any more drama.

I'm heartbroken by my family's attitude. And, to add insult to injury, Taylor isn't answering my calls. Why doesn't he ever pick up when I need him the most? Presumably he's already at Ryan's having a beer; it's New Year's Eve. I can't believe he's out enjoying himself while I've all this shit to contend with.

Fuelled by rage and sadness, I start the engine and drive to Ryan's house feeling a row brewing.

Why doesn't anyone care about how I'm feeling? I would never have treated my mum or my sister, the way they just treated me. I feel so low. They don't even care that I'm putting my life on the line to try and help bring her attacker to justice. Surely, that should count for something? Obviously, it doesn't. I never asked for any of this. I just want it to be over.

Ryan looks surprised when I barge inside his house and survey each room, looking for Taylor. He watches on mesmerised before examining my watery eyes.

"Taylor is not here," he says calmy, before ushering me to sit on the sofa.

"I'm sorry," I whisper.

I divulge the ugly truth of my life. He's a good listener. My tears saturate his shirt as he holds me close and strokes my hair, comforting me. He's always been kind to me.

I feel terrible that I've ruined his shirt. He was ready to go to the New Year's Eve party on the Grand Pier; the one Taylor and I are due to attend. I don't feel remotely like partying or welcoming in the New

Year. The only thing that 2016 will bring to my life is violence or my death.

I gulp the last of the large glass of wine that Ryan poured. It's warming on my throat and calms my mood. I'm blushing, recalling my earlier outburst. He must think I've gone crazy with my irrational behaviour. Ryan wipes my tears and pulls me back against his chest. My cheeks fuse to his cotton shirt. He smells nice. I wish I could stay and hide away from everything. I feel safe tucked away from my chaotic world that waits outside of these four walls.

\* \* \*

Objects twist out of shape, my sight distorts. My eyelids obscure them as the darkness creeps over. My wine glass crashes to the floor, falling from my limp hand.

I'm unfazed, my body comatosed by alcohol. I sleep for hours. Flashbacks of Louise and the crime scenes torment my dreams. I'm plagued by death and violence. Blood is everywhere, and the magpie's stare is burning holes in my eyes. I slam them shut shielding them.

A child's voice is humming and growing louder, it's the girl from the park. She's crying, playing with the syringe. I recognise the ominous tune. Her clothes are dirty; she's dragging her bare feet towards me across the grass, sombre eyes injecting a deadly glare. She's singing now, her childlike tone is unnerving.

'*One for sorrow, two for joy, three for a girl, four for a boy, five for silver, six for gold, seven for a secret never to be told.*'

Blood trickles from her mouth. She buckles to her knees; soul draining. My feet are cemented, I cannot reach her. Her body crumples to the ground where she studies me wide-eyed taking her last breath through her blue lips before her life evaporates.

My eyes bolt open; my chest palpitating catching breath. I lift and release my clammy cheek clinging to the leather armrest. I blink encountering Taylor through my lashes. He's staring down assessing me and eyeing the two empty bottles on the floor, one of them dripping condensation down the glass onto the carpet. I carried on drinking when I got back from Ryan's to numb my pain.

I've no idea how long I have been passed out. My mouth is dehydrated, my tongue stuck to my palate. I can't swallow.

"Have you drunk both bottles?" Taylor asks, scornfully.

"I guess so," I slur.

"Is that your answer to all of this, get plastered on your own? It's New Year's Eve for fucks sake, or have you forgotten that?"

I lick my lips trying to produce saliva and quench my thirst, but my efforts are in vain.

"What if the killer had walked through the door rather than me? You'd hardly be able to defend yourself in that state, would you?"

I start to cry.

"You don't know what it's like, I have no one."

Taylor's eyes become hostile.

"What do you mean you have no one? That's hurtful Kate; I've been here the whole time for you. I always have been."

"It's true. I don't, I've lost my mum and sister over this and now even you can't be bothered to be here for me when I need you the most."

"What are you talking about?"

"I went to the hospital. They hate me; told me to leave."

"Don't be silly they don't hate you. Louise needs time. I've been there every step of the way supporting you. Don't throw it back in my face because I'm late. It's New Year's Eve, one of my busiest days. I ended my shift early, so we could go to the party."

"I went looking for you at Ryan's."

"I literally finished work half an hour ago and I came straight home to you."

The atmosphere between us remains tense.

"I needed you tonight and you weren't here. You didn't even answer your phone."

"Well, I'm sorry for doing my job Kate. Not everything is about you. Taking to the bottle is not going to solve your problems, sort yourself out."

I study the rage in his eyes and slam mine shut to block out his tirade. I find strength, push myself off the sofa, brush past him and stumble towards the staircase. My hand grabs the cream banister and I haul myself up, climbing the stairs one by one on rubbery legs.

"That's it, walk away like you always do."

His words are muffled as I reach our bedroom. I strip off all my clothes and throw them into a heap on the floor. I can't think or speak. I've had far too much to drink. But I don't care right now. I don't care about a single thing in the world other than going back to sleep, shutting my eyes and my mind away from the torment and tragedy.

I need to be free from all this pain. I collapse face down on the bed, slamming my eyes to escape my troubled life.

# Chapter Thirty-Two – Kate

*New Year's Day 2016*

My head throbs, my skin sweating last night's Zinfandel and Shiraz. I need the pain to subside and reach for a stale glass of water at my bedside, and greedily down it.

Taylor's side of the bed hasn't been slept in.

I'm ashamed of my behaviour. I don't know what I said but my subconscious is telling me that I acted out of order and that I upset Taylor. That's booze for you. The first bottle barely touched the sides and the second knocked me plain out. I needed it. It sounds bad, I'm not an alcoholic but I needed it to make myself feel better and drift off, away from everything that I'm dealing with in my life.

My heart was crushed by the overwhelming sense of rejection, and I wanted to ease the pain. Perhaps I got carried away. My headache and dry mouth are both telling me that I did. I can't erase what's happened or take back whatever I said; it's too late.

I want to stay in bed and lock myself away from it all, but I need to get up and face the world.

My inert body skulks towards the bathroom and I stare at my reflection. I don't like what I see; a dirty face and lip creases stained crimson. I miss my immaculate bronzed complexion. My finely manicured fingernails are chewed in uneven sharp points and the flesh surrounding my thumbs is red raw. I'm dressed solely in my underwear and feel cold perched on the toilet seat lid, letting my tears flow. I reach for a piece of tissue; the quilted patterns cushion my nostrils.

There's a dark bruise on my leg. I've no idea how I got it. Drink sometimes has that effect on me, acting as evidence markers from the night before. At the time, you're so drunk you don't even feel pain. I close my eyes, searching the darkness for irretrievable memories, unsure whether I truly want to recover them or not.

I look back at the empty bed and my feelings of loneliness intensify. I've vague recollections of our argument but I can't remember clearly what was said. My stomach churns at the uncertainly. Heat rises to the surface of my cheeks as I remember crawling away from Taylor up the stairs. That's probably how I got the bruise.

I need to find him and apologise.

I wrap my dressing gown around me, walk along the landing towards the spare bedroom and push open the panelled door. The sheets are crumpled, but he's already gone. I tiptoe downstairs to the kitchen and collapse against the breakfast bar, resting my dizzy head on my palms.

The house is cold and empty without him. I'm angry with myself for pushing him away when I needed him most. Why the hell am I so stupid? Alcohol isn't the answer. It's the devil.

I do love though how quickly he forgets drinking away the weeks following Paul's death. It's OK for him to have a comforting drink but not me. I know he's bigger, able to handle a lot more booze than I can, but still, it's just so hypocritical.

I was there for him through everything. A shoulder to cry on, taking his snappy behaviour, all whilst grieving twice over. It's time he returned the favour. I'm not perfect and I'll never be a Stepford housewife, but I try my best. I will become a better person. Deep down I knew that our happiness would be short-lived; it was too good to be true.

Now my life is derailing like a train wreckage; my fate sealed. I'm only ever meant to endure pain and sadness, it follows me wherever I go. I'm not sure what I did to deserve this life.

I lift my head, half hoping to see him standing in the doorway, staring at me disapprovingly. But no, I'm alone. And perhaps that's what I deserve.

I slouch over to a cupboard, take out a glass and carry it over to the sink before turning on the tap and filling it with water.

I lift my head and catch my forlorn reflection in the kitchen window. I raise the glass of water in my hand, as if toasting my mirror image, and mutter, "Happy New Year, Kate."

# Chapter Thirty-Three – DCI Beckley

*New Year's Day 2016. 9.15am*

Kate's only been under surveillance for a short time, but I'd hoped it would have yielded a more positive result. I had hoped we would have lured him out quickly and been able to bring a swift end to this traumatic case.

I've been regularly updated with regards to Kate's whereabouts and the undercover teams claim they haven't witnessed anyone acting suspiciously around her.

It is early days I suppose, but the pressure is on to shut him down and bring him in. Chief Superintendent Harding is on my back, breathing down my neck, and I have nothing concrete to offer him at present.

The families need closure and the killer must be brought to justice for heinous atrocities he has carried out. While he's still on the streets of Weston, women are not safe, and I can't rest.

I'm intrigued by the mask he wears to shield his identity. According to collated research from the Live Cell team, Briguella is one of the most disturbing of the Commedia characters; roguish, quick-witted, opportunistic and a lascivious, cruel figure.

A superimposed image of his mask is displayed alongside photographs of the victims on the Incident Room walls. The eye slits and hooked nose convey a sinister expression; the women would have been petrified. We need to release the image to the press with a public appeal. Someone sold it, and a partner or family member may recognise it.

DI Wakeman approaches with sugar granules on his chin. He's been sat with three constables at the Live Cell desk, shoving mini doughnuts into his mouth for ten minutes. As he draws closer, I notice his belt buckle dig into his bulging stomach, having put on even more weight.

I, on the other hand, keep losing it because I'm not eating properly. I have no appetite.

"Boss, I've got an update regarding the petrol stations using Healthguard manufactured gloves. They are readily available at Sainsbury's and the Texaco garage on the main college road, which discounts the other two supermarkets and BP. Texaco is nearer to the crime scenes but we shouldn't discount Sainsbury's. I'll head down to both now and obtain CCTV footage from the nights of the murders. We might get a hit if he obtains fresh gloves en route to commit the crimes," Wakeman says.

"That's great, good work.

"We need to force his hand, dangle Kate as bait and put her alone on Millbrook."

"What are you suggesting? A sting operation?" Wakeman quizzes.

"Yes, I've been debating the idea."

"I doubt the feisty madam will agree to that."

"I'm going to discuss it with her. She won't be in any danger if armed officers are positioned within range. If the killer thinks that she's not willing to adhere to his warning over media coverage, it will anger him enough to lure him out of the shadows, where we'll be waiting for the fucker."

I leave the Incident Room and head back to my office. The desk is littered with case files. I need to sit down and go through everything but there's no time now. I need to talk to Kate and get her to agree. I dial her mobile.

"Hello?"

"Hi Kate, it's Will."

"Oh hi," she mumbles nervously.

"I wanted to check you're OK?"

"I'm fine, thanks."

"Are you sure?"

"Yes, honestly I'm absolutely fine."

"Great. I just wanted to update you with regards to the case and to check that you're happy with the surveillance methods."

"Everything seems fine. What update? Have you caught him?"

"No."

"Oh."

I hear the disappointment in her voice and try to assure her that we are making progress.

"Louise has identified a mask that the killer wore during her attack. We're putting a media release together. We need the public's help in trying to identify its whereabouts, someone may recognise it."

"OK. Surely if we run another story, it's only going to infuriate him further?"

"In a sense that's what I'm hoping."

There's a long pause on the line.

"Kate, what I'm trying to say is that I'd like to set up a sting operation. If we bombard the press with more details of the investigation, it may lure him out. I'm suggesting that we give him a little encouragement and send you to Millbrook."

"You can't be serious?" She screeches.

"Armed officers will offer protection; you won't be in any danger. Would you be willing to help us?"

"I suppose. To be honest I've gone past caring about myself, I'll do whatever it takes."

She sounds troubled; this whole situation is killing her.

"Is everything OK?"

"Ignore me, I'm just feeling a little sorry for myself. It's a difficult time. Tell me what I need to do."

"We'll need you to go to Millbrook tonight, as though you're still investigating the story, and see if he approaches you. I promise you we will be monitoring you at all times."

"Fine," she sighs. "Why not? I've got nothing to lose."

"You're certain? I don't want to put you into a situation where you feel uncomfortable."

"I have to do it, if I'm ever to regain my sister's trust. Without that, I have nothing."

\* \* \* Kate \* \* \*

*New Year's Day 2016. 9.50pm*

I feel hollow. My heart torn, and all the vessels storing affection, severed. It aches with rejection and shame caused by my erratic drinking and row with Taylor. I drank to dull the pain. Things between us were the best they have been in a long time and I ruined it.

I've texted him, apologising, but he's not replied all day. I couldn't call; I'm not ready to talk. I'm too ashamed to discuss all the things that I may or may not, have said. A part of me is angry that he can't understand what drove me to drink. Family is everything to me, he knows that. I pray that, in time, they'll extend forgiveness.

Beyond the darkness of the rear-view mirror, a surveillance van is parked. Armed officers are positioned on the rooftops directing their suppressed Blaser R94 rifles.

My legs quiver; I'm out of my depth. I slam the door shut and proceed, following my instructions from Will. I'd promised Taylor that I wouldn't come back here alone, especially at night. But he's ignoring me, obviously still disgusted with my behaviour, so why shouldn't I ignore what he's asked me to do, or not to do. Besides, I've gone past caring about myself.

I sneak one last look at my mobile; my texts remain unanswered.

The ambient street lighting disappears as I enter darkness. My orders are to walk along the alleyway and revisit Shelley Carter's crime scene, as though I'm looking for a new line on the Millbrook Murders.

Afterwards, I must approach a flat situated a few metres beyond. My fingers clutch a spiral notebook and biro, which I insert between my lips and chew nervously. A dog barks and I quicken my steps.

The alleyway entrance is deserted and my is vision compromised by the obscure sky. I feel something underfoot and step over a stray hypodermic needle. Stale urine hovers against my nostrils. I'm afraid, walking beneath birch trees, which rustle overhead.

Despite my underlying fear, part of me is willing him to confront me, so that my nightmare can finally come to an end.

I sly a quick glance over my shoulder. I'm alone and continue to the railway bridge where Shelley died. My body shifts violently, unsteadied by a reckless cyclist. The sudden presence alarms me, pumping panic through me.

I continue onward towards the flat, as agreed, and tap the front door. I've been instructed to knock twice, leave and return along the pathway. I tap my knuckles once more and walk away, passing the dense bushes. I'm gripped by dread, unable to see in the darkness. I hurry eager for illuminations to light my pathway.

The surveillance van remains positioned in the distance. They'll keep me safe, but it doesn't stop my anguish. Time is running out; he's not coming for me. I ought to feel relieved but I'm disappointed that my efforts to lure him were in vain. I'd wanted to nail the bastard.

Disheartened, my heels scuff the concrete while my fingers fidget for my keys. I unlock the car and slump into the driving seat, deflated. I'm on the edge of tears and jump, startled by my mobile. It's Will.

"Are you OK?"

"Yes. I'm sorry for letting you down."

"You haven't. It was worth a shot; perhaps we've underestimated his intelligence."

"If he's not here, then he could be out there, killing again."

"You can't control his actions Kate. Perhaps I got it wrong and he's not watching you."

"But I want him to watch me. Don't you get it?" I snap.

"I want him to get caught and bring an end to this fucking nightmare that's ruining my life. It's the only way she will ever forgive me."

# Chapter Thirty-Four

*New Year's Day 2016. 11.15pm*

Kate had remained untouchable. Tonight, that would change; he was going to take and punish her for trying to bring him down, and for not heeding his warning.

How dare she try to lure him to Millbrook?

He stood in the shadows, his breath hovering against the leaves that concealed his silhouette. He felt aroused, pulling on his gloves and mask. His fiery eyes peered through the neat incisions; breath warming his face as it clung to the interior.

This would be his finest hour, what he'd dreamt about in his fantasies. Revenge would be his at last.

She was no different to the others.

The angle from where he stood in the adjacent rear garden was perfect, allowing him to watch her undress through a gap in the curtain. He grew excited watching her fingers reach across the arch of her back to unfasten her bra. His sexual urge intensified watching her walk out of view in just her Brazilian panties. He was hungry for her but sat patiently waiting for his moment, biding his time for her to fall asleep.

His boots crept along the garden path of number 9, following the moonlight towards the conservatory door. It would provide access to next door. He plucked a crowbar protruding from his pocket and inserted its tip between the fascia edging, forcing it back and forth until the door cracked open.

He removed blue overshoe protectors one at a time, replacing them with fresh ones before stepping inside. The house was unoccupied; undergoing refurbishment by the owners. It was perfect.

He skulked across concrete, passing between structural load-bearing poles and under a clear tarpaulin sheet, which segregated entry to the lounge. At the bottom stair, he paused, licking his lips in anticipation, before continuing to the landing, where he climbed on top of the banister.

His gloved fingers opened the loft hatch and released a ladder.

Observing the silence, he continued his ascent, ducking below the attic trusses and stepping over fibreglass insulation. Carefully, he removed boxes, shielding a crawl space into the loft above number 8.

He smiled upon gaining access and crawled, ghostlike, on hands and knees, twisted the hatch latch and lowered himself down.

A small lamp lit Kate's bedroom. He peered through the mask encountering a bare thigh delicately protruding from the duvet. A black lace hem clung to her gold satin negligee, barely covering her flesh where she had tossed in her sleep.

He stared longingly and ventured closer.

He lowered himself beside her silky silhouette, stroking a hair lock sprawled across the pillow. Her comatose body didn't flinch at his touch. He smiled, dragging his hand along her back over the smooth satin and the curve of her buttock.

Upon reaching the lace he reversed direction, sweeping the material upwards to expose her while she slept. It was exactly how he'd imagined it would be.

She would not die yet; not until he had some fun.

He inserted the blade that he clutched excitedly in his palm back into his pocket. She would experience fear like the others had and he would enjoy her the most.

Her tiny body rolled over to rest on her back. He watched her chest rise and fall and wanted to touch. His fingers caressed her left breast, sending an adrenalin rush through his veins. She murmured.

He wanted her awake and yearned to see her pitiful eyes watch him claim his prize. His hand moved back to her thigh, tracing over goose bumps, which spread like fire across the surface. Her eyes flickered.

"Taylor?"

She eyeballed the mask, waking suddenly but disabled by fear.

His heavy legs pinned her to the bed. This was his best catch of all, exactly what he'd been imagining.

It was time; he was going to have his moment.

She flinched, struggling to free herself from his snare as a hypodermic needle injected her carotid artery. She fought to stay awake, but her eyelids drifted; Etorphine rushing through her system.

He tucked her arms across her chest, lifted and cradled her body against his before retracing his steps and slipping away into the shadows.

\* \* \*

Bound and gagged, her motionless body lay slumped in the car boot. He grinned, slammed the boot shut before leaping behind the wheel and firing up the engine with his frantic fingers.

The small cell space restricted the air, but Kate was unaware, still heavily sedated by the synthetic opioid depressing her central nervous system. Her corpse-like body lurched as the car mounted a series of speedbumps. She rolled over; her chest pressed sharply against jump lead prongs and a petrol can, which oozed fumes into the confined atmosphere. Neon lights flashed overhead as they travelled along the dual carriageway toward the countryside.

He maneuvered snaking gravel roads as his body pulsated against the seat. He needed her tucked securely out of sight. The headlights illuminated a dust track, the tyres spitting chippings.

Kate's ragged body tossed from side to side, her face tore against protruding metal edges.

His twitching fingertips fiddled with the radio. He smiled, tapping his palms on the wheel in pace with the music. Through the wilderness, he focused on an open rickety gate. The vehicle slowed, glided between the gaps and dipped through a small ditch. Mud splattered across the windscreen as it resurfaced back onto a grassy verge.

He checked they were still alone and swallowed to refresh his dry mouth.

Observing the barn emerge ahead, his heart raced with excitement. He slammed on the brake, smashing her head against the rear seat.

His boots sank, squelching mud as he waded through stinging nettles. He flicked his Zippo, producing a naked flame to guide him towards his prey. The boot sprung open and he stroked her face smearing crimson bloodstains.

Seemingly lifeless, she sunk into his arms as he carried her toward the barn. He dumped her body on the chippings and returned to the car, retrieving a torch. Twisting its neck, a beam emerged and blasted. He shone it briskly back and forth, scrutinising the surroundings. It was just as he remembered; untouched for decades.

His vision lowered, focusing on a corroding bolt on the arched doorway, which he unsecured. The door swung open on rusting hinges as a bat escaped overhead and soared towards the moonlight.

He draped her across his arms, stepping over fallen debris and discarded tarpaulin. They would be alone here. His eyes surveyed the scene; old wood pallets leant against the walls and hay bales stacked haphazardly.

His face burst with pride as his boots waded through rain puddles. He dropped his catch like a fisherman emptying fish from his trawl. She sprawled lifelessly amongst Guano droppings.

The room echoed the sound of his boots pacing back and forth. He removed the bloodstained gloves and chewed his nails anxiously, pausing alongside rusting farm machinery to admire her. He inhaled a fusty odour as he wrenched her by her hair across the jagged flooring, stopping to unbind and reattach her to a rusting equine chain loop wall restraint.

Water dripped onto her forehead. He wiped it away and stroked her face. She was a pretty thing before the grazes. His fingertips withdrew the mouth gag and let it fall to her neck; her lips remained parted. His slobbering tongue latched hers. She remained unresponsive.

Wet satin clung to her chest, accentuating every feminine curve, as her lungs inhaled. His eyes traveled downwards, studying her slender legs, the right thigh trickling blood from a cut.

He bent to his knees, coating the blood across her leg as he slid her nightie upwards, neatly propping its hemline around her waist. He wanted her to awaken feeling dirty, degraded and afraid.

He repositioned the mouth gag and observed her closely; processing and storing the perfect image in his mind before leaving her alone in the darkness.

# Chapter Thirty-Five – Kate

*Saturday 2 January 2016*

Daylight infiltrates my itchy pupils. I squint, trying to regain my senses and adjust to the bright, burning beams. My head throbs, my body timorous and aching. I'm confused and disorientated.

Fireworks of panic explode in my mind realising I'm restricted.

Cord snares my wrists securely behind my back. I can't breathe properly. My tongue is pressed against the roof of my mouth, constricted with sodden cotton locking my jaw. Bile fills my throat; I swallow hard. My heart is erratic. I can't imagine it ever regaining its normal rhythm. Its wild beats pound violently against my chest and my panicked breaths break the silence that echoes in my ears.

Where the hell am I? What the fuck is going on?

Memories coalesce in my mind. A flashback of his mask comes to the fore.

I remember it with total clarity before the light faded. My eyes dart around searching for him. I'm alive but alone; his prisoner. I yank at my restraints; a searing pain shoots up my arms. My muffled cries break the stillness. I need to break free, but I can't. I'm trapped.

Oh, dear God. I'm going to die.

It's so cold I'm shivering; the wet flooring bites at my buttocks. I shuffle to cover my modesty, praying to God that the sick bastard didn't touch me intimately. I can't remember anything after he pinned me to the bed. Please no.

My fear morphs to anger. Will said he would protect me! He told me that I would be safe. He fucked up big time. How did the killer get inside our house? The surveillance car was parked outside. Were the officers inside sleeping on the job?

I close my eyes, trying harder to recollect last night's events.

I remember putting the wine bottle by the sink, activating the alarm and climbing the stairs. How was I taken? I wasn't careless.

I wonder if Taylor came home or if he even knows that I've been abducted.

I can't just sit here and wait to die. I struggle against the restraints once more; they're too tight and hurt. I turn my attention to the gag and I push my tongue forcefully against the material; it loosens. It's making me retch.

After several forceful attempts, the cotton hovers on my bottom lip before dropping to rest on my collarbones. I inhale deeply and rotate my jaw in slow, circular motions, trying to ease the pain where it's been locked.

Sweat coats my temples. I honestly believed I was untouchable and that Will would protect me.

He's let me down. Everyone has let me down in the same way that I've let them down. Now it's over and Taylor won't even have my body to bury.

I wish my captor would come back and get it over with instead of tormenting me.

He wants to degrade me, make me feel like the others. That's why he's left me disheveled and exposed. It's his way of avenging women. My injuries are tame in comparison to what the others endured.

But, I suppose he's not finished with me, yet, not by a long way. I'm fully aware of that and of what is to come. A tsunami of fear drowns my mind, images of the crime scenes crashing by, wave after wave.

I won't be one of his victims, I won't! After everything I have been through this year I won't let my life end like this. I'll fight with every ounce of energy I can muster.

My body convulses violently in shock. I wonder if he's watching me. I need to focus and be strong; show him that I'm not afraid.

"Is anyone there?"

My words reverberate against the bricks, deadening the distant sounds of a dripping pipe.

"What do you want from me?"

Silence.

"Answer me you bastard," I yell, angrily.

My eyes fall to the floor surveying broken twigs and copious raisin-shaped droppings littered around me. I lift my head, tilting it backward; my eyes wander examining the beamed ceiling. I'm in an old Tithe barn; light seeping through aging roof holes illuminating my prison cell. It's ancient and abandoned, around 15<sup>th</sup> century.

If I can free myself from the binds, I can run barefoot.

I eyeball the room searching for an escape route and notice a small slatted window at the upper level. It's too high to climb. The shutters are locked in place, presumably bolted from the outside. Above them sit two tiny rectangular translucent windows, allowing further daylight in.

I count four other smaller hatches, all shielded by internal shutters and a huge arched doorway resembling the entrance to a church. I'm trapped and he's coming back to finish the job. It's only a matter of time.

"I'll do anything you want. Just untie me, the rope is hurting. Please, I'm begging you."

My pathetic voice echoes. I sob, twisting my throbbing wrists back and forth trying to loosen the cord. The rope tears deeper in, my flesh aflame.

"Help! Please help me."

"Help!"

My screams ricochet around the barn bouncing off the grey and buff irregular bricks.

My eyes leak a river of tears. I'm alone, waiting for him to come and enact his fantasy. I'm going to die an agonising death. This is retribution, God's way of punishing me for lying to Taylor about my miscarriage. That's the trouble with lies they always come back to haunt you. Karma is a bitch.

# Chapter Thirty-Six – DCI Beckley

*Saturday 2 January 2016*

It's 9.35am. I'm tired and despondent after last's nights fuck up. I know that Kate isn't to blame. I'm surprised that she even agreed to be part of a sting operation in the first place.

It's guilt, eating her up inside, a feeling that is all too familiar.

That's why she wants to help the investigation. She blames herself for Louise's attack, which is understandable. Perhaps, if I spoke with her and shared my own experience about Toby Harroway, she'd realise that she's not alone.

Guilt is part of life. You can't escape it, but you can learn to deal with it. I'm still trying to cope but it gets a little easier day by day. It's my fault Kate ran the story. I was trying to speed up the enquiry and get a result. I never thought it would backfire to this extent, and that her family be caught in the crossfire. I can't cope with the humiliation of another Force Review Team being brought in to sift through the case.

I feel even more sick having been informed that another body has been discovered and is being transported to the mortuary.

DI Wakeman was on scene and notified me that the deceased is another young, blonde woman. I spoke with Shelton over the phone; she's confident that it's one of his kills.

This victim is missing six fingertips, was stabbed in the heart and her ear was penetrated by a tool. I'm raging. He knew that we were on to him and attacked another woman in parkland, a mere three miles away in Worlebury. He's toying with us. He's making it clear that this is his game, and we're playing by his rules.

There's no formal identification yet but Shelton says the deceased was carrying a driving licence in her purse. Charmaine Morgan is just 24, the youngest of our victims to date, and the most brutally injured.

I gulp the remainder of my tea and leave the station, heading up to The Riverside Centre to witness the autopsy. I pray that Foster and the CSIs recover some concrete evidence, so that we can bring an end to his killing spree.

\* \* \*

Shelton and Delaney are scrubbed up completing digital body X-rays. From the vast array of autopsies that I've witnessed, I pretty much know the procedure step by step.

Livor mortis has set in on Charmaine's body. Her buttocks and back are discoloured, appearing a purple-red tone caused by blood accumulating in the lowermost blood vessels, where her corpse was supine.

Foster snaps away at the injuries while Shelton documents the details in her handheld recorder.

Delaney lowers the deceased down to rest on her back. Barely an inch of her torso has been left unscathed by the assailant; lacerations and bruises adorn every surface. There are grip marks on her neck where he muffled her screams.

"The distal phalanges are missing on six of the deceased's fingers. Each one severed on the left hand, and the tip of the thumb on the right hand. It's the same MO, but the level of violence has increased significantly," Shelton states firmly.

"Foster, did you recover any evidence?" I ask, praying for a result.

She approaches the viewing window.

"Interestingly, we found the imprint of a key. The killer or victim must have dropped car keys in the mud. We recovered a VW logo."

"Is there anything else that can help us?"

"Only the Casein yarn fibres; another indication that this is the work of the same killer."

My eyes move back to Shelton and Delaney. She looks brighter to-day having had time to recover from the last autopsy. Her hair is pulled into a neat French plait. She has a warm glow about her, which is nice to see given what she and the rest of us have endured lately. Foster photographs the deceased's stomach as requested.

"There's an impression on her torso. It looks like a ring imprint caused by an object striking the skin with force," Delaney says whilst taking measurements.

"It's 7mm in width. The bruising suggests a crisscross pattern on the right side with a fine line spanning the centre, and a small square posi-tioned on its side forming a diamond shape. It's pretty unusual but I've seen something like this before, caused by a sturdy, laser etched ring."

Foster records macro shots of the bruise.

"I suggest we re-examine this in a day or two when it has had time to develop."

Shelton clutches a scalpel and opens the breastplate with the usual Y-shaped incision. She removes the deceased's abdomen and places it upon the dissection table for closer inspection. She slices it open to examine the repulsive contents.

"The gastric contents indicate she had eaten a meal prior to the at-tack. The food was not digested as the process was shut down by her death. I'd put her PMI at around 13 hours ago."

I look away. No matter how many autopsies I witness, they never get any easier.

Delaney's hands inspect the deceased's open cavity. He severs the womb and carries it to the dissection table, alongside Shelton. He uses a scalpel to make a small incision. Yellow amniotic fluid gushes and spreads like urine. I'm horrified. He continues with the incision and carefully retrieves a tiny fetus.

I look away; desolate. Not only has the bastard taken Charmaine's life, he's stolen the life of her unborn baby. I can't erase the image of its minuscule arms and legs, its tiny toes. It's the worst corpse memory that is now stored in my head, forever.

I eye Shelton. For the first time ever, I witness her eyes convey sadness.

"The fetus measures 61mm and has male genitalia. It's around 9-10 weeks old," Delaney informs us.

"Why change the MO and attack a pregnant woman?" I probe.

It makes no sense.

"He couldn't have known, the deceased wouldn't have been showing physical signs of pregnancy so early on," Shelton interjects.

"My God, the media will have a field day with this."

My mobile interrupts. I vacate the CSI Suite and venture down the hallway passing a wilted plant, which longs for hydration, and press the answer button.

"Sir, Kate's gone."

My heart sinks.

"Gone?" I can barely breathe the word.

"Something's not right. Surveillance teams say she hasn't left the house, and she's not answering the door. Her car is outside, and the Chronicle says that she didn't arrive for work today."

I'm going to vomit.

"Where's the husband? Perhaps she's with him?"

"No. He's on his way home. He's been working shifts and they haven't spoken since New Year's Eve."

"Did she enter the house after the sting?"

"Yes, surveillance places her going into the house around 10.45pm last night. The lights went out at 11.30pm and there was no movement after."

"Get forensics there now. I'm on my way."

I've screwed up again, this cannot be happening. I can't lose Kate. I won't lose her.

I just hope she hasn't done something stupid to herself; I hope she hasn't found herself so consumed by guilt and rejection that she's thought there is only one way to end her anguish.

As I rush to my car, an image of Kate flashes across my mind; sprawled on her bed, an empty bottle of pills beside her, an empty bottle on the floor. And for a moment, I hope we do not find her in her house. At least then, there will be a chance that she is still alive.

\* \* \*

My knuckles pound the window of Wakeman's Mondeo. He's brushing breadcrumbs from his chin; a half-eaten ham sandwich rests upon a piece of scrunched tin foil on his lap. I don't fucking believe it. Kate's presumed missing, or worse, and he's stuffing his face with food. He wraps the remains and slams the door behind him.

"Have you tried the door again?" I ask.

"No, I was waiting for you."

I make a mental note. If she's in there, and has harmed herself, I'll ensure Wakeman doesn't have the power to issue a fucking parking ticket in the future.

The lounge curtains remain drawn. Wakeman bashes the door with his hefty fist. No response. I peer through the glass. It looks immaculate with no sign of a disturbance. Spitting raindrops fall and patter against my suit.

"Try the side gate."

Wakeman opens the oak gate to our right and we continue along the slabbed path to a rear conservatory. There are no signs of forced entry. I pull the cuff of my jacket over my wrist and try the door handle. It's locked.

I peer inside and notice Kate's handbag and keys on the table along with her iPhone.

Wakeman says nothing; his eyes confirm what I'm thinking. Simultaneously we reach for our Glock 17s, smash the glass and step inside.

"Where the hell are the CSIs?"

"They're on the way."

"Kate?" I call. "KATE?"

My cries echo around the kitchen.

An empty wine bottle is perched by the sink. Christ. Where are the pills, I wonder?

I proceed into the lounge and up the staircase, trying not to touch any surface and compromise any potential evidence. The landing creaks outside the bathroom as I continue toward the master bedroom.

The duvet is crumpled but empty.

I ought to feel relieved, that I'm not discovering her body – either lifeless by her own hand, or mutilated by him, but somehow, knowing that she's gone is worse.

Has she gone of her own accord to run away from everything? Or has the killer got to her? It's not his MO to abduct any of his victims. If it's the latter, then how did he get in? All the windows and doors appear to be locked from the inside. Nothing makes any sense.

I retreat to the conservatory and see a rear wooden gate by the garage wall. The gate is bolted from the inside. I unlock it and enter a small courtyard. He's taken her; I'm certain of it. I just haven't figured out how. Why didn't she yell for help?

"Was a squad car positioned here at the rear?" I call out.

"Sorry?"

"There's a courtyard back here. Was there a surveillance team in position here last night?"

"No. We weren't aware of any rear access. The teams were out front," Wakeman mutters weakly as he exits the house and makes eye contact.

"For fucks sake. We let him take her!"

"We don't know that. There is no sign of blood, no sign of struggle, no sign of break in. She may have left of her own free will," Wakeman answers, in a desperate attempt to cover his own arse.

"She may have gone back to Millbrook or she may even be at the hospital," he stammers.

I've a terrifying gut instinct that this is not the case; every bit of instinct and intuition is telling me that she's been taken.

"Well, at least there's a chance she could still be alive," Wakeman adds. "He hasn't left her here for us to find, like all the others, so perhaps she could still be alive."

"Perhaps, but for how much longer?" I hiss.

My body feels void, every organ stripped and replaced with empty numbness. This wasn't meant to happen.

# Chapter Thirty-Seven – DCI Beckley

*Saturday 2 January 2016. 11.19am*

Forensics teams swarm in and around 8 Waterdale Drive like ants.

Foster carefully twirls a Zephyr nylon-fibre brush between her fingers, coating the fascia surface with aluminium flake powder. She's dusting for fingerprints on the door.

Erratic camera flashes violate my eyes. CSI Tom Ford captures images of her handbag, keys and phone.

My mouth feels dry; my stomach retching. I told Kate that we would keep her safe. Wakeman believes Kate has simply left of her own accord, but deep down in my gut, I know this isn't the case. Kate has been taken. He has her. I've let her down in the worst way imaginable.

Foster peels an adhesive fingerprint lifter. She sticks it to the door-frame, presses firmly before peeling it off along with a lifted print. She mounts it on to an acetate sheet and plucks a permanent marker pen from her suit. She adds an exhibit number and job reference, today's date and the crime scene address on the outer surface.

"I want no surface untouched; I don't care how long it takes," I instruct, tone forceful.

She nods and lifts the brush back between her fingers continuing to dust the underside.

Wakeman is upstairs observing SOCOS at work in the bedroom.

"How the hell did this happen? I thought the house was alarmed?"

"It is, and the alarm was activated. All the windows and doors are locked from the inside."

"Then how the hell did he get in?"

"I don't know sir. Forensic teams are still investigating."

The mattress is now empty.

"Any semen found to suggest sexual assault?"

"The bedding has been seized and is being sent for an acid phosphatase test for semen, from which DNA can be extracted. Results will take around 24 to 36 hours."

"We don't have 24 hours."

"Do you really think he has taken her, sir?"

"Yes, without a doubt."

"Why start abducting women though?"

"He's playing with us, showing us that he's ahead of the game. He knew Kate was undercover, played us at his own game. He used the sting operation to his advantage to kill again, then he came for Kate to make her pay. We've failed her. He hasn't changed his MO, this is different, it's personal. He sent Kate a warning but, because of our sting, he felt she did not heed that warning, so he has come for her, to teach her, and us, a lesson."

Delaney opens the loft door and retrieves a metal ladder. His blue shoe protectors disappear through the dark hatch. I follow closely; the cold frame stings my palms. Delaney turns to face me, his torch beam highlighting a hole in the wall; a tunnel into the neighbouring property.

"It's the only viable explanation. There's no other way the killer could have got into a locked and alarmed house."

I feel nauseous. Any faint hope that I had of Kate leaving the house unobserved, and of her own freewill, has evaporated. My stomach contorts, accepting the likelihood that she has indeed, been taken.

I retreat downstairs and follow an excitable Springer Spaniel, sniffing the garden path in zig zag motions following Kate's scent.

"Work. Find her." Its handler commands, clutching a piece of Kate's clothing.

The dog continues sniffing, travels through the gate into the courtyard, turning in circular motions. It stops and sits upright on the tarmac.

"What is it?"

"The trail has gone cold."

"It can't have just disappeared?"

"It wouldn't if she was on foot. Your victim was transported in a vehicle after this point."

"Not unless she's being held captive next door."

The handler looks confused. Delaney follows in close pursuit. My chest feels tight with stress. The door has been forced, possibly with a crowbar. This is the first concrete, hard, evidence of something untoward having happened, which only confirms my suspicions.

We conduct a full sweep; it's empty. I let Kate be taken. If she dies, I'll never forgive myself. I promised I would protect her and she's gone.

"I need full forensics."

Delaney nods. I re-join Wakeman in the courtyard.

"Going on the assumption that she has been abducted, we need to track down any vacant, isolated buildings within a five-mile radius. He would have taken her somewhere secluded, where total privacy is assured."

I ignore the nosy onlooker stares and head back into Kate's garden encountering her husband. He's in a state of shock, face stricken. Foster approaches me.

"I'll need his prints," she whispers.

Taylor overhears and stares angrily. My guts have been ripped out by cannibals.

"Mr Rivendale, I'm so sorry."

"Sorry?" He screeches.

"We weren't made aware of the rear courtyard. Covert teams were positioned at the front."

"Not aware? You've got eyes, haven't you. I thought surveillance teams were supposed to have superb attention to detail, to notice everything!" Taylor blasts.

"Has he taken Kate?"

"Yes. I believe so. It looks like the assailant gained access via next door."

"You assured me that she would be safe on your watch."

His eyes are burning wild flames. I'm wordless, digging my hands deeper in to my pockets. His expression is dejected as Foster scans the friction ridges of his fingertips with a portable PDA to obtain a computerised impression.

He's right, of course. I assured Kate that she would be kept safe and I've messed up yet again. My career is over. Kate's blood will be on my hands and then I'll have three deaths on my conscience.

# Chapter Thirty-Eight

Blood gushed through his veins like a drug awakening every nerve, his body palpitated with excitement. The other women had given him pleasure and helped release his sexual tension until he could claim the star prize. That wait was over; she was his now.

He longed to be with her again and smirked, sipping from his coffee which warmed his throat. The police would find no forensic evidence linking him to Kate's abduction. He had been careful, like he had been with all his victims. This was his new purpose and his former pitiful self was now extinct.

He glanced at his watch and his mind pondered, thinking about their reunion in a matter of hours. He felt aroused at the thought of touching her silky skin before he drained her life. His eyes slammed shut recalling images of her terrified face. He knew from the instant he had crept into her bedroom and saw her partially clad body, it excited him. Kate was special to him; he would make her death the most memorable.

* * * DCI Beckley * * *

*Saturday 2 January 2016. 13.16pm*

Guilt is rotting my core, slowly creeping its way to the surface. Kate has potentially been missing for nearly 14 hours. If it were a missing child we were dealing with, he or she, would be dead after just four. That's fact.

Kate's a fighter, a strong character, who I believe wouldn't give up easily. I saw her feisty side during interview. I don't know her well, but I do remember the look in her hazel eyes. She won't give in.

I can't possibly be certain, but my heart and instincts are telling that she's not dead. If that were his intention, he would have stabbed her to death while she slept.

My mind is tormented; I can't bear to look at Taylor. His heavy head is hung low, his gaze remains fixed on the floor, as his boots scuff the corridor. I usher him through the wrought iron door, lock it, and lead him towards the reception desk.

Custody Sergeant Shaun Davies is poised behind the desk, signing in a scruffy bearded man in his 50s. The detainee is clearly intoxicated; an intense cider odour invades the constricted air space. Beyond him at the central bridge are two detention officers, Sergeant Ryan Hopwood and Inspector Anthony Grant, both monitoring the arrests.

Sergeant Hopwood approaches and authorises the detainee's detention, handing over a Notice of Rights & Entitlements.

"You have the right to an independent solicitor for free. You have the right to have someone told of your detention, and you have the right to consult a copy of the Codes of Practice, which govern police powers and procedures," he states firmly.

The detainee doesn't respond and staggers away to the cells. His wobbly legs sway below the ultra violet scanning lights at the cell entrance.

We continue along the narrow hallway, treading over the black bubble lino toward the interview room. Taylor narrowly misses the panic alarm strip on the wall as we stop and proceed through the double reinforced metal door, which I slam behind us. I instruct Taylor to sit at the table. He looks agitated; his body language uncomfortable.

"Why am I here? We're wasting time. We should be searching for Kate."

I stare into his bloodshot eyes. I should have offered her better protection. I was naïve.

"I have more than 80 officers working the case right now. You are of more use to us here, talking me through all the details."

"But I've already spoken with DI Wakeman and told him everything that I know."

"This is just an informal chat. We need to be certain of all the facts and ensure that we've not missed anything."

"It's a waste of time. I need to get out there and find my wife! That fucker has her and it's your fault. You assured me that you would keep her safe. You've failed her."

His eyes are fierce. My heart contorts, I want to heave.

"I'm sorry."

"You're sorry? I think it's a little late for apologies. If Kate dies, then her death will be on your hands," he yells, slamming his clenched fist sharply on the table.

I'm sweating under my jacket, nerves pumping through my pores.

"We'll find her," I assure him.

"How?"

"I've drafted in extra officers. We won't stop searching until we have her back. But first, we need to establish exactly how long she's has been missing. It's important to be as precise as possible."

"I don't have a clue because I was working a late shift. I didn't come home last night."

"Did you speak to Kate on the phone at all?"

"No."

His hands fidget. Sweat coats his upper lip; he's edgy. What does he have to feel nervous about?

"We'd argued. I was angry with her."

"Why were you angry? What did you do?"

"I didn't do anything to her, for fuck's sake, what's wrong with you?"

He shifts his weight irately against the chair, locking his arms defensively across his torso. I've angered him.

"I'm not implying that you did anything to Kate, I'm merely try-ing to establish the events leading up to her disappearance. I need to ascertain her emotional state at the time."

"We argued about Louise and she accused me of not being there for her. I was angry because she'd been drinking and had passed out, slumped in a pathetic state. That's Kate's answer to everything. She opens a bottle and drinks her troubles away. But none of this has any-thing to do with her abduction."

"I'm merely trying to piece everything together. Paint a picture, so to speak. So, she could have been intoxicated when the assailant gained access into your home? An empty wine bottle was recovered in the kitchen."

"There may well have been, but as I've already told you, I wasn't there. So, I don't know what the hell she had to drink."

I can see in his eyes that the guilt is eating him up, knowing that he wasn't there to protect his wife.

"I'm just trying to establish how your wife would have reacted. If she'd been drinking, she may not have had the strength to fight back, which is why no one heard her pleas for help. Is Kate normally fit and well?"

"Yes. She goes to the gym and runs. But I wouldn't say she'd be able to put up much of a fight; she's tiny. Are you trying to imply that this is her fault, simply because she had a drink?"

"No. Not at all. I'm trying to ascertain what happened on the night in question."

His angry tone shifts up another gear.

"The only person to blame here is you. You let my wife down. You left her without full protection and now she's fucking gone. I'm telling you now that if something happens to her, your head's going to roll."

# Chapter Thirty-Nine – DCI Beckley

*Saturday 2 January 2016. 14.45pm*

It should never have gone this far; I wouldn't have knowingly put Kate's life in danger, not for one minute.

Every operation has its threats and risks, of course, but I really thought we had every angle covered. I honestly believed that we would get a lead from the sting, and that the fucker would be in custody by now.

I never envisaged that we would screw up and that he would get the opportunity to harm Kate.

I wouldn't have taken that risk. I like her; she's young and talented with a bright future ahead. I'd wanted to help progress her career; I could see the passion in her eyes for the truth. It's my actions that have put her on a dangerous path, and right now, I have no way of knowing where it will lead.

I'd like to think her abduction is just another warning, that he'll dump her somewhere, shaken and frightened, but otherwise unharmed. But my inner conscience is telling me that's a foolish assumption; the wishful thinking of a guilty man who has seriously fucked up.

The truth, that I'm trying hard not to accept, is that she's probably lying alone somewhere, beaten to a pulp, or that she's already dead.

My head feels as though it's being squashed in a brace, my insides curdled.

Taylor's face torments my mind adding to the ghouls that already lurk there, haunting me, acting as a constant reminder of my actions.

I need to be positive; I can't allow myself to believe she is dead. Until we find a body, I have to assume, and hope, that she is still alive. I will find her and bring her home. Right now, the only thing I can do is to pull out all the stops and use every police resource I have available.

I swipe my proximity card and enter the Incident Room. My eye line immediately darts to the victim gallery. Each of them stares longingly back at me. They crave justice and I'm going to get it for them, whatever it takes.

Gold commander Greensdale is with firearms sergeant Mark Jenkinson, acting as a TAC Advisor. They are deep in conversation, discussing the case beyond the Intel 24 desk hub.

Jenkinson breaks away and heads over. I need to fill him in about Kate's abduction. He's a highly-experienced firearms sergeant and has led a team of officers at Weston for the past seven years. I've never known any of his operations to fail and I can't let this be the first.

"What's the latest Sir? Heard the sting was a no go last night and now we have a sixth victim?" Jenkinson quizzes.

"It's one big fucking mess," I confess.

"What is?"

"This case. Once the media get wind of this they are going to have a field day."

"I don't understand, what's happened?"

"It's Kate, the undercover journalist. She's been taken from her home. CSIs are combing the scene as we speak. He has her."

"Holy shit! Lads, it looks like the balloon's gone up," Jenkinson yells, turning his attention to Greensdale and his officers.

He's right the shit has well and truly hit the fan.

"I need every available specialist unit working this. If Kate turns up dead, I can't even begin to contemplate the media circus that's going to follow."

* * * Kate * * *

*January 2, 2015. Evening*

My buttocks are numb. I'm shivering in puddles that continue to penetrate my flesh; each layer of skin absorbing the damp fluid.

I draw my knees to my chest, cradling my fear inside my cramping belly. I've been awake for hours; the wait is torture, though I fear this is nothing compared to the inevitable physical torture that he has lined up for me.

My stomach craves food, but I feel sick. My mouth is parched in desperate need of rehydration. Water is all I can think about. I'm so thirsty I could drink my own blood.

I close my eyes, longing to be back in the interview suite, sipping chilled water from a cheap, clear-ridged beaker, safe in the company of Will and Wakeman. Back then it had seemed so simple; Will assuring me that I'd be kept safe fully protected by the undercover officers.

He lied to me. Everyone lies. I was bait to him. Why the hell am I so gullible?

My heart contracts angrily. I yank at the restraints. My tendons protrude as I fight their suffocating grip. The pain is immense. I slam my eyes shut; clench my teeth trying to withstand the intolerable feeling of masticating flesh. It hurts too much.

I tilt my head backwards, eyeing the high-rise ceiling, and stretch open my jaw, catching water droplets as they drip onto my frozen lips. One strikes my tonsils, catapulting my head forward. My tear ducts spew tears of frustration down my face. He's enjoying this. It's a power game; he wants me to know that he's in charge.

I'm growing angrier by the minute. The light is fading fast; I have no concept of time. I close my eyes trying to remember how the attack ensued.

I see that horrible mask again, and his evil black pupils staring into mine.

My body is rigid. I watch the hypodermic needle coming towards me. He's on top of me. I'm fighting against the weight of his body but

I'm immobile; he's crushing me. He's too powerful, I can't free myself. The needle jabs and pierces my skin. I'm shaking my head vigorously trying to dislodge it. It's too late. I've no idea what he injected me with or how long I remained unconscious.

I could have been here for days; the uncertainty is unbearable.

The only thing that I do know is that he's coming for me, and when he does my nightmare will only worsen. Louise will be delighted that I'm gone, I'm sure. She wanted me out of her life after her ordeal. She'll think I deserved this. But I didn't.

I didn't deserve to have my home invaded, be attacked in my own bed and snatched in the middle of the night. Or to be left alone feeling cold and afraid.

I didn't deserve for him to touch me, to leave me here feeling degraded and dirty. If I can't remember, I've no way of knowing what he's done to me. I draw my knees closer, my cold heels press against my buttocks, guarding me.

I'm so cold, my toes are tarnished blue. My lip quivers. If he doesn't kill me, I'll die from hypothermia. It's so cold. My eyes sting, my head aches overwhelmed by my tears, but I can't stop them. I've never felt so afraid.

My Daddy lied to me. Fear is real, it's gripping my body, suffocating me.

It's getting darker. My eyes wander but I can barely see my cell any more. I wonder if Taylor will care that I've been taken; he was so angry with me. I took everything out on him, it was unfair. It's just I had never felt so rejected in my life and it hurt. I never meant for any of this to happen. My life was finally turning around, heading back toward happiness.

Oh God, he's coming. I hear the rumble of an engine, the gravel crunching under the tyres. I yank fiercely at my wrists, using every bit of my weight to pull against the snare. It won't budge.

Oh shit, the gag! I shouldn't have spat it out. He'll know that I've been calling out. I dip my chin; stretching and lifting it back up repeatedly, trying to grab the sodden cotton. The engine stops. Shit.

Headlights seep under the door. My heart is ferocious, on the verge of explosion. Finally, I catch the gag edge and twist my head from side to side, working it upwards. I lodge my tongue underneath and slide it back into my mouth. Vomit projects from my stomach. I quickly swallow, forcing it down.

If I appear unconscious, he might leave me alone.

My eyes are wide and frantically scanning the darkness. I hear a bolt slide and the door creak.

Terror slices my body like a butcher slashing away at a fresh carcass. My stomach knots every intestine pipe with panic. I quietly tug my bleeding wrists forcefully, gritting my teeth again to suppress the pain. It's useless. I'm trapped.

His thunderous footsteps pound against rubble. My lungs gasp at the damp air. I slam my eyes shut and feel my body shut down; paralysed by fear.

Oh Daddy, please save me. Wake me up and tell me this is just a bad dream. Please Daddy.

My mind is still operational but suspended. I'm looking down on myself. I hear his laboured breaths and water splashing over his boots.

My heart is trying to beat its way out of my chest. My eyelids warm, an orange haze hovers over their surface. The flashes of light lower across my figure. I remain rigid, feeling sweat beads gather on my forehead. I need him to believe I'm sedated; buy myself more time.

The light reverts back to my face. I take slow measured breaths trying not to squint. A cold finger strokes my cheek. I won't flinch. I won't let him win. Goosebumps laminate my skin and trickle downwards, passing over each of my vertebrae.

Images of the diagonal slash wound across Louise's throat and the heavy black stitches, project in my mind. He's going to use his tools on me. I desperately want to cry and scream. His fingertips slide further downwards resting against my raging pulse. He knows I'm pretending; the pulses are too intense.

The light lowers and rests nearby but continues to illuminate me. He's watching.

I feel his presence and can smell him; a stale liquor odour. I'm his new play toy and he's going to act out some sick fantasy with me. His boots thud closer; his silhouette shields the light. His warm breath hovers over my face again but I suppress my tears.

Palms roughly grapple my breasts. I clench my abdomen to remain still. I want to open my eyes to see who he is, but I can't, I'm afraid. His perverted hand negotiates my satin nightie, dragging downwards. Tears threaten my eyes, but I remain stagnant. No one will hear my screams.

His hand slides to my thigh. My eyes bolt open, unable to maintain the pretence.

I won't let him touch me intimately.

I kick out and thrash my feet and legs against the darkness. I witness the masked figure from my bedroom and shudder, encountering pure evil. His pupils are ominous. He rises to his feet and walks away.

Water slops against his boots. My body is bursting, nearing explosion, with panic. I want it to be over. I want to be dead but he's going to make me suffer, to punish me.

A lighter ignites, nicotine infiltrates the damp air. This is a game, one he's enjoying. He wants to prolong my terror.

My wrists rotate back and forth feverishly, praying the seeping blood will allow my hands to slide free from the noose. They slacken, but not enough. The pain is immense. I close my eyes tightly, trying to escape my world and think back to my meeting with Will at Costa, recalling his words about the killer wanting to dominate his victims.

I must not fight back if I'm going to survive. I never imagined this would happen to me. I was naïve. Now I'll be among the statistics adding to the body count. But I can't die yet, it's not my time.

## Chapter Forty – Kate

He's watching me while dragging on his cigarette. I smell it. I can't see him, but I know that he's here; I can feel his evil eyes boring into me.

My blood is tricking, trailing slowly from my wrists down my fingertips and pooling behind my back.

I can't fight my fear any longer. I'm bawling, recalling fond childhood memories. I want to remember them again before it's too late and they're lost forever. I remember my gramps teaching me to waltz in a green taffeta ball gown when I was seven, at my grandparents Ruby wedding party.

I remember helping Nan to decorate Easter biscuits, with currants and sitting on sunny beaches with my parents. Dad building giant sand speedboats for Louise and me to sit in. I recall my mum's tears when we chose my wedding dress together, and dad welling up on the big day when he saw me for the first time.

Taylor flashes into my mind. He's at the end of the aisle beaming, my dress train sweeping and glistening with crystals. I'd felt like a real princess that day. The last time I saw him we argued and now that will be our last memory of each other.

I had a good life. It was happy, sad at times when confronted by grief but thinking about my recent visits to Millbrook surrounded by drug addicts and balding perverts, I know that my life was worlds apart and that I'm one of the lucky ones.

Right now, I don't feel so lucky, of course, but I brought this upon myself.

I chose to get close to the story, to cross the boundary, head down a treacherous path and veer on the side which offered the most information. My actions put me here and the odds of getting out alive are not stacked in my favour. A surge of hatred seeps through my pores; I feel so angry. I push the gag and force it out over my lips. It falls.

"Please let me go, you don't have to do this. I've learnt my lesson. I'm sorry."

Silence.

My breathing quickens, my chest rises and falls in rapid successions.

"Please, just let me go. I won't tell anyone. I'll leave Weston. I could be gone tonight. No one need ever know."

My teeth chew on my bruised lip. I flinch; a sharp pain infiltrates the nerve endings. His footsteps swish through water stepping closer. I tug at the restraint; it's pointless.

"I was just doing my job. Please, I'm so sorry."

The footsteps tread stridently, snapping twigs underfoot. I maintain my eye level, observing closely as his boots come into view protruding from the ankle of his jeans. They're brown walking boots. I'm too scared to look up. His feet are at least a size 8.

Violent force against me is inevitable but I will convey to him that I'm not going to be an easy target, once I find my courage. Perhaps I can defuse his attack, shake his confidence. Only my inner conscience is telling me that could anger him further.

Instead, I must be kind, dissuade him from hurting me, or at least stall the attack and give me time to stage an escape.

"I'm a stranger to you, why would you want to hurt me? I'm not like the others."

He remains silent; I only hear his laboured breaths under the chilling mask.

"You don't have to do this. We could go for a drink. I'm a good listener. Let's go somewhere and talk."

I have an uncontrollable urge to look at him. If I can stare him in the eye and show him that he doesn't frighten me, then I may be able to shift his rage. My eyes move slowly upwards. A flash of white comes into view. He's wearing a white T-shirt, under a black jacket. A gap between the round neck of the shirt and the edge of his mask exposes his skin; he's white.

Will would be impressed by my powers of observation, and the amount of detail I would be able to provide during an interview. If only I could get the chance.

My gaze shifts; my heart frantic, pulsating vigorously against my cold breast. He glares at me through olive eye slats. His enlarged pupils have fine white borders and do not resemble any form of normality.

I never imagined I'd end up like this. I've studied hard, worked pro-lifically to achieve my goals in life, and for what? To be his next victim and be tossed aside like the others. I won't let him do it; I won't be his prey. I'm going to fight the bastard with every breath. I inhale again, finding my voice.

"We could get out of here and go somewhere nice, just the two of us."

I can't believe the words that are rolling off my tongue. I don't want to go anywhere with him. I want to get the hell away from this vile jail. But if I can get him to sympathise with me, make a personal connection with him, it might buy time.

He motions toward me. I flinch, bowing my head back to the floor. He's fiddling with something in his hands, I hear plastic cracking. He's beside me now, clutching an Evian bottle in his left hand, which he moves toward me.

My throat feels like I've licked carpet pile. I yearn for hydration. I crave its contents like a junkie raring for his next fix. For the first time in my life I understand true desperation. It's within reaching distance; hovering near my lips. I part them and wait silently. I won't beg. I won't let him see how much I want it.

Seconds pass; it feels like minutes, maybe more, until he presses the ridge against my lips. I suck at it, greedily, gulping the fluid as fast as I can. Water gushes over my chin running down my face and neck. It feels so good.

I sly a glance of him out of the corner of my eye. My heart freezes, encountering the flicker of a blade reflecting the torch beam. I'm confused, why offer kindness if he's planning on killing me?

Maybe he wants to play a game of cat and mouse. He wants me to fight back. He needs me to regain some strength and energy for whatever it is that he has planned. He's vile and I'm going to fight him every step of the way. I won't be a submissive victim.

The blade slides behind my back, slashing away at my wrist binds. I don't understand what's happening. I'm confused.

Relief floods through my body as the cord snaps. Is he setting me free? I bring my quivering hands forward to rest on my lap. Blood smears on my nightie and thighs. The wounds look deep, oozing blood. My shoulders ache where they've been locked in place. I caress my raw wrists and stare at the blade, dangling loosely in his hand.

If I grab it, I could kill him before he mutilates me.

He's observing me in silence. I'm a fool. He doesn't have any intention of letting me go.

His eyes are on me probing, dissecting every inch of my body. He's a pervert and he's going to pay for what he's made me endure. Oh God, his hand is fidgeting in his pocket near to his crotch. He's going to rape me! Please, no!

The bottomless black pools of his eyes stare at my breasts. I tug the hem of my nightie, pulling it down to shield myself. He's motionless, watching my every move. I won't let him violate me. Bile rises in my mouth. I swallow, forcing it back down.

He suddenly lunges forward angrily and yanks my left wrist; burning pain throbs as he squeezes the gashes. He's dragging me across the floor. Coarse chippings scratch my bare skin, tearing the surface. My bravado crumbles and is replaced by terror.

"You don't have to do this," I stammer.

He pulls me to my feet and thrashes me against the wall. My head strikes a brick. I want to turn and fight him, but I feel dizzy; my legs hollow. Tiny shards of grit bite my soles; my balance unsteady. I'm shivering in the sub-zero temperature, only warming by blood seeping from my head.

My heart is vicious. I think I'm having a panic attack. He flips me around, slamming my back against the wall and frantically gropes my negligee.

I'd rather die than let him touch me. I push him away, but his hands grip my upper arms. My mind and body are shutting down; I'm in a state of suspended animation. He's gripping my hands above my head, the knife edge digging against my wrists. He has my attention. I must give into his demands or the knife will sever my veins and I'll bleed out and die here.

I'll pretend to go along with it and wait for my moment. I feel strange. My mind is swirling, head becoming heavy, and my legs rickety. The room distorts, twisting and blurring. He groans and then laughs. He's drugged me again. Why the hell did I drink the water? I'm so stupid.

My eyelids drag, legs crumble, my back scrapes the wall.

I try to speak but my jaw is locked; voice suppressed behind my tonsils. My eyelashes tickle my cheeks, plunging me into darkness once again.

# Chapter Forty-One – DCI Beckley

*Sunday 3 January 2016. Morning*

Riverwood ward is bursting with patient admissions. I've accompanied Mr Rivendale to the hospital to inform Kate's family in person about her abduction.

The swelling on Louise's face has subsided; the bruises tarnished yellow. Her frame looks fragile; hunched over, packing belongings into a holdall. Her mother, Beverly, clears the bedside locker. She spots me and nudges Louise, who lifts her head. Poised on a chair beside them is Kate's father, John. His inflamed eyes probe my presence.

"What is it?" Beverly fires.

"It's Kate. She's gone," Taylor stammers, breaking down.

"What do you mean?"

He collapses at the foot of the bed, alongside the medical clipboards.

"He's taken her."

I still can't believe this is happening, I feel nauseous.

"Who has?"

"She was trying to rectify the situation, repair the damage but the killer taken her."

His tears fall and saturate his stubble. He continues talking, his words inaudible. The trio stare at me disdainfully. I intervene and step forward.

"I'm very sorry to inform you, but we have reason to believe that Kate has been abducted from her home. I can assure you that we are doing everything we can to find her."

"Your assurances mean jack," Louise blasts angrily.

Her gaunt face reddens, blood rushing to the surface. Beverly falls to her knees, howling uncontrollably.

"We have more than 90 officers working the case. We'll find her. I don't believe he'll hurt her."

Louise stands tall, chewing frantically on her jagged fingernails. Despite their fall-out, she clearly cares about Kate. I only hope that Kate lives long enough to find this out for herself.

"Why would he take her?"

"I think his motive is purely revenge, for Kate helping us. I will find her. We're exhausting all avenues."

"How long has she been gone?" Beverly interjects through her sobs.

"We can't be precise; we believe it's around 14 hours."

"Fourteen hours? Why are we only just hearing about this? Where were you, Taylor? Why didn't you protect her?" John yells, clenching his fists.

Taylor's palms grip his forehead, compressing his skull.

"I was at work. It's my fault; I failed her. I'm sorry."

His howls reverberate across the ward. The nurses station comes to a deadening silence, uniforms paused watching the commotion.

Taylor is wrong; it isn't his fault, it's mine. I've made the biggest mistake of my life. I am the one to blame for the disappearance of Kate Rivendale.

# Chapter Forty-Two – DCI Beckley

*Sunday 3 January 2015. Midday*

Specialist firearms officers from Blackrock training facility are poised beside the armed response vehicles.

Each officer is shielded by a heavy ballistic-resistant black vest, strapped with a mobile phone, standard Airwave radio, a second radio to communicate with fellow AFOs, and a 50,000-volt Taser gun.

A Glock 17 pistol is secured neatly at each waistline, alongside an ASP baton, Pava incapacitating spray and quick cuffs. In their arms, the officers grip lightweight Heckler & Koch G36 assault rifles.

Jenkinson stands authoritatively, advising his team of the tactical operations they are to undertake. His officers listen attentively, showing their respect. He commands everyone's attention with his forceful tone and positive attitude; traits I admire. He's a few years older than me, around 40, but his muscular frame makes him appear younger.

I'm more confident about finding Kate now that he's commanding the team.

DI Wakeman takes a final drag on his cigarette and stubs out the butt with his scuffed leather shoes as I make my approach.

"Bring me up to speed."

"Intel 24 located several redundant buildings within the specified radius, all of which could be used to conceal a hostage. We're clutching at straws to be honest sir, but we've got to start somewhere. The only other option is to make Kate's disappearance public and appeal for witnesses."

"No fucking way. Kate's abduction cannot be revealed publicly, do you understand? Her family is aware that this needs to be discreet. Not only could we put her life in further danger by enraging him, the press will also have a fucking field day with yet another police screw-up."

"OK sir. Jenkinson is preparing the SFOs now. Given some of the attacks have taken place near to the railway line, Intel 24 believe a search should be conducted of the old Bourton station for a possible connection. It's three miles away, dates to 1860 and has been vacant since 1893. The site has a house which was once provided for the station master on the roadside, a couple of smaller buildings on the platform, and a derelict goods lock-up on the eastbound platform."

"Is that seriously all we have, guess work?"

"Sir, you wanted us to identify isolated and vacant properties. That is the nearest to Millbrook. Other than that, there's an old disused MOD water tower but it is surrounded by a new housing and is far too populated in my opinion."

I hate it when he rambles, it irritates me and is one of his worst qualities. He senses my frustration.

"There's also a disused airbase five-miles away. There are numerous vacant buildings on site and two aircraft hangars, one in use, the other empty. In all honesty, she could be anywhere. He could be holding her at his home. We've nothing to go on; not without any witnesses."

Wakeman places his hands on his hips as tiny water droplets descend from the ashen sky. He's right, we must start somewhere, time is running out.

"The station takes priority but proceed with caution. I want Kate alive, do I make myself clear?"

"Yes sir, perfectly."

* * *

ARVs screech towards Bourton station and halt a short distance away for concealment. Jenkinson instructs his officers to spread out on foot and trawl through wild overgrown fields.

The sky has cleared, improving visibility.

DI Wakeman follows behind, allowing the trained SFOs to execute their mission. I know that he and Kate have their differences, but it's just a personality clash; he wouldn't want any real harm to come to her, I'm sure.

I follow him closely, clearing my dry throat as the red bricked building emerges. It doesn't feel right to me; why would he bring her here? Two of the victims were found by the railway track, but I can't see any connection. Still, maybe I'll be proved wrong. I pray I am.

The building is now within metres. Two chimneys adorn either end of the rooftop, upon lead slate tiles. The majority are missing, presumably stolen. The frontage is suffocated with thick ivy overhanging warped window frames and a rotten doorframe.

Jenkinson uses hand gestures, signalling the team to split into two; heading to the east and west sides of the property, further out of my sight.

Wakeman tags the nearest team. They proceed over a rusting railway track, as they continue their tactical assault. The SFOs pause in position, covering every exit awaiting further instruction.

Wakeman pants and walks slowly, following the team through a bricked archway. Their body armour disappears. I'm immobile, my body pricked with fear that they may unearth her tortured body inside. Heavy boots thunder through the building and I wait.

"All clear," a voice blurts over the radio.

I breathe a sigh of relief, pull myself together. SFOs pass by, exiting. I tread the hallway and reach the end of the passageway; a room littered with a sullied mattress, syringes and broken glass.

"Any sign that she may have been here?" I probe.

Jenkinson lowers his Heckler & Koch and shakes his head.

"No. It's being used as a crack house. There's nothing to indicate a struggle, or someone having been held captive here."

# Chapter Forty-Three – Kate

*Sunday 3 January 2015. Morning*

Day light infiltrates my eyelids; I'm revisiting a state of consciousness. My eyeballs burn from the intense rays; they sting like I've not slept in weeks.

Fuzzy images flicker and crowd my mind as my dilated pupils scan the surroundings. Nothing is clear. My head throbs. I scutinise my body and observe my nightie. My skin is pricked with pins and needles, fear kicking in. I remember now; I'm his prisoner. What did the dirty bastard do?

A tartan blanket conceals my legs. My abdomen clenches. I close my eyes. A flashback of his mask haunts me. My eyes fire open to escape him. I scan my cell to ascertain whether I'm alone.

Tiny knots lock my shoulder blades. I'm bound again by restraints, my hands tied in front of me. I wrestle them but the cord grips and restrains my wrists like handcuffs. My fear morphs to anger. I'm infuriated that he's doing this to me and I'm incensed that Will let it happen.

I can't see a way out of this. Why is he keeping me locked up? Why not just kill me?

My skin itches; irritated by the hay underneath my bare flesh. Light dances around the room like twinkling stars boring through holes in the wall ahead. There's a window to my right. Through the gaps, I see that it's boarded on the outside.

Underneath there's a single protruding rusty nail and a hole in the beige brickwork from a missing brick. It's stuffed with blue nylon cord. I crawl over to it and draw every inch of breath I can find to project my screams. I won't be his toy or his victim.

"Help me! Please, help me. I'm in here."

Silence.

"Please. I need your help."

Silence.

Deflated, I continue my observations of the barn. There's another window to my left half shielded by a stable style shutter and a wooden plank nailed to the inside. Beneath it a small gap allows further light inside. An abundance of light orbs float purposelessly through the air. I feel as though spirits are with me, guiding me and giving me hope. I scream again through cracked lips projecting my voice toward the window. Please, someone hear me.

"Help! I'm trapped. Please help! Somebody! Can anybody here me? HELP!"

No one replies; no one is coming.

My stomach rumbles, breaking my cries.

I angle my neck, noticing a nearby object. I blink, trying to eradicate the lights that continue to penetrate my tired eyes. A tin of soup rests on a pile of bricks; a straw protruding from the rim. I lean forward, wrap my mouth around the plastic tubing and gulp its contents.

Gloopy, cold tomato liquid lines my throat, soothing my passageways. It tastes foul. It's probably drugged but I take the risk. I need to eat to stay strong, if I'm to have any chance of getting out of this alive.

* * * DCI Beckley * * *

*Sunday 3 January 2016. Afternoon*

SFOs are conducting an ambush of the old airbase hanger. The rusting roof structure zig zags, making me dizzy. I sense we're way off target.

It's been two days without a trace of Kate, and no ransom demands have been made. I fear now, more than ever, that Kate's life may already be over.

My aching feet tread past broken breeze blocks as I follow Jenkinson's lead.

Paint hangs off the walls in paper thin slices, exposing rendering. A rat shuffles over a cluster of old rags. I examine a shabby side room filled with mottled foam cushions and a white sink, stained with soot and lime scale. The silence is broken by Airwave chatter.

"All clear."

My nerves rattle at yet another failed attempt. My actions have not only attributed to the deaths of Toby and Marie Harroway, they've killed Kate Rivendale, too."

# Chapter Forty-Four – DCI Beckley

*Monday 4 January 2016. 7.10am*

Kate's pearly white teeth smile sweetly, a picture of pure, emblazoned blazoned across the front page of the Southern Chronicle, The Sun, Mirror, Express, Daily Mail and Star.

Her long dark curls are groomed neatly and draped to one side over her right shoulder. She looks young, carefree and happy.

I stare aimlessly at the photograph, duplicated across each newspaper title. Her hazel eyes bore into my soul. Guilt erupts inside my veins, merging with burning rage. I'm infuriated that the story has been leaked and that every single national is revealing facts regarding Kate's abduction. The bold headlines fry my pupils:

*"MILLBROOK MURDERER ABDUCTS CHRONICLE REPORTER."*
*"SERIAL KILLER ABDUCTS UNDERCOVER REPORTER"*
*"REPORTER FEARED DEAD AFTER BOTCHED POLICE OPERATION"*
*"KILLER STRIKES AGAIN TARGETING REPORTER"*
*"REPORTER ABDUCTED BY SERIAL KILLER"*

I knew this would happen. I digest the florid content of the Southern Chronicle to see how much of the truth has been exposed.

*"The Chronicle's dedicated Reporter, Kate Rivendale had been abducted after helping police enquiries."*

I feel nauseous and continually ping my elastic wristband to repel my anxiety. It was meant to be low key, to give us chance to find her without a media frenzy chasing our every move. Without any more media reports, to infuriate the killer even more.

I fling the articles across the desk, each dragging on one and other, as they fall to the floor. I scurry to my office window and peer through the venetian blind. The street is full of satellite TV trucks. I cower away, sickened. Wakeman appears in the doorway.

"Sir, it's a circus out there. They're demanding a press conference. Kate's parents and her sister have arrived too, and are talking openly, on the record. We need to get out there now and limit the damage."

\* \* \*

The electric doors of Weston Police Station whir open as I step outside to face the hack pack.

Kate's story has stolen their hearts; everyone wants a piece of her. I count over 100 restless reporters and camera crews, all desperate to be spoon-fed information.

The double yellow road markings are obscured by illegally parked satellite vans, all ready to broadcast live. I step gingerly towards a cluster of microphones while clutching hold of a statement in my moist palms. Cameras pan around and zoom in.

"Good morning. I'm Detective Chief Inspector Will Beckley. I can confirm that we are investigating the disappearance of Kate Rivendale, a reporter from the Southern Chronicle newspaper. Kate was last seen at her home in Waterdale Drive, Weston, at 11.30pm, on Friday January 1, 2016. A detailed forensic search of her home indicates signs of forced entry gained via a neighbouring property. We therefore believe that Kate may have been abducted sometime between 11.30pm on January 3, and 10am, on January 4."

I pause, and stare out at a sea of expectant faces, all wanting, and demanding, more.

"Kate is white, aged 34-years, 5ft 4ins tall, with a slim build and long wavy dark hair. We would urge anyone with any information regarding her disappearance, particularly any neighbours living in the immediate vicinity, to come forward and contact us on the force number, 101, quoting reference MP 5824/16, or to call us anonymously via Crimestoppers on 0800 555 111."

I make sure I give the journalists time to correctly note down the reference number, and I repeat it for them before continuing with my statement, fighting to keep my emotions in check, and to keep my voice calm.

"We are using every resource available to find Kate. We have dedicated teams of officers on the ground, and these search efforts are being bolstered by the police helicopter and the South Wales Specialist Dog Unit. We are continuing to search the local vicinity, concentrating on open spaces and parkland, which is routine in missing person enquiries. We will continue these searches, as well as conducting house-to-house enquiries. Kate's well-being is our primary concern."

Kate's voice echoes in my mind. "My well-being?" she says, accusingly. "You told me I was safe, Will. You told me you would protect me. You don't give a shit about my well-being!"

I finger the collar of my shirt, which feels as if it has suddenly been tightened around my neck. I take a moment to compose myself, clear my dry throat, and continue.

"Kate's disappearance has had an understandingly devastating impact on her family and we will continue to offer them our full support, as our search efforts continue. I would like to offer them our sincere sympathy at this most difficult time and traumatic time. Officers from across the country, including Wiltshire, Devon, Cornwall and Gloucestershire Police have been called in to help assist our search efforts for Kate. We will not rest until we reunite Kate with her husband and family."

"Don't make another promise you are not going to be able to keep," I hear Kate warn.

I catch a glimpse of Beverly and John out of the corner of my eye; both watch closely, hanging on my every word.

Their eyes radiate contempt extreme discontent. Taylor is absent. My heart leaps to my throat; tongue tied. This is the most intense press conference I've given in my career, and it's the first time I've known the victim.

Deep down I wish I'd never sought help from Kate and used her as bait. That way, she would still be a roving reporter pounding the street looking for her next story. It's my fault she's gone.

I take a deep breath and look back towards the press. Camera flashes continue to irritate my tired eyes. They sting like hell; I haven't slept properly in days.

A young slender brunette at the front inches forward during my momentary silence. She catches my attention and my heart flutters, confusing her for Kate. She seizes the opportunity.

"Can you confirm whether you are linking Kate's abduction to the Millbrook murder investigation? And is it true she was targeted because she was helping the police?"

I swallow the rock in my throat, uncomfortable with the accusations being fired. The plan was to read my statement and retreat immediately back inside the station.

I desperately want to open-up and tell them everything they long to know but my rational mind is whispering in my ear, instructing me to stick to the script, before I hinder the investigation.

If there's any remote chance of seeing Kate alive again, I know that I must play it by the book. She didn't deserve this and instead of trying to protect my own back, I must work with the press and urge witnesses to come forward with anything suspicious they may have seen on the night of her disappearance.

"All I can add at this stage is that Kate has disappeared, and we are examining a possible link between her abduction and the Millbrook murders. As this is an ongoing investigation, it would be inappropriate to comment any further."

A short plump bearded dishevelled man has shot forward with a dictaphone gripped tightly in his stocky fingers.

"Do you think that she was taken by the Millbrook murderer?"

"Again, I would like to reiterate that we are considering a possible connection."

"But Kate Rivendale was working undercover with you and your team, trying to lure the killer in, isn't that correct?"

Fuck. Where did he get that from? It must be an inside leak, or Kate's Parents. I glance at them, both exude rage. My face reddens. I've no idea what they have already blurted out.

"I cannot comment on that or release any further details of this ongoing investigation at this stage."

The pack craves more, they're impatient and angry; pen-clad hands wavewildly back and forth. I need to wrap this up fast before it gets out of control.

"I would urge everyone to get behind our social media campaign and raise awareness of Kate's disappearance using the hashtag #FindKate. We have set up a dedicated webpage for Kate on the force website detailing the exact details of her disappearance, and a contact form. I would once again renew my calls for anyone with information to come forward. We are examining new leads and are expanding our search parameters. I am confident that we will soon find Kate, apprehend her abductor and bring him to justice."

I unroll an A4 missing person poster of Kate that clings to my palm and hold it up to the cameras.

"Thousands of posters have been printed and are being distributed with a view to helping our enquiries. Our efforts to find Kate continue unabated and we will maintain our search for as long as it takes. Finally, I would like to make a personal plea to the person responsible for Kate's abduction. I ask you to search your conscience, think of Kate's family and let her return home to her loved ones. You know that it's the right thing to do."

I withdraw from the stand and urge Beverly and John forward to make an emotional plea to Kate's abductor. Both are grief stricken in front of the microphones. John, the more composed of the two, takes the lead, while clutching Beverly's trembling hand.

"Be brave my darling girl."

Tears leak from his eyes; overwhelmed with emotion. He wipes his face and squeezes Beverly's hand. He looks back at the cameras, fighting the urge to collapse to his knees.

"You are strong, bright, and confident. We have every faith in you that you will not give up without a fight. If anyone knows where you are or what's happened to you, please just tell us and end all of our suffering."

"What about her abductor, what words do you have for him?" The chubby balding reporter interrupts.

"Please just leave Kate somewhere we can find her. We just want her home; that's all. Please do the right thing and give us back our daughter, Kate has done you no harm. She is a kind, funny, caring person, who does not deserve this. Please search your conscience and return our baby girl."

Beverly has broken down in floods of tears. She looks terminally ill, as if her life is slipping away.

"What about Kate, do you have any words for her?" A voice blurts from the crowd.

"Kate, we want you to know that you are so loved, and we will do whatever it takes to find you and bring you home. Please be strong and keep us in your heart; we love you to the moon and back," John stammers, clutching his palms over his face, a broken man.

He removes himself and Beverly from the spotlight.

This is not how I wanted things to pan out but I realise now that all that matters is finding Kate alive, no matter the consequences for my career. This cannot be her end. I won't let it.

## Chapter Forty-Five

His teeth clung to his curled lip as he viewed the official announcement on ITV news. Blood pumped through his constricted veins, listening to their claims about finding Kate.

He sipped from a freshly poured mug of coffee and slid back in his chair. His heavy eyes closed, conjuring images of the reunion he craved.

Kate was special. She wasn't like the others. They were trash, that needed cleaning up off the streets. Erasing their lives gave him fulfilment, particularly the first girl. It had given him release, allowed him to enact his revenge over the parts of his life that ruined him.

He was damaged goods, a broken puzzle with a missing part. He could never be put back together; the picture would always be incomplete.

For years, he'd tried to live happily, forget the past which haunted him. But now he could see that all women were vile and needed to be eradicated. Kate's death would be the most fulfilling. He knew she was frightened, but she would understand his motives.

Tonight, he would embrace her, hold her close to make her feel safe, and ask for her forgiveness before plunging the knife into her heart.

* * * Kate * * *

*Monday 4 January 2016. Evening*

I'm so cold. I don't ever remember feeling this numb. An icy urine puddle bites my flesh. I've never felt so degraded in my entire life.

Why is he doing this to me? I feel weak and empty. The restraints chafe my lacerations. I pull at them and wince, it feels like my muscles are tearing away from my bones.

I'm so thirsty. I lick my lips, trying to ease my discomfort.

It's been days now that I've been held prisoner, I'm certain of it. Why hasn't anyone come to help? Taylor would have reported me missing, surely? He would do everything in his power to find me, I'm sure he would. I know that he loves me despite our argument.

Will and his team must be aware I am missing, by now. They can't be that incompetent. I was under their protection. They must realise that I've been taken. Surely, someone is out looking for me?

I can't sit here and wait for him to return.

My heart is frozen by fear, my mind conjuring images of his lifeless stare eating away at my soul. I don't want to face him again. I need to summon up as much inner strength as I have left, and not be a victim.

I draw my grazed soles to my buttocks, use my weight to push against my right elbow and tuck my legs underneath. I inhale my own wee, as I stand on shaky legs. A sharp pain shoots down my calf and I feel dizzy.

I scour the room searching for a way out. I could break through one of the window shutters. I just need to free my hands. I'm not ready to die, not now; not like this.

# Chapter Forty-Six – DCI Beckley

*Tuesday 5 January 2016. 8.10am*

It's been four days. A body hasn't been unearthed and there's still been no ransom demand made. The uncertainty is killing me. I dread to think what has happened to her and, if she is alive, what on earth she is going through.

What must be going through her mind? She was meant to be under our protection, how could this happen?

What does he want with Kate; a girl that doesn't even fit his profile? It can only be revenge, a way of getting one over on us for acquiring Kate's help with the investigation. He wants to show us that he's in charge, always one step ahead.

Countless search and missing persons' experts have joined the investigation from The National Crime Agency, The National Missing Persons Organisation and The College of Policing, yet to me it feels as though we're not making any headway.

We are further extending our search parameters, due to some Intel we have received and will be conducting a detailed forensic search of a property on the Millbrook Estate today. Meanwhile, searches of open spaces across Weston, near to where she was taken, continue.

Police divers will also conduct a full search of a nearby lake. I'm not implying she's dead and that we're trying to recover her body. I still haven't completely given up hope of finding her alive yet. These searches are merely routine and are not due to any specific intelligence. We must exhaust all avenues to find her; dead or alive and bring her home.

Officers have been joined by hundreds of volunteers giving up their time to help look for Kate. Among them are her friends, colleagues and family.

It must be tough for them fearing they may stumble upon her body. Hope is the driving force pulling everyone together in a desperate attempt to find her.

Kate's face is everywhere. Posters adorn every street corner, they're pinned in shop windows and she's on every news channel. It's sad how the dead are soon forgotten.The emphasis seems to have changed to be more of a search for a missing person, rather than the hunt for a murderer.

With no body people have hope. But as each day passes I fear the worst; that she's been tortured and brutally murdered, and he's left a trail of her scattered body parts for me to find. I cannot let that happen.

\* \* \*

SOCOS in paper suits carry thermal radar equipment and digging tools into 68 Lasmerton Drive. The two-bed property is tucked in the corner of the cul-de-sac, on the opposite side to the alleyway entrance where some of the victims were killed.

Forensic teams will be carrying out an extensive search of the property and combing over it in microscopic detail, paying attention to the rear courtyard garden where there are reports of recently disturbed vegetation.

The tip-off suggests the occupant is a single man with few acquaintances. He lives alone and moved to the area approximately two months ago. He has not been seen entering the house over the past day and the Intel further insinuates that he was seen leaving in a hurry.

If it is him, and he's killed Kate, why bury her, if that's what the disturbed vegetation suggests? Why not leave her out in the open for us to find like the others? He likes to feel admired. The others were left on display; he wanted their deaths to be acknowledged.

Concealing Kate's body does not fit his behaviour patterns.

A chopper swirls overhead capturing live video footage and photographs of the forensic tent that's been erected in the garden. The rotor blades slash through the dense air, attracting further attention as neighbours gather and flank the tape cordon.

Satellite trucks arrive and park beyond the crowds. Crews disembark in haste with their cameras to capture on-the-ground action of the CSIs. I shouldn't admit this, but I have this dull ache in the pit of my stomach, the type you encounter during grief. It's constricting my insides in tight cramps and the pain will not ease.

The longer this goes on, the more I think that Kate's husband and family may need to prepare themselves for the worst.

I weave through rustling suits documenting potential evidence. Delaney and Shelton are poised at end of the hallway in the kitchen doorway.

"Are there any developments?"

Shelton turns to face me and nods.

"There's a raised profile in the lawn; a sign of disturbance, suggesting there may be something buried beneath. We've secured the ground to examine it closely."

"Any blood traces anywhere or signs of a struggle?"

"Nothing that stands out sir, but the team will be here for several hours yet."

"Do you think you're going to unearth something sinister out there?"

My eyes move to the blank tent and back to Shelton.

"I can't possibly say without closer inspection. But it all feels too convenient if you want my opinion."

"I share your thoughts exactly. It's the ideal location, minutes from where the girls were found but he wouldn't bury her. Someone's either fucking with us, or he's trying to buy himself more time."

Despite my views on the matter, we must explore every new lead and therefore this forensic examination must be followed through.

I could be wrong, but I desperately hope that I am not. I cannot imagine watching the earth being lifted and soil being dusted off to expose her pretty face. Her marbled eyes would be open, transfixed on me, firing blame and anger. I close my eyes, but the image continues to haunt me. I see Kate's bludgeoned body being zipped inside a cold body bag, joining strangers in the mortuary fridge. I hear her voice again, whispering in my ear, "It's your fault I'm dead, you did this to me."

Protective plates are laid down on the garden, which Shelton stands on to avoid contaminating the scene in any way. The teams have already scanned the area with a ground penetrating radar. She clutches a garden spade and carefully lifts a layer of turf off, examining it closely to ascertain if there's been any disturbance to its natural soil profile.

Samples are taken to examine the colour, mineral content, particle size and inclusions, which can later be used as a comparison on the offender's boots. If Kate were buried here I'd feel something, I'm sure I would, but I feel nothing. I pray to God that my instincts are correct.

\* \* \*

Three hours into the excavation, nothing has been unearthed. Shelton and Delaney are confident that this property is a wild goose chase and that drugs were probably stashed deep in the soil and later removed.

They assure me they're merely tying up loose ends before finalising their search. SOCOS haven't discovered anything of notable interest inside the house either; no blood or semen.

I slip away under the taut tape, eluding the rubberneckers and head over to Summer Lane Pond. It is situated at the end of a long green corridor stretching westward from Plumley Park, less than a mile from Kate's home.

The pond and surrounding low-lying fields protect the Summer Castle housing development from flooding. I park alongside the site's iconic living willow structure, which stands proudly like a Wiccan pentacle symbol, opposite a pathway of weathered Sarsen stones. It's eerie, yet the sunbeams and blue skies warm the morbid atmosphere.

Padlocks on the olive metal gates, which shield the Batch sewage pumping station, have been cut and rest loosely where forensics have examined the bricked building beyond the curved sewer pipes. I continue onwards, eyeing a small clearing within the trees to view the activity amongst the wooded landscape.

My heart is in overdrive, desperate for knowledge. Police divers from the Underwater Search and Recovery (UWSAR) team, are positioned in each quadrant scouring every inch of the murky, tea-coloured water, looking for her body.

Ducks continue to swim regardless and a huge heron swoops low, landing on a pontoon in the centre of the lake. My eyes focus on tree shadows and the lattice reflection of a mammouth steel electricity pylon, which towers above, dominating the skyline. I look to the lake boundary; countless volunteers stand at every fringe, all forming part of the search party. Everyone is rallied, pulling together to find Kate.

Kate's parents walk hand in hand, their faces convey pure devastation, as they hand posters to passers-by and rescue volunteers.

Louise stands somberly a few steps behind her parents, unaccompanied. Her eyes focus on the floor; her back rests against the wooden Summer Land Pond information board. She doesn't want to be here, this is too much for her to cope with.

I slip away and proceed towards the lake entrance, following black silhouettes and shadows that engulf the stone path with every footstep. Gold commander Greensdale and TAC advisor Steve Kent are positioned ahead, liaising under the native alder and pollarded white willow trees. Stone chippings scrape and leaves crunch underfoot, replacing the faint drum of car engines passing by, as I approach.

Taylor is perched before the gated entrance to the woodland track; the lake's perimeter. He and a group of three men and two women, around the same age or a few years older, are resting on a semi-circle of sarsen stones, which bear a resemblance to Stonehenge.

Daylight seeps through the overhead trees creating illuminated patterns by their feet on the grey chippings. My eyeline is distracted by dark spinning objects; sycamore keys spiral down like tiny helicopters to the ground. I revert my gaze back on them. Their eyes probe me. I assume that they're Kate and Taylor's close friends and I can already see the hatred in their eyes; they blame me, too. As well they should.

I observe Greensdale and Kent, now stood beyond a wall-mounted red lifebelt on a low-level wooden fishing platform, overseeing the dive team. I'm desperate to speak to them for a progress update but Taylor's presence has me secured to the spot. I daren't move. His fierce eyes fulminate with wrath and grief.

I recognise the dark-haired woman with him from Kate's Facebook pictures. I believe her name is Dawn. Most recently, they dined out at the Le Chateau bistro. I remember the image, as it's one of my favourite restaurants. Her eyes look sunken today, through sadness and sleep deprivation.

"Taylor."

He hears me despite the sound of two choppers swirling overhead; one a police helicopter, the other press.

"DCI Beckley," he greets, tone sharp, forceful almost.

He still blames me for all this; who wouldn't?

"I have an update."

I take a deep breath.

"As you are aware as a result of new information received, we have been carrying out a forensic examination of a property in Lasmerton Drive."

I study his face; the colour in his cheeks fading. It's not the news that he wants to hear, that we've found her. Still, I'd rather be telling him that it was a false lead, than informing him that we unearthed Kate's remains.

"We didn't find her; but there's still hope."

"You must have some clue, I thought it was classed as a major development this morning."

Dawn rests her palm on his arm.

"Calm down Taylor, you need to stay focused."

"I can't help it Dawn, this imbecile is the reason Kate was taken and now he can't even find her. It's been four days; four fucking hideous days, the worst time of my life. He could have done anything to her within that time, she's probably already dead."

She dips her head, distraught and deflated, twisting her short wavy curls around her fingertips. The man to her left, presumably her husband, grasps and squeezes her other hand, offering reassurance. He looks uncomfortable, like he doesn't want to be here. To me, he appears unnerved. His stare remains fixed on the soil avoiding all eye contact.

"Come on mate, that's good news surely; we can't give up hope."

I drag my eyes to the guy on Taylor's right, who's talking.

"Kate wouldn't want us to," he continues; placing an arm around Taylor's shoulder.

He stares back at me and eagerly introduces himself as Ryan Rickard, 'a close friend'.

"It's great that you're all offering your support," I reply.

The slender blonde girl next to him remains consumed with emotion; her eyes trail a river of black mascara. I presume she's his girlfriend. A lone figure paces quietly behind Dawn. He, too, appears anxious, chewing his thumbnail. I study him closely; he doesn't fit in the group, though I can't place it. He catches my attention, reaches out his hand and introduces himself as Todd McCarthy, another friend.

I can't help it; I don't see Kate's friends before me, I only see potential suspects. I know that is wrong, but jealousy or anger can turn even the most placid person into a coldblooded killer.

"I'm sorry but I really need to liaise with the gold commander and TAC advisor," I state, nodding in their direction. "They'll be able to provide a better picture of how the search is progressing."

Taylor's eyes well and he gives me a simple nod of approval. I retreat and step onto the planked jetty over the lake, between two thick bundles of pond grass, protruding from the water ripples. Beyond them UWSAR divers equipped with Interspiro DP1 respiratory apparatus study the water closely. They're using Sonor technology to interpret sound waves in the water and create high-resolution computer images of any underwater objects.

"DCI Beckley," Greensdale greets.

"What's the latest?"

"We're entering our fifth search hour, but we've found nothing related to Kate."

"How much more ground do you have to cover underwater?"

He presses his fingertips into his chin, resting his head on their surface.

"Couple more hours at least, just to be certain."

"What about the teams scouring undergrowth surrounding the lake?"

I watch the PolSA (Police Advisory Search) teams scrutinising the scene, shrouded by an array of trees.

"PolSA are about half way around, there are a lot of dense bushes to be examined."

"Are we deploying sniffer dogs?"

"Yes, we have a few that have joined the search from the specialist unit in South Wales."

I'm not sure why, but I suddenly feel queasy again.

Taylor and Kate's family must be thinking this is a lost cause and suspect we think that she's already dead. That's not the case; I'm feeling more positive again that she's alive. Don't ask me why, but my gut and my heart are telling me not to give up. Not just yet.

Taylor and his friends have vacated the rocks and entered the woodland. I follow the continuous stream of bodies, joining the police and forensic teams via the stocky rotten oak gate. Heavy ivy clings and sprawls across the path edge like forest fire, dotted between fallen alder leaves and catkin. Tree branches hang overhead and form a canopy, which obscures the sun, creating a dark atmosphere. Birds chip harmonious melodies and their wings flap, rustling against the leaves. I proceed, following the solid, cracked mud path that looks like shattered glass.

Intertwined blackberry bushes merge with overgrown stinging nettles, which hug and creep their way up the railings protecting the railway boundary. Peering through at the steel and iron tracks, a jab of fear impels me as a train thunders past, couplings clanking with high speed motion.

I had no idea that the site ran alongside the railway track. Fuck. What if this is our connection? What if he has dumped her here; discarded her alongside the track like he did with the others?

I feel empty, lost and suddenly very afraid that I could be wrong after all and she might not come out of her ordeal alive.

I quicken my pace, overtaking search teams who are probing the shrubbery, until I reach a clearing. Sunlight blasts down, and I blink to accustom myself.

To my right, Taylor and Shane kneel on a fishing pontoon overlooking the lake. They're silent, watching the divers dipping below the surface; oxygen tanks skimming the water's surface, which glistens like diamonds.

I saunter on through another set of gates into a second clearing, containing a large cluster of boulders. A lone pensioner in a traditional brown wax jacket sits at the centre, peering through his spectacles at his black Labrador. He's clearly exhausted by his efforts or overcome with emotion. I want to sit with him, close my eyes and shut my mind off to escape this tormented world.

As an onlooker, I witness teams break away from the lake perimeter, entering an open space with a tarmac path on the right and a row of trees to the left, blocking the housing development.

The open clearing is vast. Electricity pylons disperse the scattered clouds and stand like soldiers on military parade. The line of white suits and police uniforms walk shoulder-to-shoulder in a straight-line sequence, probing the grass with rakes, looking for any evidence.

I take an alternative path which leads to the left-hand side of the field, stepping over a discarded crushed energy can with a shark logo, resting upon stinging nettles. A rat scuttles away into foliage. It makes me think of wild animals gnawing on her abandoned corpse and I want to vomit or die.

# Chapter Forty-Seven – DCI Beckley

*Tuesday 5 January 2016. 17.05pm*

Members of the press are here in droves awaiting further information regarding today's searches. They gather alongside the willow sculpture, almost shielding the exit to prevent me from leaving.

It's getting dark; my jacket does little to repel the chill in the air. I make my approach and inform the pack that I will be holding a press conference in five minutes. First, I need to check in with Shelton and Delaney to ensure nothing of significance was unearthed after I left the Lasmerton scene.

Gold commander Greensdale has told me confidentially that the search here today was a waste of time and resources.

I don't share his view; I'd rather be 100 per cent certain her body is not decomposing at the bottom of the lake than left wondering. We owe it to her family to be absolutely thorough.

I approach a cluster of boom mics. Cameras already click concurrently, their flashes illuminating the quickly emerging dusk.

"I'm Detective Chief Inspector Will Beckley and I have an update into the Kate Rivendale investigation. As a result of new information received, we attended a property in Lasmerton Drive on the Millbrook Estate early this morning. The information suggested that a body might have been buried in the rear garden. The area was immediately cordoned off and an extensive forensic search of the address has taken place throughout the course of today. I am now able to confirm that, following those examinations, we did not recover a body, or any evidence to suggest that Kate had been held captive at this particular address."

I feel deflated, not being able to give them any positive news. And they look equally disappointed. I want to be able to stand here and proudly say that Kate's been found alive and well, but as the hours and days pass it somehow feels less likely that those words will ever leave my lips. I must keep my mind sharp and continue updating them with the latest developments.

"In addition to the forensic search of the house, a major search operation has been under way at Summer Lane Pond, which is just over a mile from Kate's home.

"This area was identified for a routine search due to its proximity to Kate's address and the fact that it is a wide-open space. Forensic teams, police divers and hundreds of officers from four different forces, formed part of these efforts today. They were assisted by hundreds of volunteers, including Kate's family and friends, conducting searches of undergrowth around the lake's perimeter."

"But you haven't found me, have you, Will?" Kate's voice invades my mind again, distracting me momentarily. "Tell them why I was taken, Will. Tell them it's because you fucked up, and didn't keep me safe, like you said you would."

I shake my head, trying to silence her accusations. I need to stay focused. I need to show the media and, through the media, the man who is truly responsible for Kate's disappearance, that I am not broken.

"Police divers used specialist equipment to tirelessly search underwater, but this lengthy operation did not yield any notable results; nor did those searches of the surrounding woodland. I would like to take this opportunity to thank everyone who has supported this investigation from the outset. We have been humbled by the sheer volume of people who have given up their own time today, to help look for Kate. Kate's family is naturally very distressed, and they are growing increasingly concerned for her welfare. I offer them our heartfelt sympathies at this incredibly difficult time. We will continue to offer Kate's family our full support as this investigation progresses."

There's another chorus of camera clicks.

"I would like to offer my reassurance that this investigation remains very active and our search efforts for Kate will continue unabated. We also still need to find the man who has brutally killed several other women, and who may well be responsible for abducting Kate, too."

"I would kindly ask that any further public searches are coordinated through the force, so that we can dovetail our efforts. We know Kate's last movements on Friday 1st January 2016, before she mysteriously vanished without warning from her home in Weston. We know she was abducted from her own home; her phone, keys and handbag were found inside the property. Access to her house was gained via a neighbouring house, where signs of forced entry were discovered. What we now need to figure out is why she was taken and who was responsible."

"It's the Millbrook Estate murderer, isn't it?" one of the national journalists shouts out. I ignore him, more determined than ever to demonstrate – at least to the outside world – that I am a man in control.

"Officers have been working meticulously to find the answers to all those questions. They have now been joined by experts from the National Crime Agency, National Missing Persons Organisation and The College of Policing, who are offering us vital assistance. There are many other lines of enquiry that we are pursuing as part of this complex investigation."

"Is Kate the next murder victim?" the national hack persists. Again, I do my best to ignore him. I will not let the media dictate the agenda for this conference; I will stay in control.

"Someone out there knows what happened to Kate or may have seen someone acting suspiciously in the area at the time of her disappearance. There may have been pedestrians and drivers travelling on paths and roads near to Kate's home, at the time of her disappearance. We would urge anyone who was in the Waterdale Drive area at around 11.30pm, to please come forward and help us with our enquiries."

"I would like to thank everyone who has supported our social media campaign #FindKate. The online engagement we have received from this has been phenomenal; already reaching three million people worldwide. I would ask that everyone continue to support and share details of this campaign to further raise awareness of Kate's disappearance. Finally, I would like to renew calls for anyone with any information whatsoever regarding the disappearance of Kate Rivendale, on Friday 1st January 2016, to call the Force on 101, or contact us anonymously on 0800 555 111. Alternatively, there is a dedicated page for Kate on the force website whereby you can make direct contact with us."

"Our investigations into the deaths of the six murder victims remain fully active. We will leave no stone unturned until the killer is caught and prosecuted for his crimes. I would once again reiterate my pleas to stay safe and not walk out alone. Thank you for your time. Again, anyone with information with regards to any of their deaths can contact us via Crimestoppers."

I briskly walk away; I won't be taking any questions. I simply don't have the answers, and I won't find them by being interrogated by the media.

# Chapter Forty-Eight – Kate

*Tuesday 5 January 2015. 9.30pm*

He's left me in this shit hole for days now. I've been slipping in and out of consciousness. The last thing I remember was standing, trying to find a way out in the dark. I must have collapsed.

When I woke, it was light; sun shone through the aging bullet type holes in the brickwork and roof, illuminating my squalor. I'm not sure what time it was but I'm guessing it was mid-morning. The second time I opened my eyes the sun had disappeared; the temperature had dropped, and I felt cold again.

Now, I'm lying here in the pitch black again, fully conscious. I'm trying to swaddle under the flimsy blanket to retain heat. It's not big enough to cover my entire body. I remain worried that I'll catch hypothermia.

If that sets in, then my body will go into shock and I'll die. Either way, it's probably only a matter of time before I meet my end. And I think I'd rather die from hypothermia and shock than at the hands of monster who has put me here.

In fact, if I am going to die here, let it be soon, before he comes back. Let me have this one tiny victory and deny him the pleasure and satisfaction of physically ending my life himself.

My nose is dripping. I feel lost and afraid. I can't remember if he raped me and it's making my stomach curdle, despite my hunger. I don't remember the last time I ate a meal. All I taste is the remains of the gloopy tomato soup that is latched on my taste buds, making me thirsty. My throat and palate feel like I've been on a massive drinking bender.

It's that horrible feeling you get when you wake up the morning after the night before, severely dehydrated through alcohol. I'd do anything for water, or better still some wine and copious amounts of it, so I can get completely wasted, pass out and escape this chamber of horrors.

In all honesty, I just want to go home have a soak in the bath, snuggle under the duvet and pretend none of this happened.

I'd even be prepared to do that, if he set me free. I'd do anything to step back in time and relive the night he took me all over again. Why didn't I prepare myself for such an eventuality? I should have kept a weapon under my pillow, like you see in the movies. Why didn't I try harder to fight him? I should have bit, kicked, scratched; anything to stop him in his tracks and show him that he couldn't take me. Why am I so weak?

I thought that I was safe, under police protection 24/7. I'm so pathetic and gullible. Will doesn't give a shit about me or my safety. He only cares about solving and closing the investigation. I'm such a fool.

The silence is unbearable; I'm not used to it.

All I hear are thoughts roaming in my mind, everything playing in sequence repeatedly. What if I'd done this or done that. I could have done so many things differently looking back, starting by not choosing to put my own life in danger by going undercover.

At the end of the day though, if he was out to get me, he was always going to hunt me down and kill me. The fact that he took me while I slept in my own bed, with officers poised, outside makes me so angry.

I'm reeling right now, I feel let down and humiliated. I want to spit in his face and let him know how it feels to be degraded.

I'd also like to kick Will in his fucking balls so hard that he can't walk for days. He promised me that he would protect me; he's a prick. I'll only ever regard him as a big fat liar, who led me up the garden path with his false promises. If I ever get out of here alive, he's not going to know what's hit him.

I guess you can never judge a book by its cover. Will always looked so kind, a figure of authority, someone I saw as a great protector. I never thought he would let anything happen to me.

In a way, I thought that he liked me and that he had great respect for me. Maybe I was wrong and that was all in my head. Though I'm certain it isn't, I'm normally good at reading people. There was a connection between us, professional or friendly, I'm not sure which but I know I felt it. I'm sure he did too.

Now I just feel repulsed that I allowed myself to fall for his charm.

At the end of the day I'm a mug, he just used me for his own gain. Perhaps underneath that tough exterior, he's cold, ruthless and only interested in himself and his own career.

If I saw him in Costa now, instead of being captivated by his alluring eyes, I'd stare into them with pure hatred, tell him how I feel for what he's done to ruin my life and then I'd punch his lights out.

I'm no longer in control of my body; my mind is still active, but my body doesn't want to respond. Maybe it's the cold. I feel numb; barely able to wiggle my fingers. The enduring pain in my wrists is excruciating; I've never known anything like it. This must be what it's like to feel abandoned by everyone that has ever cared out you.

In a way, I feel Taylor has abandoned me, too. He was so angry after our fight and just walked out on me with not so much as a note. That would have been the decent thing to do; or he could have responded to one of the 11 text messages I left him. But I had nothing.

Maybe I screwed things up forever that night. Perhaps he's finally had enough, and he doesn't care if I'm dead, or alive. Maybe he's relieved that he's rid of me.

I've been locked up in this hell hole being abused, degraded and God knows what else. I don't want to imagine, it is better that I don't know. What you don't know can't hurt you, isn't that how the old saying goes?

The thought of him doing anything sexual to me makes me want to end my own life. I couldn't cope knowing that someone had violated me intimately, without my consent or even my knowledge. I feel so dirty and cheap.

I just want my mum, and if I can't be free of this torment, I may as well end things now. I already feel as though my life is over, it's slipping away.

Maybe the world would be a better place without Kate Rivendale in it.

# Chapter Forty-Nine – DCI Beckley

*Wednesday 5 January 2016*

Criminal profiler Victoria Archer has joined me to discuss information acquired by Live Cell regarding Kate's background.

We wanted to ascertain as much information about her life as possible to help us understand her abductor's motives. Kate is 34, has been married for almost two years, and gained employment at the Southern Chronicle after graduating from Southampton Institute.

Her life appears normal. There's nothing of any significance that stands out to me; this is purely a case of revenge, a way of silencing Kate and putting an end to her coverage of his crimes. She was leading the press pack, had the inside scoop, which I now regret deeply, because that was down to me.

She could have escaped all of this. It's my fault.

"Why do you think he took her?"

Archer's eyes lock on mine.

"The killer panicked. Kate's the one that's been exposing all the details of the investigation and been pounding the street talking to women. Her stories have seen a heightened exposure of the case, with sensational national accounts following. At first, the killer would have been excited reading her reports. He would have gained sexual gratification, 'got off' on it, so to speak, seeing the headlines and knowing that he was responsible. That however, probably pushed him into overdrive. He stepped up his game and shortened the timeline between each victim to fulfil his urge. Only Kate was making everything 'too public'. It was becoming, for him, very unwelcome attention; too much and he feared that the net was closing in on him. He snapped, turned his attention and rage on her. He wanted to shut her down and eliminate her."

I watch Archer intently, studying Kate's medical notes. Her vision focused in on a recent insert. She leans back, lifting the page closely to her face, eyeing and digesting the contents, confirming beyond doubt, in her own mind, what she is reading.

"What is it?"

"A potential motive."

"What?"

"It says here that Kate miscarried at 15-weeks."

I move closer, maintaining our eye contact.

"I don't understand the relevance, how is that pertinent to this investigation?"

"I may be overstepping the mark, but perhaps you should interview the husband again."

"Taylor? Why?"

"Violent actions are usually triggered by something occurring in the offender's own life. Up until this point, life has been normal but when something tragic occurs, such as a death or relationship breakup, it can cause the person in question to behave irrationally and out of character, completely overstepping the line."

"I've not heard anything to suggest that Kate has ever behaved irrationally," I say.

"Not Kate. What I'm suggesting is that maybe her husband didn't cope after the loss of their baby. He blamed Kate and to get over his bereavement, he directed and inflicted his pain on other women until he finally plucked up the courage to tackle the root cause, the mother of his child."

"That's ridiculous. It doesn't feel right. If you saw the pain in his eyes yesterday during the search; he was a broken man."

"I'm probably wrong, but as you know murderers often tend to be someone close to the victim."

"Taylor wouldn't have it in him, plus he didn't know the other victims."

"He didn't need to know them."

"But he has an alibi for the night of her disappearance."

Archer looks agitated.

"All I am saying is that I think we should get him back in for further questioning."

\* \* \*

Taylor's eyes are enraged as custody suite officers sweep electronic metal detectors over his body. I'm stood at the central bridge alongside Archer, who's monitoring his body language and behaviour.

His cheeks are pale and his eyes sunken behind heavy black circles. To me he doesn't look culpable; he looks devastated. Normally I get a feeling about a suspect but on this occasion, I feel hollow. This case has ruined me. I am numb, helpless and I cannot seem to get any closer to the truth.

We escort him into an interview room and instruct him to sit. DI Wakeman joins Archer and me, as we proceed with informal questioning. We have no basis to charge him; only Archer's theory.

"Mr Rivendale, this interview is being tape recorded. I'm DCI Beckley and this is Victoria Archer."

"And I'm DI Wakeman."

"What is your full name?" I ask.

"You know my name, why are you asking me that?" Taylor snaps.

"Could you answer the question, for the tape please?"

"Taylor Rivendale."

"And what is your date of birth?"

"10th June 1979."

"Please confirm there are no other person's present."

"That's correct."

"The date is January 6, 2016, and the time by the interview clock is 14.07. This interview is being conducted at Weston Police Station. At the end of the interview I will give you a notice explaining what will happen to the tapes and how you may gain access to copies of them."

"OK."

I study him but cannot read his face.

"Mr Rivendale, you are not under arrest and are free to leave at any time. You are entitled to free independent legal advice. Do you understand?"

"Yes."

"Mr Rivendale, I wish to check that you understand everything that I have said to you. Do you have to answer my questions?"

"No," he replies abruptly. Then he sighs heavily, and adds, "Could we please hurry this up as we are wasting valuable time trying to find my wife after yesterday's botched attempt," his eyes glancing at the tape recorder.

I ignore his remark and continue to follow procedure.

"Mr Rivendale, you are entitled to free and independent legal advice, which includes the right to speak to a solicitor on the telephone. This interview can be delayed for you to obtain such legal advice. Do you want to have a solicitor present at this interview or do you wish to speak to one on the telephone?"

"No, I'm fine."

He lifts a glass of water to his mouth and slurps the contents. "What are your reasons for declining legal advice?"

"It's not required; I've done nothing wrong. I wouldn't harm a hair on my wife's head. I just want her home safe, with me, where she belongs. It's your fault she's gone, not mine."

There's an element of truth in what he's saying. I did promise to protect her, but I never envisaged I would need to protect her from her own husband. I eye Archer who continues to examine Taylor.

"I allowed Kate to be placed under surveillance by you and your officers to help catch the sick bastard that's killing all those girls. I have no reason to want to harm my wife, I don't know how I can be any clearer on the subject. Could we hurry up and conclude this interrogation, so that I can look for Kate?"

"Mr Rivendale, I will expect you to listen carefully to my questions and I will give you time to think. I will be expecting you to give me as much detail as possible, don't leave anything out. If you do not understand something please tell me," I continue.

"I understand, and I will cooperate fully with your investigation. At the end of the day I want my wife back and as much as I don't like, or understand this questioning, I will go along with it."

"During this interview, I will be asking most of the questions and my colleague, DI Wakeman, will be taking notes."

Wakeman nods with his usual blunt, no nonsense stare.

"As you are aware we are investigating Kate's abduction and I am asking you to account for your whereabouts on the night in question. Can you please clarify for the tape where you were when your wife disappeared?"

"I already told you, I was working."

"Could you confirm what your job is and your place of employment?"

"I'm a taxi driver; I work shifts."

"So, even though you knew your wife was in a potentially dangerous situation, you chose to go to work. What kind of a man does that? Most husbands would be waiting for their wife's return."

"Firstly, you insisted my wife would not be in any danger, so you obviously lied to me at the time to get her on board with your operation. Secondly, maybe most men would have, but I was not aware that she was taking part in any fucking sting operation. I genuinely thought she was under your protection, but you fucked up, didn't you?"

My cheeks scald and I wipe my sweaty palms on my trouser legs. From deep in my mind I recall the many times I let Jen down, always putting my job first. I'm no better than Taylor.

"If we could not detract and get back to the line of questioning please. Can your taxi firm corroborate your alibi?"

"Yes."

"Our records indicate that Kate was last seen at 11.30pm. Are certain you did not see or speak to Kate after this time?"

"Yes, that's what I've said. Your DI here called me to say Kate was missing. I came straight home and found you lot sniffing around the house."

"I would remind you that a record is being made of this interview and it may be given in evidence if you are brought to trial. Do you understand?"

"Yes. Fully," Taylor answers, hastily.

I pluck an evidence bag containing a fingerprint sample and slide the sachet across the table.

"I would like to refer to exhibit 4471/MDJ/1."

"For the tape, DCI Beckley is handing the suspect a sealed evidence bag," Wakeman interrupts.

"This is a fingerprint found on the loft hatch of the crime scene, which we have reason to believe was the entry and exit point of her abductor. The print has been uploaded to the NAFIS database and it came back with a match to you, Mr Rivendale. I believe this may be due to you having taken part in commission of the offence in question. What do you have to say in reply to that?"

Taylor pushes the evidence bag back across the table, narrowly missing Wakeman's water.

"I live there. It's my house. Of course, my fingerprints are going to be in my own home, imbecile. I've never heard anything so fucking ridiculous. I also obviously have a key to my house, why would I need to go to the effort of breaking in?"

"Perhaps you wanted it to look like someone else was responsible for her abduction? I suggest that is why you forced entry to the neighbour's door, to make it look like someone broke in. My suggestion is that you were the person responsible for the abduction of your wife."

Taylor's face looks fierce. In the blink of an eye he's on his feet, the chair smashes against the wall.

"Please calm down," Wakeman orders.

I smile to myself.

"Now, that's the type of aggressive behaviour I believe you exhibited on the night in question, when you abducted your own wife."

Wakeman picks the discarded chair from the mottled carpet and instructs Taylor to sit.

"I didn't do anything of the kind."

I notice his hands tremble on his lap.

"Are you OK Mr Rivendale? You're shaking. Perhaps I've hit a nerve?"

"I'm shaking because I'm fucking angry. How dare you accuse me of kidnapping Kate?"

"My suggestion is that you snapped. Kate devoted all her time to her job, so much so it cost the life of your unborn child, and that's why you're punishing her."

"What did you just say?"

Taylor's eyes widen, his enlarged pupils engulf his irises. I lean closer, maintaining full eye contact.

"I said that perhaps Kate's work stress killed your baby, and you blamed her. You're making her suffer for putting her job first."

My throat is parched. I pour a glass of water from the jug and gulp the stale contents in one swift action. Taylor's eyes are watery. I stare at him trying to decipher whether it's anger or sadness.

"Well?"

"Kate hasn't lost a baby; get your facts right."

"Her medical records say otherwise."

I slide a document from Kate's medical notes across the table. Archer looks uncomfortable. Perhaps she's got it wrong. From the blank expression his face conveys, I genuinely feel he had no prior knowledge of his wife's pregnancy.

"This is a serious investigation and we need to ascertain as much information about the victim as possible. This miscarriage gives you motive. Perhaps she lost your baby and it triggered your anger. You flipped out, lost it and made her pay."

"You are twisting everything to make me look guilty. I had no idea Kate was ever pregnant. Why would she keep that from me? What the fuck is going on here? It's fucking crazy!"

His face is grey, as if on the brink of death. He then takes a deep breath and composes himself. Perhaps he knows that if he loses control here, he might inadvertently confess. "I find it disturbing that you would breach my wife's privacy and divulge such sensitive information without her consent. You can come up with whatever conspiracy theories you like but I can assure you I didn't know she was ever pregnant, and I did not do this."

Wakeman directs a stare at me. We nod in agreement. I know that we have no real evidence to go on.

"Do you wish to clarify anything you have said?" I ask.

"Only that I am not responsible for any of this. I would never hurt Kate and I've no reason to harm any of those other women. This is ridiculous."

"Do you wish to add anything else?"

"Yes. You have wasted valuable time which would have been better served hunting down the real culprit and finding my wife. I'll make you pay for this when this is all over."

"Is that a threat, Mr Rivendale?"

"No, I'm just saying that your career is over."

"This is the document DCI Beckley told you about at the beginning of this interview," Wakeman states impassively, presenting an A4 sheet to Taylor.

"It outlines what will happen to the tape recordings," he declares.

"The time is now 14.55. The interview is now being concluded. You are free to leave pending further enquiries," I state firmly.

I'm angry and disappointed. It was not the outcome I'd anticipated. I hoped that I could push Taylor over the edge into a confession but deep down I knew I was barking up the wrong tree. Still, we must explore all avenues if we are to get any closer to finding Kate.

Wakeman switches off the recorder, removes the tapes and prepares a label seal, which he hands to Taylor for a signature. I watch his trembling fingertips grip the black biro, complete the tag and promptly slide it back across the table. Wakeman and I insert our signatures and seal the tape securely.

"Thank you for your cooperation."

Taylor's bloodshot eyes stare into mine. He's full of rage, or grief, or perhaps a mixture of both. I cannot figure him out. It's a look I do not wish to encounter again. He wishes I were dead.

# Chapter Fifty – Kate

*Wednesday 5 January 2016. Evening*

I paw at the flaking surface of the rusty nail embedded in the wall. It's my only chance. I'm weak but must keep fighting.

I visualise his face, trying to muster all my strength and determination. He will not succeed this time. I will fight this.

I press the orange nylon cord against the nail and begin rubbing it back and forth. I'm tired and the pain is unbearable, but I won't give in. I need to stop the cord's suffocating grip; it's gnawing away at my tendons and against my carpal bones. I need them free, no matter what injury I cause to myself. I increase the intensity, grating my wrists in frantic motions. My heart bolts, feeling a sense of hope as friction severs the fine rope section by section under the pressure. I need to keep going. I can do this; I can fucking do this. Yes!

My detached soul has been injected back into my body with renewed force. I'm alive; I'm a fighter.

I lurch forward, adding my weight onto the cord as I continue to slice through it. My wrists sting, as tears wet my cheeks. A second and third thread snaps. My heart is racing, adrenalin fueling my mind, awakening my senses. 'Keep going, come on, keep going,' my inner spirit screams in my ear.

I think about Taylor, and his face spurs me to increase the momentum. I need to see him again; to say sorry. I cannot die and leave behind our last memory where we're fighting.

I'm almost there. The burning friction on my sore wrists is almost too much to bear, but this is the only way if I'm to escape this chamber and be free.

\* \* \*

His foot slammed hard against the accelerator, speeding through the darkness along the country roads. Kate had been left alone for far longer than he anticipated, without food or drink. He wanted her alive.

A carrier bag stocked full of bottled water and snacks rested neatly on the passenger seat. The engine revved as the car raced through waterlogged fields. He had to hurry; make sure he wasn't tailed.

Excitement and testosterone drowned his veins as he neared. They would soon be reunited, and he would then enact his revenge. Kate would become another addition to his trophy collection; his most prized possession.

\* \* \* Kate \* \* \*

Blood trickles down my fingertips as the nylon invades my flesh. I don't care about the pain; it's minimal compared to the pain he'll make me endure if he catches me trying to escape.

My breathing is erratic; I'm hyperventilating or having a panic attack. Oh shit! He's coming. I hear his engine. Please, no. Not now, I'm so close.

My eyes slam shut, listening, as I pray for help. My time is up. I find every ounce of strength in me and continue shredding the cord. My nose cracks as I fall forward, smashing my face against the wall. The pain splinters my entire face. Blood gushes and floods my mouth, clogging my throat. I don't care about the agony, I'm finally free from his snare.

My icy numb hands fumble the brickwork, until I stand tall.

This is my only chance. I survey the room, I haven't much time. The doorway is bolted from the outside. The engine hum grinds to a halt. My soles sting as shards of gravel already embedded into their surface dig further in, as I stumble through my prison.

I can't see properly, my vision obscured by blood and tears. But I know that I need to keep moving, get the hell out. I won't be a victim any more. Every step hurts as if I am tip-toeing across a bed of nails, but I need to find a way out of my nightmare.

Light enters the darkness beyond the stack of hay bales to my right. His headlights shine against the brickwork, illuminating a crawl space. I don't have time to wrestle the boarded windows, I need to act fast.

The car door slams shut; he's coming.

I grapple against the straw, heaving myself up, mounting the bales one by one. The light continues to illuminate the square cut-out as I reach the top. I force a smile at the irony; the headlights from his car is helping to show me how I can escape from him. I pull myself through the slot and jump down into an adjoining room.

An agonising pain spears my foot as I land on the other side. A piece of wood splinters my sole; the pain piercing. I fumble my way through the darkness treading over what feel like fence panels. I pause, give myself time to think and scrutinise my surroundings.

I make out the outline of a ladder on the floor and machinery. Wait, there's a bloody door! Yes! This is it; my escape, oh thank you God.

I stagger towards it, every hair on my body pricked on end. I hear my heart's thunderous rhythm echoing in my chest. I keep swallowing my own sick, as it projects in violent waves up my throat, merging with blood. The taste is foul.

Shit! It's propped against the wall, it's not real. Tears burst the banks of my eyes again. My body trembles, fear igniting every nerve. His boots scuffle across stones. He's coming, I'm going to die.

Wait, there's a small wooden hatch, and it isn't bolted from the inside. I crawl as fast as I can towards it; wood and stones abrade my tender skin. I can't think about the pain, I can only focus on staying alive. I yank at the pallet edges; it comes crashing down on my chest, jabbing my back against the floor.

I find strength to force it off me, not having time to wonder where that strength came from and toss it to one side. A gaping hole lies ahead. It's dark. I don't know where it leads or what's inside, all I know is that if I stay here he will find me, and he will kill me.

I wipe my flooded tear ducts, summon all my strength once more and inch forward through the crawl space, dragging my blood with me. I only see darkness but feel cold air on my face. It's getting colder with every forward motion; I must be getting close.

The door bolt echoes in the distance. Time is running out. I quicken my pace until a gust of wind pelts my cheeks. I'm at a standstill; my route impeded by a metal criss cross grating, blocking my escape. I clench my teeth and wrap my fingers around the metal. It's fixed and won't budge.

I can't let this be the end, not after coming this far. I lash out, slamming my head forcefully, butting its surface. The pain is excruciating and throbs like my skull is being squeezed in a vice jaw clamp. I close my eyes, retreat, bite down hard and head-butt the metal again.

I'm almost paralysed by pain, as hairs rip from my scalp. I feel dizzy. I grapple the metal; the casing has loosened.

A gush of relief dispels some of my pain. I can't hit it with my head again; I won't withstand another smash to the skull. I lie on my side, draw my knees close to my chest, curled and tucked into a tight ball. I work my body around in the cramped confinement, so I'm feet first instead.

Using my good leg, I lash out stamping and kicking for dear life until I'm free. Icy air bites savagely. I drag my body across what feels like thick, gloopy wet mud. Its gluey consistency clings to my skin with every glide as I pull free.

The full moon shines like a flashlight, lessening the inky darkness of the sky. It illuminates my escape.

Angry howls erupt from inside the barn. I'm frozen with fear, panicked and suffering unbearable pain all over. I push myself to my knees, listening intently to muffled screams. I don't know what he's saying. I don't know what I'm thinking any more, everything's a blur. I want to be so wrong it's unreal. My mind is weighed down, boggled by confusion and pain. Maybe it is the drugs playing tricks. Only there's this pang eating at my guts, rinsing them in long tight twists. It hurts.

## Chapter Fifty-One – Kate

I reopen my eyes, I've no idea how long I've been slumped in the mud. I'm wet and freezing, I can barely feel my fingers or toes. But I must keep moving.

He's going to figure out my escape route, I'm sure, and then he'll follow. If he does, he's going to find me and murder me. The only way to make the pain and torment I've endured worthwhile is to survive this and tell my story.

My feet sink, wading through the mud, hindering my escape. It squelches between my toes. I fight its suffocating grasp, withdrawing my heavy legs quickly to pick up speed. Itchy overgrown weed grass viciously whips at my calves and thighs.

I know he's already coming for me, I feel it in my bones. I won't be weak, I can't be. I'm running faster; my legs resemble jelly shaking through darkness. The only sounds I hear are my snatched ragged breaths and grass dragging underfoot.

I can't focus; everything is blurred scarlet with blood. I wipe my eyes with my soiled hands. I don't know where I am or which way to run. All I know is that I need to keep putting one foot in front of the other or I'll die.

The drugs must still be in my system.

I feel them worsening my head injuries. I'm dizzy, tumbling; my knees slap the wet mud. My chest is constricted; I can barely breathe. I know that if I stop, even for a second, he'll find me. I can't afford the luxury of a rest; if I give in to the urge to close my eyes, he will find me, and then I will never, ever, open my eyes again.

I stumble back to my feet, fighting the dark shadows that engulf me. Stinging nettles prick my legs, but I won't stop. I'll either die alone from my injuries, slumped in a water filled ditch, foxes feeding on my scrawny carcass, or he'll catch up and steal what little life is left in me.

Oh, God. His engine roars in the distance. I turn around and survey the sound, trying to focus on its direction. I only see blackness, everything remains distorted. Please don't let him find me. Every limb in my body is screaming for me to run.

My lips quiver with every breath, the intake struggling to infiltrate my restricted throat and fuel my starved lungs.

Jagged branches slice my arms as I continue into the darkness, stretching for miles. I'm incapacitated. A dense branch jabs my throat, sending me tumbling backwards with a thud. My back ruptures the surface of a mud pool; it sucks at my satin nightie. I'm numb, struggling to breathe, desperately snatching gasps of air quickly as I fight its grip and crawl back to my feet.

The engine grows louder. I see headlights frantically zig zagging through the darkness, coming for me. I stagger onwards gradually picking up speed again. I will not surrender.

I will not give him the satisfaction of finding me and finishing me.

If it's the last thing I do, and it probably will be, then I will die in defiance, denying him the satisfaction of watching me die at his hands.

I drag my feet onwards, running through a cornfield; leaves and stems whip and scratch my skin. I can't stop my tears. I've never felt so much pain. My whole body wants to shut down, but my mind won't let it; it's willing me on, making me run for my life. Mind over matter.

I'm scared. It's so much darker in here, the leaves are taller, engulfing me; I can't see in front of my face. Maybe I should hide. He won't find me in this maze. No. I won't risk it. I run on, enduring the persistent flogging; my steps growing faster and faster as my chest wheezes, sucking in the damp air.

BANG! Fuck. The gunshot deafens my ears; I'm on my back, winded. I'm disorientated, grappling my body for a bullet wound.

I roll onto my knees, cowering with my hands shielding my ears. I was repelled; hit a trip wire, igniting a flashbang to scare away birds from the crops.

Holy shit! My palpitating heart is on the verge of its own explosion; my head banging, ears ringing. I'm dazed. I crawl on hands and knees, staying low, wading through the leaves until I only see darkness approaching at the boundary. I stagger to my feet; barely able to stand and run. My hands tear through brambles and blackberry bushes, which prick my flesh. I'm bleeding from every orifice imaginable but force my weary legs onwards, heading toward a clearing ahead. This is my chance; if I want to survive.

Barbed wire perforates my palms and soles; I climb over it regardless. It hitches and slashes my nightie. I don't care what state I'm in, I just need to be free of the malicious mask, and the evil stranger hiding behind it.

I stagger forward; sharp gravel crunches below my toes and spits away with every step. A surge of fear forces me onwards. I'm running with every tiny ounce of fight left in me. I can do this, I know I can. I won't be beaten. Not now; not ever.

I'm running faster, heading downhill. Cold wind slaps my face; it smells of freshly cut grass.

My soles tread over solid mud tyre tracks; they're uneven unsteadying my balance. Shit, something's snagged my ankle. My face and hands smash into the tarmac, grit splitting my palms. It stings. I fumble, frantically tugging at a fallen branch which entraps me. I yank myself free and rise back on rickety legs.

There's not a single part of my body that doesn't hurt. I thought I'd experienced pain in my life, but nothing compares to this.

The fierce wind pushes me backwards as I run up hill, slowing my steps. I can barely fight its brutal force, trying to lure me back to him. Fuck you. Fuck your little game. You've lost me, and you won't find me.

I drive my whole body onwards battling against its reins. I won't stop running. I can't stop. It's not an option.

Intense beams pierce my distorted sight as I stumble through pot holes underfoot. I lift my achy head toward the light, it is close. I can make it to safety.

I stagger, it is growing closer, quicker than I thought.

A thunderous blow catapults me into the air. I hear glass crack. I'm rolling over metal in 360 degree turns and falling like a rag doll being flung from a buggy.

I land like lead; crumpled and broken. I'm dying. This is how it must feel, I'm slipping away. It wasn't meant to end like this. Oh Taylor, I'm so sorry! A crimson river surges from my head cascading over my eyes, slamming them shut, presumably forever.

# Chapter Fifty-Two

*Wednesday 5 January 2016. 11.26pm*

"Oh Gordon, what have we done? Is she dead?"

"I don't know. Kathy; she just came out of nowhere. For Christ's sake call 999."

The elderly couple stand in a state of shock, observing the lifeless body mashed into the tarmac like pulp.

"There's so much blood. Oh, please don't die on us. Should we try and move her?"

"No, don't touch her."

"Emergency, which service do you require?"

"Ambulance, please."

"Ambulance service, what is the address of the emergency please?"

"We're on Collum Lane on the outskirts of Weston. We live at Lye Farm. It's about half a mile away from here. The postcode is BS22 9YX."

"Thank you; help is being arranged. Can you tell me exactly what has happened?"

"I've hit someone with my car; a woman. She just ran straight into the road. I didn't see her until it was too late."

"Are you with the casualty now?"

"Yes."

"Is she conscious and breathing?"

"She's unconscious. I can't tell if she's breathing."

"Does she have a pulse?"

"I don't know. I didn't like to touch her in case I caused any further injury."

"Are there any signs of serious bleeding?"

"Yes, she's covered in blood, it's everywhere. It's seeping from her head. Please help her, send an ambulance."

"An ambulance has been dispatched and is on its way to your location. Can you see her chest moving up and down?"

"I can't tell it's too dark to see anything clearly, she's on her side."

"OK, can you hear any breathing coming from her mouth?"

"I think so."

"Could you please get closer to the casualty for me and listen carefully for signs of breathing?"

Silence.

"Sir, can you tell me what's happening?

"Yes, she's breathing. There's so much blood, you need to hurry."

"An ambulance is on its way to you, sir. Please try to stay calm and the paramedics will be on scene shortly to help. Can you give me an approximate age of the casualty?"

"It's hard to tell, she's probably in her 30s."

"Can you give me the model and colour of your vehicle?"

"Yes, it's a red Ford Kuga, registration PZ14 BYV."

"And are you the registered keeper of the car?"

"Yes, my name is Gordon Hawkins."

"Thank you. Would you like me to stay on the line until help arrives?"

"No. It's OK."

"That's fine. If the casualty's condition changes in anyway, please call back for further instructions."

"Thank you."

\* \* \*

*Wednesday 5 January 2016. 11.42pm*

Erratic emergency lights illuminate the crash site. Her legs and arms lie sprawled in a pool of blood, twisted like a bendy Barbie. Paramedics John Carter, and Lucy Armstrong, place green rescue pack bags, a spinal board and an oxygen kit beside the casualty. Their reflective strips highlight their arms and ankles.

"Is she still breathing?" John asks.

"Yes," Gordon falters, wiping perspiration from his head.

"Have you moved her at all?"

"No. She just ran out in front of us; she literally came from nowhere."

"Is she going to be OK? Please don't let her die," Kathy begs.

"She's got a weak pulse and an increased respiratory rate. She's in shock from blood loss."

Kathy breaks down in floods of tears.

"Is she dying?" she stammers.

An oxygen mask is applied and seals the casualty's mouth and nose, as a spinal board is slid into position. She's fitted with a neck brace and head blocks; lifted and strapped to a stretcher for transportation. Police sirens wail nearby as the stretcher is placed inside the ambulance, allowing the paramedics to assess the full extent of her injuries in the light.

"We need to stem the bleeding from her head or she'll die on route," John exclaims.

Lucy applies swift pressure to her head with gauze.

"Why was she running barefoot? It doesn't make sense." She averts her gaze from the bloodied fabric; their eyes lock.

"I think this girl has been through a far worse ordeal than being hit by the car. Just look at her wrists; she's been restrained."

* * *

The doors of Weston General Hospital's Accident & Emergency department crash open, as both paramedics wheel the casualty inside.

"Unidentified female involved in a high impact RTC. There's significant blood loss. She has severe chest, facial and abdominal trauma, and a possible compressed fracture to the skull. Her GCS level has been three throughout, her heart rate is 110 and her BP is 90 over 60. She's had 1.5 litres of saline."

Benjamin Harris, consultant general surgeon, clinical lead, assumes responsibility for the patient.

"Let's get her straight over please. Call X-ray and tell them we need a full CT and give ICU the heads-up."

"Nice and gently please ladies and gents. On one, two, three," Lucy instructs, transferring the casualty over from the stretcher.

Harris removes his chrome stethoscope from his neck and places the disc-shaped resonator onto her slashed torso, observing her heart rate and chest.

"Pneumothorax on the right side, we need to get a chest drain in."

Zoe Brooker, consultant trauma surgeon, co-clinical lead, steps up. She makes an incision and inserts the drain on her right side into the fifth intercostal space to reach the pleural cavity and allow drainage of air, blood and fluids. Harris awaits her instruction before proceeding to re-examine the chest.

"Sats are improving. I want a full blood count, BM, Us, Es and LFTs," he yells.

"Body temperature is 30C; we need to warm her up. Get me another IV of saline."

Harris examines visible bone fragments on her forehead.

"We've got a compressed skull fracture; she's at risk of a hemorrhage. We need that CT ASAP. I also want full X-rays and an ECG. She's fitting. Sats are dropping; she's going into respiratory arrest. She's in pulse-less VT. Defibrillator, now!" Harris screeches.

Nurse Campbell rushes to assist, handing over the device.

"Oxygen away. Stand clear please. Charging. Charge to 200 joules. Stand clear, shocking."

Harris grips the paddles, applying them to her chest; her body jerks violently. He fixes his gaze on the heart monitor before performing CPR for two minutes.

"Again. Stand clear."

A second spasm judders her lifeless body. Nothing. Harris repeats CPR.

"Again. Charge to 360. Stand clear."

He places the paddles back on her chest. Silence. He pauses awaiting a reaction. Sweat beads swarm on his temples; the machine emits a bleep.

"We have a sinus rhythm. Pressure's coming back up."

Brooker examines the patient's lacerated left wrist.

"She's almost severed her ulnar and radial arteries."

Harris examines the bloody wound and assesses her right wrist.

"She's been restrained. We need to alert Weston CID. We're not solely dealing with an RTC victim here."

Brooker nods, as she tucks her jet-black hair behind her right ear.

"She's endured a horrific ordeal by the looks of it."

Harris studies her face, marred by violence and blunt force trauma.

"What is it?" Broozer quizzes.

"I think she's the missing reporter."

"The girl from the Chronicle?"

"Yes."

"It's hard to tell due to the swelling, she's barely recognisable."

"It would explain her restraint injuries and why she ran barefoot into the path of an oncoming car."

"Inform the police that we suspect it's her. We need a formal ID ASAP for her medical records."

Brooker's eyes narrow, studying her face.

"If it is who you say it could be, we may need a sexual nurse examiner to look for signs of sexual trauma."

"I agree, we will get that arranged once she's stable and conscious. Most of these injuries were inflicted prior to the collision. This woman has had a close shave with death."

# Chapter Fifty-Three – DCI Beckley

*Thursday 6 January 2016. 00.20 hours*

Accident & Emergency overflows with admissions. A teenage boy presses a bloody cloth against a gash on his head while staring at a teenage mother and her screaming baby with total contempt. Its high-pitched wailing reverberates around the room, irritating my ears.

To her right, a frail pensioner clutches hold of her arm; its surface weeping from a superficial burn.

I hate hospitals, I hate everything about them; their stench, their lack of privacy and the endless wait. It's hard to describe the way I feel right now, knowing that you could be lying in a bed here fighting for your life.

I pluck out my badge and press it against the glass reception window to bypass the queue.

"Can I help?"

I stare back at the clerk, a woman in her late 40s with gold rimmed glasses and a neat blonde 80s bob, complete with a heavy blunt fringe.

"A young woman was brought in within the past hour; a collision victim."

"Yes, she's in ED, through the double door and turn right. They're expecting you."

Her words slice through my empty stomach. I feel as though my insides have been torn out and pulverised with a meat mallet. I long for it to be you but at the same time I don't, if that makes any sort of sense.

I wanted to be the one to find you Kate; alive and unharmed. It wasn't meant to end like this; your tiny body macerated on the tarmac. Please don't die.

I follow a woman in her mid-50s with matted, faded, rainbow streaked dreadlocks, eyeing her attire; yellow Crocs, Minion pyjama bottoms and a leopard skin mohair cardigan. She drags one crutch along; the other weighed down with carrier bags on the handles. I wonder whether they contain her worldly possessions.

I continue into Minors; each cubicle concealed by disposable turquoise curtains. A young copper-haired staff nurse stands behind the desk, talking on the phone. I scour the room and catch the eye of a sister, who emerges from one of the bays to my right. Her silver pocket watch rattles against her large breasts as she walks toward me.

"Can I help you?"

"DCI Will Beckley, Weston CID. I'm looking for the young woman involved in a collision this evening."

"Come this way." Her eyes express concern and sympathy; it's a look I don't wish to encounter. I know what's coming; I want to heave.

This is surreal. My stomach is flipping, like a washing machine on full spin. I can't believe there's a possibility that the girl fighting for her life in here could be you, and you're alive. What the hell happened? I don't understand. Did he let you go or did you escape? If it's the latter, then you're in immediate danger and require police protection. He's already probably out looking for you.

I failed you once; I won't be made to look a fool twice over. I will not let him come for you, not again. Oh, please, let it be you.

I remember the first time that I saw you. Your cheeks were flushed a warm rose tint, feeling all eyes in the press conference on you. You were self-assured grilling me in front of the cameras, but I could tell by the colour radiating your face that it was a front.

Underneath you're not quite as confident as you'd have people believe. I recall your reaction when I bumped into you on ICU; you wanted to bolt but were frozen. I also studied your body language at Costa; you're shy really, a timid little kitten.

If it is you and you've fought him, I'm impressed that you found your inner strength and determination.

My heart is asphyxiated with apprehension; I suppress a shiver creeping up my neck. I need to make things right, keep you safe and take you home. I follow the sister, passing two giggling trainee nurses who offer a smile. Another set of doors lead us into ED.

"Nurse Campbell, could you locate Dr Harris? DCI Beckley would like to speak to him as a matter of urgency."

I glance at Campbell; a petite blonde in her twenties, about 5ft 2ins tall. Her navy tunic is too tight squashing her buxom breasts together in a pillow-like shape. She sidesteps the desk.

"Sure, give me a moment." I turn to thank the sister, but she's already disappeared.

My pulse is racing, adrenalin thrashing through me awaiting Campbell's return. Anything could have happened since you were brought in. What if you've died? What do I tell your family? "Oh, yes about Kate, she' was found alive, but she's since died."

Those words won't leave my tongue. I clear my throat pushing the repulsive image of your butchered corpse out of my mind. I can't think like that. I need it to be you. I want it to be you so bad, it hurts.

"DCI Beckley, Dr Benjamin Harris, Clinical Lead."

He's tall, around 6ft 3ins with toned biceps bulging against the snug sleeves of his teal scrub top. He's young, around 33, with a sun-kissed complexion and dark brown hair pulled back, exposing his chiselled jawline. He grips my palm in a firm handshake.

"Are you certain it's Kate Rivendale?" My heart convulses awaiting his response. He tilts his head to one side, hesitating before answering.

"The girl bears similarities to the missing reporter. She's badly in-jured, so it's difficult to be certain, especially as I've never met her. Due to the nature of her injuries, and her presentation on arrival, I do believe it's her," he whispers through his bearded chin.

"What do you mean by her presentation?" His fingers caress his chin; eyes full of sorrow or maybe confusion. I can't tell which. It's a frightening expression.

"Aside from her impact injuries from the vehicle collision, there's sign of significant trauma on her body."

I force bile back to my stomach as my fists clench together angrily.

"Her wrists are brutally lacerated, indicating she's been restrained. Her feet are severely abraded which suggests she had been running barefoot for some time. She was only wearing a nightdress when she was brought in. It's these factors which make me certain that the girl in that bed is Kate Rivendale."

## Chapter Fifty-Four – DCI Beckley

A surge of dread engulfs me. I'm afraid of what he's done to you.

"What colour is her nightdress?" My words quickly spew out.

"It is antique gold with black lace."

A stab of fear hits my frantic heart; confirmation it's you, surely.

"Will she make it?"

"It's hard to say at this stage but she's a fighter. It's been touch and go, to be honest; we've nearly lost her once since admission. I'm not sure how her small frame has fought the extensive injuries she's sustained. She suffered severe head trauma during the vehicle impact." I'm listening to Harris as we continue toward the cubicle, but the words aren't sinking in. They're racing through my mind like a racehorse on the final stretch at Goodwood.

"She's about to go for a CT scan, I need to ascertain if there's a bleed on the brain." Harris adds, studying me closely.

I feel drained; face colourless.

"Are you okay?"

"Yes, I'm fine. Please continue."

"She's suffering from mild hypothermia, which we're continuing to monitor closely but that's no surprise given her presented attire and the low temperatures she endured."

I'm in shock; jaw locked, body numb with guilt. Your face keeps replaying over in my mind. I remember you twiddling the ends of your curls in Costa, being inquisitive. Please don't die.

Harris stands tall, his scrub top pulls tightly against his pecs as he reaches and grips the curtain that protects you. I take a deep breath, trying to calm my frazzled nerves.

"I've also examined the X-rays. The Cervical, Thoracic, Lumbar and Sacral vertebrae in her spine all appear intact despite the impact. She does however have fractures to her right arm and left leg. She's one lucky girl to be honest. I've not detected any permanent damage which would prevent her walking again. In all honesty, she should be dead."

A bludgeoned head rests against the pillow, shrouded by a thick bandage protecting a wound. A blade plunges into my heart and viciously twists, severing all the vessels. The sight before me is harrowing; I look away. I can't breathe; my chest is tight as if I'm having an asthma attack.

I steady myself against the foot of the bed, trying to anchor my weight and maintain composure in front of Harris as I will myself to look back at you.

My eyes fix on your lips; they're swollen and grazed, and your bulbous eyelids are a deep damson like the colour of rigor mortis. You look dead, but I can hear your heart beeping on the monitor. You're a fighter. I knew you would be. I ought to feel relieved, seeing your face again, but I feel empty; the pain unbearable.

What did he do to you? Every inch of your arms is scratched and torn, held together by black snaked stitching and steri-strips. You look like you've been attacked by Freddy Kruger; both wrists heavily bandaged, presumably from where you were detained. An intravenous drip pumps fluid into your dehydrated body. I lift my eyes back up. Clumps of hair have been brutally ripped from your scalp; the remainder matted with dried blood.

I want to wash it, make you clean. I know that sounds odd, but you would be mortified by your reflection. You take great pride in your appearance. The Kate I see before me is a shadow of the girl that you were.

Lacerations and a black bruise suffocate your throat. What the hell happened? Harris is correct; you should be dead from what you've endured but by some miracle- it can only be described as that- you're still here.

"Is it Kate?" Harris probes, eyes flashing a spark of curiosity.

"Yes." I whisper, barely able to get the answer out.

You're hardly recognisable but I'd know you anywhere. You're wearing your diamante tennis bracelet; the one you twiddled nervously in the interview suite, and the white gold and diamante pendant on your neck. I feel as though I've been kicked, I'm doubled over with nausea. I should feel elated to have you back but seeing you like this is torture.

I'm not sure why I feel so much pain, perhaps it's my guilt. When you wake and remember, your pain will only worsen. I'm so sorry. I truly am. I wish it were me in that bed, not you. I'd do anything to swap places. I deserve to die.

If only I'd offered you better protection, I could have prevented all of this. Now you and your sister are 'damaged goods' and I'm responsible.

Well, the fucker won't get away with this, I promise you that, Kate. I'll bring this fucking bastard down, if it's the last thing I do.

A surge of anger hammers my skull. I stare at Harris. He's been studying me for a while, trying to figure out the nature of our relationship. He suspects that I care about you. Surely, it's natural to feel like this. If I didn't care, I wouldn't be human.

I know you're married. I just feel a connection to you and an overwhelming need to protect you, given that I've failed you so badly. I need to make things right and I will Kate, I promise. I won't let you down ever again.

"Did you know her well then?" Harris probes, voice low.

Colour brightens my cheeks.

"Sort of. It's complicated."

He rests his head on his hand.

"She was helping you, wasn't she? Assisting with the Millbrook murders investigation?"

I detect a scornful tone, as if he's accusing me of failing you. I don't need him to tell me that, I know what I've done.

"I can't discuss ongoing investigations or tactical operations."

"I understand. Try not to worry. She's safe here. She's in good hands," Harris answers, offering a weak smile.

Maybe I read him wrong. He is only interested in Kate's welfare, not attributing any blame.

I exhale the trapped anxiety from my lungs.

"Is she going to die?"

"I can't give you an answer. Like I said, it's been touch and go but from what I've witnessed so far, she's determined to fight for her life. After the CT, we'll have a better picture of what we are dealing with."

I'm looking at your face, holding back my threatening tears. I can't appear weak in front of Harris. He wouldn't understand, and it would be unprofessional.

"Was she sexually assaulted?"

"There's bruising to her thighs but we have not examined her intimately. We wouldn't without her consent."

Your arm feels cold to the touch. Why did he keep you out there for so long? I want to swaddle you in blankets and help you in any way that I can but that's not my field of expertise. It's Harris that you need right now, not me. I'm useless. That's what Jen said; I was 'a useless waste of space'. She was right. I'm the one who put you in this bed. I'll never forgive myself.

Harris closely examines your obs.

"Have you ever dealt with anything like this before; a patient who was held captive?"

He looks up from the machine, a frown spanning his forehead as though he's delving his mind for information.

"Yes, once. Some time ago. The girl awoke in a psychotic state believing she was still being held prisoner, it was horrific. She fought all the nurses and ran into the hospital grounds. She was suffering Post Traumatic Shock. I'm no expert in that field, but if Kate lives it's highly likely that she could suffer psychological damage."

He pauses, realising that his words have turned my face grey.

"Although, she's suffered severe head trauma and may have no recollection whatsoever of the events which brought her here."

I'm watching you breathe through the tubes taped to your lips; his voice trailing off. I don't want to hear any more. I need to shield myself, I can't think about how you'll respond when you wake up or how you'll react when you see me. I know you'll be mad. That image ignites a burning pain in my chest; its coiling around my heart and setting fire to it.

I don't care how angry you are with me, so long as you live. I need you to live, Kate. Be the fighter that I presumed you to be. Don't let the bastard win. I will get him for what he's done to you and that's a promise I intend on keeping, even if I swap my life for yours.

\* \* \*

I've been lying in my bed for hours staring up at the blank ceiling. I needed to separate myself from the investigation, just for a few hours, to process everything.

I couldn't bear to look at you, knowing that it's my fault you were taken. My body desperately wants to surrender to sleep but my mind won't allow it the victory. Every time I close my eyes, I see your battered face haunting me. I can't sleep while you're fighting for your life and not while the vile bastard is still out there. I wonder if your abductor the man responsible for the deaths of all those women, or are there two different assailants at large?

My insides feel like they've been scraped out, I'm completely hollow, like a carved pumpkin with guilt clawing away at the bare cavity.

I wanted to stay by your bedside. That's wrong and totally inappropriate, but I feel responsible. I should never have put your life in danger. I acted stupidly. It's 5.30am. Sod it, I'm coming back. I need to be with you. I know that you're under police protection but it's not enough.

This time I will protect you myself. I won't give him the chance to finish the job. There cannot be any room for error this time around.

I won't let you down again, just please forgive me and let me make things right.

# Chapter Fifty-Five

He stared at his reflection; bloodshot eyes hidden beneath bulging bags. He no longer recognised himself. He was out of control.

His heart thumped raucously, recalling her distorted twig-like limbs sprawled on the tarmac like puree.

The prospect of Kate being alive and talking hit and impaled him like a train at high speed. She wouldn't bring him down; he wouldn't allow it.

Soap suds cleared the windscreen as the car disembarked from the ramp.

All other evidence linking him to her was smoldering ashes in the woods. Police search teams would be canvassing the area; retracing their way back to the den where he had played out his fantasies, but they would not find any trace of him. He'd been careful, as he'd always been.

There was no way he would let that jumped-up little bitch expose him. Not now, not ever.

* * * DCI Beckley * * *

*Thursday 6 January 2016. 6.46am*

Harris's eyes looked strained; the result of a 17-hour shift.

"She's stable and her obs are improving. The CT revealed no bleed, either; it's quite remarkable. She's fortunate that no damage occurred to her spine from the impact trauma."

His eyes remain transfixed on the medical chart at the foot of the bed which he completes with a Montblanc fountain pen.

"Will she regain consciousness anytime soon?"

"I suspect it'll be days, not hours, until she's conscious and coherent."

I'm staring at your crumpled body; wires and tubes protrude from every orifice. I think you're breathing on your own; the machines are just there to assist. I can hardly bear to look at you. Your face has deteriorated; severe swelling and a huge crimson bulge is forcing your taut skin outwards and encroaching your right eye socket.

Your cheekbones and under eyes look like you've done ten rounds in the boxing ring. Your neck bruising has worsened too. Did he try to strangle you? The thought is repulsive. All the scratches and bruises will fade in time, I just wonder what emotional scars you'll be left with. They might never heal.

I hope you're not in any pain. Dr Harris appears to have everything under control, I must thank him. I wonder if you could hear me if I spoke to you? I want to tell you how sorry I am. I want you to know that I would never have knowingly put you in harm's way.

"Can she hear us?"

"It's possible."

Harris's brow deepens.

"People have woken from comas and recalled not just words of comfort but entire conversations, word for word. Would you like me to give you a minute or two with her?"

"Please. Is she stable enough for a forensics examination? If there's a remote chance of getting any DNA transfer, we need to take it."

"I've no objection to you gathering evidence. She certainly deserves justice."

You and I are alike Kate, in the sense that we are both determined, and career driven. I admired that trait in you. I saw it the moment that I laid eyes on you; you have a real passion for the truth. Maybe that's why I felt some sort of connection with you. We're cut from the same cloth, you and I.

And it's that drive that put you in this bed. I must inform Taylor and your family that you're alive. I'll make it my next priority. They deserve to be here when you wake up. I'm sure the first thing you would rather see is Taylor's face, not mine. After all I'm the one that got you into this mess. I'm the one that put you in this bed fighting for your life. But right now, I want to sit with you and tell you how very sorry I am.

I encase your delicate fingers in my hand, eyeing your ragged nails. You fought him every step of the way, didn't you?

I knew that you would. I just knew it, deep down. I saw a glimpse of your feisty side. I wonder if you obtained his DNA. I want to nail the bastard so very much, it hurts. Not just for you but for all the girls. None of you deserved to endure such horrific pain and suffering.

All of you were so young, had your full lives ahead of you and poor Charmaine lost her baby too. You are the lucky one Kate. I know that sounds crazy, I just mean that you were the only one strong and determined enough to fight back. You will survive this, I'm certain of it.

I gently squeeze your hand so you're aware of my presence.

"Kate, it's Will. I hope you can hear me. You're safe now. I swear on everything that is holy. No one is going to hurt you. You are in the hospital and you have full police protection. I'm deeply sorry, I never meant for any of this to happen. This will soon be over, and I will make him pay for what he's done to you."

I jump, startled by a twitch. I'm certain you squeezed my hand, or maybe my mind is playing tricks and it's just wishful thinking.

"You are so brave, you put your life on the line to help the investigation and I want you to know that I will never forget what you did for me; for the case, for justice, and for those girls who did not get away. I promise you Kate, I won't stop hunting until I have the bastard under lock and key for life."

# Chapter Fifty-Six – DCI Beckley

*Thursday 6 January 2016. 9.33am*

As much as I didn't want to leave you, I was in the way of Foster's forensics examination. I hope that she extracts his DNA from under your nails. He needs to pay for his crimes and while I'm still breathing air, I won't stop investigating this case until I hunt him down and bring the full force of the law raining down upon him with such force, it will crush him.

I've arranged a press conference at 3pm. I'm being hounded for an official update regarding Charmaine's murder.

I've been unable to make a full announcement regarding her death, as we had to await formal identification from her next of kin, who were flying back from Australia. I must tell the press that he not only took her life but that of her unborn baby.

I still cannot erase the image of the tiny fetus being extracted from her womb, I've never seen anything so disturbing. It was bad enough having to inform her family, none of whom knew that she was even pregnant.

Now I must notify the media circus. They'll have a field day with the information. That's the worst part of my job, Kate; those words having to leave your lips and witnessing people's lives come crashing down to ruins, obliterated as would a bomb destroy its target. I hate it, yet I cannot complain; I chose this life.

The media also want to know about you. Your face is on every TV channel, the front page of every national newspaper and your name is on repeat across radio news bulletins. They are hungry to know what's happened to you Kate.

You always dreamed of breaking the news; I bet you never imagined that you would be making the news. It's kind of ironic. I didn't expect it either, and for that I am sorry.

You know how your profession works. A pretty, young face helps sell the story and capture people's hearts. The photo they are using of you is stunning, with a beautiful natural smile across your face and sparking eyes that reach into people's souls. The fact that you were also trying to help us to avenge your sister's attack just cemented the nations admiration for you.

Informing them that you've been found alive and survived a prolonged ordeal will be difficult, it makes us look incompetent. But it's better than reporting that you're the latest murder victim. And the media – and the world – need to know that despite what you've been through, you're a fighter. You will keep on battling, I know you will. You want justice as much as I do.

I want the fucker to know that you're alive and that you beat him. You're our game changer Kate. You've won and when you come around you'll help me piece everything together.

First, I need to see your husband and family. I need to tell them. I want them to hear it from me, that you're alive, not learn it from a media report.

They take priority; they need relief from their enduring suffering. I feel terrible for questioning Taylor, but Archer insisted. I also need to liaise with Jenkinson for an update regarding their search efforts. The teams have been out since first light working alongside forensics, searching the surrounding area of the crash site. We will find where he held you captive by working slowly backwards from where you were found. Then we will pin this on him.

\* \* \*

Taylor's head is slumped in his palms, gazing down at the beige carpet avoiding all eye contact with DI Wakeman and me. His body rocks gently, listening as I inform him about you. He remains silent as I outline your injuries.

His jaw is locked with anger, his fists scrunched. He can't take the news in, maybe he's in shock. I felt like that when I took the call saying you were alive. I couldn't believe what I was hearing, it all seemed unreal. To be honest this does feel like a weird dream. Soon I'll wake up and instead of you being hospitalised, I'll be standing over your corpse at the mortuary and then singing hymns at your funeral.

"We can take you to the hospital if you're unfit to drive?"

Taylor lifts his sluggish head; his bloodshot eyes meet mine staring with pure contempt. I study his unkempt face as I continue talking, offering reassurance.

"She's stable and is making good progress." He breaks his silence, his pupils scorn with hostility.

"Lucky for you, she is."

"Sorry?"

"I said it's lucky for you she's improving, or you'd have another death under your buckle. I heard how you screwed up that other case too. It seems to be a habit of yours."

Shit. I swallow phlegm clogging my throat. How the hell does he know about that? His tone is clipped, angry even. Rage ignites a fire in his eyes which lock and probe mine.

"I'm not here to discuss my past cases Mr Rivendale. Your concerns would be better focused on supporting your wife."

I know he's right. I am a fuck up, but this time I will make things right.

"Perhaps you can pack her a bag? Then we'll accompany you."

"Am I still a fucking suspect?" he yells, rising abruptly looking for a fight. His eyes are wild.

"Is that why you feel the need to accompany me?"

"No. You need to calm down, we're just trying to help you, Mr Rivendale. When she wakes up it's your face that she needs to see."

He rubs his head as if trying to erase his pain and anger.

"We need to inform Kate's parents too. We could visit them on route?"

"No. I'll tell them. They deserve to hear it from me."

His gaze lowers, his face crestfallen.

"They think I failed her that night, at least I can be the one to tell them she's alive."

"If that's how you want to handle things Mr Rivendale, that's fine. You're her next of kin."

"I'll call them. They can meet us at the hospital. I need to be with my wife."

I don't understand why, but his words slit my stomach in half, my emotions pouring out tarnishing the perfect cream carpet.

* * *

Beverly is inconsolable, clinging hold of your frail hand as she examines your bludgeoned body and the wires protruding from your skeletal frame.

You're still unconscious; body absorbing fluids from the IV drip bag which hangs from the pole above your head. I hate to admit this, but every time that I see you, you look worse. The guilt is weighing me down like an anchor, pulling me to the depths of deep despair.

Black thread snakes across your skin binding your wounds and protruding in between the bruises, which have deepened in colour.

John is silent, but beneath his calm exterior I can tell that his blood is raging through every vein in his body. I see them pulsing on his temples. His face paints a picture of harrowing distress. Seeing both of his girls beaten and fighting for their lives will haunt him for the rest of his life. Dads always think they will protect their daughters at all costs, and not let anyone harm a single hair on their head.

Only, in real life, that never happens, people's daughters are beaten and murdered every day. He feels as though he's failed you too, I see it in his eyes. It's a look, and a feeling, that I'm far too familiar with.

Louise is perched on a plastic hospital chair against the turquoise curtains which flank your cubicle. She's not uttered a word to anyone and stares at her interlaced fingers. I study her; she appears traumatised by the state of you. Maybe it's like looking in a mirror, only your reflection is more damaged.

She feels culpable, knowing that she forced your hand, pushed you into this.

She was the one insistent on you working with us; she made you feel accountable for her attack. Had she not insisted that you go undercover, you probably wouldn't be here. I suspect she also feels guilty for her self-indulgent behaviour and for acting like a bitch toward you.

Perhaps it's also remorse. Her wounds have healed, but her heart hasn't. It's probably beyond repair.

I notice that she's lost weight since she was discharged from hospital. Her clothes hang off her frame and her face is sunken. To be honest she looks like the ghost of the woman she was before her attack. I didn't know her, but I've seen pictures. What I see before me now is a broken woman, floating around like a lifeless ghost trapped inside her ordeal, unable to escape.

That fucker has destroyed both of your lives with his twisted mind. I can't let him claim any more victims; not now, not ever. I will find him. That's a promise I plan on keeping.

Taylor looks thunderstruck observing your motionless body. His cheeks are milk white; eyes scarlet where he's been crying. He's stroking your hair; his other hand is wrapped around yours. He paints the picture of a loving husband. He adores you. I'm certain you share a loving relationship.

A pang of jealousy whips my heart. Jen and I were that close once; until I screwed up like I always do. I'm destined to be married to the force; my company will only ever be my colleagues and that's a sad future prospect.

It sounds crazy, but I wish I hadn't told them about you just yet. That way I would still be the one sitting there holding your hand; not him.

I know that's totally out of order and very odd behaviour considering I barely know you.

But somehow, I feel responsible for your welfare. I knew you were married, I wanted to get closer to you, even if it were just a friendship. It was never meant to be like this. I've ruined your life; I've ruined everything. You won't ever forgive me.

And maybe, you don't have to. Maybe that's what I need.

Perhaps, if I can catch the vile, pathetic excuse for a human being who is behind all this, then maybe, just maybe, I can learn to forgive myself.

# Chapter Fifty-Seven – Kate

*Thursday 6 January 2016. 11am*

Why is everyone around my bed? It's odd. I can hear you all talking about me. But none of you are speaking to me, if that makes any sense?

Will was talking to me earlier, or was it last night? I can't remember which. It was weird. He was holding my hand, which was extremely odd. Taylor wouldn't have liked that; he would have been jealous. Will kept telling me that I was safe now and promised that he would protect me. I'm safe from what? What do I need protecting from? Or who? I don't understand what's happening or where I am. Obviously, I'm in bed, but it's not my own bed. Has something happened to me, or is this one of those dreams that makes absolutely no sense at all?

Will's voice sounded soothing, yet sorrowful.

He kept apologising to me, saying that everything was his fault. I don't know what he's talking about. I quite liked him holding my hand, though I probably shouldn't admit to that. It reminded me of being a teenager going on my first date with Mark Timpson.

I remember my hand trembling as he held it and kissed me. I was so excited, like my heart was going to detonate inside my chest. I couldn't wait to tell my friend Sam. I haven't seen her in ages. Anyway, back to Will. He was holding my hand; I tried to squeeze his back, so that he knew I was OK. He stayed with me for a while, talking about some case and how he would make things right. Maybe he wants me to write a story about it.

Suddenly he freed my hand. He was talking to another man. They were discussing me saying that I was lucky. Why am I lucky? I tried to figure out what they were saying but then they both just left me here and disappeared.

I was alone for hours, just lying here, wherever here is. I'm not sure if he's back now, well I haven't heard his voice. I've only heard mum and dad. Mum is holding my hand now. Why is everyone holding my hand? I'm starting to freak out, worried that perhaps something seriously horrible has happened to me.

Surely, I'd know though, if it had, I'd be able to feel something; I'm numb, like I've a dead leg from sitting down too long. It's like I'm in a deep sleep and I can't find my way back to reality.

Where's Taylor? I haven't heard his voice.

Perhaps he's still in a mood with me. I hope not. I want to make things right between us; re-enter our perfect little bubble. I do love him despite everything we have been through this past year. I know that things have been difficult, but our Christmas together was amazing. It cemented us back together and set us back on our pathway of happiness.

Is it the New Year now? I don't remember what day it is.

What's that annoying bleeping sound? It's by my ear, irritating me. I want mum to turn it off. I don't know what it is but it's really getting on my nerves. Mum isn't listening; well she's not answering me back, which is odd. She never ignores me. Why can't she hear me? Maybe I've lost my voice? What the hell is going on? She's tucking me under a blanket; I'm swaddled like a baby. She's treating me like a child. I don't like this, I'm scared. Please mum, please dad, wake me up from this vivid nightmare and tell me everything is going to be all right.

# Chapter Fifty-Eight – DCI Beckley

*Thursday 6 January 2016. 10am*

Blue and white CSI suits are dispersed along Collum Lane placing yellow evidence markers around the damaged Red Ford Kuga.

Foster is knelt beside Shelton, both studying and capturing images of a giant blood pool at the vehicle's rear. You lost one hell of a lot of blood, it is no wonder you had to have a transfusion. I retrieve a neatly folded paper suit and blue shoe protectors from Tom Ford and quickly oblige to prevent contaminating the scene.

I step closer to the car; its roof has a hefty concave indentation and the cracked windscreen resembles a woven spider's web. There's also a deep depression on the bonnet presumably from where you hit the car.

Delaney is further to my right, scrutinising the surrounding brambles.

He is underneath the weighty branches of a mammoth Ash tree that overhangs the hedge, dipping low into the road. The team has been here for a couple of hours, documenting the scene.

Delaney is following a blood trail, trying to ascertain the direction from which you fled.

Jenkinson and the SFOs are poised in their van; I fear there's a potential firearms threat. Dr Harris told me that your feet were badly abraded having ran some distance. I didn't see them myself, your legs were swaddled. I understand that you're a capable runner, you could have been held captive miles away. We're searching for a needle in a haystack, but we will sew all the pieces together, Kate, I promise.

Delaney surveys the tarmac and the loose chippings that tore at your soles. He's dotting the bloody pathway with further evidence markers as he follows the trail, passing around potholes and twigs.

Your blood has darkened but remains visible. You must have been bleeding when you were running. It's good for us though, Kate; you have given us visible clues to follow.

Forensics can piece everything together and help the search teams work backwards and find his lair. The attacker would have felt powerless after losing you and had little time to clean up. We will find it, along with all the evidence we need. It's only a matter of time.

"Sir, over here," Delaney yells.

He's studying a piece of bloodied gold satin flapping ferociously in the wind.

"It looks like she fled into the road from this field."

I run over and eye the material, pierced by barbed wire. I feel his hands choking my throat as we get closer to the truth.

"It's Kate's. I've seen her nightdress; Foster bagged it earlier."

I try my hardest to pull my gaze from the sullied rag. All I can envisage is you running for your life, the wire piercing and slicing your skin as you continue onwards, desperate.

I shake my head to return my mind to its normal state. My stare lifts, examining two chrome gates smeared with blood. Beyond them my eyes capture varying shades of green, bursting from the leafy cornfield before us.

I don't need to get closer, I see flattened vegetation. Your bedraggled body is running, zig zagging toward me, you're mouth screaming. Your eyes are frantic, tears erupting and diluting your blood. I hear your snatched breath screaming my name, begging me to help you. I shut my eyes unable to endure the fear I see in yours. It's like I've been stabbed, then gutted with a fisherman's filleting knife.

* * *

White suits and the black bullet proof vests of the PolSA search teams stand shoulder to shoulder, conducting a straight-line method forensic search through the cornfield using wooden rakes.

Delaney holds back, collecting soil samples of the surrounding vegetation for potential evidence comparison. I follow them until we reach its boundary. Beyond it, I observe sweeping grassland, a patchwork quilt of greens in every direction. There's nothing here Kate. Just open emptiness. Where did you come from?

I'd hoped this was going to be simple, that we would have unearthed your prison before noon but it's 12.25pm and we've barely touched the surface of your escape route.

The only thing we can rely on is your bread crumb blood trail and scent, however minuscule. You must have been losing blood for quite some time. I'm unsure how you found the strength to keep running. I admire you; I honestly do, for having such fighting spirit.

We've been walking for 10-15 minutes. The field boundary seems to get further with every step and this appears a pointless task, with very little progress being achieved. But I can't think like that. The brisk sea air whips off the sand dunes at Sand Bay, slapping my cheeks, as we continue onwards looking for the answers I so desperately need.

Archer was correct, the killer chose an isolated location where your screams would never be heard.

The gap between us and the perimeter is closing in. We reach a muddy clearing and absorb the scene before us. Another field, double in size, shrouded with more trees and shrubs. My hopes are gradually fading.

Far in the distance, I notice a blot on the landscape; tucked in the corner and out of place within the green woodland. I focus my stare to the best of my ability. A flashback of your broken body, twisted, and bleeding haunts my mind. My heart pulverises to slush. I want to snare the evil bastard before he can kill again or returns to end what he's started with you.

I cross behind the horizontal line of CSIs and continue to finger through the wet grass blades. We trace our way slowly towards it ensuring we follow the evidence. There's a paper-thin slice of wood protruding from the ground. Half of it has snapped underfoot and is laced with blood. Beyond it, I see your footsteps. It's almost as if you're here again, showing us the way, leading us right to your place of captivity. They've been disturbed by rain but they're visible. We're getting close.

On closer inspection, I realise that the blot on the landscape is a timber clad shed with a red ridged metal roof. It's tiny, decrepit and its bramble contents overspill toward us. The surrounding ground is a mixture of twigs, leaves and mud. I follow the waterlogged pathway, with fresh tyre marks bursting from the mouth of a mud pool.

Foster is capturing images, Delaney ordering track impressions. They resemble thick, diagonal slash wounds.

A disused metal gate, similar in nature to the one we entered to gain access, rests on its side. It's perched at a 25-degree angle, squashing weed grass and nettles underneath. I take a closer inspection of the windowless shed. Brambles and blackberry bushes protrude like the wires on your body. It's clearly derelict, the wilderness taking over inside from floor to ceiling. I feel deflated; this isn't your cell. It's a shitty old abandoned shed that's been left to rot, in the same way he left his victims rotting under the railway tracks.

# Chapter Fifty-Nine – Kate

*Thursday 6 January 2016. Afternoon*

Mum has gone but Taylor is here. I can't believe it. Despite our fight, he does still care about me, after all.

Our fingers are interlaced; it feels warm and comforting in the same way it did when Will was holding it. Only this time it feels right.

Taylor's wedding band is cold to the touch against my skin. His other hand is running through my hair. It feels nice, though it's knotty and he's tugging a little too hard. He keeps saying that everything will be all right. I know it will be, we just suffered a blip through my careless drinking. I am stupid sometimes. Still, he's here now and that's all that matters.

Earlier, I could hear that unfamiliar male voice again. He was talking about good progress being made. It's deep, slightly husky and seductive.

None of Taylor's friends sound like that. I wonder who he is and why he's at my bedside. Why on earth are they talking about us making progress? It's no one else's business but ours. I need to wake up; this is one hell of a fucked-up dream.

Mum is back again. Her hand is resting on my opposite arm. She's pulling a blanket up over it. I'm relieved as there is a chill in the air. She's sobbing, muttering my name. Why is she crying? Have I done something wrong to upset her?

I don't think I have, except for the fall out with Taylor. But he's forgiven me now. He's here, so things must be OK? I feel bad that she's crying. I want to give her a hug but for some reason I can't move; maybe it's that heavy blanket weighing me down.

Oh my God, Louise is here. Mum just thanked her for a coffee. I thought that she hated me? I'd done something bad. I can remember that. I did something that really pissed her off. That's it, I'd upset her, not mum. Louise was hurt; I can picture her bruised face. It makes me feel sick. I'm sure I wasn't responsible for hurting her physically, but I know from the curdling feeling in my belly that I was involved in some way and that makes me sad.

I don't like this dream. It's more like a nightmare. I want to wake up snuggled against Taylor. I want it to be a Saturday morning, so we can lie in past 9am. I can have a long soak in a nice bubble bath, while inhaling the lush smell of bacon cooking as it wafts upstairs. That prospect is lovely.

The trouble is I'm getting a burning pain in my chest that's making me feel that the end of this nightmare is a long way off. I want to cry.

# Chapter Sixty – DCI Beckley

*Thursday 6 January 2016. 14.36pm*

I've been forced to abandon the search and leave everything with the PolSA search teams.

We have meticulously searched the surrounding crime scene for a couple of miles, yet we still haven't found where he held you prisoner.

I'm sorry. Though, I'm sure that we're getting close. You can't have run too far, not in the state you were in. Or maybe you did, I guess I don't know what you're capable of. Taylor says you're a keen runner, perhaps you ran a longer distance than I'd anticipated. Time will tell, I just need patience but mine is wearing paper thin.

I've returned to HQ for the press conference. I need to tell them about Charmaine, and about you.

I thought that the last press conference, about your disappearance, was the most intense one I'd delivered in my career but judging by the sheer number of reporters and TV crews outside, this will far surpass that.

I feel queasy, almost seasick and I'm sweating, despite it being a freezing January afternoon.

I've been tugging my elastic wristband almost hourly since your disappearance, but it doesn't work anymore. I've never felt more anxious. After this is all over I'm going to frequent Dr Patterson more regularly. I thought that I was getting over Toby Harroway's death but instead I feel guilt over you. I screwed up.

The press pack is hungry outside the foyer doors. They resemble a sea of wolves waiting to attack me and bite the flesh off my bones. I don't want to face them; they're going to ask me questions that I don't want to answer.

Information is being leaked. An insider is sharing knowledge about this case, which pisses me off. And that's something else I am going to deal with, as soon as I get time. And I'm going to come down on whoever is doing it like a ton of bricks.

The media probably already know Charmaine's identity and about you. They just need me to say it on the record, so it can't come back to haunt them if they publish or broadcast the information without their being an attributable source.

I wipe my brow and step through the circular glass atrium. Erratic camera flashes snap away as I approach the press stand. I observe a sweeping ocean of unfamiliar faces, all eyeing me, eagerly awaiting vital information about the investigation. It's like animals in a zoo, when the keeper steps into their cage carrying a bucket of food.

They are broadcasting live, too, so I need to ensure I appear cool, calm and collected; I hate seeing myself on TV. Still, I'm offering good news about you. Despite that being the news, they crave, deep down inside of me I know it won't be good enough. They want answers and his blood; I just can't give it to them yet.

"Good afternoon. I'm DCI Will Beckley, leading the investigation into the deaths of six Weston women, and the abduction of Kate Rivendale."

I scutinise the crowd seeing frantic fingers at work.

"I can confirm that the sixth victim, found in woodland in Kewstoke, on the 4th January, has now undergone a full autopsy and has been formally identified as Charmaine Morgan, a 24-year-old local woman. I would like to offer our deepest sympathies to her family. Due to the nature of her injuries and her cause of death, we believe that she was killed by the same perpetrator as Shelley Carter, Nicole Hall, Cheryl Gray, Hannah Green and Jesse Cooper."

"Isn't it true that this latest victim was pregnant at the time of her death?" A young reporter screeches.

I pause and inhale, infuriated that details regarding her pregnancy, have been leaked.

"Charmaine Morgan suffered a single stab wound to her chest and a brain hemorrhage caused by an incised wound to her ear, the result of which killed both Charmaine and her unborn baby."

As soon as the words roll off my tongue, their expressions morph to shock. Nausea creeps to my throat.

"This is an ongoing investigation and therefore it would be inappropriate to comment further, other than to say Charmaine's body was found in shrubbery off the coastal toll road. It is believed she was killed sometime between 11pm, on Friday 2$^{nd}$ January 2016, and 10am, on Saturday 3rd January 2016."

"Charmaine was last seen leaving her place of work, the Sandy Hotel, half a mile away, shortly before 11pm. We would appeal for anyone with information regarding her death, no matter how small, to come forward and contact us on Crimestoppers on 0800 555 111."

Hands are already wildly pointing trying to reel in my attention for questioning. I ignore them and continue.

"I would like to stress that significant progress is being made towards catching the person responsible for all these deaths. We are currently examining several high priority leads and can reassure you that every effort is being made to bring the killer to justice. We will leave no stone unturned until he is apprehended."

My stomach revolves, and the incessant camera flashes do nothing to repel my headache. I bite my lip in anticipation, preparing myself to tell them about you. They're going to hang me out to dry, as will Detective Chief Superintendent Harding. I'll deal with him later.

"I now turn the focus of this update to the abduction of Kate Rivendale, a 33-year-old local reporter. I can confirm that Kate has been found safe and well and is receiving the medical care she requires at Weston General Hospital. She has sustained significant injuries, but I am delighted to say that she's making good progress. Our thoughts are with Kate and her family at this difficult time. We wish her a speedy recovery."

I pause again to acknowledge and gasps and surprise on the faces of some of the journalists. They might be able to blame me for putting Kate in danger, but at least they won't be able to accuse me of being responsible for her death. I grasp a crumb of comfort at this thought.

"Kate had been assisting us with our enquiries at the time of her disappearance and we do have reason to believe she was abducted by the assailant responsible for the Millbrook Murders. Once Kate's condition is stable, we are certain she will share vital information with us which will assist this investigation considerably.

In the meantime, it would be inappropriate to comment any further, other than to thank everyone who has offered their assistance to date in searching for Kate."

Hands raise again, like children in a classroom desperate for permission to be excused. They wave, and stretch, as if they think the more effort they make, the more chance they have of me inviting their interrogation. I won't give them the pleasure.

"I would further like to reiterate our advice about women not walking out alone at night. Our previous warnings have been ignored, allowing the killer to take the life of four further women over the past few weeks. I am urging you, please, to not put yourselves in danger. The killer has expanded his killing zone, attacking women in other parts of Weston. Personal attack alarms are being issued as a safety precaution, free of charge; if you have not received one, please visit Weston Police Station reception."

I study their faces, full of scorn. It's not my fault that there's a psychopath out there killing innocent women. I'm not responsible for his actions and I won't be held accountable for their deaths. You, on the other hand, Kate, I do deserve to be held accountable for what you've endured. I know that it's my fault you were taken, and I will do what I can to make it up to you.

A fine misty rain emerges, landing like tiny beads on Marela Flynn's hair. She's a feisty little madam from the Weston Observer, always trying to impede our investigations. She looks the part; the jumped-up bitchy stereotype you see in ITV dramas. The arrogance she exudes beggars belief. She's flapping her hand at me. I offer a gentle nod to allow her questioning. She flicks her long hair away from her face, eager to have her shining moment in front of her peers.

"Would you care to comment on the nature of Kate Rivendale's injuries and can you tell us when, and how she was found?"

Her questions make my hairs stand on end. I hesitate, wondering if I should give them the full picture and decide I need to be honest.

"Kate managed to escape her abductor and was found in Collum Lane, a countryside road that runs toward The Priory. Unfortunately, as she fled, she was involved in a road traffic collision."

Marela's face offers no sympathy. I'm forming the impression that there's no love lost between you and her.

"So, despite a major police operation, you didn't actually find her, she escaped?"

Her eyes narrow, voice forceful.

"That is correct."

A skinny young guy to Marela's right, who's as tall as Lurch, interrupts.

"Have you identified the location where she was being held?"

"Extensive searches are currently under way and we are confident we will unearth where Kate was being held shortly. Once we have confirmed that location, forensic experts will work tirelessly to gather any associated evidence that will link the scene to her attacker. I am confident that we are close to making an arrest and will bring justice to all of his victims."

A balding older man in his sixties, with bushy eyebrows and a bulbous nose, catches my attention. He's wearing a black mac and brown brogues. He bears a faint resemblance to the character Gargamel.

"Do you have any words for the Millbrook murderer?"

I don't hesitate; words roll quickly off my tongue.

"We are closing the net on you. We are coming, and we will find you. You will be held accountable for the six young women you brutally murdered, as well as the unborn child. I will have justice for all of them, and for Kate Rivendale. Hand yourself in and make things easier for yourself. It's only a matter of time until we come knocking at your door."

# Chapter Sixty-One – DCI Beckley

*Thursday 6 January 2016. 16.15pm*

"We've located it." Jenkinson's tone is eager.

"We have found Kate's hostage site. Continuous tyre tracks and her blood led us straight to it."

I open my mouth to speak but my words are guillotined from my tongue.

"Sir?"

"Where is it?"

"An old tithe barn approximately half a mile from the shed you examined. It's totally isolated; abandoned for decades. Forensics found blood on a metal grate used as an escape route. There's blood inside too, and signs of restraint."

"I knew you wouldn't let me down. Send me the GPS coordinates."

My hands sweat profusely. I know you endured a horrific ordeal; in fact, I can't begin to imagine what he put you through. What I do know is that you're the key, you've unlocked this investigation and led us to the killer.

\* \* \*

The sky darkens as I negotiate the winding country road. It's unlit and eerie, my pathway ahead lit solely by my car headlights. It's going to be difficult for forensics to examine the crime scene, but I won't let the teams stop searching until they have combed every single inch of it.

He might think he's been clever evading detection but not for much longer. He fucked up, we have his tyre tracks and I'm going to get the motherfucker.

Floodlights illuminate the quarry stone barn. I step out of my car; the subzero temperature snaps at my ankles as I wade through the dark. The veins on my temples are thumping with adrenalin giving me a head ache. I pass under the cordon and follow the SOCOS. Their blue shoe protectors tread carefully inside; each officer carrying evidence bags.

I suit up and enter his lair. Tears swell, overwhelmed. I imagine you trapped here, cold, alone and frightened for your life. The vision makes me miserable.

Archer, Delaney and Foster occupy the scene documenting your torture chamber. I spot a pile of clear bio-hazard evidence bags. The yellow strips on their outer surface glow in the light. Delaney completes an exhibit label on a further package and places it in the outer pouch. I've no idea what he's bagged but I feel a sense of hope that it could be vital evidence linking him to you.

A pipe drips tarnished water near to where Tom Ford is shining a white light torch on to the ground. He's moving it back and forth in slow motion, scrutinising the surface. I watch him bend to his knees, closely examining a substance. Shelton joins him, removes her mouth protector and gives me her eyes. I can read her face.

"Sir, I've found traces of semen."

My guts feel like they've been wrenched out. Kate, I'm so sorry.

"It's only a small trace but it could be enough to extract a sample for DNA analysis." Shelton smiles reassuringly, as if to say, we've fucking got him.

"Where did Kate escape?" I probe, changing the subject.

Shelton turns and directs me to a hay bale stack behind her. My eyes follow blood spots and bloody marks smearing the wall. I begin my ascent and observe a tiny chamber below. Saddle racks hang from the walls. It's an old stable cluttered with wooden planks and junk. I inhale the unpleasant stench of your blood and urine. I imagine the torment you endured as his prisoner. I've never felt so incensed. I am sorry that I allowed this to happen to you.

"DCI Beckley," Wakeman yells, tone urgent.

He's at the arched entrance, resting his heavy frame against the oak door, face panicked. I feel the blade of a knife twist in my gut again, skinning my insides.

"What is it?"

"Kate, she's in pulseless VT again sir. Resus teams are working on her."

My body is rooted to the spot; heart shredded like an egg slicer. I can't lose you Kate, not now. We need you. You found the strength to escape from this hell-hole, come on, Kate, dig just a little deeper, find just a little more, and hold on!

"How long has she been like that?"

"I don't know, I just took the call."

"Fuck," I yell.

Delaney and Shelton both look perplexed. My mind is floating but my hollow legs are running, tumbling down the hay to get to you. I pound through mud, duck under the police tape and screech away. This can't be the end.

# Chapter Sixty-Two – DCI Beckley

*Thursday 6 January 2016. 17.26pm*

On arrival Dr Harris informed me that you pulled through again and are on ICU. Being here seems strange. I keep imagining you staring back at me from the other end of the corridor, like the day I caught you sniffing around for information on Hannah Green.

You looked so petrified, yet adorable. You were blushing, clearly devastated that you had been caught in the act. I knew that you were in search of the truth. But standing in the doorway now, the canvas painted before me is somewhat different. I barely recognise you. Your body better resembles a decomposing corpse.

I feel like I'm stuck in the most horrific nightmare I've ever had and cannot wake up. Your body is motionless, aside from your chest very gently rising and falling as the nasal cannula discharges oxygen through your nostrils.

You're alone; there's no sign of Taylor or your parents.

Every time I look at your face guilt spreads throughout my blood like a deadly virus poisoning me and snatching my last breath. I deserve to be in that bed and if it were possible to swap places with you, I do it in a heartbeat.

I'd do anything to turn the clock back and prevent this from ever happening to you, but I can't. You have a life to live, a husband, a loving family, a career. I have nothing; only the force and that will soon be a distant memory when I'm fired.

That is my fate. I understand that, and I must face repercussions for my actions. I will hold my hands up and I'll resign; if necessary. My life couldn't get any worse than it is. There is nothing left for me anymore.

Your hand feels colder than the last time I held it. I'm worried that your hypothermia may have worsened, though Dr Harris knows what he's doing; he's saved you twice now and brought you back from the brink of death.

I wonder if you're aware of what's happening to you. It is better that you don't know but the selfish side of me wants you to, so that you know I am here and that I'm so very sorry.

I keep imagining how things could have panned out differently. If only I'd never taken your telephone call and agreed to work with you. But I saw a passion in you Kate, I wanted to help you. I don't like that other reporter, Marela. You, on the other hand, are assertive and sweet. I wanted to kick start your career; help propel you into the spotlight, so you'd be headhunted by the nationals. You deserve it. I've followed your stories. You always made me laugh with the exclusives that you pulled out of the bag; Copping Off and The Dogging Copper. My story is not quite as exciting. If you wrote about me, it would read like an obituary, or a scandal involving police failures.

"Kate, it's Will. I know that I am probably the last person that you want to see but I want you to know that you've helped us. We worked backwards from the crash site. You're one hell of a runner, you ran some distance. We found the barn where he held you."

Your eyelids are moving; hand twitching. You can hear me. I'm certain of it.

"We know that he kept you there as his prisoner. Forensics are combing the scene, gathering every trace of evidence we need to nail him. I'm going to catch him Kate. I won't let you down this time around."

You're blinking; grip suddenly fierce around my fingers. I don't know whether to keep talking.

"Dr Harris!" I yell. I yank the bedside device and press the nurse call button.

"It's OK, Kate. I'm here and you're safe. No one can hurt you."

Nurse Campbell and Dr Harris, rush in. I prise your hand away and step back, granting them access to your bedside.

"I think she's regaining consciousness." My hands tremble, watching your eyelids flicker. You're murmuring, trying to speak. Come on Kate, you can do this.

Fuck, what are you doing? Your hands are frantic, grappling at the wires on your chest trying to dislodge your breathing tube. Don't do that, please, Kate, no. You're going to hurt yourself. Shit, you're in a state of panic; you don't know what the hell you're doing. Your eyes fire open; petrified pupils darting around the room, arms and legs kicking out frantically with distress.

"Kate, calm down. It's OK you're safe. My name is Dr Harris, you're at Weston General Hospital."

Your head twists from side to side, eyes trying to focus on your surroundings. You're dazed and confused; in a state of shock or panic.

"Please, stop struggling Kate, the wires and tubes are to monitor and help you. Please calm down and leave them alone," Harris begs, gently touching your hand.

I watch in horror as your eyes roll into the back of your head. Your bony hand falls limp on your thigh as you slip back out of consciousness. It's as if I have just watched you die, right in front of me.

# Chapter Sixty-Three – Kate

*Thursday 6 January 2016. 19.36pm*

I had the weirdest dream. I was in bed and randomly Will was beside me holding my hand. That's the second dream I've had about him doing that to me.

It's weird and wrong in so many ways, but it was comforting, and I enjoyed his touch. He was talking to me and said something that frightened me. I can't remember what it was, but his words terrified me, and I woke up. Only, I didn't know where I was.

There were bright lights and they stung my eyes, so I closed them again. Now, I'm sleeping or daydreaming again, I'm not quite sure which.

I'm wondering what on earth he said to make me so afraid. I don't know why I'm worrying really, this is all just a messed-up dream after all. I'll soon wake up properly and I won't remember any of it.

* * *

Every time he closed his eyes he recalled the rush he felt as Kate wept with fear. This one wasn't Kate, but she was the next best thing, and he craved fresh meat to take the edge off.

She was pretty; about 24, with blonde curls to her waist and full, meaty breasts. He stood in the shadows watching her outside the university campus flirting with two men. She was asking for it, dressed in a short skirt and boots, behaving seductively.

She wanted it; and he was going to give it to her, and then kill her.

He waited patiently, closely following her heels as she ambled slowly toward the bus shelter, fiddling on her mobile.

His hand muffled her screams. He yanked her by her hair into the bushes, so they could be alone. She fought his grip but a vicious kick immobilised her.

He flipped her onto her back, enjoying the terror etched across her sweet face. A gash on her temple seeped blood. She laid cowering beneath him; his eyes hungry and menacing. Tears fell and collided with the bloodstain, cascading along her cheek. Her hands grappled the ground, as his fists pummeled her face.

His gloved palm slid across her breast and down her ribcage to her pelvis. He yanked her hair backwards, tilting her head to expose her throat, and then reached for his blade. It glistened in the moonlight; tip poised against her neck as he watched her breasts rise and fall.

He felt so aroused as the knife penetrated her flesh and her soul drained away. He tossed aside her lifeless body and his deadly footsteps disappeared into the darkness.

# Chapter Sixty-Four – DCI Beckley

*Friday 7 January 2016. 7am*

It's been 12 hours since you regained consciousness. Taylor and your parents look deflated. You've had countless visitors; you're clearly well-loved.

Dawn was here earlier with her shifty husband and that odd fella, Todd. She brought you pink roses and lilies. I heard her telling you that they were your favourite, which strangely made me feel sad, listening about your favourite things; it made me realise that I don't know you at all.

I thought I did but you're a stranger to me really, a mere acquaintance I crossed paths with at a specific point in time. Had that never happened, you would have avoided all this pain and suffering. I am truly sorry for that.

I never meant for any of this to happen. It's not something I could have envisaged, yet at the same time I should have better ensured your safety. The whole of your bedside is adorned with bouquets. Ryan brought some too, a cheap flimsy bunch; the type you buy on a petrol forecourt. I admit I've bought plenty of those in my time.

Taylor's, on the other hand are huge, a bouquet bursting with white lilies, pink roses and pink Gerberas, encased in pink tissue paper, clear cellophane and tied with a bow.

Ryan and Taylor were at your bedside for ages, both clutched your hands. Though when I caught Ryan's eye, he coiled and dropped your hand, alarmed. It sent a shiver through me; I saw a glimmer of deceit and I didn't much like it.

Was there some aspect of your life that we missed?

I still can't shake that image from my mind. It was the look in his eyes. I need Wakeman to do a background check on him. Something doesn't feel right.

I know that I held your hand, but I wanted you to know that I was with you, that I was sorry and that you were safe. His touch seemed inappropriate, especially with your husband sitting opposite. Shit, was the baby not even Taylor's, was it Ryan's? Is that why you kept your pregnancy s secret from your husband? Sordid theories roam my brain. Did Ryan try to kill you because he thought you aborted his baby?

If he was responsible for your abduction, he wouldn't have the balls to come and sit with you, would he? I feel a panic attack coming on. I need to lock your visitors down, restrict it to only your parents and Taylor for your own safety. Everyone's a suspect.

Your mum is with you now, clutching a kidney-shaped cardboard bowl. She's dipping cotton balls into it, squeezing out the water and wiping your face to remove bloodstains.

"Are you OK?" I whisper.

Her eyes are desolate, as she turns from her daughter and glances at me.

"I can't bear to see her looking this way. She doesn't look like my Kate."

The gentle pressure causes water droplets to ooze from the padded bud, along your bruised cheek and trickle onto your pillow.

"Just leave it, love," John blurts.

"No. I want to clean her up, she can't see herself looking like this when she wakes up."

I understand. I, too, want to clean her face. I would if I could. The tension mounts in the air. I quietly slip away, allowing you to be with your family.

\* \* \*

I've not slept for approximately 46 hours. My eyes sting, staring at the bloodied naked corpse before me; eyes locked with terror transfixed upon the clouds.

Tiffany Myres aged 24; his latest victim spread dead on the Millbrook Estate fringe. Only this time, her body is staged. Her stomach is smeared with blood and turning purple with rigor mortis. Seven of her fingers are severed. We know that she's one of his kills. Shelton believes she was sexually assaulted, too, unlike the others.

She swabs her inner thigh and seals a fluid sample in an air tight vial. Was this punishment for letting you get away? Tiffany is the spitting image of you. Same slim build, neat curls. Only she's dead, not you. You traded your life for hers. Not intentionally, I'm not saying that or attributing any blame. What I'm suggesting is he's vented his anger for allowing you to slip away and deviate from his plan.

I thought that your escape might frighten him, might force him to go into hiding, to lie-low. But no, it seemed to inflame him, to re-ignite whatever it is that made him start doing this in the first place.

Delaney is bagging bloodstained clothing into biohazard bags. There are scratches on the victim's hips. "Have you bagged her knickers?"

"No, they aren't here."

He looks at me wide-eyed.

"Do you think he's taken them as another trophy?"

"It's the most probable explanation."

"What evidence has been recovered?"

Delaney finishes sealing the bag in his hands and signs the evidence label to ensure chain of custody.

"Nothing substantial. He's punctured her ear. I expect we'll find traces of the casein yarn on closer inspection."

"With regards to Charmaine, I've sent you greater detail images of the bruising on her stomach. It's from a ring and it's an unusual. You should be able to identify it and link it to the killer."

"What about Kate's crime scene? Are there any results yet?"

"We're waiting for the blood and semen results to come back from the lab. The restraint rope is still being examined for DNA. We also took shoe impressions outside the barn; killer must have fled in a hurry."

"What about the tyre tracks?"

"We can't give you a make or a model, they're too generic."

"Shit."

"But if you find the car, we can match the tread and place him at the scene."

\* \* \*

*Friday 7 January 2016. 11.52am*

Greensdale and Kent are in the Incident Room discussing the case. Images of Tiffany's body have now joined the corpse library on the wall. It's already stored in my mind with the other souls.

The poor girl's dignity was stripped when he left her lying there bare. What a sick bastard. I hate seeing them like that, fully exposed for everyone's eyes to pore over.

Not that anyone would be aroused by a naked corpse, it's just the fact that their privacy is invaded.

Shelton's certain that he assaulted her given the swabs she took. I pray to God that he didn't touch you. The thought is repulsive.

Images of the bruising on Charmaine's stomach also adorn the evidence wall. Intel 24 officers are trying to search for an exact image match and find a replica piece of jewellery, so that we can send an image to the press and jewellery shops.

It's our best way of linking him to Charmaine's body.

We're getting closer. I know he's taken another innocent life but bit by bit he's coming unstuck, as Archer insinuated he would. He's leaving crumbs, and those crumbs make for a recipe of success.

Delaney and Shelton will give us what we need to nail him of that I'm certain and when they do, I'm coming for him, like a bat out of hell.

# Chapter Sixty-Five – Kate

*Friday 7 January 2016. 20.11pm*

I can't breathe, I'm retching. There are pipes lodged in my throat. The room is swirling, I can't focus or see anything clearly. Where am I? Oh, God what's he done to me now? Is this a torture device?

I pull the tube harder, trying to remove it from my throat, and tug at a wire embedded in my hand. Oh shit. What have I done? Blood is squirting everywhere.

I blink erratically, trying to correct my vision. My heart strikes my chest; afraid. My entire body hurts; my head feels like it's been struck with a crow bar. Hands are on me weighing me down, restraining me. Oh, please no, not again.

"Kate, I'm Dr Benjamin Harris. Please try and stay calm. You're at Weston General Hospital. No one is going to harm you."

My head relaxes, sinking back into the pillow. My eyes follow the voice; it's calming. I recognise it. I've heard it before; in my dreams. My eyes focus on his face. He smiles; a wave of relief floods my blood. His face is kind with faint dimples either side of his pearly smile, which is striking against his olive skin and dark hair. His eyes fix on mine; their green and blue tones glisten.

I know I'm free and safe with him.

His lips remain fixed in a smile.

"Welcome back. Try and stay calm, OK?"

I nod my head slowly. It hurts, sending a spasm down my back. Someone is applying pressure to my hand, trying to stem the bleeding. I didn't mean to do that, I panicked. He removes the tube from my throat; I'm almost sick in the process.

"You've sustained some significant injuries, and we're treating you for those. This tiny plastic tube under your nose is to help you to breathe. Keep it there."

"OK." I inhale deeply, drawing its contents deep within.

He pours a glass of water, inserts a straw and places it between my swollen lips.

"Take a sip," he insists. I obey him and gulp the contents; mouth starved of hydration. I keep sucking until it's gone and eject the straw with my tongue, the under-surface running over chapped, flaky skin.

I must be frowning; he senses my confusion.

"Kate, you were involved in a road traffic collision. Do you remember anything?"

"No."

"OK. It's not important, we need to focus on getting you better. Are you in any pain?"

I nod again. I want to scream out, the pain is so bad, but I can't muster the energy to utter a sentence. I close my eyes, absorb the silence and search my mind for answers. A memory jabs me; a flashback of me sprinting into darkness, running for my life. My body is trembling; I'm backing away. I draw my knees to my chest under the sheets, protecting me from him. His hand touches my arm. I flip out thrashing my arms and legs wildly, kicking and punching to get away from him.

"Kate, stop it. You're safe. I told you, I'm Dr Harris. You're safe now. I'm here to help."

The words slowly sink in and my arms and legs fall limp on the bed. I'm dazed and confused. My head hurts so much that I want to cry.

"I'm going to administer some morphine to lessen your pain, OK?"

"OK."

My memories slowly resurface, remembering that I was abducted, and I escaped. I hurt myself in the process. All I cared about was getting away, no matter what the consequences. I had to get away from him; that mask. He was going to kill me like the others. Oh, God, that mask! That horrible mask.

I've been studying the machines attached to my body and the vast sea of flowers at my bedside. I want to remember everything that happened, but I fear my memories will destroy me.

Maybe I'm better off not knowing all the intricate details. What I don't know can't hurt me, right? And I'm already hurting enough, I don't want any more pain. Right now, all I do know is that I was held somewhere and escaped.

Another memory flashes; I'm snapping restraints. I wiggle my nose, remembering how my face smashed against the wall. Every muscle in my face hurts.

Something bad happened; something far too wicked to think about but I'm alive. I beat him; he lost the game and soon it will be over.

\* \* \*

Dr Harris accompanies DCI Beckley into the room. He's beside me, head bowed, eyes on the floor; he can't look at me. God, I must look ugly. Is it that, or because he feels too guilty to look me in the eye? I suspect it's both.

"Kate I'm so sorry," he whispers.

I don't know whether to cry or shout. I'm furious because he's partly to blame. He promised he would keep me safe, he didn't. I don't know what day it is or how long I was gone. All I know is that my body hurts, and my memories will hurt a hell of a lot more when they eventually come back.

I don't want to remember; I can't think about what he did to me. He kept drugging me, everything's a blur.

"I know that I'm probably the last person you want to see Kate, but I wanted to see you. I had to know you were OK. I'm at fault and I hold my hands up for not giving you better protection. I expect you think my assurances mean nothing, but I promise you, Kate, I'm going to get him for what's he's done to you. He won't get away with it, even if I spend the rest of my life hunting him down. I won't rest until he's behind bars."

His hands tremble; face sullen. He looks awful, as though he hasn't slept in weeks. His eyes mimic those of a frightened puppy. I believe his words are sincere. I did blame him. I remember that. I felt so angry that I'd been taken. I'd promised myself when I came face to face with him that I'd look him in the eye, and make sure he knew exactly how hurt and angry I feel.

But now, after everything I've endured, I don't have the energy to hold a grudge. And he looks as if he's suffered enough.

"I was helping you, wasn't I?" I breathe.

"Yes. You were undercover, part of a sting operation to help us catch the Millbrook murderer. We had every reason to believe he was following you, after what happened to your sister."

A tear falls over my lashes, his words cut deeper than a knife. Images of Louise's battered face conjure in my mind. I knew something had happened to her. I dreamt it. That's why she was so mad at me. I must resemble her now; broken and unfixable.

Will reaches forward and wipes my bruised cheek with his fingers. I flinch at his touch feeling a sharp pain burn my face. He withdraws his hand quickly and apologises, taking a deep breath.

"I'm going to be straight with you."

I inch forward, paying attention.

"He took you, held you captive."

"I know."

"You have to remember exactly what happened. Who was he?"

"I can't."

He places his hand on mine.

"Please try, it's the only way I can get him."

"Can I have a moment, DCI Beckley?" Dr Harris asks.

The duo stare at each other in a macho standoff.

"Sure."

I observe them in the corridor. I can't understand what they're saying; I only hear raised voices. I feel violated. How can I ever rebuild by life when he's still out there? He's going to hunt me down and kill me. I know it. It is just a matter of time and the clock is already ticking.

## Chapter Sixty-Six – DCI Beckley

"Kate's clearly traumatised and her memory is blocked. I did warn you this could happen," Harris blurts.

"Will she remember anything?

"It's hard to say. Often, victims of such abuse don't want to remember, the thought is too disturbing and so they purposely lock it away for their own protection."

"The question is, will you allow me to help her to remember?" I probe. "Kate is the key to this investigation. We believe her attacker has killed seven women."

"I understand that, but she's in deep shock, she needs time and patience."

"We don't have time."

Harris ponders, pacing the corridor; fingertips rubbing his bearded chin.

"I'll allow you to question her a little further, but if she shows any signs of distress, you're out, understand? Kate's welfare is my priority."

We step back inside. Kate looks bewildered and pissed off. I sit beside her, studying her bludgeoned face. She's barely recognisable; it hurts.

"I'd like to try something on you, a cognitive interview technique. It will help me to take you back to the scene to describe him, what he did and recall sounds and smells."

"I don't want to go back there, aren't you listening?" She answers testily, eyes full of scorn.

I know I fucked up, but I must push her. It's the only way I can get to him.

"It would just be the two of us talking. Dr Harris can stay."

He's stood with his arms folded across his chest. Kate eyes Harris, who offers a smile.

"He can stay," she falters, appearing more relaxed.

"This could help you to remember something about him, something incriminating. We've already found where he kept you."

Her eyes widen demanding answers.

"Where?"

"It was an old barn near to The Priory."

I can see by her expression that she's picturing it in her head. I explain to Kate everything about cognitive interviewing and how she needs to be calm. She closes her eyes and looks surprisingly peaceful, given her ordeal, and her understandable reluctance to want to re-live what she has been through.

I tell her that I'm going to take her back to that night, so she can tell me what happened. I also inform her that while it may be upsetting, I'll try not to hurt her any more.

"If something is scaring you, lift your left hand. If you need more time or want me to slow down, lift your right hand."

After a few minutes, Kate appears relaxed. I hope I can help her remember the suppressed memories. Harris looks very uncomfortable. He's worried that this might set you back. But I promise I'll take this slowly. I don't want to hurt you; you've been through enough. All I want is for you to remember something that is of key importance, something that can identify him.

"You are at home and there is a man. Can you see his face?"

"No, he's wearing a mask."

"What happened to you Kate?"

"He's in my bed, pinning me down. I can't fight him; he's too strong."

A tear leaks from the corner of her eye.

"It's OK Kate, I'm here.

"A needle is coming toward me. He's too strong, I can't fight him. It jabs me."

"He took you somewhere while you were unconscious. But you're awake now, what do you see?"

"It's cold." She inadvertently pulls the blanket over her chest. Tears snake her grazed, puffed cheeks and soak into her hospital gown.

"It's all right to feel scared, anyone in your shoes would feel the same, but I'm here. He's not going to hurt you. Breathe deeply."

She visibly relaxes again.

"Tell me what you see."

Her chest is beginning to rise and fall; her breathing quickening.

"It's dark. I can't move. My hands are tied. I'm scared."

Her head tosses from side to side; trying to shake the memory away.

"Kate you're safe, he can't hurt you. Stay still."

She lies still, resting her head deeper into the pillow. I pause and allow her time to think.

Her memories return gradually; she remembers hearing his tyres on the gravel, his boots thudding the floor and splashing through water, branches snapping under foot.

"Can you describe those boots?"

"They're brown with laces, around a size 8."

"That's good, Kate. Well done. What else is he wearing?"

"Jeans, a white T-shirt and jacket."

"Does he have any rings on his fingers?"

"He has blue gloves on, I can't see any rings. He's white."

"Are you certain?"

"Yes, I see a patch of skin on his neck."

That's great Kate, you're doing really well."

"He's coming for me."

Her left hand starts to rise.

"It's OK to feel scared. Breathe deeply."

"Do you know who he is, Kate?"

"No. He's wearing a mask!"

"What does he say?"

"Nothing. He doesn't speak, just stares. His eyes are black and sinister, like nothing I've seen before."

Her forehead furrows, eyes scrunch. She's traumatised by the events.

"It's OK. I'm here."

"He's standing in front of me, I lash out trying to kick him and keep him at bay."

She breaks down, sobbing.

"I don't want him to touch me."

I take her hand and squeeze it gently, reassuringly.

"He can't hurt you now, Kate. He'll never hurt you again. Try and stay calm. I'm here. What is he doing now?"

"He's smoking. I smell menthol cigarettes."

"He's finished it now Kate, what's happening?"

"Oh God, he's coming, I hear his boots. He's dragging me by my hair."

Her hands shield her head. Sweat beads layer her temples. She's panicking.

"It's OK, he can't hurt you."

"His hands are on me. I want him to stop."

Rage spreads through my bones. I feel hatred. "He's given me water, but I feel woozy; he's drugged it."

Her tears morph to howls.

"That's more than enough, DCI Beckley," Harris interrupts.

I ignore his remark. I know I should stop, but I need Kate to remember. She's already told me so much. She really is so strong. I just need to push her a little further.

"When you woke up, what do you remember?"

"I broke the restraints and found a way out."

"What do you see?"

"It's dark, blackness stretching for miles. I'm running through it. It is cold, my legs are heavy. I hear his engine; the mud entraps me pulling me down."

Her face is contorted by fear and distress re-living the ordeal. Harris is fuming, his teeth are clenched but he allows me to continue with my line of questioning. He has to prioritise Kate's welfare, of course. But even he can sense that there's the chance of the biggest breakthrough yet in this case; a chance to end these killings.

"His headlights are bright, stinging my eyes. I get up and run. Branches snap in my face. There's a gunshot."

"No, it wasn't a gun, Kate. He's not shooting at you."

"Where are you now?"

"In the road; the tarmac hurts my feet. I'm running toward the light. I can't go back. He's coming for me. He's going to kill me."

Her body is trembling. She cups her hands over her face, howling into her palms.

"That's enough," Harris orders.

"You've done great, Kate, you really have. You are so very, very, brave. Thank you."

She reopens her watery eyes; gaze fixed on the drip attached to her frail hand. She can't look at me. I feel utter remorse for putting her through that.

# Chapter Sixty-Seven – Kate

*Friday 7 January 2016. 22.11pm*

I should feel safe, but I don't, not even in the slightest. I'm fearful that he could track me down and kill me at any minute and I'm dreading facing Taylor.

The last time we saw each other I was shit-faced. We rowed and then I was taken. I was cruel to him. I didn't mean for us to argue, I was merely trying to drink away my anguish. I'd do anything for a glass of wine now, just one to diminish my nerves.

I'm not sure if Taylor's forgiven me yet or if he ever will. I've damaged us, just when our relationship was working again. He'll blame me; say that it was my own fault for getting too involved with the operation. He did warn me, after all. I never do listen, do I?

My hands tremor watching Taylor and Dr Harris through the glass; mum and dad follow closely behind. Mum is sobbing into a crumpled tissue; dad's head is hung low. Maybe they still hate me, too. Mum had taken Louise's side after all; she was the one who told me to leave the hospital.

I remember it all now. Everything is coming back to me. They were all so angry with me, they blamed me.

I don't want to see anyone, I can't face them. The thought of another lecture is not appealing, and I know that if they kick off and rant at me, then it's going to get heated. I've been through enough shit; I won't and can't take any more.

"Hey sleepyhead," Taylor smiles, planting a gentle kiss on my forehead.

His eyes are sincere; he clutches my hand tightly, warming it between his palms. My anxiety diminishes; a wave of affection comforts me.

"You have no idea how good it is to see you awake, I thought I was going to lose you. I thought I already had."

Tears teem from his eyes. I feel my own tears start to swell, as I'm overwhelmed by so many emotions. Sorrow, guilt and, above it all, such incredible relief; he doesn't hate me!

"I'm sorry."

I've no other words.

"Kate it's not your fault."

"I'm sorry for fighting."

"That's history, baby, it doesn't matter. I have you back, that's all that counts. I love you so much."

"I love you, too."

Mum and dad join us. Dad looks grief stricken, as if he's attending a funeral. Witnessing both of his daughters beaten has taken its toll. His face is gaunt; eyes bloodshot, the vessels swamped with pain and hurt. I smile, trying to ease his suffering.

"I'm OK, Dad."

He and mum wrap their arms around me. It hurts but I remain silent, letting them comfort me. I want them to comfort me.

"I'm sorry, Kate," mum whispers.

Her tears drip on to my pillow sullying the surface with mascara. Taylor retreats. But I don't want him to move away from me.

There's an awkward silence and a clear uncomfortable atmosphere between my parents and my husband. They blame him, I know they do. Dad would have condemned Taylor for not protecting his little girl, that much I do know.

I hope that I can prove to dad that none of this was Taylor's fault. I know that dad does not offer forgiveness easily; I'm his baby girl after all. But the last thing I need is another rift. I could not cope, I want everything to go back to normal.

"Is it bad?" I ask. Mum doesn't answer.

I'm frowning, my head hurts. I'm trying to gauge her expression. "What is it?"

Her face slips avoiding eye contact. "Mum tell me what it is."

She lifts her head noting the urgency in my tone. Her eyes lock on mine as they burst their banks. I grapple at my face, fumbling my fingers over my swollen cheekbones. I paw at crusting scratches. I move to my head, fingering though my hair. I touch something cold, clammy.

"What's that?"

I'm starting to freak out, and I feel scared.

Everyone is staring, no one will answer me. They're making me angry. I only want the truth. Oh, please don't let me be disfigured.

"Get me a mirror," I demand.

"I don't think that's a good idea, love," mum says weakly.

"Why?"

"Your face is bruised and scratched. Give it a day or two."

"What's happened to my hair? Please let me see."

Mum finally reaches into her bag, and with hesitation plucks out a compact mirror. She's crying. I stare at my reflection; shock and violence mar my features. A bald patch exposes my crown. I slam my eyes shut, shielding me from the creature that's staring back at me. I can't open them; I don't want to face my reflection, or anyone else. Maybe I am going to have to wear a mask. Like he did. The bastard who did this to me.

# Chapter Sixty-Eight – DCI Beckley

*Saturday 8 January 2016. Midday*

Wakeman and I are in my office discussing case developments. The media is aware of the latest victim; film crews were at the scene boundary, capturing footage of the forensic searches.

I've returned from the Riverside Centre, having witnessed yet another autopsy. There was bruising to her thighs, and evidence that she had been sexually violated, which is disturbing. He's changing his MO.

Archer and Shelton discussed his change in behaviour. Archer believes we're looking at an Anger Retaliatory Killer, who is crossing the threshold, expressing signs of an Anger Excitation Killer on the latest victim.

He's always asserted his masculinity over his victims through excessive violence. His primary focus is to inflict pain and terror for his own sexual gratification. It's the only way he can bring relief to his past or whatever the issue it is, that's spurring him to act the way he is.

He resents how life has treated him and feels compelled to kill. Now, having lost Kate, he's fueled with increased rage against women. Archer claims that's why Tiffany was left in a state of undress. He wanted to degrade and punish her.

"It could be a copycat?" Wakeman suggests.

"No, it's him. Everything was identical, aside from the body staging and sexual assault. Her fingers were severed, she suffered a single stab wound and her ear was also pierced with a tool from his murder kit. We're just fortunate it's not Kate's body in the mortuary."

"The press is gathered outside."

"I'm fully aware."

"They're also surrounding the hospital, trying to get access to Kate."

"That can't happen! The visiting stipulations are to remain in place. She is to have no contact with anyone other than her parents and Taylor. I won't be making the same mistake twice."

"You think he's coming to finish the job?" Wakeman probes.

"Yes, that's something that both Archer and I agree on. It's only a matter of time. He won't want her divulging anything she knows; not if he wants to get away with his crimes. I've already briefed her protection detail. Everyone is aware of the medical staff undertaking Kate's care. I have stressed to Dr Harris that this cannot alter, not without my prior consent. The killer's clearly intelligent. I wouldn't put it past him to feign a fake employee identity and try to get to her while she lies recovering."

"Results are back from the lab from Kate's bedding."

I feel a pang of hope, until Wakeman shrugs his shoulders.

"No semen was present only hair, which matches Kate's DNA."

It is just as I suspected. Of course, I'm relieved that no semen was recovered. The thought of him raping her in her own bed is absolutely repellent. But I fear, given the samples extracted in the barn and what he's done to Tiffany, that he may still have sexually assaulted Kate at some point. The thought of hearing her say those words, when she remembers, is unbearable.

Hopefully she'll block that particular memory away. I shouldn't push her any more. It's best she doesn't know the full extent of her ordeal. She's suffered enough.

\* \* \*

*Saturday 8 January 2016. 16.00pm*

The full media glare is upon me outside Weston Station. It's freezing, dusk looming. Cameras flash as I approach the microphones.

"I'm DCI Beckley, leading the investigation into the Millbrook Murders. I can confirm that a 23-year-old local woman, identified as Tiffany Myres, was killed near the university campus on the fringe of the Millbrook Estate. It is believed she was killed sometime between 10pm, on Thursday the 6th January and 9.30am on Friday the 8th January."

I pause gripping my statement nervously.

"We are investigating her death in connection with the six other women who were killed on the Millbrook estate and other areas across Weston. We believe Miss Myres, a university student, at the Broaden Campus, was killed by the same person who is responsible for the deaths of Nicole Hall, Cheryl Gray, Jesse Cooper, Shelley Carter, Hannah Green and Charmaine Morgan, and Charmaine's unborn child. At this stage, we are exhausting several lines of enquiry, and we are confident that the net is closing on this evil killer and that we WILL bring him to justice."

"Our thoughts are with Tiffany's family; who have asked for their privacy to be respected at this incredibly distressing time. We will continue to offer support to them and to all the affected families, as this investigation progresses. In the meantime, I urge all women to be on their guard until the suspect is apprehended. He has taken enough lives. Please be sensible, do not allow him the opportunity to take any more. As soon as I can update you further, I will do so. I assure you the net is closing in and we will bring an end to this killing spree."

The reporters surge forward waving their hands, desperately seeking more answers but I honestly don't have them.

I need the lab results for the blood, semen and the rope that were recovered in the barn to come back.

Why does everything take so long? I can't stand here and tell the press that we are still no closer to finding the killer. That will only cause further alarm and panic in the town.

I just want this to be over with. It's draining every ounce of energy that I have. I wish I was a fighter like Kate, but this case is pulling me under. I feel like I'm drowning.

# Chapter Sixty-Nine

He closed his eyes, revisualising the panic in Tiffany Myres's eyes. It excited him. She was beautiful; her body perfect. She was almost identical to Kate, which dispelled his rage.

Touching Tiffany excited him, but he had enjoyed watching the terror in her face more, as her life slipped away.

They all deserved to die, every one of them, Kate especially. Her time would come; she would complete his puzzle.

* * * DCI Beckley * * *

*Saturday 8 January 2016. 19.14pm*

I'm back on ICU with Kate. I'm being tough and giving her little time to recover, but the truth is he's coming for her. We both know it, though I not sure she'll admit that to herself.

I can't let that happen, I need to get to him first. The only way I can do that is to extract more information from Kate. I need her to remember no matter how painful it is. There's something that she can tell me about him; I'm certain of it. Something that can be the turning point, that can identify him and put an end to the killings. I just need her to open-up and let me into her nightmare.

Her facial swelling has subsided but she's burying her head into the pillow.

I think she's embarrassed about the bald patch, but it doesn't bother me in the slightest; it's the least of her worries. Shelton says she did it to herself during her escape. That girl has some serious balls. I suppose you do anything when there's a threat to life.

She looks like a woeful, injured lamb lost in thought. There's nothing I can say or do to help her, or to undo the damage that I have caused.

"I'm sorry that I've put you in this situation, truly I am," I whisper.

She remains silent staring out of the window watching tadpole raindrops trickle.

"Kate, we will get him."

Her right arm and left leg are encased in plaster casts. The pain she must have withstood is unimaginable.

"I keep having flashbacks, bits and pieces. I haven't told anyone any of this, not even Taylor. Please don't say anything. I don't want to hurt him."

"What do you remember?"

"My captor, he was punching and kicking me. His gloves dragged over my body."

Her face conveys repulsion. I want to hold her hand, tell her it's going to be OK. But how can it be? How can she recover from something like that?

"I don't know whether he… everything's a blur. But I have this pain inside of my gut telling me I was violated."

She's crying but trying to hide her tears.

"I pray that you're wrong. Has a nurse examined you?"

"Yes. I couldn't feel any more degraded than I do right now."

"He may have slipped up. We found traces of semen at the crime scene. That's not to say it came from any contact with you."

I'm mumbling, trying to cite a reasonable explanation for its presence.

"Our criminal profiler says killers often masturbate in front of their victims."

That sounds just as bad. But at least it's not as bad as raping her.

"What I'm trying to say is it might be all we need to nail the fucker."

She turns to face me; eyes tormented. They've lost their sparkle. I need to bring the old Kate back, but I don't know how to reunite her soul and bring her back from the depths of despair.

# Chapter Seventy – DCI Beckley

*Monday 10 January 2016. 9.56am*

"Sir, Shelton and Delaney are in the conference room with the lab results," Wakeman mutters.

He looks like shit too. Neither of us has slept since the body count started to mount.

Every time I close my eyes, I imagine Kate's bludgeoned body. Her face has replaced Toby's. I don't see him anymore. It's not that I've forgotten him; that guilt will remain with me until my dying days. It's more that Kate has become a prominent fixture in my mind. He's what went wrong in my past; she's what went wrong in the present.

My whole focus has been on finding her and bringing her home. Only now she's back, I still can't get her out of my head. I feel so guilty and the only way I can ease my conscience and the heavy burden that I'm carrying is to unveil who he is.

Wakeman and I vacate my office. There are still no leads with regards to the mask. The ring has proved a hit though. We have two stores currently examining their purchase records. Hopefully, we get a match to the bruising found on the victim.

I've finished cross examining all the CCTV footage of the fueling stations. We may have something."

I suddenly find myself paying attention to Wakeman.

"What?"

"Foster said she found the imprint of a VW key. That made me pay attention to this vehicle model when examining the footage. The same VW blue Golf visited Sainsbury's forecourt on the night of each murder."

"Have you run a PNC check?"

"They're false plates. But what you can clearly see is the driver getting out of the car, not to refuel, but to discard something inside the bin beside the pump and acquire new gloves."

"Fuck."

Pins and needles of adrenalin swarm my skin. We're getting close.

"Can you see his face?"

"No, he's hooded and hangs his head low to avoid detection."

"Then we can't identify him."

"Not unless we find the car and any evidence within it. We have the tyre impressions from Kate's crime scene. If we find the car, we can place it at the scene. All we need are his prints inside the car to link him to the vehicle."

"I'm tracking the plate via ANPR for recent sightings. It will show up at some point and then we can close the net. Forensics has also collected the bin contents. It's not been emptied since Tiffany was killed. We might get lucky."

Shelton and Delaney have presented their findings on the table surface.

There are images of a shoe imprint, the rope used to detain Kate and the tyre tread patterns. My nerves are frazzled. Their optimistic faces say they've unearthed something. Shelton's eyes fall on to mine.

"As you're aware we collected several samples from within the barn; blood, hair and semen. The blood on the rope matches Kate's DNA, along with the blood spatter throughout the premises and the hair sample."

My patience is fraying; I just want her to be blunt and get to the point.

"Do we have the fucker?"

"Not yet. The semen sample only gives us a partial profile."

Her words rupture my spleen like a bullet; pain engulfs my entire body while thick vomit plugs the back of my throat. My pain morphs to anger.

"So, you don't have a complete DNA profile?"

"No."

Her cheeks redden. I know that I shouldn't take my anger out on her, I just thought we were finally closing the net. I had him, I felt it, he was in reaching distance and now it feels like he's slipping from my grasp. I cannot lose him. I won't lose him.

# Chapter Seventy-One – Kate

*Monday 10 January 2016. 15.30pm*

I'm being discharged from hospital. The doctors say that I don't need to be here any longer and can recuperate at home.

In other words, it's about budgets; they need to free up a bed. I don't want to leave, I'm not ready. I'm scared to face what's outside of those doors. He wants revenge; he will punish me for ruining his game. I'm the only girl who got away, aside from Hannah but she's dead now too.

He won't let me talk; he's going to silence me. I'm fully aware of that, as is Will. He and I have discussed my position at great length and he's assigned me a protection detail. We joked about them screwing up again, but he won't make the same mistake twice.

Despite my fears, I cannot stay in hospital forever and if Dr Harris says that I'm fit for discharge I can't argue. Taylor wheels me toward the exit. Will is ahead, protecting the entrance like a nightclub door bouncer. The smell of coffee mixes with my nerves and makes me want to heave.

"Shit." Taylor blurts, pausing and retreating backwards into the glass atrium, away from the cameras.

"Stop, what are you doing?"

"I'm trying to protect you, shield you from the media circus."

"I know you are, but I am going out there with my head high. I want him to know that he failed, that I'm alive and I'm not afraid."

Will examines the press pack, whispers on his radio and then his eyes slip on to me.

"You don't have to do this."

He looks concerned.

"It's OK, I need to. If he's not here, then he'll be watching on TV."

Taylor pushes me into the spotlight. I'm shaking and terrified, observing the dark sky, which hangs low overhead, threatening rain. My chest is tight, burning anxiety. I'm struggling to breathe; I feel like his hands are on my throat constricting my airways. I'm having a panic attack. Taylor squeezes my hand offering his support and reassurance.

"It's OK honey, take a deep breath."

I inhale and seize damp air. Marela is positioned nearby, gawping. She's speechless, her big mouth suspended wide with shock. Tom is behind her looking equally repulsed by my appearance. I've become accustomed to it. The cuts are healing quickly; my hair another matter. I can't think about vanity while he's still out there claiming innocent lives. My only interest is telling the bastard that it's over and letting him know we're coming for him. It's only a matter of time.

"I'm DCI Will Beckley. This is Kate Rivendale. She is prepared to give a short statement."

He looks at me sincerely, passing over the attention. I break our stare and turn to face the crowd. The camera flashes hurt my eyes. I cannot find my voice; it's trapped behind my tongue. I never imagined being at the centre of a full media glare; it's intimidating. My chest is gripped in an intense rush, my hands tremor. I want to cry. I bite the inside of my cheek to ebb my tears. I won't let him see me cry. I'm a fighter; I've come this far. I will be strong.

Will's hand squeezes my shoulder gently. I take a deep breath and exhale.

"I'm Kate Rivendale; the girl who got away."

Camera flashes invade the hospital entrance.

"To the Millbrook Murderer, you may have taken me while I slept in my own bed and held me captive for days, but I would never be your prisoner. You've failed. You are a failure, you need to stop all this and get the help that you need. I know I've infuriated you by escaping, but I would never be your victim. Take this as a lesson. You are not invincible, and you will come unstuck. The game is over."

Cameras click relentlessly, as the audience hang on my every word.

"I am my own person and I would never allow someone to lock me up like a caged animal. I will never be a victim, it's not in my nature. I want you to know that I remember everything that you made me endure and I remember you. I am fully cooperating with the investigation. Your time is running out. There's nothing more you can do to me now. The police are coming for you and when they do, you will suffer far greater than I ever did."

I pause; I want every one of my words to be recorded correctly and broadcast to the world, so that, ironically, he will not be able to escape from me.

"To the families of the other women whose lives you took, I am sorry for your loss and offer my sincere sympathies. But mark my words, I will not stop assisting the police investigation until the killer is apprehended and behind bars for the rest of his life, so that no other families have to suffer the way you have."

\* \* \*

Squad cars and surveillance teams are positioned outside our house. DI Wakeman is at the front door, his hand hovering over his Glock pistol. Even his eyes convey sympathy studying my battered, wafer-thin body, as I emerge. Maybe I misjudged him. He has his own issues that he's trying to hide beneath that stern exterior.

Taylor lifts me from the passenger seat and carries me to the door, passing the keys to Wakeman who obliges. He remains silent. My heart feels as though its embedded with a blade. This will always be the place where he took me. It will never be home any more.

"I promise you that the house is secure; I've fitted panic alarms. You couldn't be safer," Taylor says assuring.

I feel sick, my stomach under torsion with stress. Taylor lies me down on the sofa.

"I'll make you a hot drink, and then take you up to bed."

His words gut me; my insides explode with fear. Taylor observes my panic.

"Hey, it's going to be OK."

He puts his arms around me. Flashbacks of the macabre mask attack my mind; only he's pinning me to the sofa. I'm hyperventilating, crying uncontrollably. The barrier is crashing down; I can't keep up the pretence.

"Calm down. Breathe. I'm so stupid, what was I thinking, bringing you back here? I'm sorry."

I can't speak; my sobs uncontrollable.

"You're safe I promise; I won't let anything happen to you."

I know Taylor was being thoughtful, adding additional security measures, but how can I feel safe when he's still out there plotting my death, especially when he knows where I live? Taylor may as well have taken me back at the barn; this house is where all my torment started, when that monster snuck into my bedroom while I slept.

"I can't stay here."

I'm scared for my life. Part of me wished he'd taken it, that way I'd be free of this nightmare.

* * *

I've never felt so empty in my life. Taylor is beside me, being my rock, but my life has been stolen. The killer is out there laughing, waiting for his moment to strike. He's now forced me out of my own home and I feel isolated from everything that I knew.

My life will never be the same again. I'll always be 'that girl', the poor girl who was abducted and tortured by a serial killer. That label will always stick. People don't forget things like that. It will always follow me wherever I go, like a ball and chain, a burden I will always have to drag around with me.

We're hiding out in Church Gate guesthouse near the toll road. It's a stone's throw from Le Chateau Bistro. Taylor thought being near to somewhere I love would help me feel safe but that's far from how I feel. It's a stately home set amongst sweeping lawns with huge sash windows, tall ceilings and chandeliers hanging from the floral ceiling roses.

It should be lovely, but it feels so cold, given the state of my mind. The orange and peach hallway walls are segregated by a dado rail and clash with the patterned Axminster rugs. Our room feels icy and I'm numb.

This is not home. I shouldn't be here. The trouble is, I'm not sure where I should be, anymore. I'm letting him have the upper hand. He's still in control, ruining my life.

I'm exhausted, sat propped on the bed, the weighty casts imprisoning me, acting as a constant reminder. The magnolia walls feel as though they are closing in.

If he came for me now, I wouldn't be able to run. I'm immobile and weak. Tears drain my eyes as I examine both the solid casts on my arm and leg. I'm a complete mess. I hurt everywhere, in my bones, my flesh, my heart and my mind. I feel so low, I've lost myself. I'm not even sure that there is a way back from all of this. He's ruined my life, broken me and I don't know how to put the pieces back together.

Taylor re-emerges in the room, carrying two large glasses of red from the bar.

His lips are warm on mine. I can't tell him that I'm afraid. It would break his heart after all the effort that he's gone to in taking me somewhere safe. He stretches out next to me, watching TV. He's acting as if nothing has happened; treating this like a mini break. Maybe that's his way of coping; pretending everything's normal to stay sane.

Truth is; I don't think he knows what to say or he doesn't want to know what really happened in my prison cell.

I'd love nothing more than to confront my abductor, unravel the man beneath the mask and make him understand the damage that he's caused. Not only did he ruin the lives of the women he killed, he ruined those of their entire families.

I won't forget the violence that he inflicted upon me. He was so full of rage. Something must have happened in his life to warrant a distaste of women. He needs help, not that he deserves my sympathy.

If I had the chance to kill him I would. I'd end his life in a heartbeat.

Taylor wouldn't believe me if I told him that. He'd say I don't have it in me to kill. I do; we all have it in us, buried deep. We are either born to kill, or it takes one trigger to make us snap. Either way, it's in all of us, an animal instinct.

My heavy eyes keep surrendering; a mixture of wine, medication and emotion.

Taylor remains engrossed with the TV, distracting himself from the situation. I don't blame him. I just wish that he'd talk to me and make me feel safe.

I want to close my eyes; shield them from the horrors that I've endured. Only, every time they're closed, I see the mask suspended above me. I feel his weight, his hands and smell his sour breath on me.

Either way, asleep or awake, he haunts me. I'm never going to be free of him; I'll be forever plagued. He may not have taken my life, but it's tarnished forever, beyond repair.

# Chapter Seventy-Two – Kate

Panic erupts and flushes through my bones like I've taken a bullet to my spleen and I'm bleeding out on the bed.

I awake covered in sweat; my back adhered to the sheet.

I'm alone, Taylor's left me. Why would he leave me unprotected? I feel betrayed. I thought he loved me and that everything was OK between us now. I rub my eye sockets, refreshing them and scour my surroundings, checking for an unwelcome presence lurking; weapon in hand.

My heart is ferocious, a dull ache growing inside like a fetus. I resemble a broken china doll; the pieces sharp, uneven and laid bare.

Why would he abandon me?

The stillness is broken. Water jets echo from the en-suite. A surge of relief washes over me. Taylor hasn't left my side after all. Part of me didn't think he'd really leave me like a defenceless newborn lamb, unable to stand.

Panic just set in; I feared I was alone. When I am, it acts as a vivid reminder of my time spent in isolation; the hours of enduring silence, while the cold gnawed at my bare flesh. Memories of my ordeal resurface. I want to shut them away under lock and key forever, so that they never reemerge and further torment my mind.

I snuggle my heavy head back into the duck feather pillow, trying to dismiss the recollections. My pain has subsided unlike my fear, which remains vivid.

Wine made me drift off last night. Ever since I regained consciousness, I've been unable to sleep. I close my eyes and see him, taunting me. So, I stay awake night after night. I can't let him near me; ever again. I won't subject myself to the terror I felt in his presence. I can't erase my memories, if only life were that simple. He's imprinted on my brain. My life may as well be over.

I notice a pile of newspapers on Taylor's side of the bed; my own tormented face staring back at me under the bold headline: "*THE ONE WHO GOT AWAY*".

My insides double knot.

I've written hundreds of front page stories; I never thought I'd become one. I want to read it, though my subconscious is telling me to ignite it and burn the reminder to smoldering ashes.

I can't do that; I need to know what's being said. I drag The Sun newspaper over, studying the rancid image of my wheelchair-bound body outside the hospital, and the "before" picture that was taken at Christmas in my blue dress. To me, that person now looks like another girl, in another life. It's not me, not any more.

I've morphed from a girl into a woeful, ugly creature. He did this; but I will have my revenge. He's going to wish he were never born. I'll help the police to catch him, even if I die doing it.

Taylor emerges from the bathroom with a white towel wrapped around his waist.

He kisses me awkwardly with wet lips but says nothing.

He doesn't know how to handle me and keeps treating me like a china doll. That's men for you; unable to share their emotions, or properly understand anyone else's. I've only ever seen him cry once, at his twin brother's funeral. People handle things in different ways. I'm over emotional, I cry easily. Only I can't shed my tears in front of Taylor; it will break him. If I rupture he will go in to meltdown. I've seen him in that state before and it's not something that I ever want to revisit again.

I slide my legs out of bed, stagger on my uncomfortable crutches toward the bathroom. I want to be alone when I see my reflection in the mirror; it can't be as bad as it looked in the papers. Goose pimples crawl over my anaemic flesh that protrudes from my black pyjamas. Flashes of yellow and purple bounce back as I study all the bruises. I look like a dying beast. The lump on my skull has subsided, however the prominent bald patch makes me look like a radiotherapy patient with only hours to live.

I snatch a facial wipe from the packet and run its damp surface over my face, refreshing my eyes.

The image is clearer now; and worse. I hate the monster staring back.

My cuts and grazes will heal and fade in time; unlike the damage to my mind. I'll never be free of it. This is my life now. I slump my weight on the toilet seat lid, clutching a hand towel to my face to muffle my cries. It is better I keep my pain from Taylor; I can't let him see me suffering. My life will never ever be the same again.

Water jets spear my back, my arm and leg protected by a waterproof wrapping. Taylor can't hear my tears in here.

The cubicle cocoons me and masks my pain. No matter how hard I try, I cannot wash him off me. His touch is tattooed on my skin. Although I cannot see it; I feel it. It won't go away. I lather yet more soap, vigorously rubbing my flesh to get him off. The bastard is winning the game. I slam my eyes shut, allowing the water to wash away my tears; I hear his boots again, splashing coming close.

My body trembles violently, memories invading my thoughts; ones I don't want to remember. They can't be real. They hit me like the cleaver blow to my skull. I vomit and clog the shower drain. I don't understand what's happening. None of this can be real. Maybe I'm still dreaming; I'm going to wake up any moment now.

But my heart is telling me otherwise. It's being ripped from my chest by a hungry wolf and savaged. This is real and there's no escape.

Questions pound my mind, but I don't have the answers. My head is spinning out of control; my rapid breaths inhaling urine where it's clinging to my legs. My fear is real; my life is near its end.

# Chapter Seventy-Three – DCI Beckley

*Tuesday 11 January 2016. 7.16am*

The investigation is picking up pace thanks to Wakeman's lead on the VW vehicle; the net is closing. We are going to get the fucker and have justice for his victims.

The National ANPR Data Centre (NADC), which scans vehicle registrations and checks them against the Police National Computer, has captured images of the suspect's car.

It places him on the Millbrook Estate during the nights of each murder. It was last captured entering the estate at 9.30pm, *on Thursday January 6*, and again fleeing the scene at 11.01pm. That puts the car in the area at the time when Tiffany Myres was killed.

CCTV captured the same vehicle at the Sainsbury's petrol filling station at 11.25pm.

The suspect is seen dumping gloves in the forecourt bin. Forensics should come back with a result on the gloves any time now. All we need is a print and we've got him.

In the meantime, we're concentrating our search efforts for the vehicle within that vicinity. Squad cars are combing the surrounding streets and housing estates; unless of course it's picked up again first via real-time ANPR imaging.

Once we have the vehicle, Shelton, Delaney and Foster can process it for DNA and any evidence associated to all seven murder victims.

The clock is ticking; he's running out of time. He will not take any more lives, I won't allow it.

The body count ends here; his sick game ends now. We're coming for him. We will get our man and I will bring closure to all the victims' families, and Kate.

I swore to her that I would catch him. I won't break that promise. I've already failed her miserably; I can't screw up. I need to rectify my mistakes; only then can I ease the heavy burden that I carry.

# Chapter Seventy-Four

It's her fault that I killed them. If she hadn't ruined everything then things would have been different. Her actions tore my world apart and actions have consequences.

The inquest changed me. I had to relive his ordeal; a graphic and clinical account of how he died. The coroner spoke as if he were talking about a broken toy. I didn't deserve that; he should have shown more compassion. His words still echo in my ears; all the internal and external injuries, every contusion described in microscopic detail.

I couldn't bear to listen to it or see her every day. That bitch ruined everything; she took half of me.

How dare they treat him like that; as if his life was nothing? He wasn't just a corpse; he was my brother, so for that I made her pay. I stole her life in return and made sure that she suffered in equal measure. The skewer: for what she made me listen to at the inquest. The heart: because she broke mine.

One day I'll tell them where she rests.

They say revenge is sweet; it was at the time, but it didn't fully dispel the rage that I feel. The only way to relieve my anger is to keep on killing anyone who reminds me of her. They all deserve to die; every single one of them.

## * * * Kate * * *

Blood weeps from my scalp tarnishing the water. My nails have unsealed the crust of a scab. The oozing gash is wide open, as is my memory which has hit me like a giant tidal wave.

I see it all now.

I hear his voice; the muffled screams coming from the barn. The one that I recognised; the sound that I didn't think was real. My mind was playing tricks on me, I was sure. I was dazed, disorientated. But I heard him, I know I did. My tears equal the water intensity that's ejecting from the shower.

I don't understand what's happening.

Why him? Why would he do this to me; to the others? Nothing makes sense. Has his smile masked a monster within? He's not capable. I recall my head resting on his chest; my tears falling onto him. Why didn't I see it? How could I have not known? Everything is a lie; a sham. Everything!

Why I am so stupid? Nothing adds up. I don't understand his motive. What did those women do to justify their deaths? I didn't do anything either, to warrant abduction or abuse. My head hurts; swamped with fear, physical pain, and most of all, deceit and betrayal.

## * * * DCI Beckley * * *

SOCOS bag and seal evidence from within the vehicle discovered at Worle industrial estate, a short distance from Sainsbury's. It's parked in plain sight. He must walk to it or swap vehicles when he's on a killing spree.

We're inches from the truth; I feel it in my nerves. Shelton catches my attention; eyes vividly bright and intense. My bones rattle; chest tight. I've been holding my breath awaiting answers.

Red fabric radiates against Shelton's white gloves. She kneels on the ground placing the package upon the tarmac. I watch on, engrossed, as she carefully unfolds the material, almost in slow motion.

Metal glistens in the daylight. I can barely believe my eyes, which fixate on the blade, then shift to the skewer. We have his murder kit. I exhale; my pent-up anxiety and frustration seep from deep within.

Neither of us speaks. Shelton smiles and gives me an acknowledging nod. She refolds the casein yarn blanket and secures it within a clear bag.

Delaney approaches carrying a photograph, and a brown biohazard bag.

"Tyre tread matches the impressions taken outside the barn. We can place the car at Kate's hostage site."

He presents the bag.

"Lace knickers," he states.

I presume they belong to Tiffany Myres. My heart is gripped with anger. He's an animal that needs to be slaughtered.

Foster and Harlan empty the car boot. Harlan removes the base protector, exposing the spare tyre and a carrier bag. They pause while Foster captures images of the content. My heart is contracting in quick successions pumping blood excitedly.

I watch them finger the plastic; carefully tugging the tied handles before reaching inside. My stomach is hollow with suspense. The duo pauses and stares at one another, mute.

"Foster?"

She turns. I see a fire ignited in her eyes by the discovery. I step closer as Harlan spins around. His palms clutch an olive mask. It's Briguella.

\* \* \*

The Riverside Centre is a hive of activity. Foster places the knife into a Cyanoacrylate Fuming Chamber. Superglue vapours attach to amino acids and develop latent fingerprints.

The gloves from the petrol bins have also yielded a print, which Delaney is processing.

The killer was always going to trip up- criminals always eventually make a mistake. They're always going to leave behind that one piece of key evidence.

The blower runs for five minutes before the knife is removed and placed under the Crime-Lite imager. The print is captured, and the ridge characteristics run against IDENT1, the national database, for a match.

I stare at the screen; it's a hit.

Vomit rises; my chest feels as if he's skewered it with his own murder kit.

I've been so stupid. My teeth tear loose skin on my bottom lip angrily; it stings, drawing blood.

I'm horrified, suddenly recalling a flashback of them at her bedside. I see the ring on his finger, his hand on top of hers. It was there all along, in plain sight, right in front of my eyes.

Why didn't I connect it to the case? All this time hunting, and he was right under my nose. I've allowed her to walk right back into the lion's den.

# Chapter Seventy-Five – Kate

*Tuesday 11 January 2016*

I slump on the bed pulling a woolen grey jumper over my head. My shaky fingers peel damp hair off my neck. I hold my head low to avoid detection. A tap at the door sets my heart racing. Taylor answers and retrieves a breakfast tray.

"Come on," he states firmly.

I hobble on crutches and sit at the table. My fingers tremble, picking up the fork. He studies me in silence. I can't look him in the eye.

"Kate are you OK?" I nod, maintaining my fixed gaze on the scrambled eggs.

My entire body quivers; fear wrapping itself around my bones and throat suffocating me. He lifts my chin and stares in to my eyes.

"Why didn't you tell me about the baby?"

His words are cold, like nothing I've heard before. I don't understand how he knows.

"Wasn't it mine?"

"Of course, it was yours," I stammer.

"I couldn't tell you."

"Why not?"

"You were grieving for Paul, I didn't want to add to your pain."

"You hated the fact that you were going to have to put someone else first, didn't you? That's why you killed our child."

"I didn't, I lost him."

"Maybe so, but your selfish behaviour caused it to die."

I swallow.

"That's unfair and untrue. It wasn't my fault."

"You were strutting around chasing stories like you're the big I am. You're a selfish bitch. I should have finished you off when I had the chance."

I gasp; winded by his words.

"The only time there was a real connection between us was when you were writing about me."

"That's not true Taylor; I love you, you love me. This isn't you."

"You should have told me about the baby back when I loved you, when I would have traded lives with you in a heartbeat. Instead, you pushed me away, Kate, and made me feel inadequate. I always came second."

"I was sparing you the pain."

I can't believe the man I love is capable of rape and murder. I can barely breathe. I'm snatching short breaths, my heart vicious, heartbroken.

"But why kill all those women, what did they do to you?"

"Because she took Paul from me; that silly little bitch."

"Who are you taking about, the motorcyclist?"

"Yes."

"I don't understand."

"That stupid blonde took him from me, so I stole her life in return. I had my revenge; she was my first victim. She was loathsome, just like my blonde junkie whore of a mother."

I don't understand any of this. I don't know what he's talking about.

"Your mum isn't blonde."

"My adopted mum isn't, but that dirty scumbag who gave birth to me and abandoned me was. They're all filth; they needed eradicating. You couldn't mind your own business, could you Kate? You had to get involved, get in my way."

I feel weak and fragile; I cannot fight him.

"No one will ever know the truth. I'll say I found you like this."

"Like what?"

"Dead."

His deathly stare crushes my heart. I slam my eyes shut, shielding myself from the truth.

His hands are on my neck, crushing my windpipe.

"You ruined everything, Kate. You should have taken on board the warning that I gave your sister. But no, not Kate, she can't mind her own fucking business, she's always searching for the truth. Everything's always about her."

My heel digs and scrapes the carpet as I struggle under his weight.

Rage radiates his eyes, pure evil lurking beneath. I now see the same dark eyes that had glared at me in the barn. All I ever did was love him, how could he treat me like this? We were going to be a family.

His fingers squeeze harder; choking me. I'm going to die. My shallow lungs are starved of air. I'm slipping away.

The door crashes open as I gasp my final breath.

Will points his Glock pistol. Taylor doesn't acknowledge his presence. His mind is focused on draining my soul. I'm drifting away; dying. The little girl with the syringe from my dream is stood beside the bed, waiting for me. She's holding out her hand, urging me to follow her toward the light.

"Back off," Will screeches.

Taylor's lips stretch into a twisted smile as my breathing fades. He releases my throat at the sound of a gun click; safety catch releasing. I gasp for air. The girl disappears.

"I let you get away with it once, mother fucker. I'm not about to let it happen a second time," Will yells, pointing his pistol with intent.

Glistening metal emerges from Taylor's jeans; the blade slashing the air towards my neck.

I screw my eyes, protecting them from my impending death, and brace myself for the fatal blow.

An explosion pounds my ears; the sound electrocutes my spine with fear.

Blood and brain tissue spatter my face. I flinch, sickened. My eyes flick open, observing the gaping hole in Taylor's skull as his corpse crashes to its knees.

I see a different darkness cloud his eyes as he falls to the floor. I don't recognise the creature before me. His blood cascades and saturates the beige carpet. I dart my panicked eyes away from the horror, my aching heart shattered beyond repair. Will's alluring eyes quash my terror.

"It's over now," he says calmly, offering a weak smile.

* * *

I'm not the only serial killer survivor. Many of you evaded death without even realizing it; all because you trusted your instinct, didn't engage in contact and get into that stranger's car, or help him to look for his "lost" puppy.

Taylor never gave me the chance to disengage.

I wasn't a victim of chance; I was destined to be the final piece of his jigsaw. His smile masked a monster. I truly believed I could spot evil; I was wrong, deceived twice over.

Why didn't I see what lay right in front of my eyes?

Maybe those strange red fibres should have made me think about that old red blanket that Paul gave as a present to Taylor. He thought it would be perfect for our summer garden BBQs.

I'd forgotten all about it. It wasn't important to me, unlike Taylor, who must have treasured it as keepsake. I see it clearly now; a fitting tribute to Paul. He avenged his brother's death by stealing the motorcyclist's life, and then wrapped his murder weapons in the blanket to keep Paul's memory alive.

I can only presume that taking her life wasn't enough. It didn't dispel the burning rage he felt inside, stemmed by his abandonment as a child. Rejection of that magnitude has consequences; it damaged his soul and twisted his mind.

I wonder if I hadn't lost the baby whether any of those women would still be alive. Would parenthood have suffused his darkness so that he didn't seek revenge? I honestly don't have the answer, and I'll never know.

What I do know is that I didn't think my own husband would be capable of such horrific crimes.

You think you know a person, every little last thing about them. How could I have not known or seen the warning signs? I'm foolish. Perhaps I loved him too much; they say love is blind. I'll never forget this chapter of my life but slowly, day by day, I'm getting better. I'm rewriting my story, only this time it will have a happy ending.

THE END

Dear reader,

We hope you enjoyed reading *Briguella*. Please take a moment to leave a review, even if it's a short one. Your opinion is important to us.

Discover more books by Vicki Fitzgerald at https://www.nextchapter.pub/authors/vicki-fitzgerald-crime-mystery-author

Want to know when one of our books is free or discounted? Join the newsletter at http://eepurl.com/bqqB3H.

Best regards,
Vicki Fitzgerald and the Next Chapter Team

You could also like:

Inside Sam Lerner by Gwen Banta

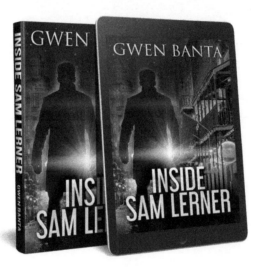

To read the first chapter for free, please head to:
https://www.nextchapter.pub/books/inside-sam-lerner

Briguella
ISBN: 978-4-86752-672-9

Published by
Next Chapter
1-60-20 Minami-Otsuka
170-0005 Toshima-Ku, Tokyo
+818035793528
6th August 2021

Ingram Content Group UK Ltd.
Milton Keynes UK
UKHW040701210423
420559UK00004B/462